FORCED VOWS

by Lucy Monroe

1st Printing 2024

FORCED VOWS

Lucy Monroe

Lucy Monroe LLC

For my writing besties, Carrie Nichols, Aleksandr Voinov, Traci Douglass and Tracy Goodwin. Where would I be without you? When Róise needed I posse, I gave her the best friends I knew. You all!

ITALIAN MAFIA HIERARCHY*

Cosa Nostra Territories:

New York: Five Families

Bonanno (Queens), Colombo (Bronx), Gambino (Staten Island), Genovese (Manhattan), and Lucchese (Brooklyn): each founding mafia is led by a don who could be from any of the families loyal to them.

New York Genovese family

Don/Boss:

Severu De Luca

(Also known as The Genovese and King of New York)

Underboss:

Miceli De Luca

(Severu's brother)

Consigliere:

Big Sal De Luca

(Severu's uncle)

Capos:

Domenico Bianchi

Salvatore De Luca

(Severu's cousin)

Tomasso Marino

Niccolo Costa
Lorenzo Ricci
Stefano Bianchi
Head Enforcer:
Angelo Caruso
(Also known as Angel of Death)
Soldiers:
Luigi, Carlo, Aldo (Severu's men)
Fausto, Marco (Big Sal's men)
Las Vegas
Don/Boss:
Patrizio Mancini
Underboss:
Raffaele Mancini
Detroit
(Don: Pietro Russo)
New England
(Don: Unnamed)
Boston
(Don: Lombard)
The Cosa Nostra is known as the Lombardi Family, despite the Americanized name for the don's family.
Chicago aka The Outfit
(Don: Unnamed)
* All names and positions are fictional or used in a fictional capacity, a product of the author's imagination, loosely based on La Cosa Nostra structure in America.

CHAPTER 1: RÓISE

Facing the guillotine to my dreams, I wait with my uncle while Don De Luca's secretary opens one of the imposing double doors to his office.

A foot taller than normal doors and each of them at least six inches wider, the entry to the Italian mafia don's office screams power and wealth. Right along with the twelve-foot ceilings.

In Manhattan every inch of real estate is precious, including vertical space. Having an entire floor in their building with twelve-foot ceilings tells everyone who comes to meet the don that he can squander that space on aesthetics because unlike normal people, his access to square footage is virtually limitless.

His ridiculous wealth and far-reaching influence are why my uncle is so ready to sacrifice my future.

Some might think I'm being dramatic.

I'm not.

Every one of my dreams dies behind those doors when this blood alliance becomes a reality.

When my engagement to a member of the Cosa Nostra becomes official.

The low timber of masculine voices leaks out as the door opens.

One of the voices sounds familiar. I shake my head. It's not possible.

No way can *he* be *here*.

Then one of the men laughs darkly and the cold dread of certainty freezes me in place.

My first lesson in the cost of being part of a mob family came when I was nine years old. I loved to play dodge ball during recess. Until one day, a classmate filled one of the balls with water instead of air.

When it hit me dead in the center of my stomach, all the breath in my lungs gushed out in a gasp. Unable to yell, or even cry, I stood there as pain like I'd never felt radiated out from my stomach.

The classmate was the son of one of my grandfather's men. He was angry about something my grandfather had done to his father. The boss of the Shaughnessy Mob, my grandfather was untouchable.

I was the easy target.

It was the first time I hated being the granddaughter of the mob boss and part of a world where violence was the go-to solution for conflict. But it wasn't the last.

Furious when he found out what happened, my dad wanted to pull me from the private Catholic school where the other children of high-ranking members in the Irish mob went.

He and my grandfather argued for days, but eventually my dad won. That grade school was my first taste of life not overshadowed by my family's criminal world.

Two months ago, when *I* chose who to take as my first lover, I thought I'd had my last. But even that was tainted by my family's world.

Because the man I can't stop thinking about...the one who stars in my dreams night after night and my fantasies while I touch myself just as often...*is in that room.*

I went across the country and evaded my bodyguards so I could choose who to have sex with the first time. All to give my virginity to a freaking member of the New York Cosa Nostra?

There is no way this goes well.

Whoever it is will have leverage with my future husband. Like all syndicate men, he'll use it. And once again, I will pay the price because I am the easy target.

"Come on, Róise. This is no time to get up the high doh." My uncle grabs my arm and tugs me forward.

Who wouldn't be stressed under these circumstances?

Even if my one and only sex partner wasn't in the same room as my future fiancé, meeting said fiancé for the first time is enough to make anyone's nerves riot.

And not in the way Ares made my nerves riot that night two months ago.

There are three men waiting in the room, but my eyes lock on only one of them and refuse to move on.

Ares.

He's wearing a black suit, either tailored high end designer or bespoke because it fits him perfectly despite his extra broad shoulders. He's not wearing a tie and the top two buttons on his shirt are undone, revealing the strong column of his neck and a hint of dark chest hair.

The gray silk shirt is smooth over his muscular chest, no straining buttons and no wrinkles from having to tuck too much fabric in at the waist either. Thighs ropy with muscle that only my mind's eye can see are encased in dark slacks.

My gaze finally travels up to his handsome features. His gorgeous lips capable of eliciting so much pleasure are set in a firm line and he's not looking at me.

A breath of relief escapes my lungs.

At least I have a few seconds to pull myself together before he notices me.

Will he say something? Will he pretend not to know me?

His gaze, along with everyone else's, locks on me expectantly in the suddenly silent room. Everyone else is looking at me too.

Heat crawls up the back of my neck and into my cheeks. "Uh...hello."

"Severu, this is my niece, Róise. Róise, this is Don De Luca, his underboss, Miceli De Luca and the Genovese consigliere, Sal De Luca."

"Keeping it all in the family," pops out of my mouth, but my brain is scrambling to make sense of the introductions.

My uncle did not point as he introduced each man, like I'm supposed to know who is who. My guess is that the consigliere is the older man.

That leaves the two men who look like brothers. The don and his underboss.

Which one is Ares?

"Family is important," the man who is not Ares and not Sal De Luca says. The don?

But that would mean that Ares is the other man. The man I'm supposed to marry?

I cannot believe this. I traveled nearly three-thousand miles to a city with no mafia or mob presence and didn't just give my virginity to a Cosa Nostra soldier, but ended up sleeping with my future fiancé?

Fate isn't done screwing with me either because there is not a single glimmer of recognition in Miceli De Luca's eyes.

"A pleasure to meet you, Róise," Ares...no, *Miceli*...says in his deep tone, stepping forward with his hand outstretched.

I don't move.

Uncle Brogan nudges my shoulder. Not gently. I stumble forward, my hand rising of its own volition toward Miceli.

He takes it, his big hand dwarfing mine, just like it did the night in Portland.

His fingers are an inch longer than mine. I know because I measured my hand against his during one of our lulls in lovemaking.

Am I going to have to tell him that it was me in Portland? I can't imagine anything more demoralizing in this situation. My classmate's job on my makeup and the blonde wig made me even more unrecognizable than I thought.

"Nice to meet you, Miceli." My voice catches on his name.

I can't help it. That night two months ago was a fantasy, but this is reality. This man is not Ares, god of war and Aphrodite's lover.

He is Miceli De Luca, Genovese underboss and my future husband.

Miceli's espresso eyes narrow and he looks more closely at me, his hand on mine tightening when I try to pull away.

His gaze boring into mine, he turns my hand so my inner forearm is exposed. I know what he'll see when he looks down.

A flicker of some dark emotion tells me he does too. Or at least he suspects.

Was it my voice that gave me away?

Is this worse, or is it better that I don't have to tell him?

Dropping his gaze to my arm, he sees the distinctive tattoo. Two butterflies that starts off vibrantly colored at the top and fades to grayscale at the bottom of their wings. The symbol of two souls lost to this world too early.

Underneath are two dates. My parents' deaths.

I got the tattoo as soon as I turned eighteen and could sign the consent form for myself.

"Cazzo." His tone is low and angry.

I know what that word means now too. Fuck.

Cursing? Angry? What does he have to be mad about? I'm the one who got played by fate. Not him.

It all started with that damned doctor's report.

CHAPTER 2: RÓISE

Two Months Previous

Patient's hymen intact.

Fury knocks the lid off the simmering cauldron of emotions I've kept in check for the past week.

With a primal yell, I throw my phone against the wall with all my force. It hits with an unsatisfying thud before dropping, unharmed to the floor.

Darn indestructible phone case.

Chucking it at the window wouldn't give me any more satisfaction. All the mansion's windows are made with double glazed bullet resistant glass.

Throwing my head back, I scream again until my voice gives out.

It doesn't help and now my throat is sore.

It's bad enough that my uncle is forcing me to marry into the Italian mafia. The Cosa Nostra is responsible for my mom's death and probably my dad's too.

Uncle Brogan says mom's death is one of the reasons we need to cement an alliance between our family and the Genovese mafia.

To stop the same thing from happening again, despite the truce between the Shaughnessy mob and the Five Families of New York.

But this? This nod to the archaic customs of the Italian mafia? It pours fuel over the fire of rage that's been smoldering inside me, its eruption inevitable.

Patient's hymen intact.

Unless he's different than every other made man I know, my future husband isn't a virgin. The fact that I am has nothing to do with personal conviction and everything to do with circumstances of birth.

No way was I going to pop my cherry with an ever-present bodyguard lurking nearby. I've dated. Kissed some. Touched some. A very little of some, to be honest.

Again, refer to the lurking bodyguard.

I haven't found anyone I liked or trusted enough to go to the trouble of slipping my bodyguard's protection for the necessary privacy. Ergo, an intact hymen discovered by the doctor I believed was checking for pretty much everything else.

A couple of days after I reluctantly agreed to marry into the Genovese mafia (I would rather do almost anything than marry my enemy.), Uncle Brogan informed me that I would have to undergo a medical exam, including genetic testing.

He's the boss of the Shaughnessy mob and the only man who could have convinced me to agree to this travesty of a wedding. Not because he's the boss, but because of who will pay the price if I don't.

My too accommodating and vulnerable younger cousin.

Uncle Brogan says a clean bill of health is necessary for my part as temporary guarantor of the blood alliance he is negotiating with the Genovese mafia.

Considering the fact that I had to negotiate to be on birth control for the first two years of marriage, the request didn't surprise me. I'm only twenty years old and I'm not ready to be a mother.

Besides, I've got another year and a half of my Bachelor in Fine Arts program before I graduate. I had to make finishing my education a non-negotiable item too. With my uncle!

I haven't spoken to a single Cosa Nostra soldier.

These mafia men see marriage as a business transaction.

You don't sign a business contract without knowing the other company is able to fulfill its commitments. In my case, that means carrying a De Luca heir, the permanent guarantor of the alliance between the Genovese mafia and the Shaughnessy mob.

For the right to wait two years to get pregnant and finish my education, I agreed to the exam and signed my consent to the genetic tests. I didn't agree to having my virginity confirmed.

They don't have any right to that information, much less to expect me to be untouched sexually. This blood alliance might be right out of a chapter in history when women were treated like possessions, but I'm not.

Love for my cousin might force me to marry a man chosen for me by my uncle, but I don't have to go into the marriage with a submissive attitude. I'm not sure I've even got one of those in my acting repertoire.

No matter what the men in my family and the Genovese mafia might think, I am my own person.

All of my choices are being taken away though. There's one left I just realized I won't let them take: who I give my virginity to.

I'm not engaged yet.

For cripe's sake, I don't even know the name of my intended groom. I doubt my uncle does either. All I'm sure of is that he'll be a high ranking De Luca in the Genovese mafia. That's what Uncle Brogan says, anyway.

Which means I'm not betraying anybody by having sex for the first time *before* I enter into the *bondage* of matrimony.

How do I have sex before my groom is chosen and the engagement becomes official?

I could ask a friend to help me out, but afterward, would I ever be able to look my friend in the face? Not that I have a bunch of male friends. But the few I do have are *only* friends.

Okay, friends are out.

Uncle Brogan has some hot guys on his payroll, but I'm not looking to get anyone killed. And my uncle will murder any man who works for him that touches a woman in his family.

Right. No bodyguards or other mob soldiers.

Using a dating app leaves a trail I don't have the skill to erase. So, that's out too.

There's only one option I can see: a one-night stand with a stranger at a club, or something. Somewhere and someone not connected to the Irish mob in any way.

A one-night stand isn't exactly fairytale fodder, but neither is an arranged marriage to create an alliance between two criminal syndicates.

And sex with a stranger is better than losing one more decision to the machine of two syndicates aligning.

CHAPTER 3: MICELI

The thump of the bass beat from the club's speakers reverberates through my body, going straight to my cock. Beautiful women writhe sinuously on the dance floor, a buffet for my senses and my neglected libido.

Some are partnered. Some are not.

A few have definite potential for tearing up the sheets with me in my hotel room later.

I'm celebrating, even if I have one more job to do before returning to New York.

The operation in Colombia went smoothly. It was a good call for Sev to send me to Colombia with Cian Doyle's man to oversee the destruction of the Guiterrez cartel.

The cartel leaders that threatened *la famiglia* are dead. The new leader of the cartel is our man. Beholden and loyal to *us*. He's made a blood vow to keep his syndicate's activities out of New York and Chicago.

Key members of his new organization are on our payroll too. Because you don't leave shit like that to chance.

After the op, our alliance with the Doyle & Byrne mob in Chicago is as tight as a capo's fake smile.

Working with mercenaries instead of our own soldiers allowed me to let loose the rage that has festered inside since finding out Giovi-fucking-Revello betrayed us. I've sated one primal instinct. Now it's time to sate another.

Before I return to New York and my next assignment: marriage.

Sev wants to secure an alliance with another Irish mob, this one in New York.

After the cartel's attempt to sew discord in New York, Brogan Shaughnessy offered his niece for a blood alliance.

Not just a marriage, but a marriage with guaranteed issue, a child that carries the De Luca name and the Shaughnessy genes. He even had his niece tested for fertility and genetic health concerns.

There'd been one more piece of information on that report. My future wife, if I agree to the bargain, is a virgin.

It's fucking unreal that I know she's never had sex but can't bring her facial features to my mind.

That's my choice. After a single glance at the picture that accompanied the file Domenico put together on her, I didn't look again. It showed a woman with a sea of pink hats in the background, holding a picket sign that read, *My voice. My story. My body.*

The capo thinks he's funny. The mafia is no place for placard wielding activists. We stay in the background. How did this mob princess miss that memo?

The innocent fervor on her too young face has no place in my tainted life and after the first glance, I didn't look at her again. Nor did I look through the other pictures included in the report.

I didn't read the rest of the file either. The summary sheet told me everything I needed to know.

Name: Róise Shaughnessy

Only daughter of deceased heir to Shaughnessy empire and niece to the current mob boss. Born into the Irish mob.

Height: 5'4"

Nearly a foot shorter than me and too damn small for a man of my size.

Eye color: green

Hair: brown

Age: 20

Not even old enough to drink legally and thirteen fucking years younger than me.

Relationships: none

Of course she hasn't had a serious boyfriend. She's barely out of her teens.

Some men might look forward to marrying an innocent with no sexual history. I'm not one of them. She'll be eaten alive in my world. Probably by me.

But once I officially agree to the marriage, I'm committed to her.

Cazzo.

Her willingness to be the other sacrificial pawn in this game of chess means that despite her feminist activism, she is under Shaughnessy's thumb. Is he planning to use her to gather information on our mafia?

Will my wife be a spy I have to watch as closely as a new recruit? And less loyal than one?

I'm not looking for a marriage like Sev's.

My brother is so gone on my sister-in-law, her happiness is more important to him than his own. That's not the example our father set for us.

He only ever had eyes for our mother, but that affection and care was always tempered by his responsibilities as don. I don't think *anything* tempers my brother's love for his wife.

I like my sister-in-law. A lot. Her brain and perspective on life is unique and I can't wait to see what kind of kids she and my brother make.

But I don't ever want to be that wrapped up in a woman. Not my wife. Not even my daughter if I have one. Caring too much is dangerous. Emotions cloud the judgment and make doing the hard things even harder.

I'm not capable of that kind of devotion anyway.

I don't know how Catalina broke through the scarred walls of my brother's heart, but I'm pretty sure that there's nothing left of that organ behind my own.

My sister-in-law is the reason Sev is so determined to cement an alliance with the Irish. He'll keep her and any children they have safe at any cost.

The other reason Sev wants this alliance, one he's never said aloud, even to me, is my brother's plan to be the next godfather.

Don Caruso's health is failing. Our intel is that he has a year, two at most. When he dies, Sev will need alliances both inside and outside the mafia to guarantee his succession to the title.

A blood alliance with the most powerful Irish clan in New York and one of the most powerful mobs in the country is a good start.

Even if it means marrying his brother to the enemy to get it.

CHAPTER 4: RÓISE

My heart is beating so hard it hurts.

Waiting in line to be admitted to a club in a city with no mafia or mob presence, I rub damp palms down the short black skirt of my dress.

I'm dressed for the part I'm playing tonight: young, twenty-something, looking for an anonymous one-night stand.

No mob princess here.

I let one of the makeup artists in my acting seminar do my face. With the dramatic makeup bringing out the green in my eyes and contoured to make my cheekbones pop, even I don't recognize myself.

She also put me in a platinum blonde wig so tightly attached to my head that if I yank on it, it won't budge. I tried.

This chick knows what she's doing.

Silver strappy stiletto sandals add three inches to my five-feet-four inches. My tight black dress lifts my boobs and creates cleavage, making my breasts look bigger than they are. Which is necessary.

The hem hits high on my thighs, adding to my persona for the night. And bonus? My stubby legs look borderline long and sleek.

Although I drugged my security detail and left them sleeping peacefully at the hotel...what? I didn't hurt them. They're fine. Just...tired. And unlikely to remember anything tomorrow morning.

But seriously, I can't afford to be recognized while I'm out on my mission to choose my first sex partner. For his sake as much...or yeah, let's face it, or definitely more than for mine. No one can ever know who he is.

Mafia men make Cro-Magnon man seem advanced in certain ways.

I mean, I wouldn't even take the risk if I wasn't on the other side of the country from my family right now. This acting seminar in Portland, Oregon is part of my Fine Arts program and has been on the calendar since September.

Lucky for me, the timing is perfect for my plan to take back a tiny slice of control over my life and person.

The fact Uncle Brogan would have an aneurism if he knew? Totally a bonus.

The doorman gives my fake I.D. a once over before letting me inside without a word. I immediately head to the bar for some liquid courage. I wish I could have invited one or all of my classmates to come with me tonight.

There's security in numbers, but no one can know what I'm doing, or who I do it with.

Waiting for the bartender to mix my Manhattan feels right. In a few months, maybe a year? Wow, how do I not know the timing on this marriage thing? Anyway, sometime in the near future I'll be moving to Manhattan, territory for the Genovese mafia.

The bartender hands me my drink, but someone bumps me from behind and it spills all over the bar. Some of the amber liquid splashes back on me.

Feeling good about choosing an LBD for tonight's adventure, I take the stack of napkins the bartender offers me and start patting at the wet spots almost invisible against the black fabric.

"Let me buy you another. I didn't mean to bump into you like that." The deep voice cuts through the loud music and sends French love poems floating through my brain.

I turn to face the man.

Taller than me, with muscles his suit jacket can't hide, the gorgeous guy smiles. "Things can get rowdy in here on a Friday night."

"That's okay." I smile back at him through my lashes.

Flirting already. Go me.

He puts his hand out. "Helios."

"Helios? The ancient Greek god of the sun?" I ask.

"Well, I'm not ancient, but I am Greek," he says suggestively.

Is Greek a euphemism for sexy? Because I'm thinking yes.

"Should I call you Aphrodite?" There's definitely a suggestion in his voice now, but it's got nothing to do with wanting to know my name.

Anonymous sex. That's what I'm here for, right? "Yes."

Perfect white teeth slash in a smile on his swarthy face.

"Helios, tell your brother I'll see him tomorrow." The man who arrives to stand beside me is even taller than Helios, with short black hair and a magnetism that sends my nether regions into pulsing awareness. "I've got things to do."

Dark eyes in a mature face skim over me with interest. But...there's a tall, slender brunette hanging on his arm.

His *things to do*?

Something twinges in my chest. Disappointment? Nah. I shouldn't have had the Szechwan shrimp for dinner. Too much spice.

Helios salutes the other man. "Will do."

With a nod, but no more words, the man and his date turn to go.

Helios tries to take the napkins from my hand. "Let me help you."

"So, your name really is Helios?" I bat his hand away with a laugh.

"That's me, the sun god," Helios says with a smile.

For some reason, French love poems are making my ovaries yawn now.

"He doesn't look like the kind of guy who goes for short and fat," the brunette says loud enough to be heard over the music as she and the black-haired hottie walk away. "She doesn't even have impressive tatas to make up for it."

Heat crawls up my neck and into my face. For a second, before I remind myself that shallow and bitchy doesn't get to ruin my night, my body freezes.

A lot of women my size wear at least a D cup. I'm barely a C. I've never been naked with a man, so I don't know how a lover will react to my attributes. I'm planning to find out tonight though.

And I'm not worried about it. I'm not looking to be some man's dream girl. Just his sex partner.

Helios laughs. "Ignore her. I enjoy women of all shapes and sizes. If she's only been with men who don't, that's her loss."

"Sure." There's still a tiny part of me that feels small from the meanness.

Not what she said so much as why she felt the need to say it. To put me down. If she was annoyed her date looked at me with interest, she could have left me out of it.

Whatever her reasons, I don't need shallow and bitchy adding to the nerves jumping to a Zydeco beat inside me.

What I do need, I realize, is time to psyche myself into hooking up with a complete stranger.

I throw the wadded-up napkins on the counter. "I'm going to dance."

"I insist you allow me to replace your lost drink." Helios grabs my arm, before I can walk away.

Why not? Liquid courage sounds better than ever.

I nod.

He makes a gesture to the bartender.

"After you enjoy the best Manhattan west of the Rockies, we can dance." Helios smiles down at me.

Those French love poems are sounding more and more like a lullaby, sending my ovaries to sleep.

"Not best in the country?" I tease, reaching for that initial spark that went out without even leaving a puff of smoke behind.

"I only care about being better than our sister clubs in California." He winks. "Don't really care about clubs on the East Coast."

He consigns the Midwest and the South to nonexistence in his drinks competition. Interesting.

A server comes rushing up and asks something in urgent tones. There's no disappointment in me when Helios grimaces ruefully.

"Duty calls. Maybe we can catch that dance later, Aphrodite" he offers.

I shrug noncommittally.

"She'll be busy." It's the guy with the rude date.

But the brunette is gone and the dark-eyed hottie is looking at me so intently, I worry one of my fake eyelashes is falling off.

Helios says something in a language I don't understand. Probably Greek. The language might be indecipherable to me, but the tone is easy to interpret.

He's swearing.

The older man...he's at least thirty, I'm sure of it...maneuvers his big body between me and Helios. My ovaries wake up like they just got a caffeine I.V. and butterflies start doing the mamba in my stomach, drowning out the Zydeco beat of my nerves.

I take a big gulp of my drink.

He smiles, the expression not reaching his dark eyes. "I apologize for Lala. She would say she is sorry herself but she's no longer here."

There are people named Lala? Who knew?

"Okay. That's not sinister or anything. What did you do, play bouncer and kick her out?"

He shrugs his massive shoulders. "I told her I was no longer interested in fucking her."

"And she just left?" And also, why is he no longer interested in the other woman?

"As a friend of the owners, I could get her blacklisted from the club."

"You're a friend of the owners?" I ask.

"Friend might be stretching it, but she offended one of them already. I doubt they'd deny me."

"You mean Helios?"

"Yes."

"Oh." Had Helios only been flirty because he made me spill my drink and he's ultra good at customer service?

"He called you Aphrodite."

I nod.

"Your name?" His confident demand for information draws me in a way none of the college age guys I see daily do.

I take another drink of my Manhattan and answer over the rim of the martini glass. "Tonight, it is."

"If you are Aphrodite tonight, then I will be Ares."

"Not Eros?"

He shakes his head decisively. "Eros was the god of carnal love, but Ares was Aphrodite's lover."

He was also the god of war. I can see this man in that role. He's big. Intense. Moves like a jungle cat and exudes an aura of power.

"Why not Adonis then?" It fits too. He's the most beautiful man I've ever met.

Including the gorgeous Helios.

"Ares is more fitting."

Because he was Aphrodite's lover? That sounds promising.

I know why I'm so up on the Greek gods and goddesses. Because a course in Greek Tragedy is part of my College of Fine Arts curriculum.

Why does this man know so much about them? I shove my curiosity into a dark closet and shut the door.

I'm not asking him.

Rule one in one-night stands to lose your virginity: don't get to know your sex partner.

Even if he's an intriguing older guy who sends alien sparks of want through your ladybits. Especially then.

That's how hookups work. Right?

If I'm wrong, I don't want to know. It's how it has to work for me. I can't let myself get to know him.

Whoa.

When did I decide he's going to be the guy to pop my cherry? Probably sooner than I should have. My ovaries cast their vote when I first heard his voice. Not French lullabies but deep, rich Jazz.

"Would you like to dance, Ares?" I ask in my best sexy-times-are-coming purr.

Which is a brand new voice element to my acting repertoire.

It must be on point because his dark eyes burn me up. "Yes."

CHAPTER 5: MICELI

S he asks me to dance.

I like her confidence. Lala's snark hasn't fazed my beautiful Aphrodite.

The anonymity of the pseudonyms fits my mood tonight too. Across the country from the territory I help my brother rule and the home I will never leave, the only option between us is a one-and-done.

Although that *one* is going to last all night if I can trust my instincts.

I take her hand in mine and lead her to the crowded dance floor. The press of bodies only means we have to stay close together.

Spinning her around, I slide my hand over her stomach and pull her generous ass against me. She jolts into stillness, like I surprised her?

Did I misread the situation? I take an immediate step back, but she follows me, her smaller hand pressing over my own. Her other hand reaches up to latch onto the back of my neck.

I lean down. "This okay?"

I'm a forceful lover, but until the terms are set, I don't take anything for granted.

Wiggling her ass, she nods.

This is one of my favorite positions with a woman. Her body in front of me, every juicy curve accessible to my touch. I'll like it even better when Aphrodite is naked.

And we *will* be naked together.

The chemistry between us could power nighttime in Times Square.

Aphrodite's fingers play with the hair at the nape of my neck while her body shimmies enticingly to the music. Her hand on mine guides our entwined fingers in a circle over her belly.

Cazzo. That's sexy.

My cock rises to meet the little temptress. Even in her heels, she's several inches shorter than me so her backside presses against my upper thighs.

I'm tucked to the left and my semi-hard cock grows with my arousal so she can't help but feel the bulge as she grinds against me.

She pauses again, her body going unnaturally still. But then she presses even harder against me, massaging my erection with her bouncy curves.

We dance like that, close together, our bodies teasing each other, regardless of the beat of the song. When it's fast, we increase our speed. When it's slow, she seduces me with every leisurely glide of her ass.

I let my hand slide lower until my fingertips are just above the apex of her thighs.

She turns suddenly, not trying to get away, but pushing closer. One of her hands is against my chest, her fingers kneading like a cat's claws and the other grips my hair hard enough to sting.

An atavistic growl rumbles my chest.

Her eyes go hazy with passion.

I lean down and demand close to her ear, "Come back to my hotel room with me."

"Yes."

I turn us both and head toward the exit, weaving my way through the crowd while keeping my body between hers and everyone else.

One of my men falls into subtle position behind us, keeping his distance. Although we used mercenaries in Colombia, I took my personal crew with me. I don't travel anywhere without them.

The five men have tonight off, but they followed me to the club and of course one of them plays bodyguard when I leave. Ordered to, or not.

Silvio, one of the deadliest men alive, follows us across the parking lot on silent feet.

When we reach my rental, a sleek black Mercedes SL-Class, Aphrodite pulls up short and steps away from me. "Wait, um…"

I don't crowd her. If she wants to come with me, she will. And she wants to. The proof is in the pheromone saturated air around us.

"Is something wrong?" I ask, my libido riding me as hard as the steel pipe in my pants.

"Tell me where you're staying, and I'll meet you there."

Good girl. I like that she's watching out for herself. She should ask for my driver's license, but that would negate our anonymity. Not that I'd show her the Miceli De Luca identification.

I didn't travel to Colombia under my own name and I'm not giving it out to this stranger. Even one as sexy as Aphrodite.

"I'm at the Ritz-Carlton. Meet me in the lobby."

She nods, her platinum blonde hair looking white under the parking lot lights.

"Order your ride share and I'll wait with you until it gets here." Silvio will follow the rideshare to the hotel.

I wouldn't let women under my protection take one at all. Tonight, this woman is mine and I'll make sure she's protected.

"You don't need to," she says softly, unconsciously biting her bottom lip. "I can wait for my driver in front of the club, near the bouncer."

"No."

Her eyes narrow. "Wanting to have sex with you does not make you the boss of me."

"In the bedroom it does."

She sucks in an audible breath. "You want to get kinky?"

"It's not kink. It's me. I'm a controlling bastard in the bedroom, but I promise you the pleasure I give you will make up for it."

"What does that mean?" She blinks up at me, her perfectly made-up features reflecting unexpected innocence.

"Don't worry, I'm not going to tie you up." Not on our first time together and since there won't be a follow up fuck, not at all. "But I won't stop to ask if every kiss is okay with you or if I can fuck you now."

"But—"

I put my finger against her lips. "You can always say *no*. Or *stop*. Any time. And I will listen. But I will take your silence as consent."

"You won't hurt me?"

"Fuck no. I might fuck you until you are too sore to walk tomorrow, but I don't hurt women."

"I believe you."

"You probably shouldn't." I give her my most charming grin. "But I'm glad you do."

She definitely should not trust a man she just met, but I *won't* hurt her. I know she's safe. She doesn't, but she believes she is.

If she belonged to me, I would spank her ass for following a strange man to his hotel.

Manaja. What the hell? I've never spanked a woman and don't intend to start, no matter how much her luscious ass tempts me.

If she asked, on the other hand…

Hell, if she belonged to me, I'd kill the man and tie her to our bed until she repented even thinking about letting anyone but me touch her.

Where in the three hells is this possessiveness coming from? And the need to protect her?

Both have no place in a one-and-done sex encounter.

It's that damn marriage of convenience hanging over my head. It's short-circuiting my brain.

While I've been thinking ridiculous thoughts, she's been ordering her rideshare.

She looks up from the phone she pulled from the tiny evening bag she's wearing on a gold crossbody chain. "Done. He'll be here in six minutes."

"Just enough time."

"For what?" she asks with more innocence than a woman who dances and looks like she does should be able to project.

"This." Cupping her face, I tilt her head up.

Her lips part on a small gasp and I swallow the sound with my mouth.

CHAPTER 6: RÓISE

Ares's lips demand my submission and I give it. Eagerly allowing my mouth to soften against his, following his lead without hesitation.

Our tongues tangle and I go as high on my tiptoes as I can, but it's not enough. I can't get as close to him as I want.

Strong arms wrap around me and lift.

Yes. Something falls from my hands and I lock them behind his neck, helping him lift me until my breasts are squashed against his hard pecs and my feet are dangling above the ground.

Alien sensations zing through my body. Sparks of want. Starbursts of pleasure. The desire to spread my legs and wind them around his torso.

Moaning, I bend one leg, using my thigh to push me upward.

This. This is what kissing is supposed to feel like.

The sound of a honking horn breaks through the frantic lust building inside me.

Miceli ignores the interruption and keeps kissing me, but my brain is starting to come back online. It's telling me that honking is for me. Or us.

Either way, I pull my head away and drop my leg, embarrassed I was climbing Ares like a tree in the parking lot.

I look around and notice a car idling with its lights on only a few feet away. My rideshare.

My phone. Where is my phone?

It's not in my hand. Memory of dropping something during that scorching kiss has me scanning the pavement around my feet. There it is.

I kneel down to grab it. The movement lights up the screen which is *not* cracked. Another point for my shatterproof phone case.

My driver's name is Evan and the license plate on my app matches the car and I take a step away from Ares. "That's my ride. I'll see you at the hotel."

He nods and then walks to the driver's side door of the rideshare.

Evan drops his window. "Ann?"

"No, but I will be following you all the way to the hotel. Don't try anything with her if you value your life."

"Dial it back a notch, god of war," I order, even though his protectiveness stirs things inside me I don't want to think about.

That I *can't* think about. Not in this situation.

The driver isn't as impressed as my ovaries. "Forget this," he says firmly. "Get your girlfriend a different ride."

The driver's window starts going up.

Ares grabs it and stops it.

"Knock it off. You're going to break my window, man." Evan doesn't sound panicked. He sounds pissed.

"Do not lose me my rideshare, Ares," I warn.

"You will drive my date to the hotel as promised." It's not a question.

I rush to the car and give Evan my most winning smile. "It's fine. I'm harmless, I promise and he's not coming with us."

"He threatened to follow us." He tilts his head and mouths at me, "Are you safe?"

I smile and nod. "My date is a little intense, but he's just looking out for me. You don't have to worry about him."

Suddenly five hundred dollar bills drop through the driver's window into his lap. "Drive Ann to the hotel and you will be fine."

The rideshare driver looks from me to the money. "You promise he's not going to beat me up once we get there, or something?"

"I promise. He'll be too busy with me." I wink.

The driver shakes his head. "Whatever you're into."

Ares opens the back door for me.

I move around him and slide onto the small backseat. "See you soon."

"Yes, you will. Ann."

Something twinges in my chest. The anonymity of made-up pseudonyms is fun. Having him call me by the fake name on my fake I.D. feels deceitful. Especially considering what we plan to do later.

"Aphrodite tonight, remember?"

White teeth flash in a masculine grin. "As you wish, my goddess."

The door shuts and Ares sprints to his car. He's right behind us as we pull out of the parking lot.

"That guy is intense. Are you sure you're safe?" Evan asks me. "I can drop you off at the police station instead, or a friend's house."

"You're a good guy, Evan, but I'm fine. Really." Ares *is* intense.

As much as that kind of arrogance in my uncle and his men irritates me, in Ares it's like catnip to the sexy kitty that wants to come out and play.

Losing my virginity to him will have her purring. He'd be a little too much for day-to-day living though. I have a feeling trying to keep up with him would keep any woman on her toes.

But especially one with as little experience as I have.

"To each her own, but I'll stick with my cinnamon roll boyfriend."

I laugh. "I'm pretty sure Ares would be too much for me as a boyfriend too. Tonight is a one time thing."

"It's like that, is it?" Evan teases.

"For tonight." The rest of my life will be spent with a man I've never met and who I can never love.

How do you love a man who works for the same syndicate that cost you both your parents?

CHAPTER 7: MICELI

*P*resent Day in Severu's Office

I avoid looking at the young woman I have been instructed to marry. I will do my duty to *la famiglia*, but I can't drum up any excitement for tying my life to a woman more than a decade younger than me.

And fucking Irish to boot.

When she fails to respond to something Shaughnessy says, I finally focus my gaze on her.

Brilliant green eyes stare back at me, her expression a strange mix of trepidation and dislike. Something about her is familiar. Have I seen her at one of the clubs? No. She's not twenty-one yet and a mob princess isn't going to risk getting into a mafia owned club with fake I.D., is she?

Too big a chance her actions will blow back on her family.

Then she speaks. "Uh...hello," she says after a short hesitation.

I know that voice.

Aphrodite.

The woman who has haunted me for two damn months.

Other than her voice, the woman standing in front of me has nothing in common with the siren who gave me the best sex of my life.

And a gift I had not looked for.

It can't be her.

But then she speaks again, a wisecrack about keeping it in the family when she's introduced to my don, me and Big Sal. That snarky tone is pure Aphrodite.

Róise...*cazzo*, I thought her name was Ann...is wearing black like that night in Portland.

The color of the dress is the only similarity between then and now though.

This black dress has a full skirt that reaches past her knees like something from the 1950s. It hides the perfect curve of her lush ass and although it highlights her waist, her tits with their raspberry pink nipples are hidden behind a conservative bodice.

Not a single inch of the creamy skin I spent so much time licking and marking is on display. Her black leather flats add nothing to her diminutive height.

My intended fiancée's outfit wouldn't be out of place at a funeral.

The platinum hair is gone. Her waxed pussy hadn't hinted at the dark brown curls that shine with rich copper glints under the bright office lighting.

If she's wearing any at all, Róise's makeup is subdued and does nothing to give her the look of false sophistication she had two months ago.

That woman's innocence better matches this woman's presence.

Accidente. She definitely didn't come with the intention of impressing her future fiancé.

Not like two months ago when she'd been dressed to kill with makeup that changed her features more than I realized.

Or my mind is just playing fucked up tricks on me. There's one way to know for sure.

With a perfunctory greeting, I put my hand out to shake.

Her uncle has to prod her, but Róise takes it. Her fingers slide against my palm and the electric current that jumps between us from that simple touch is as familiar as her voice.

Unwilling to put off learning the truth, I turn her hand over so I can see the memorial tattoo on her forearm. It's there. If it were angel's wings, or something common, I could believe it was a million-to-one coincidence, but this?

No.

The overlapping butterflies in flight are distinctive both in design and coloring, going from vibrant blues and purples to black. There are two dates under them. Her parents' deaths, she'd said.

Fury battles with shock and *relief* that only increases my rage.

What is there to be relieved about?

She's a good lay. So are thousands of other women in New York. Her charade only goes to show how good she is at deception.

"You tricked me," I accuse.

She tries to yank her hand from mine.

I don't let go.

"We can talk about that later," she hisses.

"How did my niece trick you?" Shaughnessy demands. "You two have never met to my knowledge."

Something flashes in my soon-to-be fiancée's emerald eyes. Fear? Anger?

"As you well know, I didn't even know his name until this morning," she says in an even tone to her uncle.

Her quick sidestep only increases my distrust of her, but her implication is unacceptable if it is the truth.

I wouldn't lay odds on that though.

"Is that true?" I demand of Shaughnessy in a voice that lets him know I expect an answer and no damn prevaricating like his niece.

"She agreed to the blood alliance," Shaughnessy says without actually answering my question.

"It runs in the family," I say with disgust and squeeze Róise's hand before repeating my question. "Is. That. True?"

Her too young features set in a mutinous frown, but she nods.

"Why wouldn't you tell her who her intended husband is?" my brother, Don of the Genovese, asks.

Shaughnessy hems and haws, but doesn't say anything that explains it.

"If you let go of my hand, I will tell you," Róise bargains.

This woman. "I shouldn't have to make a deal to get honesty out of you."

"That goes both ways."

Not sure what the hell she means by that, but I let go of her without putting distance between us. "Start talking."

"He didn't want to give me any reason to back out of the deal. Though he should have realized that learning who you are would only make me more determined to go through with this unholy bargain."

Unholy bargain? Melodramatic much?

"Why is that?" Severu asks when I don't.

Róise looks at him. "Your brother's reputation precedes him. He is both ruthless and a womanizer."

"And that made you *want* to marry him?" Severu looks at me like I should know what she's talking about.

I don't have the first clue, unless she's planning to spy on us for her uncle. Despising me will make that easier for her to justify to herself.

"It made me *not* want my cousin offered up in my place."

"Your cousin is already married." To Shaughnessy's underboss.

"My *younger* cousin."

The Irish mob boss only has one other daughter. No way is Róise talking about Fiona Shaughnessy.

"She's still in high school for fuck's sake." The look of disgust I give to Shaughnessy is lost on him.

He's too busy glaring at Róise. "She'll be eighteen before the wedding."

"I would not agree to marry a damned teenager." Róise is almost twenty-one and that is bad enough.

"If I back out, then you won't agree to the blood alliance?" Róise asks with enough hopefulness to do serious damage to the ego of an average man.

Good thing I am not average. I'm starting to get amused. Róise clearly does not want to marry into our family. That bodes well for her *not* being a spy.

"You have already given your word," I remind her. "If you back out now, not only will the blood alliance not happen, but our two syndicates will become enemies."

She crosses her arms over her sweet little curves. "Aren't we already?"

"No."

"We have a truce," Severu adds, looking at my almost fiancée like he's trying to figure her out. "That truce would end."

"More blood would spill," Shaughnessy says with a meaningful look at his niece. "Innocents as well as soldiers would be caught up in the conflict."

"We don't hurt innocents," I bark.

Róise's expression is pure disbelief. "Tell that to my mom. Oh, wait, you can't because she's dead."

"Your mother died ten years ago." Big Sal speaks directly to Róise for the first time since she and her uncle entered the office.

"Eleven, but who's counting?" she demands caustically. "In case you are wondering, that would be me."

Okay, two things Aphrodite and Róise have in common. The voice and that sarcastic attitude.

Sal nods ponderously. "Your mother's death was unfortunate."

"Agreed." Shaughnessy frowns at his niece as if daring her to continue.

I could have told him that would only spur her on. And I only knew her for one night when she was pretending to be someone else.

How does he not realize it?

"My mother died after being hit by a stray bullet fired from a Cosa Nostra gun during our so-called truce." The look she gives me says she holds me personally responsible.

My dick twitches with inappropriate interest. That angry fervency is too close to the sexual passion she met me with that night in Portland. A perfect match to my own despite the innocence I discovered too late.

Big Sal clears his throat. "The Bonanno Family and your grandfather had bad blood between them."

"Cleansed by the spilling of my mother's."

As brutal as that truth is, she is right. Her mother's death absolved the former mob boss's sins in the Bonanno don's eyes.

"We are not the Bonannos," I point out.

"You swore on the godfather's ring, just like every other mafia man in this city."

Every high level made man, but she's not going to care about the distinction. "I did."

"Which makes you Cosa Nostra."

"It does." Part of the syndicate responsible for her mom's death.

I get it. She doesn't like that, but I'm proud to be Cosa Nostra. Even prouder to be the Genovese underboss.

"Enough," Shaughnessy barks. "You agreed to this betrothal, Róise. It is done."

"But it's not done is it? Not until I give birth to a De Luca baby."

Which according to the agreement won't happen for at least two years because that's when she goes off her birth control. I didn't argue about that addition to the contract between our families.

My nephew is precious to me and I hope Severu and Catalina have lots of kids for Neri to play with, but I'm content to wait to be called papà myself.

There's no rush. Unlike my brother, I don't need heirs to take over from me one day.

CHAPTER 8: RÓISE

"Take a seat." Don De Luca indicates a seating area similar to the one in my uncle's office.

But unlike Uncle Brogan's penchant for traditional furniture in dark wood, Severu De Luca favors sleek, modern lines. And his office is even more massive than my uncle's.

There's room for the traditional office suite of executive desk and visitor's chairs, plus the seating area. Three dark leather couches form three sides of a square, while two matching chairs with a table between them make up the final side.

It reminds me of the main living room in the mansion.

Across from the seating area is a glass conference table with twelve chairs. A pile of documents and folders sits at one end.

Everything is staged to set a tone. That tone is wealth and power with a dash of prestige.

I'm in my third year of theater study at college; I know something about staging.

So does the don apparently.

I make a beeline for one of the chairs, but Ares...darn it, *Miceli* grabs my wrist. "Let's sit here."

Here is one of the sofas. He neatly maneuvers me to one end and sits smack in the middle, right beside me. His arm stretches across the back of the couch, surrounding me with his heat and scent.

The familiar peppery fragrance, with earthy undertones and a hint of lemon is enhanced by something I discovered that night in Portland is pure *him*.

I snooped in the bathroom of his suite and discovered the cologne is Dark Lord by Kilian. Two months ago, I didn't think anything of it. Now? It's funny, in a macabre way.

The mafia underboss is definitely a dark lord.

"Would anyone like coffee?" the don asks.

My gaze locks on the low table in the center of a seating area. It holds a tray with a gold rimmed China coffee service, complete with the obligatory pot of coffee, five cups and cream and sugar.

"No thank you," I say politely.

This meeting is stressful enough. Holding a hot beverage right now is just asking for trouble.

"I'll have a cup." My uncle sits back on the sofa with a complacent look directed my way.

In our home, men never pour their own coffee. Lucky for me and my feminist sensibilities, my uncle (and sometimes his men) only join us for dinner.

Grateful to put some distance between me and Miceli, I stand quickly and lean over to pick up the coffee pot. After pouring my uncle's cup, I add a splash of creamer, stir it with one of the small teaspoons and put it down in front of him.

I lay the teaspoon on a napkin on the tray since there are no saucers.

I'm about to sit back down when Uncle Brogan clears his throat meaningfully.

Since it will keep me out of my seat a little longer, I indulge his chauvinism and ask, "Can I pour for anyone else?"

Mamo would be proud of me. Not for the polite question, but for asking it in an even tone with no sarcasm.

Pick your battles, Rosy-girl.

"Thank you, I will have a cup. Two lumps of sugar. No milk." Big Sal watches me like he's measuring my every movement against a ruler in his head.

I do not roll my eyes. Go me.

I pour the consigliere's coffee, doctor it and put it down on the table near him. His eyes narrow, like it offends him I didn't pass it directly to him.

Oh, well. I guess that's one ding against me.

"Sit down, Róise. My brother and I are capable of pouring our own coffee." Miceli casts an irritated glance at Big Sal De Luca.

The older man stares back blandly.

Miceli pours him and his brother cups of coffee, putting nothing in either. I suppress a shudder of revulsion. You cannot convince me that coffee without flavored syrup and oatmilk (other milk will do in a pinch) is meant for human consumption.

Black coffee is the worst.

"Do you want something cold to drink?" Miceli asks me.

I start to shake my head, but my throat is suddenly parched and I swivel so I'm nodding. "Yes, thank you."

"What would you like?"

To leave? To go somewhere private for five minutes to process the fact this is the man I had sex with two months ago?

Not happening. "Water is fine."

Miceli grabs his phone and sends a text, putting it back in his jacket before sitting down again. His thigh brushes mine and I jump.

Good thing I wasn't holding coffee, isn't it?

The don crosses one ankle over his knee and takes a sip of the unappealing coffee. "Your uncle tells us you are studying theater, Róise."

"Yes."

"You went to Portland to take an acting seminar a couple of months ago." The don's dark gaze penetrates so I feel like he's reading my mind.

He can't though. Right? Right.

No mind reading.

Miceli tenses beside me. His arm shifting so it lands softly over my shoulders. Is he trying to warn me not to say anything?

He doesn't need to worry. I'm not about to say anything about my wild night of freedom in front of my uncle.

"Uh, yes."

"Miceli was in Portland at the same time I believe. But you wouldn't have run into each other."

Something garbled comes out of my mouth that is supposed to be agreement.

"I spent the night I was there at the club and then went back to my hotel." Miceli's words *sound* like an agreement.

If you're his brother, that is.

To me, they sound like a taunt.

"Um..." I cast around wildly inside my head for something to say to change the subject, usually my specialty.

Then a woman arrives with a Karafe of water and glasses on a tray. She transfers them to the larger tray on the table and leaves without a word.

No one seems to think that's weird.

"Thank you," I call after her.

Don De Luca's lips tilt in the tiniest of smiles. Huh.

My uncle grunts. We've had the "Don't thank the staff for doing their jobs," conversation too many times for him to even bother anymore.

Big Sal is putting another mark against me in his mental tally. I just know it.

If he checks off enough negatives, will he advise his don to cancel the marriage part of the alliance?

Miceli pours a glass of water, drops a lemon wedge in it and hands it to me.

"What if I didn't like lemon?" I ask with enough snark that my uncle clears his throat again.

This time it's all censure. Ooops.

"Uncle Sal is the one who convinced me this blood alliance is good for *la famiglia*," the don says.

The sip of water I'm trying to take spills down the front of my black dress.

I narrow my eyes at him. "Did you take a class in mind-reading?"

"Your face is very expressive."

When I'm not thinking about it. Which is most of the time, to be honest.

"You like lemon." Miceli pats at the wet spots on my chest with a napkin. "You're too tart not to."

"Ha ha." I grab the napkin from him.

Memories from that night two months ago spin to the forefront of my mind again, but I shove them back.

This is now. And now my Ares is actually a Cosa Nostra underboss with a brother who sees way too much for my own good.

And apparently an uncle who went to the same school for hidebound patriarchs as my own.

CHAPTER 9: MICELI

Róise does her best to answer monosyllabically as both Severu and Uncle Sal subtly grill her. But I want more and I push for it.

She looks at me with pure dislike after I ask her to elaborate on something she said again.

"My plan *was* to be an actor. Now it's to get my degree and try not to kill the man I'm supposed to marry."

Uncle Sal and Brogan make matching sounds of disapproval. Sev looks amused, damn him. But I'm tempted to laugh too.

"I never realized Irish mob princesses were so bloodthirsty."

"I'm not a princess and I'm only half Irish."

Her uncle pounds the sofa arm. "You're a Shaughnessy. You're Irish."

This is an argument they've had before.

"Organized crime families are as close to royalty as you get in America." Severu stands. "Miceli, a word?"

"No need. I'm ready to sign the contracts now."

He nods, showing me the respect of knowing my own mind. "Let's move to the table, gentlemen. Are you ready to make this official, Róise?"

Her emerald eyes widen in shock, but she nods. "I don't have much choice, do I?"

Severu shrugs. He can be a ruthless son of a bitch and he wants the blood alliance with the Irish.

He's not giving Róise an out.

If I was a better man, I would suggest another way of guaranteeing the alliance, or at least waiting to formalize it.

I don't.

This is about keeping *la famiglia* strong and safe. And if I have to have the same woman in my bed for the rest of my life, it might as well be one I want as much as I do Róise.

Even if she is too young and irreverent for an underboss's wife.

Everyone sits down when we reach the table. Again, I make sure Róise is beside me, with no other man on her other side.

She gives me a disgruntled frown. "You're clingy for a leader in a criminal organization."

Big Sal finally allows the humor that has been building in him since Róise opened her mouth the first time to burst out in a big guffaw.

She thinks he doesn't like her, but he's been using his disapproving face to hide his mirth for the last hour. Will he be as amused if our cousin Salvatore marries a woman with so much sass?

Róise is staring at Big Sal like she's never seen him before. "Is he alright?"

"Fine."

"But he's laughing."

"At you," her uncle grumbles.

"At your niece's sass," Big Sal corrects. "She'll be a good match for Miceli."

"You think I'm a good *match for him*?" Róise demands, sounding disappointed. "But—"

My uncle interrupts her. "It takes a strong woman to stand beside a Cosa Nostra underboss."

"But I think it's stupid for women to serve men like they're the superior species."

"Humans are all the same species and lucky you, my nephews see things the same way."

"You do?" Róise asks me suspiciously.

"I think you'll find the Genovese mafia a little more progressive than the Irish," my brother answers for me.

"It's not progressive to let women into your ranks, it's foolish." Brogan shakes his head. "But you run your mob your way, I'll run mine."

"You allow women to be *made*?" she asks, incredulous.

"Don't tell me you think women can't be just as ruthless as men?" I mock.

"Of course they can, but I'm shocked you believe it too."

"My daughter is my son's underboss," Big Sal says proudly. "She's fierce."

"Wow. I want to meet her."

"You'll get to meet Nerissa and the rest of the family at your birthday party," Sev says.

"My birthday party?" She looks at her uncle, clearly confused.

Brogan pats his pockets, finds a cigar and pulls it out. "Miceli will be hosting your 21st birthday."

The mob boss chews on one end of his cigar but doesn't light it. Sev does not allow smoking in his office, or any other part of the Oscuro building.

"What? No, we're going to—"

"You know birthdays and holidays have to be sacrificed sometimes."

"For the good of the mob." Róise's tone reveals what she thinks of that truth.

And it's not good.

Brogan is unfazed.

"What were you planning to do for your birthday?" I ask. Maybe it can be incorporated into the plans.

But she shakes her head, clearly unwilling to share.

Róise insists on reading every line of the prenup agreement before she's willing to sign it. Brogan blusters, but I push the document toward her and ask her uncle a question about a weapons shipment we are getting from him.

It's small arms and ammunition, not like the large weapon purchase I was in Portland to negotiate with the Hades Brotherhood. The first rocket launcher they sold us came in handy down in Colombia.

After reading the first couple of pages, Róise looks up. "Why are we signing this when divorce is not an option?"

"Once we have a child together, the alliance between our families is set."

"So we can divorce after that?" she asks a little too eagerly.

"Under certain circumstances." The De Lucas don't divorce, but neither am I going to kill my wife if we find ourselves egregiously incompatible.

She grabs the prenup and starts to read again.

Putting her finger down to hold her place on the page, she looks up. "You retain full custody of our child, or children?"

"Only if we divorce."

"Duh." She bites her lip and looks at her uncle furtively.

He's busy talking to Big Sal.

Róise's shoulders relax. "If you're too much of a manwhore for me to stay married to you, I'm not giving you custody of my child."

"Read the next page." It spells out what happens if either of us is unfaithful.

After I kill the man who touches her (which is not spelled out in the prenup, but should be obvious), the divorce terms will not only grant me full custody, but discretion about visitation. And her settlement goes from ten million to zero.

If I cheat, which I won't; a De Luca's word is binding. But if I did, I would have to share custody equally with her.

Since there is no settlement for me in the event of divorce, that punitive result does not apply.

"You're not that progressive after all." Her frown judges me and finds me wanting. "You only have to give me shared custody, but I lose all access to my child."

"I won't cheat."

"Neither will I."

"Good." Then no one has to die. "The point is moot."

She grumbles something about still living in the last century and goes back to reading. When she's done, she pushes the stack of papers back toward me.

"Do you want to change anything?" I ask.

"Of course not," Brogan says, proving he was paying attention even while talking to my uncle. "I already approved all the clauses."

Róise frowns at her uncle and then turns that disgruntled look on me. "Are you willing to change the custody clauses?"

"No."

"Then no."

"Are you sure?" Sev butts in. "You could get another ten mil out of him easily in your settlement."

"The money doesn't matter."

"Says a woman who has never had to go without it," Brogan says patronizingly.

"Every man in here inherited his wealth." Her eyes flash with anger. "None of you has gone without either."

Brogan puts his hands up as if surrendering. "Don't be getting angry, lass. Na, and we haven't gone without but when I was twenty, I was working the family business, not taking classes teaching me how to play make believe."

If the mob boss wants to calm his niece down, he's going about it ass-backwards.

"And I'm signing away my life for the family business, despite wanting nothing to do with it," Róise points out, scorn vibrating from every pore. "That prenup is nothing more than a seedy offer of ten million dollars for my child."

"Against my advice, Miceli is offering an out that most women in our world don't get," Big Sal informs her. "Most prenups in our world are written to discourage filing for divorce by withholding any financial support."

"For the wife. And if the mafia man divorces her? There's no punitive clause for him, is there." Róise shakes her head. "Typical men. I'm not surprised a Cosa Nostra underboss puts such a negligible value on his child."

The look of derision she levels at me exponentially outdoes the one she gave her uncle. "Miceli could triple the settlement without putting a dent in the public account he keeps for the IRS, but that's not the point, is it?"

Stung at the implied criticism of my provision for her if we should separate, I slash through the ten million and write one-hundred-million before initialing it.

"Unless you're changing the custody clause, I'm not impressed." Her glare stays fixed on my face.

"One hundred million doesn't earn even a smile?"

Not a flicker of surprise, much less appreciation lights her green gaze. "No. Money is currency. Children are life and you're not buying mine."

She can't know it, but every word out of her mouth shows how well Róise will fit in with my family.

The mafia is important. They are family as well as business, but the De Lucas come before all others.

I am not taking on a twenty-year old virtual stranger for the profits we will get from joint ventures with the Shaughnessy mob; I am marrying Róise because this blood alliance is another wall of protection around my family.

CHAPTER 10: RÓISE

The two-ton boulder of fatalism sitting on my heart since agreeing to this marriage alliance, grinds and shifts ominously.

I have no choice about marrying Miceli De Luca. Because it's not just a matter of protecting Fiona now. It's the only way to protect the rest of my family from ending up like my parents in a war with the Genovese mafia.

I might hate my future husband for it. I might despise my uncle. But I will do it.

What I will not do is sign this horrible prenup.

I put the pen down on top of the papers. "You are not buying my children," I repeat.

My uncle curses virulently in a mix of Irish and English. He knows I mean it. That I will not be moved. Like the Shaughnessy women before me, when I take a stand, I keep it.

I ignore him, staring Miceli De Luca down.

"I'm not trying to buy *my* children." His anger is rising to match mine. And I like it.

I want to get under his skin. Make him mad. Make him feel even a tiny drop of the helplessness I do.

"That document says you are." I nod toward the offending papers. "If you mean what you say, then change it. Take out the settlement entirely. I don't care, but if we divorce, we share custody."

"I'm not removing the clause about adultery."

"Fine..." I pause.

He looks triumphant.

"But it has to be reciprocal. If you take a lover outside our marriage, I get full custody."

"Agreed."

The instant capitulation stuns me.

"De Luca men don't cheat," the don explains.

I cross my arms and glare at the most powerful Cosa Nostra leader in New York. "Neither do Shaughnessy women."

"Good to know."

"You cannot move out of New York," Big Sal says firmly. "It would be too hard on the children."

In other words, even if I do divorce Miceli De Luca, going to Los Angeles to pursue an acting career is out. There's plenty of live theaters here in New York, though.

It's not my dream, but it's something to hope for. In the future.

Give Miceli a child, divorce him and my life is my own again.

It's a better future than I thought I could have walking into this office.

"If you file for divorce before our youngest child is six, the custody arrangements remain as stated."

"What? Why?"

"Because we owe our children a home and you can't make a home when you have one foot out the door."

He keeps saying children. Plural.

"What if you file for divorce before then?"

"I won't be filing for divorce. I keep my promises."

Implying I don't? "Even those made under duress?" I taunt.

"I will keep every promise I make to you."

I have to look away from his intent gaze. "I still want the agreement to be reciprocating."

"Agreed."

He really believes he won't divorce me. Will I divorce him? I don't know, but I do know that I need this out.

"Regardless of the custody agreement, I will provide full time security for our children and you," he adds.

Does it really matter who hires our bodyguards? With his experience in the underworld, Miceli is more qualified than I am to hire the security personnel.

Unable to see a downside, I nod slowly. "Okay."

Miceli gets up and goes to his brother's desk. He opens the computer and is soon typing away. It's weird to see him do that. Doesn't he have someone to make the changes for him?

Maybe the De Lucas consider the contract too sensitive to let anyone else see it. It is different than what they say mafia couples usually sign, if they have a prenup at all.

The whir of a printer comes from near the big executive desk.

Miceli returns to the table a few seconds later and places two stacks of paper in front of me. "Read it, initial each page and sign both copies."

There's no reason to argue, but I want to. He's just so freaking bossy. It's really annoying.

When I'm done, I slide the papers over to him. "You didn't remove the settlement."

"No, I didn't. It wasn't in there to buy my children." His offense at my accusation makes his voice hard.

I refuse to be intimidated. That's how the contract read to me. "Child," I correct him. "Twins don't run in our family."

"You assume we'll divorce after our first child is born."

Of course I do. "First implies more than one. We're having one kid and then we are both free." That's the hope of a future I'll cling to walking down the aisle. "Wait, can we have a civil service and skip all the religious stuff for the wedding?"

The don, my uncle and Big Sal all say, "No," at the same time.

Miceli doesn't say anything. His expression is almost pitying.

I don't need his pity. I might be younger than him and have no part in organized crime, but I just negotiated a future for myself with a mafia underboss, his don and my mob boss uncle.

"Your turn to sign," I point out.

He does it without comment, initialing each page with dark black slashes and signing with the same confident strokes.

When he's done, the woman who brought the water returns and notarizes the document. I thought a notary had to watch a contract being signed, but this is the mafia.

The fact everything but the spot on the page she's supposed to emboss with her stamp is covered supports my assumption they don't want anyone but us to know the details of the contract.

Too bad. I'm telling my grandmother and cousins all about this meeting. And every detail of the prenup.

"Now, it's time to sign the contract that matters." My uncle rubs his hands together.

I disagree. Whatever is in the alliance agreement between the two syndicates, it will never be as important to me as the one I just signed.

My uncle reads through the documents and then grunts. "It's all in order."

"Naturally." Severu pulls a knife from a hidden holster.

Uncle Brogan pulls his own knife out, a switchblade he always keeps handy. He flicks something with his thumb and the wickedly sharp blade pops up.

My heart hammers in my chest. "What are you doing?"

They just agreed everything is in order. Why are their knives out?

"Signing the contract," Big Sal says, like it should be obvious.

"With knives?" I demand in disbelief.

Miceli pulls his own knife out and sets it on the table between us. "With blood."

My uncle offers his hand to the don, palm up. Don De Luca slices a shallow cut across my uncle's palm. At least I hope it's shallow.

Blood wells immediately.

After dipping his thumb in the blood, Uncle Brogan presses it down on the top right corner of each page until he gets to the last one. This time, he leaves his thumbprint beside his printed name at the bottom.

After tying a handkerchief around his hand, my uncle cuts the don's palm the same way. Then Don De Luca goes through the same process, leaving his thumbprint right beside my uncles on each page until the last one. Where he leaves it beside his name at the bottom like my uncle did.

"You couldn't have just signed it?"

"The cuts show their trust in each other. The fingerprint and blood DNA are irrefutable evidence that they signed the contract." Miceli puts his hand out to me, palm up. "It's our turn."

"But I don't trust you and you shouldn't trust me."

"Are you going to cut my finger off?" he asks, sounding too darned amused.

"I could and not because I want to." I have training in self-defense.

I can even shoot a gun and hit what I'm aiming at. Something my father insisted on after my mother's death. I have never trained with a knife though.

"You'll do fine."

"I haven't read the contract."

"And you won't," Miceli says implacably.

I cross my arms, relieved, because I'm pretty sure none of them want me reading the contract. "Then I'm not signing it."

"Your signature isn't necessary, just your cooperation," Uncle Brogan says.

"Is there anything in there that affects me other than the marriage and giving birth to a child I already agreed to?" I ask.

"No."

"Then you don't need my signature," I agree.

And if my uncle isn't being 100% truthful with me, I can't be held to the terms of a document I haven't signed.

Miceli flips his knife over his fingers, the hilt landing in his palm. "You will put your bloody thumbprint beside mine on the page that refers to our marriage and offspring."

"Offspring? Who says that?"

His eyes don't reflect a single glimmer of emotion. "Contracts say that."

"I'm not signing a contract I haven't read," I say again, stubbornly.

"You can read the page your thumbprint is on." Don De Luca's voice brooks no further argument.

My stomach roils. Because I'm going to argue. "No."

"Damn it, Róise, now is not the time to be stubborn. I told you there's nothing in there you need to worry about."

Part of me believes my uncle. He's spoken truth I don't like. But to my knowledge, he's never lied to me. It's that *to my knowledge part* I can't get past.

Not after the blackmail.

"I promise on my vow as a made man that there is nothing else in that contract beyond our marriage and the promise of a child carrying both our DNA that pertains to you personally. All the terms will eventually effect you as a Shaughnessy and a future member of our family." Miceli's words ring with truth.

To doubt them would be a huge insult considering he vowed on his honor, or you know...the equivalent to a mafia man.

Even so, I should definitely not trust my future Cosa Nostra husband more than I do my own uncle. But I do.

"Róise," Uncle Brogan says warningly.

I look into Miceli's eyes and warn him with my own that I will do whatever I have to get back at him if he's lying to me. And then I nod. "Okay, I'll sign it."

Miceli places the sheet of paper in question in front of me.

I read each word, heat prickling along my arms and legs and up the back of my neck as the words sink in.

This is really going to happen. I am going to marry Miceli De Luca, a member of the syndicate that killed my parents. And I'm going to give him a child for the sake of peace between our crime families.

We, the undersigned, Miceli Mars De Luca...

"Your middle name is Mars?" I ask in a strangled voice.

"Our parents named him after the Roman god of war because as the second son, it is his role to wage war on behalf of our family," the don answers.

When he called himself Ares in Portland, he was giving me a sliver of truth about himself. My heart kathunks in my chest. What does that mean?

Do I even want to know?

and Róise Aisling Shaughnessy, agree on this X^th day of April in the year of 20— to join in holy matrimony to bring together the De Luca and Shaughnessy families of New York in a blood alliance, described herein.

We agree to the following terms.

> 1. *This legal marriage will take place no later than the 30th of Jun in the year of 20—.*

> 2. *Róise will remain on birth control that does not compromise her long term reproductive capabilities, at her discretion, for the first two years after the marriage takes place.*

> 3. *The marriage will have issue of at least one living child.*

> 4. *Róise Shaughnessy will be loyal and faithful to the Genovese Family as well as the De Luca family, causing them no harm and keeping their secrets.*

> 5. *Miceli De Luca will be loyal and faithful to the Shaughnessy mob insofar as such loyalty does not compromise his vow to the Cosa Nostra, causing no harm and guarding their secrets.*

Miceli De Luca

Róise Shaughnessy

The wedding has to take place the same month I graduate from college. That's only a little over a year away.

Clammy sweat forms on my forehead and in my armpits.

"Give me your hand, Róise." Miceli puts his hand out, palm up like the other men.

Only he wants me to place mine on top, not cut him.

I look at him and try to speak past my suddenly dry and tight throat. "I don't know if I can do this."

My words are barely above a whisper, but he hears me. Maybe the others do too, but my focus can't move beyond Miceli's handsome face.

The face of a man who should be my enemy, but will one day be my husband.

"I'm not your enemy, Róise. I never will be."

Did I say those words out loud? I must have. I'm pretty sure Miceli does not have his brother's gift of reading minds.

"But—"

With a gentle grip on my wrist, he lifts my right hand and places it in his outstretched palm. "It will be alright."

Nodding, I look away like I do when I'm getting a shot or having blood drawn and feel a tiny prick on my right thumb.

Shocked I jerk my head forward and look down. A drop of blood is welling on the pad of my thumb.

"Squeeze it a little and there will be enough blood to sign the contract."

I can only stare at the tiny drop of welling blood.

He squeezes my thumb between his and his forefinger and the drop grows. He releases the pressure on my thumb and rubs the blood around so it covers the pad completely.

"Do it quickly before the blood dries," he says.

I press my thumb down beside my name under the promise to marry this man.

He pulls my hand to his mouth and sucks the blood away from my thumb. Erotic chills replace the horror of seconds ago. Will I always react to him like this?

My body going up in flames at his slightest touch.

He releases my thumb from his mouth. "Now it's your turn."

He means for me to cut him.

I shake my head, putting my hands under the table so he can't put the knife in them. "I don't want to. Have my uncle do it."

"No." Miceli doesn't say anything else, but he waits.

Like he's confident I can and will do what is necessary.

"Say something to make me mad," I tell him. "I think I could cut you then."

"Bloodthirsty, I like it," he teases.

I shake my head. "I mean it."

"No."

"Can't you say anything else?"

"I'll help you if you want."

My head is nodding before my brain catches up, but then I'm locked in.

He curls his hand around mine and guides the dagger to the pad of his thumb. He exerts pressure and suddenly it's his blood I see. I don't know why, but I squeeze his thumb increasing the size of the droplet. He could do this himself, but for some reason I don't understand, I have to.

Like he did with me, I smear the red viscous fluid around the pad of his thumb.

It feels as intimate as his mouth on mine.

He puts his bloody print beside his name on the contract and I hear the click of a padlock going into place.

It's done and my future is locked into place, inexorably connected to his. We haven't spoken any vows and we're not married, but I'm tied to Miceli De Luca all the same.

CHAPTER 11: RÓISE

Irritation makes my steps faster than normal heading to the armored SUV that will take us back to Long Island.

Okay, maybe my comment was a little awkward. "I guess you have my number to call with any questions about my birthday party."

I was still feeling a little out of it after that whole *sign it in blood* thing and maybe even a tiny bit grateful to Miceli for how he handled it.

But the underboss looked at me like I was a mafia groupie hitting on him and said, "The call will come from my sister-in-law."

Right. Why bother calling the woman you've just signed a contract *in blood* promising to marry?

The whole episode felt like it came right out of a period drama. Right up to Miceli's offhand dismissal of me afterward.

Only my life isn't a television series. There was real bloodshed and there are genuine long term consequences for me. I'm eventually going to have a child with Miceli De Luca. Divorce, or not, he will always have a role in my life as the father of my child.

So, sue me for thinking that means we should maybe get to know each other. Enemies, or not. Because we *are* getting married next summer.

And I would prefer not to walk down the aisle with a complete stranger waiting at the other end.

We're going to be living together for at least nine years. *If* we don't have any other children.

Nine years!

Because I am not giving up my child. Not for anything.

If I go off my birth control early, I could maybe shave a year, or so off of that. That's still seven to eight years living the life of an underboss's wife, surrounded by the Italian mafia.

Why did I agree to that clause?

I glare at my uncle, sitting in the back of the SUV with me now, on his phone and oblivious to the cauldron of anger bubbling inside me.

Why didn't he stick up for me, even a little?

Because the old dinosaur thinks I should stay married to Miceli. Till death do us part.

In the mafia world, that isn't the promise of relationship longevity some people think it is.

I respect the sanctity of marriage which is why I wanted to get married in a civil ceremony. I don't want to make vows in a church that have an expiration date.

And no, I don't want Miceli to die to set me free. The image of his inert body, lying in a pool of blood tightens my stomach with nausea.

I wish I could crack my window, but that's a security no-no.

Gah!

And my uncle just sits there, not even a little bothered by how his plans have hijacked *my* life.

"I guess I passed inspection," I grumble, wondering if Uncle Brogan will even bother to respond.

But that first hour we were there? That was so the De Lucas could size me up. So Miceli could decide if he wanted to go through with the marriage alliance.

Because unlike me, he has a choice. Had one, anyway. Before the whole blood thing.

Him, his brother and uncle were looking me over like a new car. Miceli has even had a look under my hood.

Not that I'm telling my uncle that.

I'm still furious with Fate for that trick.

"It wasn't an inspection."

"Oh, please. It so was an inspection."

"The De Lucas wanted to get to know you, that's all."

"Funny, you didn't seem to care if I got to know Miceli," I accuse.

"He will make you a good husband."

"Temporarily."

Uncle Brogan's eyes the same green as mine snap with impatient umbrage. What can I say? My uncle's temper makes him easy. And right now, I want to vent my anger. He's not just an easy target, he's the perfect one.

It's his fault this morning even happened.

"Don't be a child." He looks at me with patronizing disapproval. "You are not divorcing him."

"You just keep telling yourself that. I didn't fight over those custody clauses because I don't intend to utilize the divorce option if I need to."

"You won't," he assures me. "The De Luca family believes in fidelity, and they actively try to suppress domestic violence within their ranks."

"Do you?" I ask, the need to know superseding my anger.

"Mob wives can't go to the police, but every woman in the Shaughnessy clan knows she can come to me, and I will deal with it."

"Personally?" It's a big mob.

"Yes."

"Oh." My desire to pick a fight with my uncle wanes a little.

"As the weaker sex, our women need to be protected."

Just like that, I'm furious with the old chauvinist all over again.

"I can't believe we all signed the alliance contract in blood." I give an exaggerated shudder, but my memories aren't the queasy ones from when the don and Uncle Brogan cut each other's palms. "Where do you file contracts like that, with the devil?"

"None of your concern," he dismisses.

"Like the terms of the alliance are none of my concern? Even though they cost me my future?"

"Enough!" My uncle's bellow reverberates in the car, his temper finally slipping its leash.

I don't flinch. Uncle Brogan won't hit me, and I refuse to be cowed by his shouting. That doesn't mean I like it.

I don't.

"My reproductive system is the guarantor for the contract," I remind him in case he forgot. "That gives me a stake in it."

"Don't be crass, Róise."

I can't help rolling my eyes. "You're such a dinosaur. Mentioning my uterus is not crass. It's biology."

The argument is taking my mind off of Miceli's curt dismissal, and I might be having fun too.

Just a little bit.

Maybe I should say the word vagina next. I doubt Uncle Brogan has ever heard the word said aloud by any of the women in our family.

Chances are none of the men have said it either. They're more likely to use another word. One that would really send my uncle through the roof if it came out of my mouth.

Oooh, the temptation.

"Leave biology out of this, young lady."

"I'm almost twenty-one, Uncle Brogan."

"Old enough to know better."

"Old enough to be spoken to like an adult. Especially as it is my status as an adult with a vagina *and* a uterus that makes me your ideal tool right now."

"Róise!"

Gotcha.

An answer to my own earlier question pops into my head. "The bunker."

Of course he keeps contracts for the illegal mob dealings there. And now a blood alliance contract, complete with my marriage to the Genovese underboss.

Uncle Brogan's brows draw together in a thunderous frown. "Where did you hear about the bunker?"

Unwilling to rat on my grandmother, I shrug. "Could have been one of the times I listened outside grandfather's office."

It wasn't, but it could have been.

Mamo tells us all sorts of things I'm sure my uncle wouldn't approve of, just like my grandfather before him.

But my grandmother says that a woman born into the mob has to be as canny as any mobster. That's why we started playing the listening game. She taught us girls that too.

We still play it, but now we know it's not a game. My uncle is a lot more careful about shutting the door to his office when he's talking mob business than my grandfather was.

Which is how Uncle Brogan blindsided me with the arranged marriage thing.

"You'd better have outgrown listening at doors," Uncle Brogan says ominously. "And forget whatever you heard about the bunker."

What does he think? I can just erase a memory like I delete a file from the cloud?

I don't answer, letting him read what he wants into my silence.

But that doesn't change the fact I know the bunker is a warren of sub-basement concrete corridors and rooms under three of our mob-owned buildings in Queens. Access to the buildings is protected by technology and highly trained soldiers.

"Is it really necessary to have the De Lucas host my 21st birthday?" Miceli fobbing the plans off on his sister-in-law is more hurtful than it should be.

It's fake. All for show. And I want someone planning my birthday that cares about me. Not the right mob mentality, but it's how I feel.

"Wouldn't it be better to let *mamo* organize things like usual?" I wheedle.

Uncle Brogan is tapping on his phone. "Not the De Lucas," he says absently. "Miceli."

"I'm sure he'll make every plan without any help from his mother or sister-in-law." I don't have to roll my eyes for my uncle to know I'm being sarcastic.

Miceli all but said he doesn't plan to lift a finger for it.

"It doesn't matter who calls the caterer." Uncle Brogan goes back to his phone, clearly believing the discussion is over.

But I'm not done. "Only the perception of who throws the party is important."

Irish or Italian, organized crime families are all about appearances.

"It will let the rest of New York know that our families are joining," my uncle says, confirming my thoughts. "The other syndicates will speculate about an upcoming alliance between us and the New York Cosa Nostra."

Uncle Brogan's now benevolent, but patronizing tone shows he thinks he's doing me a favor by explaining.

It's my turn to correct him. "The Genovese Family you mean."

"They are the most powerful mafia in New York. If we have an alliance with them, we have an alliance with The Five Families."

A sudden thought sends cold chills through me. "Are we announcing the engagement at my party?"

"No." My uncle lifts one shoulder in an indifferent shrug. "When the time comes for that, the PR team will take care of it."

The modern criminal syndicate. We have a PR team and investment advice for our people to invest in a 401K.

Something I learned listening at grandfather's door and didn't understand until my high school economics class.

"For now, we let them know you are dating Miceli De Luca."

Great, I'm fake dating a mafia underboss, even if the marriage that's going to take place someday is 100% real.

"When will the PR people announce the engagement?"

It's possible I missed this key piece of information because of the six-foot-four-inch distraction that sucked my blood off of my thumb.

"Not right now. Severu wants to wait."

"Why?" I definitely didn't hear that.

Not that I mind. The longer it goes unannounced, the longer I can keep my connection to the Italian mafia from my friends at college. I don't want to think about what's going to happen when the engagement is made public.

Some people will be fascinated, others will cut me out of their lives. Like when my school friends discovered my grandfather was the Shaughnessy mob boss. Somebody knew somebody who recognized my dad when he came to the first play I had a leading role in.

And then *everybody* knew that I wasn't like them.

My uncle shrugs. "He's got his reasons."

"And that doesn't bother you?"

"Why should it?"

Isn't it obvious? "He could back out of the agreement."

"Not without forfeiting territory, which Severu De Luca will never do."

That must be one of the terms in the contract they didn't let me read. "Because he signed it in blood?"

"Because Severu De Luca doesn't go back on his word. And yes, signing the contract in the old way is unbreakable. For men like us, reputation is everything."

Assuming Severu De Luca is a man like my uncle. One whose word is his bond and who has a code of honor, even if people outside the mob would not understand it.

"The old way is right. You could have warned me you were going to whip out a knife and slice each other's palms." Not to mention that I would have to participate too.

I know my uncle thinks I'm young and naïve, but I'm only one of those things. What is naïve is to believe that your enemy will keep his side of a bargain because of a bloody thumbprint.

All contracts can be broken. And not all forfeitures are paid.

Why do you think warfare breaks out like it does in the criminal under-world?

If I can get Miceli to break this one though...

The Genovese Family and the Shaughnessy mob will become straight up enemies, not tangential ones because of the tension between us and the Bonanno Family. Our mob might even go to war with the Genovese Family over it.

Yeah, no. Trying to get Miceli to back out is not an option.

Disgruntled, I frown out the window. "At least I won't have to play the part of adoring fiancée for a while."

"I'll settle for polite girlfriend at your 21st birthday party."

I'm not making any promises.

CHAPTER 12: MICELI

Candy Shop blasting, I do the last rep in my pull day and deadlift the 500 pound weighted bar bell. Every muscle in my posterior chain burns as my body shifts up, my hips hinging, my grip solid.

The music cuts off in the middle of my favorite line.

"You got enough weight on that thing?" My cousin Salvatore stands in front of me, eyeing the number of 45 pound plates on each side of the barbell.

Sev stands to the side.

"I could do more." Not a lot more, but damned if I'll tell my cousin that.

Doing everything I did to lift it but in reverse, I bring the heavy barbell back to hip level and then let it drop.

The plates clang loudly even though the mats muffle the impact.

"You in the thousand-pound club yet?" my brother asks.

"Like you aren't. When are you going to have our t-shirts made?"

The thousand-pound club is a competition some gyms sponsor, giving their members recognition for lifting a combination that equals 1,000 pounds in squat, bench press and dead lift.

As soon as I learned about it, I challenged my brother and cousin to make it. We've all hit the number and Sev knows it. He's just giving me shit.

"When I start wearing a friendship bracelet instead of a gun." Sev wraps tape around his hand, protecting the cut he made on his palm this morning.

It's an archaic tradition, but it has its power. No way in hell will I break that contract, or allow my little Aphrodite to either.

I saw the speculative look in her green eyes. Even though she signed the prenup just like I did, the Irish princess was plotting before she and her uncle stepped past the threshold to leave.

A mob princess who goes looking for a hookup without her bodyguards has to be watched. And watched over.

I've got that covered.

I stretch, starting with my arms and moving down my body one muscle group at a time. "You two going to lift?"

Sev and Salvatore are both wearing workout gear, but the tension in my brother's shoulders says he's in our home gym for another reason too.

"Yeah. Leave the plates on the bar. Today's a pull day for me too." Salvatore does a few stretches before grabbing a jump rope to warm up his muscles.

Severu does the same and I grab one too. Might as well. Sev's got something on his mind. I can stick around to find out what it is.

He's on our customized rack while Salvatore does bicep curls with dumbbells when he finally starts talking.

Sev does one measured lat pulldown after another. "I went to see Don Caruso after our meeting with Shaughnessy and his niece."

Salvatore pauses, but when my brother doesn't add anything else, he goes back to lifting.

The visit isn't a surprise. Our godfather had a supposed heart attack early this year. Supposed because it's more likely it was a stroke, but the risk of a stroke compromising his mind as well as his body means no one on his medical team is going to admit it.

He doesn't leave his house, citing security concerns. But again, doubtful.

"And?" The jump rope creates an air current as it whizzes over my head and under my feet in quick succession.

"He's a tough bastard." Salvatore sets the dumbbells down and breathes evenly, before doing his next set of reps.

"No argument there," I agree. But I watch my brother.

"He said it's time to start planning for his retirement."

Godfathers retire when they are dead. Which means the prognosis after his recent collapse isn't a good one.

"Is he going to back you?" Sev is young for a godfather, but that's what everyone said when he became the Genovese don.

He proved he could do the job with as much wisdom and ruthlessness as any man twenty years his senior. He is the man our father raised him to be, but even more he is the man he is determined to be.

Sev's features are set in satisfaction. "Yes."

"Good," Salvatore and I say at the same time.

"What about Henry Caruso?" The godfather's nephew is a potential problem we are going to have to watch.

The Americanization of his good Italian name, Henrico, is only one strike against the asshole.

"He'll be the next Lucchese don, but Caruso doesn't think his nephew is up to the task of being godfather."

"Neither does anyone else." I stop jumping rope and wipe the sweat from my face and neck with a gym towel.

"We need a plan for swaying the other families to vote for you, Sev. The godfather's endorsement will go a long way, but some are so damn hidebound they might as well be in the rhino exhibit at the zoo."

My cousin is not wrong.

"Vegas and Detroit will support you." After wiping down the jump rope with sanitizer, I wind it into a neat coil and put it away.

"Detroit's a maybe," my brother disagrees. "And that still leaves New England, Boston and the other four families in New York."

The godfather is voted on by all the dons in the Cosa Nostra. Although most godfathers have come from New York, they don't always. And there are at least two New York dons who might challenge Sev's run for the position.

Salvatore dries his hands before moving on to his next set of reps. "I've got an idea about how to get leverage and/or good will with the Gambino don and Henry Caruso."

The plan my cousin outlines is a good one. There are five properties in New York state about to come on the market. Two are outside the city, but three are in Five Families territory.

Of course, my sister-in-law, Catalina, noticed the opportunity during her daily information gathering. She's the only one in the family interested in weird shit like I am, but she outdoes me for sheer volume of information processed.

Some of the men think she's part computer. I think she's part witch and a powerful one at that.

Sev pulls his body upward in a TRX row so smoothly, I swear he doesn't even displace air. "Get those properties, Salvatore."

CHAPTER 13: RÓISE

There are no alarm clock emojis from Ollie in my texts this morning. He doesn't respond to my message telling him I'm almost ready like he usually does either.

I run late. It's a thing. Ollie, on the other hand, is always early.

He assures me it's a bodyguard thing.

When I get downstairs, there is no Ollie finishing a cup of coffee in the kitchen. No Ollie brushing crumbs from a piece of toast off of his tie while he flirts with the cook, who is the same age as his mother.

I can hear her in the pantry, muttering to herself about people who raid her pantry shelves and have no more manners than wild boars. Not in a good mood then.

Maybe that's why Ollie isn't in here. Maybe he's the miscreant who got into her baking chocolate.

He's the one that taught me and my cousins how delicious Irish milk chocolate is, in or out of cookies. His absence is weird but not unprecedented. Even if he didn't eat the chocolate.

Ollie is assigned to both Fiona and me. If my cousin needs a bodyguard at the same time I do, Ollie's priority is her. Not because Uncle Brogan decrees it that way, but because I do.

Fiona does better with people she likes and trusts like Ollie. He's been part of our security team since we were children. When Kara married, she got assigned her own team, but Fiona and I still share one.

In his mid-forties with graying red hair and a ready smile, Ollie is her favorite.

My cousin always tells me if she's leaving the house though and she hasn't said anything.

The sound of raised voices draws me out of the empty kitchen to the side porch we use to exit the mansion. The front door and its impressive steps and entry are for guests and formal occasions.

Raised voice. Singular. Ollie is the only one shouting. And he's on a rampage, throwing out Irish invective and questions about somebody's parentage.

Two people I've never met are facing him. Both are wearing dark suits tailored to conceal shoulder holsters, standing with the confidence of made men. Except the younger one is a woman.

She looks about my age, but that's where our similarities end. This woman is syndicate soldier from the top of her closely cropped hair to the tips of her shiny shoes made for quick movement, not showing off the curve of her ass.

The man's expression is implacable, but the woman looks ready to let loose on Ollie. No wonder. The last two insults were directed at the pair's boss and their parents in that order.

"Róise is my responsibility!" Ollie shouts in the man's face. "I've been protecting her since she was a toddler."

"Our orders are to take point on her security going forward," the stranger responds.

Ollie shakes his curled fist at him. "Repeating it isn't going to make me go away!"

"You're not going anywhere," I insert, drawing all eyes to me. "Ollie, we need to go. I'm running a little behind."

A brief flicker of indulgent humor flares in his pale blue gaze. "If you weren't I'd think you were sick, Rosy-girl."

Hitching my backpack more firmly on my shoulder, I head toward the door. The two strangers follow me, putting themselves between me and my bodyguard.

Discomfort crawls up my spine like a spider on a quest.

I stop and turn. "I don't know who you are, or what your orders are, but I'm not going anywhere with you. Let Ollie pass."

"We're your new security detail," the woman says with a sneer for Ollie.

"Yeah, no. I don't want or need new bodyguards."

"Miceli sent us." The man says, like that explains everything.

It doesn't.

"Miceli has no authority over me or in this house. Ollie is my body-guard."

"Text Mr. De Luca and he'll tell you," the woman suggests.

Even if I wanted to, I couldn't. I don't have Miceli's number. And doesn't that just say it all?

"You're not that bright, are you? I just told you that Miceli De Luca is not my boss. That means I don't care if he sent you, or not."

I'm sure he did, the arrogant jerk. These two never would have gotten past the gate guards and into the house otherwise. At least not without bloodshed.

Since no alarms have gone off and Ollie looks angry, not worried, I'm going with these mafia soldiers are here with my uncle's permission.

"How about this?" I speak slowly for the made men, whatever their gender, in the room. "*You* text him and tell him that I don't need you."

The woman crosses her arms. "We have our orders."

The man pulls out his phone and taps on the screen. Sending a text, but I doubt it's to inform his boss that I don't need the new bodyguards.

This is because of Portland.

The hypocrite. It was fine for him to be out trolling for a sex partner without security, but not the woman he now plans to marry.

Someday. In the very distant future.

A girl can hope.

Ollie's phone pings and premonition makes my stomach queasy. Or is that lack of breakfast? It's a good thing Ollie keeps meal bars in the glove box for me.

"Fecking hell," my bodyguard mutters as he reads the text. Then he looks up at me. "The boss says these two puffed up Jackeens are now on your security detail too."

"No." My denial is visceral and heartfelt. "I'm not trusting my life to Cosa Nostra gangsters."

Foxes and henhouses come to mind, the words spoken in *moma's* soft Irish burr.

"The Cosa Nostra is the strongest syndicate around."

This woman is really getting on my nerves.

I smile sweetly at her, if sweet comes with a side of shark's teeth. "Tell that to the network of Irish mob families with control of territories the Cosa Nostra can't touch."

Yes, the Cosa Nostra is *one of* the strongest criminal organizations operating, but there's a reason the powerful and ruthless don of the Genovese wants an alliance with my uncle.

Through our ties in Ireland and here in the U.S., the Shaughnessy mob has alliances and/or influence with most of the Irish crime families in the world.

I used to think that made us special. Because it made my dad proud. Now, I think it makes us at the top of the rotting heap of organized crime.

If I'd been born into a normal family, I wouldn't be forced to sign my life away at the age of twenty for the sake of alliances and more power. If my dad were still alive, he wouldn't have allowed it to happen either.

But Uncle Brogan is different. There's family love there, but the mob comes first. For my dad, me and my mom came first.

"Rosy, what are those people doing here?" Fiona's voice wavers with stress.

I look past the two would-be bodyguards and force a genuine smile. "Nothing to worry about, Fi. They work for Miceli De Luca."

Fiona's gaze doesn't meet mine. It's stuck on the Cosa Nostra soldiers. "Why are they here?"

The woman steps toward Fiona, smiling. "You must be Fiona. I saw your picture. I'm Zoey." She indicates the man who is at least ten years older than us both. "This is Allessio. We're your cousin's new security team."

Oh, crap. The flirty tone in Zoey's voice coupled with her nearness to my cousin sends alarm bells clanging in my brain.

Recognizing the stressor minefield for what it is, Ollie jumps between the two women. "Step back."

Zoey stops, but her hand is still out and her gaze is locked on Fiona.

Allessio curses in Italian.

My sentiments exactly.

Instead of retreating like I expect, Fiona smiles shyly and moves to shake Zoey's hand. "Nice to meet you, but we already have a security team?"

My cousin, who avoids strangers as much as possible, and can have a panic attack triggered by bumping into one, is shaking this mafia soldier's hand. With no sign of letting go.

I glare at Zoey. "If you read a file on us, and you must have in order to have seen Fi's picture, you know she's only seventeen."

Finally letting go of Zoey's hand, Fiona puts her fists on her hips and frowns at me. "I'll be eighteen soon."

Which is one of the reasons I agreed so quickly to Uncle Brogan's blackmail. I'll be twenty-one in three weeks, but Fiona turns eighteen over the summer.

He would have had her married off before she'd had her first kiss, just like Kara.

Fiona would be utterly miserable married to any man, but especially one as cold and deadly as Miceli.

"I'll be twenty in the fall," Zoey says.

I roll my eyes. "Good for you. I hope that means you really are just security and not made already."

"Róise! Don't be rude," Fiona censures me.

Life in the mob: where asking someone if they've killed before is both normal *and* rude. And also, sometimes necessary.

Why is Fiona still standing here in the hall? Why is her jacket hood still down, revealing her face?

Don't get me wrong, every time she overcomes her anxiety, it's a win. But does my cousin need to find a Cosa Nostra soldier the reason for doing so?

"I'm not made. Allessio is your new bodyguard, but he's training me. So two-for-one, right?" Zoey grins at Fiona.

Nipping this in the bud right now.

"As fun as this is, if we don't leave right now, I might as well skip my first class. And I am *not* doing that." I point at Allessio. "You're driving. Ollie, you're in the backseat with me and the teenager flirting with my cousin can ride shotgun."

Three bodyguards is total overkill. The only reason I had that many in Portland was because I was out of town. This? Is ridiculous.

I'd laugh if I wasn't so irritated.

"I don't take orders from you," Zoey says loftily.

"You do if you want to ride in the same car." Yes, I'm twenty.

No, I'm not ready to get married and start popping out mob babies.

That does not mean I am a pushover. I was raised in this life. I've been protecting myself and my cousins since my dad died and before that, I'd witnessed too much to ever be a regular kid.

Allessio barks something in Italian and Zoey snaps to attention, all emotion wiped from her face.

"Follow us, Miss Shaughnessy, but do not exit the house until we give the all-clear sign."

"Which is?" Does he just assume we all use the same one?

I guarantee we don't. When we were kids, Ollie taught us it was safe to move when the bunny said so. We still use the bunny signs.

Two fingers spread slightly and pointing upward means the bunny is on alert. When they twitch like a happy bunny, it's safe to move, or enter a new environment. When the bunny ears curl down, he's hiding and so should we.

Allessio holds his index and middle fingers together, straight and pointing upward. "This is all clear."

"Got it." I wait until Ollie gets close enough to whisper. "I like the bunny ears better."

"Using universal symbols telegraphs your purpose." My still irate body-guard doesn't bother to lower his voice.

No way can the Genovese soldiers miss his criticism. For once, Zoey doesn't respond. She's too busy checking for bogeyman in the naturally secure exit from the house.

The standalone garages with soldier's quarters on the second floor create a barrier parallel to the side of the mansion. The walkway between the two buildings is covered, limiting line of site from the only two directions not blocked by the garage or house.

And one of them is the bay.

My irritation goes through the roof when we reach my college and Allessio tells me they plan to follow me around all day.

I don't have time to argue because I really am late, but I try.

I'm in the middle of a reasonable and compelling (I think) argument for why they should leave when I receive my own text message from Brogan Shaughnessy.

I glare at Allessio. He's not just a Cosa Nostra thug. He's a tattletale.

BS: *Behave, Róise. I don't have time to deal with your tantrums. Your new bodyguards are under Miceli's orders. If you don't like the way they guard you, take it up with him.*

Yes, I have my uncle listed as BS in my contacts. For Brogan Shaughnessy. If it implies he's full of something else, that's okay too.

It's a long message for Uncle Brogan and that shows how annoyed he is. Unlike some men, the angrier my uncle gets, the more verbose. It's pure BS.

Both kinds.

But the text tells me one important thing. My current situation is 100% on Miceli. Sure, Uncle Brogan could kick up a fuss about it, but why would he?

I'm not a multi-million-dollar weapons deal he doesn't want to sour. I'm just his niece.

Every question I get from classmates throughout the morning, every curious look is fuel to the fire of my growing indignation.

This. This is the one thing I've worked so hard to avoid for the nearly three years I've been attending the university. Being seen as different from the other students with wealthy parents.

This is me being singled out as having a level of danger in my life they don't.

Ollie drops me off and picks me up every day, but that's not so unusual around here.

A security detail trailing me, checking every classroom for threats before going to wait outside? It's a level of intrusion in my life I won't put up with. I have a year and some change before I graduate.

Is it too much to ask for that year to be mine? Me living like the normal woman I won't get to be once I marry a mafia underboss?

Apparently for Miceli De Luca, the fake boyfriend from hell, it is.

CHAPTER 14: MICELI

The door to my office slams open and Róise storms in, a five-foot-four avenging fury in an oversized flannel, khaki cargo pants and...

"What the fuck are you wearing?"

She ignores me, her fury incandescent. "How dare you? You had no right to set these two rottweilers on me!"

Allessio texted to tell me she insisted on being brought to me, "Wherever the fuck he is."

The text was accompanied by another.

Allessio: *This is the first time I've heard her swear.*

That doesn't surprise me. Like his father before him, Brogan Shaughnessy has some old-fashioned views about women, especially those in his family.

An Irish mob princess doesn't talk like a made man and those men don't drop the f-bomb in a princess's hearing.

I've heard Róise say the word *fuck* though. In bed.

Fuck me, Ares. Fuck me now!

I fix my gimlet glare on Allessio. "You let her leave the house like that?"

I sweep my hand toward my soon-to-be fiancée whose entire midriff is bare. The drab greens in the plaid on the flannel shirt are fine, but they're accented with thin pink lines. Every fucking button is open and her fucking little pink bra is on full display.

"You didn't tell me to play fashion police," Allessio replies with a sardonic twist of his lips.

Zoey's eyes are wide and she looks concerned for *me*, not the little hellion still shouting about inconsiderate jerks who make an ox look savvy.

It's a convoluted insult, but I'm impressed all the same.

"Uh, it's a bralette, boss," Zoey informs me.

"And that is better how?" I demand.

"It's uh, cotton and it doesn't show her cleavage."

"Just all the skin above and below that tiny band of fabric."

"Are you still harping about my clothes? Seriously? Did we go to sleep and wake up in the Dark Ages? Oh, yeah, I guess we did because I've got Thing 1 and Thing 2 following me all over campus!"

Okay, security detail first and appropriate clothes to wear out of the house second.

"Close the door, Róise, and we can discuss the change in your security like adults." Her flaming temper turns me on, but she's going to have to learn to curb it.

At least when others are around.

"If you considered me an adult, you would have *discussed* them with me before they showed up at my house this morning."

"Your uncle knew they were coming. I assumed he would inform you." Which was an error on my part.

I'm not usually that obtuse. As in almost never. I'm the underboss of the most powerful crime family in New York. I can't afford to misread even minor situations like this one.

"You mean like he told me who I was marrying?" she asks with scathing accuracy.

I silently signal to Allessio to clear the room and close the door.

But Ollie, Róise's Irish bodyguard, refuses to budge. "I'm not leaving Miss Shaughnessy alone in a room with a Cosa Nostra underboss."

"You are mistaken, Ollie. That is exactly what you are going to do." Remaining seated, I stare the other man down.

He doesn't shift or drop his eyes.

I'm surprised. Few people can hold my gaze when their imminent pain is in my eyes. I would be more impressed if his charge hadn't gotten away from him and the other guards in Portland. For the whole damn night.

"Your vigilance is a little late, don't you think?" I taunt.

Róise jerks, her face paling and she glares at me. "Shut up!"

Did she just tell me to shut up? She did. Not sure which shocks me more. That she'd say it, or that it would fucking turn me on instead of pissing me off.

My sexy hellion turns to Ollie, her green gaze full of appeal. "I prefer not to have an audience for this discussion, Ollie. Not even you."

"But, lass—"

Róise lays a hand on his bicep. "It's alright. Nothing is going to happen to me. My uncle would not have let Miceli's people accompany me today if I wasn't safe with them."

She sounds like she's pushing her words through gravel. She hates saying that, almost as much as I hate the sight of her touching Ollie. It's not personal.

She's mine and my woman doesn't touch other men. That's it. "Take your hand off his arm unless you want him to lose it."

Róise drops her hand to spin around so she can scowl at me when she yells again. "That's not funny. Ollie is my friend."

"He's your bodyguard and not a great one."

"That's not true!" She worries her lip with her teeth, showing temper isn't the only emotion she's feeling.

She's afraid I'm going to reveal his dereliction of duty to him. The fact that he hasn't figured it out yet only shows how important it is for Allessio and Zoey to remain on Róise's security detail.

Allessio is the only man I trust as much as I do my brother and cousin. His family joined the Genovese four generations ago and have been loyal ever since.

He trained with me and Sev for most of our teen years and is not only an expert marksman, but is a Judo *Godan* as well, holding his fifth black belt. Zoey is one of his students and already holds her first black belt. She is also a soldier in training.

If Allessio and Zoey were not such a lethal combination, I would have assigned a larger detail to Róise instead of assigning her the equivalent of a second bodyguard and his trainee.

But having Allessio there is almost as good as me being there myself.

"Ollie, please, I need to talk to Miceli privately. You can wait in the outer office."

It takes more cajoling from my mob princess before she convinces Ollie to leave and every soft, imploring word said to another man is nails on a chalkboard in my ears.

I'm ready to shoot the damn bodyguard and be done with it by the time he finally follows my people out and shuts the door behind him.

"Do not beg another man ever again."

"Get over yourself. I agreed to marry you in a year...ish," she corrects herself. "From now. Not to obey your every command."

"There's a promise to obey in the wedding vows." That's what I've heard anyway.

Neither Giulia, nor Catalina, promised to obey in theirs, but pushing Róise's buttons is one of my new favorite things.

Eyes flashing, breasts heaving, she glares at me. "And I promise you, I won't be saying it."

The temptation to touch is going to override my good sense. There's a reason I haven't moved around my desk, but I can't get the image of fucking her on top of it out of my head.

"As sexy as I find acrimony on you, I have things to do today." Like figuring out how much of a problem Henrico Caruso is going to be in my brother's eventual bid for godfather.

"Of course you do." She jerks her thumb toward my office door. "Fine. Pull your soldiers from my security and I'll leave."

"I should have contacted you directly rather than trusting your uncle to tell you about the change in your security." Acknowledging my error should calm her down. Unfortunately. "But that's not happening."

She storms across my office and stops right in front of my desk, vibrating with fury.

Then she slams her hand down with a loud thwack. "You should never have assigned me a Cosa Nostra security detail in the first place."

"That's going to hurt." My desk has clean, Danish lines and looks lighter than it is, but it's made of hard, solid maple.

I could fuck her until she screams and it wouldn't break.

"What hurts is trying to get through to your thick brain." But she presses her hand to her side, mouth drawn tight.

Damn it. I jump up and open the minifridge hidden behind a cabinet door. There's fresh ice in the fridge's tiny freezer compartment. Like there is every day.

I pull some out and wrap it in a bar towel. "Hold this. It will take the sting out."

She glares at the icepack, but then takes it with a muttered thank you.

"Getting bawled out by a woman is a new one for me." Playing with temptation, I lean back on my desk next to where she's standing, so much smooth skin on display. "Mamma is too refined. My sister, Giulia, lives in Las Vegas. And Catalina doesn't yell."

She gets her point across, but the only man my sister-in-law gets really hot under the collar with is Sev.

"I'm not like them," Róise says defiantly. "I yell when I get angry."

"And hit desks."

"I was making a point."

"Next time, do it without hurting yourself."

"Gladly." She sighs, seemingly calmer. "I don't need Allessio and Zoey following me around."

"I disagree. Your actions in Portland made it unquestionably necessary. If your bodyguards were adequate to the task, you would not have been in the club that night. The fact you stayed in my room until the wee hours only proves my point."

She waves away my logical and legitimate concern with a flick of her wrist. "It's not like I'm going to do that again."

She'd better not, but I'm smart enough to keep those words in my head. Róise Shaughnessy has a fiery temper and is as likely to do the opposite of what I tell her just to prove that she can.

She sits down in the chair furthest from my desk, and furthest from me. "I don't want your bodyguards."

Irked at her obvious rejection, I say, "I don't want to deal with a child-bride prancing around in a pink bralette either, but here we are."

Hurt flickers in her eyes, but she tries to mask it with belligerence. "Leave my clothes out of it. Plenty of women older than me dress like this."

"Not in my world."

"Well, in your world, or out of it, I'm not a child. I'm twenty years old."

"Start acting like it." I shove down the guilt hurting her feelings causes. Neither of us can afford for her to act her age.

She's going to be the wife of an underboss.

"Just because I don't act like an emotionless toad doesn't mean I'm acting like a child. I have feelings and I'm not afraid to acknowledge them."

"That might work with your college friends, living in your protected student bubble, but if you wear your emotions on your sleeve around the mafia, you'll be eaten alive."

"I know when to hide my feelings," she claims.

"Really? Because so far I haven't seen you do it." And part of me hates that she has to change to fit in my world.

Brogan should have taught her this, damn it. He knew she would marry into syndicate leadership one day. He's the one that suggested a marriage based alliance with his niece as the bride.

He's probably been planning it since her father died.

Róise pulls the ice away from her hand and gingerly shakes it, wincing before she wraps her fingers around the icepack again. "You're such a jerk."

"Most people would call me an asshole." Though not to my face. "I'm not removing my guards from your detail."

"You have to." This time the soft, begging eyes are fixed on me. "Before today no one at my college knew there was anything different about me." She gives a disconsolate shrug. "Not even the administration is aware I'm connected to the Shaughnessy mob."

That's safer for her, I suppose. Especially with her security so lax. However, it's not sustainable. Her uncle must realize that.

"Allessio and Zoey aren't going to link you to your family's criminal enterprises. They're too discreet for that." Where is this need to reassure her coming from?

"Discreet? Are you kidding me?" Disbelief overrides the sadness in her tone. "A lot of students at my college come from wealthy families, but none of them have bodyguards trailing them to class."

I shrug. "Maybe they should. The world is a dangerous place."

"Says one of the men responsible for making it that way."

"Organized crime is a hell of a lot safer than chaos." We are ruthless with each other, but not the general public.

Making that same oblivious public safer than they would otherwise be. Not always. No system is perfect. And while the average citizen doesn't have to fear me, any that think to get in the way of my mafia do.

So-called law enforcement do as much to foment violence as we do. The CIA banked the start of the major drug trade in North America and instigated more cartel wars than any mafia family ever has.

"My dad always said that." She looks away from me. "But he understood that I didn't want to be part of the mob."

"I hate to break it to you, but you were born into one of the oldest mob families in New York."

"That's not the point."

"No, the point is your safety."

She shakes her head, reddish-brown curls bobbing softly around her pretty face. "Even if they don't know it's because I'm from a mob family, having Allessio and Zoey trailing after me like oversized lemmings is going to change how my friends and the other students see me. How they treat me."

"They'll be more cautious around you." That's a good thing. Especially when it comes to the male students.

"More cautious? They'll start avoiding me. How long do you think it will be before my professors begin asking the administration if it's safe to allow me to attend classes?"

"You're exaggerating." No wonder she's studying acting. Róise has a flare for the dramatic.

"You think?"

"I think your actions in Portland were reckless, ill-conceived and danger-ous."

CHAPTER 15: RÓISE

Miceli's words flay me like a whip, every single one scoring me with dead-on accuracy.

Skin prickling with embarrassment, I defend myself. "I was never in any danger."

"If I had been a different man—"

"I wouldn't have gone with you." Which I don't like admitting, but it's better than letting him accuse me of being too ignorant to protect myself.

"Fucking hell, Róise. You left that club with the most dangerous man in the building."

"Oh, please."

His jaw looks like it's made of rock. "If I had been one of your uncle's enemies and recognized you—"

"You were and you didn't," I say, cutting him off again.

"The Shaughnessy mob and the Genovese Family are not enemies."

It's not what I expect him to say and I should take the pass he's giving me, but I can't seem to stop myself pushing further.

"Tell that to my dad. Oh, wait, you can't ask him either, because just like my mom, he's dead!"

"You say that like it has bearing on this discussion. It doesn't," he says calmly.

Too calmly.

I don't want him to be calm. I want Miceli to feel as out of control and trapped as I do, but he never will.

How can he? He's not only a made man, but he's the underboss. The only person in the Genovese Family with more power, is his brother, the don.

He could have refused this alliance marriage, but he went along because like so many men in the mafia and mob, he doesn't care who he marries. I'm just a walking reproductive system to him.

A way to cement an alliance neither family would trust completely without the promised child.

Because of all the deaths. "Just because we could never prove it, doesn't mean I'm ignorant of who killed my father."

"Who?" Miceli has the gall to ask.

"No culprit was ever identified." Like he doesn't know this. I let every bit of contempt I feel for the mafia show in my face. "But I know who my money is on."

"The Cosa Nostra?" he asks like it's the most ridiculous idea ever.

"Bingo."

"We didn't kill your father."

"How would you know? You didn't even know your people killed my mother."

"Eleven years ago, I was a low-ranking soldier. Six years ago, I was not. I would have known if one of the Five Families took a hit out on your dad."

"He's dead."

"Which is not irrefutable proof that it was at the hands of the Cosa Nostra. If it will make you feel better, I will dig into it further."

I shake my head. "You think I will trust you to tell me if you find out his murderer is one of your own?"

"I'm not going to lie to you about it."

His words have a ring of certainty I can't allow myself to trust, but a tiny part of me...hello, vajayjay...wants to.

"You promise me you will tell me what you find out?" Did I really ask that, like I could trust his vow?

"On my oath as a Genovese."

I suck in a shocked breath. *That* kind of promise is binding. No matter who it is made to. Man or woman. Enemy or friend.

One of the things my cousins and I learned about Miceli during our research is that he does not break his word. Neither does his brother.

Which might be something to hold onto if it wasn't the very trait that has me trapped in this deal.

"Now, *you* promise *me* on the memory of both your parents that you will never do anything so fucking stupid and dangerous as ditching your guards so you can get away to have sex with a stranger again."

"Wow. You went from almost human to overbearing ogre in a single sentence. You're talented."

"This is not a damn joke, Róise."

"No, it's not," I agree with venom. "Two months ago, I was blackmailed into agreeing to a marriage I don't want. To a stranger I wasn't even given the name of."

"Your uncle should not have been so secretive with you. Withholding information is sometimes necessary, but this time it wasn't."

He's preaching to the choir on this one.

"I know why I didn't recognize you, but why didn't you recognize me that night?" I ask, something that has been bugging me. Yeah, the makeup job was sick, but come on. "You can't tell me you didn't know who you were supposed to marry.

"Yes, I knew." He frowns.

"But you didn't recognize me."

"No."

"Of course you knew who you were supposed to marry," I accuse, my anger kindled all over again. "Because you are a man."

"Because my brother treats his family differently than your uncle treats yours."

"Are you saying your sister knew at the same time as her future husband?" I ask suspiciously.

"My father informed her as soon as the agreement was made."

"Did he even ask what she wanted?"

"Not as such, no, but my father made sure she and Raff met and got to know each other. That they liked each other."

I roll my eyes. "What a great reason to get married. They *liked* each other."

"That wasn't the reason for their marriage but it is the reason my father agreed to it."

"But you and I didn't like each other. We'd never even met when you agreed to marry me." I shake my head, knowing there's no point in going over this again.

"You want to know why I didn't have a clue who I was really fucking that night?"

"Sometimes you're really crude." And sometimes he talks like a literature professor.

A really good looking one.

He ignores my insult. "I barely looked at the file Domenico provided on you. Your looks didn't matter. The fact you're too young for me doesn't matter. My brother wants me to marry you for the sake of our family."

His shrug says, if that's what the don wants, that's what he gets. Duty. Obligation.

"But we don't even like each other." I was yelling a minute ago and now I can barely get my voice above a whisper.

Miceli thinks I'm too young for him? Of course he does. I bet Miceli has been a made man for more than a decade.

I'm not even done with college. I'm an adult woman, but my life experience is light years behind his. Even after witnessing my mom's death.

I've never killed anyone and I never will. I'm not the mobster.

"Again it doesn't—"

"Matter," I finish for him. "But why? You're the underboss. The don is your brother. You could choose your own wife if you wanted to."

"That's not the way it works. Even my brother didn't choose his wife."

"But he did! Everyone knows. He switched Catalina for her sister at the wedding."

"One day, when I trust you not to share what you learn from me with your uncle, I'll tell you a story about Catalina and Severu."

"You don't trust me?" I mean, I know I don't trust him, but that only makes sense.

Why wouldn't he trust me? I'm not part of the organization. I have nothing to gain by betraying him.

"You're the niece of our rival. Shaughnessy might be arranging this marriage to gain information about our family."

"My uncle wouldn't do that." Uncle Brogan might see us as pawns on his chessboard, but not as cannon fodder. "If I were a spy, you'd kill me. *Mamo* told me what your cousin did. Uncle Brogan knows about it too."

And doesn't care because in his words, "There's nothing for you to be afraid of. You're not going to betray Miceli or his family."

He's got that right. Everyone in New York knows what the Genovese do to traitors and death isn't the worst of it.

"You might not even know you are doing it."

"Thanks so much for thinking I'm that easy to dupe." What a superior jerk. "I might not be as old as you, or as experienced, but I know what it means to betray a secret."

His gorgeous face shows nothing, certainly not belief. "A lot can be learned in normal conversation."

"Which would require my uncle talking to me. That's not as common as you think it is. Remember, I didn't even know your name until the morning we signed the contract."

"But you do talk to your cousins."

"He's no closer to his daughters than he is to his niece." Is the De Luca family really that much different from ours? "If you distrust me so much, why are you going through with this?"

"I told you, the alliance is good for the Genovese Family. Besides, I won't be telling you anything I don't want your uncle to know."

"How do we make a marriage work when we don't trust each other?"

"The same way everyone else in our families have done. We work at it."

"By we, you mean me." The walls are closing in again, but they have been since that day in my uncle's office.

I should be used to feeling like this by now.

"You'll have to make the most changes in your life, yes." There's no apology in Miceli's tone.

He's so darn complacent. And sure of his view of the world. Was my dad like this with my mom in the beginning? No way. My dad was *never* like this.

"And that's why what I did in Portland was necessary," I say helplessly.

The look he gives me is incredulous. "In what way was anticipating our wedding vows necessary?"

"Do you hear yourself? You sound like a Victorian spinster. *We* weren't anticipating anything. *I* was choosing my own partner to have sex with for the first time."

"You were a virgin!"

"I know exactly how much sexual experience I have and I also know that there was no way I was getting married without having had sex with at least one other guy."

"At least?" The tendons in his neck look ready to snap. "What the fuck does that mean? You're not letting another man touch you."

"Oh, so you were a virgin too that night?" I don't give him a chance to reply. "Of course you weren't. You were just another Cosa Nostra leader with the same double standard as every other made man."

"What double standard?"

I've heard the term, *a voice that could cut glass*, but never really understood it until this moment.

"The one where it was okay for you to be out on the prowl for a one-night-stand, but you're now having a tantrum because you learned the woman you're supposed to marry was doing the same thing."

"You planned to give what should have been mine to someone else."

I do not believe this guy.

"I didn't owe you my virginity." I jump up from my chair and shout, "My body was and is mine!"

"That might be true, but it doesn't justify what you did in Portland."

Might be true? Is this guy for real? If I took his knife and stabbed him with it, would anyone really blame me? Would they?

"I know you're not stupid," he says, offering the words like a panacea. "But what you did that night was."

There it is. The screw he's determined to twist. But he's wrong.

"It wasn't though. Not for a normal person. And that night I thought that's what I got to be." I'd done everything I could to have one, solitary night of normalcy.

And it backfired spectacularly. He assigned Allessio and Zoey to stick to me like glue because of it. Now, even the parts of my life that *were* normal won't be.

"Going home with a stranger isn't smart, for anybody."

"You did it."

"I was armed. Were you?"

"You know I wasn't."

I hate that he is right. I created a fantasy in my head of what it meant to be normal and try to live it out for one night.

But I didn't do it in complete ignorance. "I did my homework. There are no mafia or mob ties in Portland. No one knew me there. It was my one chance to taste freedom."

"That taste of freedom could have cost you yours." He pauses to let that sink in.

Even though my stomach churns with the reality of what *could* have happened, but *didn't*, I glare back defiantly.

"As for the lack of a mafia presence," Miceli says, sounding like one of my professors. "The Hades Brotherhood took over territory there recently, but the bratva were looking for a foothold already."

I suppress a shiver. Like the mob, some bratvas have a code of honor that doesn't allow human trafficking. Others don't.

"And we have ties with the Greek mafia now. Even when the Cosa Nostra doesn't have a presence in a territory, that doesn't mean we don't have influence, or even people on the ground."

"I know that now." Do my grandmother and cousins know?

They will after I tell them. Among the women in our family, when it comes to information, it's share and share alike.

He nods. "Good. You need to stop living with your head in the clouds and accept your life for what it is."

"You sound disgustingly like Uncle Brogan."

Miceli shrugs his broad shoulders. "Accept the bodyguards with grace, or I'll tell your uncle about Portland." Miceli lets that sink in.

Blackmail: the one toy in the made man's closet he never hesitates to take out and play with.

"He'll make sure I don't have to worry about you slipping the leash again," he continues with unnecessary detail.

"I'm not a dog!"

Miceli's jaw sets implacably. "The bodyguards stay with you."

"Why did I even bother trying to reason with you?"

"Yelling at me like a harpy isn't reasoning."

"If I was a harpy, I'd carve that black stone you call a heart right out of your chest."

CHAPTER 16: RÓISE

"You did not say that to him." Kara's laugh is almost worth the confrontation with the most stubborn underboss in history.

My older cousin doesn't smile as much as she used to, not that my uncle notices. He's too busy growing his kingdom. When he does notice Kara, it's to pressure her to give him another grandchild.

She's not the same girl she was at sixteen when she agreed to marry a man she'd never met from a different country. And the eighteen-year-old with stars in her eyes who thought that marriage might be like my parents is long gone too.

Fiona's spoon filled with pistachio gelato dangles from her hand inches from her mouth as she stares at me with wide eyes. "He's the Genovese underboss."

"That doesn't make him a god." Not even the god of war.

I can't believe the Ares I shared my body with so enthusiastically is Miceli-the *asshole*-De Luca.

My cousins still don't know that Ares and Miceli are the same guy and I have no intention of telling them.

Besides, they're not the same. Not really. I wasn't the only one playing a role that night. Ares had a sense of humor and he rocked my world.

Before kicking me out of his hotel room. Maybe they're not so different after all.

Two Months Prior

Ritz-Carlton, Portland

Ares slides his hand down my back and lets it rest right above my bottom, using it to guide me to the bank of elevators. His room is on a floor that requires a keycard to access.

He doesn't kiss me on the silent ride up and I'm glad.

My mind is spinning with what I'm about to do, but my body is so eager, my panties are soaked. Excitement thrums through me making it hard to think.

To even breathe.

If I hyperventilate in this elevator, I'm going to drop dead from embarrassment.

Suddenly two hands cup my face and tilt my head so I'm looking into a pair of unfathomable eyes. "Okay?"

I try to nod, but it's an abortive movement, my muscles jerking from conflicting fight or flight signals.

And my brain is screaming, "Stay."

This is exactly where I want to be. About to have sex for the first time with a man of my choosing.

"Do you want this?" he asks again.

"If I say no?"

"I order you a car and make sure you get home safely."

Not a rideshare. Not for a man who stays on a private floor of a hotel like this one.

"I want to stay. I choose you." He can't know what I mean, how profoundly those words impact my own mind.

But I am taking back my choice for tonight. This is my stolen moment to be the woman I always wanted to be and will never get the chance to know again.

"I'm glad you chose me. Helios was pissed though."

"Was he?" How did Ares know?

"Because I would have been if you had chosen him to dance with instead."

"You make it sound like you were both fighting for my attention."

"Weren't we?"

"There was no fight." The second he returned without Lala, my focus was entirely on Ares.

He spins me around and slams his lips down on mine.

Okay, so we're done checking in.

Kissing him back, I mold my mouth to his and get lost in the sensation of our lips and bodies pressed together so intimately.

I'm climbing him like a tree when the elevator dings. Moaning, my lips cling to his but he doesn't break the kiss. He wraps an arm tightly around me and there is the sensation of movement while our mouths eat at each other.

This is passion. The stuff you read about, but I sure as heck have never experienced.

Every place our bodies touch is on fire, including my lips. I wrap my legs around his torso and don't care that my short skirt is riding up so high my panty clad butt is on display.

He stops and there's movement behind me. Then we step into darkness, no light flickering against my closed eyelids.

My back slams against a wall and I use the leverage to push my aching ladybits against his hard abs. I writhe and buck, so close to something cataclysmic, but I can't quite reach it.

Ripping my lips from his, I pant, "Help me, Ares. Make me come."

I've climaxed before. On my own fingers, but this is already so far beyond that for sensation, I'll probably pass out when I actually come.

"*Cazzo*. You're a wildcat." He bites my earlobe and presses into me, forcing my thighs further apart.

"Aphrodite, not Cotso." Whoever that is, she's not here.

"*Cazzo* means fuck. Exactly what I'm going to do to you after I make you scream my name."

After? I can get behind that.

He slides his forearms under my thighs and lifts until my most private place is level with his face. He leans in and inhales, nuzzling right into my intimate flesh through the soaked crotch of my panties.

Jayzuz, Mary and Joseph!

He chuckles, sending hot air against me and making me shiver. "Are you Irish, Aphrodite?"

Shoot, I said that out loud. "Know a lot of blonde Irish women?"

It's pretty artful prevarication for how muddled he's got my brain right now.

All my thoughts are sitting in my cooch.

He doesn't bother to answer, his mouth is too busy exploring. Sparks of ecstasy are exploding all over my ladybits and I grab his hair because that's all there is to hold onto.

Ares growls, the sound vibrating against my clitoris. And I lose what's left of my rational thought.

Riding his mouth and yanking his hair, I babble about coming and gods among men and all sorts I won't want to remember later.

He bites my swollen bud right through the scrap of fabric covering it. And I detonate, screaming, "Ares!" at the top of my lungs.

That's not enough for the god of war though. He rubs up and down over my sensitive nub, not letting me catch my breath, but hurtling me toward another explosion.

When it comes, my body arches until every muscle is contracted, my shout incoherent and long.

Then everything releases, pleasure driven lethargy taking over my body. I lose my hold on his hair. My legs dangle bonelessly and my head lolls back against the wall.

With a masculine sound of pure satisfaction, Ares shifts me down his body so he can carry me with one arm under my bottom. His other hand grips the nape of my neck, keeping my boneless body from listing to the side.

Light comes in through the floor to ceiling windows and I get the impression of a large living room with a truly spectacular view of Portland at night. Ares doesn't stop until we're in the bedroom. Then he drops me onto the bed and I flop onto my back.

"Don't go to sleep." He rips his shirt over his head without unbuttoning it. "We are nowhere near done."

"Not sleeping." I wave my hand languidly. "Just resting up for the next round."

My eyes lock onto the tattoo of a snarling wolf that covers the bulging muscles of his right arm. Below are two words I don't recognize, but I guess what they mean. *Famiglia sempre.* Well at least the family part.

Sempre probably means loyalty.

Unlike the one on my inner forearm, there's no color in any of the ink.

The intensity of this man tells me that his tattoo probably carries as much meaning for him as mine does to me.

Stop it, brain. Not speculating on who Ares is under all the sexy.

I'm here for one reason only. To turn in my V-card.

CHAPTER 17: MICELI

Aphrodite devours me with her eyes.

The drapes are open, letting in the city's light, but it's not enough for me. I want to see everything when I get her clothes off.

With the flip of a switch, both bedside lamps glow, bathing my disheveled lover in their warm light.

Her little black dress is shoved up so high over her hips that it's more like a crop top. Wet panties cling to her puffy pussy lips.

A shoe dangles from the toes of one foot. The other dropped in the hall.

Platinum blonde hair is spread around her head in a messy halo on the duvet.

Shucking my slacks and boxers at the same time, my cock bobs free and points straight toward the sensual woman on my bed.

Aphrodite's eyes widen and her little pink tongue comes out and wets her lips. Lips I want to see wrapped around my dick.

But I want inside that sweet pussy even more. Her arousal smells so good and tastes honey-sweet.

"You're big." She licks her lips again.

Nervously?

"I won't hurt you." I don't hurt women. Not even in sex play.

It's just not my thing.

But if this woman wants a sensual spanking? I might overcome my personal preferences.

That round ass is so fucking tempting.

If we had more time, I'd fuck it, but for all her bravado and unrestrained passion, I sense a streak of innocence in my exquisite goddess of love.

She's experienced enough to let a man pick her up in a club and to ride my face like she was born to it though.

I'm pretty sure she's too enthralled with my dick to answer. Which is an answer in itself. Aphrodite wants to feel my thick meat filling her up.

Some thought spurs her into action and she rips her panties off. Then sits up and does the same to her dress. She's not wearing a bra and my mouth waters when her pretty tits come on display.

"You're in a hurry all of a sudden." I reach out and cup those soft mounds and squeeze.

She might not have a big rack, but her tits are a perfect raspberry tipped handful and bouncy as fuck. There are no hard edges on her. My sweet Aphrodite is all soft curves.

"Pretty." I give both nipples a little tweak.

Her moan goes straight to my balls. "Do that again."

"Bossy. I like it." There's no bigger turn on for me than a woman who knows what she wants and tells me.

This time I pinch the little berries and pull before twisting them gently.

She breathes in deeply, her eyelids going half-mast in pleasure. "You're really good at that."

There's no chance to reply before her small hands are wrapped around my turgid shaft. She squeezes and twists, following me move for move.

And fuck if it doesn't feel amazing.

I show her what I want by doing it to her nipples and she follows my lead without hesitation. Until a drop of my precum falls onto her leg.

"Oh," she gasps.

Then she swipes it up with a fingertip and sticks that finger into her mouth. "Yum."

"You can have it from the source."

"I am," she says and then her eyes light with understanding and she leans forward. This time it's her tongue swiping right over the bulbous head.

She opens her mouth and takes my whole tip inside, stretching her lips obscenely.

I let her suckle the end for a few glorious seconds, but I want inside her pussy and if I come down her throat I'll have to wait.

Though with how she turns me on, it won't be that long.

Cupping her cheek, I pull back. "Let's save that for later. I want to be inside you."

She nods enthusiastically, sending her messy hair swinging. Flipping over, she crawls up the bed, giving me a tantalizing view of her jiggly ass and bare pussy as her thighs shift.

I'm so caught up in the view, I don't realize what she's doing until the lights go off casting her curves into noir relief.

"You don't like light while you're fucking?" Some women don't.

One lover told me, the light hurts her eyes when she's that sensitized.

"There's enough coming in from the windows and it's silvery."

At least she doesn't say romantic. The death knell to a good night of sex is trying to bring romance into it.

"Whatever you want." I've seen every square inch of her.

Nothing will erase her bare, pink pussy or the way her nipples look engorged and tipping her deliciously pale breasts from my mind's eye.

"I want to be in the bed," she says decisively.

"Are you cold?" I'll keep her warm, but if she wants to start with the covers on, I can do that.

It's a surprising choice for a woman like her though.

"A little."

I run my hand down her backside and she shivers. Do I have the A/C set too low? I like a colder bedroom.

"Come on, little love goddess, I'll keep you warm." I pull her under the covers with me.

Her giggle cuts off abruptly as my fingers unerringly find the wet folds of her slick snatch.

"Since I can't see you, I'll have figure out where everything is by touch," I tease.

"Like you don't know." Her voice rises on the last word.

Maybe because I let one fingertip slide over the rosebud at her back entrance.

"Ares?" she asks uncertainly, confirming her innocence of this act.

If only she lived in New York. We could be lovers until the blood alliance with Shaughnessy's mob is formalized.

We only have tonight, so we'll have to make the best of it.

I'm so lost in her body, I almost forget the condom and have my head inside her before I remember. I *never* forget.

But when she goes stiff under me, I remember. "Don't worry. I'll put one on. Just give me a second."

"T-take your time," she says between stuttered breaths.

She's as turned on as I am, which makes me want to tease her and go as slow as my own libido will let me. So, I don't slam in with a single thrust like my balls are aching for.

No, I take it one slow inch at a time.

"Just do it, Ares, please."

"Do what?"

"Fuck me!"

I do. She just lies there at first and I think she's not into it. How is that possible? But then she thrusts upward and by the next thrust her nails are scoring my back.

She comes with a sob and I let her pussy milk my own release out of me.

For the first time in my life, I resent the condom stopping my semen from pouring directly into her body.

Marking her as mine.

Unable to look away from the beauty in the bed, I remove the condom and toss it in the trash without looking at it, before putting another one on my still hard cock.

Begrudgingly.

I bite back the urge to ask if she's on birth control and offer to show her my latest clean bill of sexual health. What the fuck is wrong with me?

I don't go bareback with my sex partners. Ever.

But fuck do I want to mark her. I settle for sucking up pretty purple marks on her breasts and throat throughout the night as we make l—fuck that. As we fuck over and over.

I don't know what time it is when I wake up, but it's still dark outside. Aphrodite is curved into me like a kitten, her body molded perfectly to mine.

"Mmm...Ares..." she slurs in her sleep.

Ares, the god of war. More fitting than she'll ever know. A woman like this can't live in my world and I don't have any business in hers.

That thought gets me moving. I order her a car, pull on my trousers without boxers and then wake her up.

She rubs her eyes sleepily. "I don't think I can again tonight."

"It's time for you to go home. Your car will be here in twenty minutes." It's enough time for a quick shower but not enough for a drawn out goodbye.

She stares at me like my words aren't registering. "A car?"

"To take you home."

"To take me home," she repeats and shakes her head as if to clear it. "To take me back," she says more firmly. "I can get my own car."

"If you want to, but this service is bonded and guarantees discretion." I show her the car service on my phone.

It's a national company well known in my circles, but that doesn't mean she'll trust them. No doubt, she'd rather go with some stranger driving a rideshare.

But her face clears and she nods. "Okay. Let me get dressed and I'll be out of your hair."

It's only after she leaves and I go to take the shower she refused that I notice the red streaks of dried blood at the base of my cock.

I run back into the bedroom and yank the duvet away from the bed.

The streaks on the bottom sheet are unmistakable. More blood.

She could have been in her period, but I inhaled her feminine arousal like I was huffing a popper and there was no telltale scent of copper. She wasn't bleeding when she got here.

My goddess of love was a damned virgin.
And she didn't say a word.

CHAPTER 18: RÓISE

"Okay, you sure you've got this, Fi?"

Fiona waves her hand around the media room like a game show presenter. "I've got three of *my* favorite movies queued on the big screen for an all-night binge watch with enough snacks and drinks to keep me until next week. What's not to love?"

"You're right." A night all to herself in the media room, watching whatever she wants is her jam.

It's kind of mine too, when I'm not doing my best to ace all my college classes. I don't remember the last time I binge watched my favorite show, much less a bunch of movies.

I'd be jelly if I wasn't going into the City to watch Drunk Shakespeare.

"What happens if someone comes looking for us?" Kara asks, looking around the media room like a bodyguard is going to jump out from the shadows.

But our security teams respect our privacy. We don't even have to have someone in the hall outside the room when we're home.

Uncle Brogan has plenty of security, both bodies and technology to keep the mansion safe from intruders.

"The only security that might do that are gone for the day." We all know I'm talking about Allessio and Zoey, who are assigned to be with me whenever I leave the house.

Since I had no *official* plans to leave the house tonight, they left before dinner.

"No one will question that you're not in here with me," Fi answers her sister. "No one ever checks on us when we're having a movie night."

That's the main reason we're pretty sure we can get away with this. Because no one *does* check on us when we do our movie nights. Unless you count Kara's husband and tonight, he's in Queens with Uncle Brogan at a mob meeting.

So, tonight Kara and me? We're meeting my friends from college and going out to celebrate my 21st. Which technically isn't for another week but who's going to tell?

"I can't believe I'm doing this," Kara says her eyes alight with excitement. "I have never snuck out of the house before. Not even when I was younger."

"You talk like you're an old woman and you're only four years older than me, three as of next week."

"And then it will be four again in October," she responds with the familiar argument. "I guess that's what comes from getting married when you're eighteen."

Kara doesn't sound bitter, just pragmatic.

But tonight we're not two women trapped in a world we were born into and can only leave by death. Unless we want to leave all those we love behind.

Tonight, we aren't two mob princesses. We are just two young women having some innocent fun.

There's a door in the back of the movie room, hidden in the wall. It's for staff to use and leads to the inner hallways they use to move around the mansion efficiently and unobtrusively.

They have more direct routes from one area of the house to another, which we are using tonight to reach the backdoor.

Of course, the passageways are monitored, but Kara is some kind of genius with technology and she's programmed a glitch into the system that will give us three minutes to get out the back door unseen.

If she weren't a mob princess who married at eighteen, she'd probably run a dot.com or one of the big software companies by now.

We're both breathless when we reach the backyard. We have to wait one minute for the sensors in the backyard to glitch like those in the house.

"Remember, we have one minute to get down to the boathouse," she says.

I nod. "Pull up your hood."

We both tighten the drawstrings so only a little bit of our faces show and then we run toward the boathouse, using the route we carefully mapped out to decrease our chances of getting caught.

My cousin insisted on disabling the security systems for the shortest amount of time possible, staggered like this so no one trying to breach the property could take advantage.

Not that anyone knows the systems will be down. Or that we are leaving. Not even *moma*.

Because of Kara's scary smart brain, the biggest problem we face is timing our movements to avoid the perimeter guards. If one of them deviates from their routine by even five seconds, we're not going anywhere.

But our sprint across the lawn, past the pool and down to the boathouse goes unseen. Not even by the backyard cameras. Kara disabled those too.

The rest of the plan is my idea, including the dark camo clothes we're wearing. I pull the inflatable lifeboat out of the bathroom that I took off the yacht earlier this week. Fi inflated it this morning.

She spends more time in the backyard and the boathouse than the rest of us, so her being there today didn't cause any suspicion.

"This is fun," Kara says breathlessly.

I grin at her. "Just call me 007."

"Oh, I want to be Salt."

Crossing my fingers for calm waters, I drop the waterproof duffle with our clothes for tonight in the bottom of the dinghy.

The yacht has a full size, motored lifeboat of course. But there are four dinghies for backup only the family and my uncle's most trusted men know about.

Men like Uncle Brogan have to be prepared for any eventuality. Including having his yacht sunk and the lifeboat disabled. Mob life.

What can you do?

But that extra precaution is working in our favor. If I had to order an inflatable rubber raft off the internet, it would never be delivered without being checked by security.

All packages are.

Adrenalin pumping, we each take an end and lower the boat into the water beside the speedboat. Like Kara planned it (which she did), the bay door opens halfway.

"We've got two minutes to launch."

This isn't new to us. We used to have a rubber raft both of our parents let us use as long as we didn't paddle too far from shore. It sprang a leak and dumped us into the bay one day and disappeared the day after.

Too dangerous.

Kara gasps and starts tipping toward the water. I grab her hoodie and yank her back. We don't have time to exclaim over her close call.

We need to launch. Like now.

Which we do, falling into a rhythm with our paddles pretty fast. Is it a little risky? Maybe. But we're both strong swimmers and it's not like this boat is going to spring a leak.

Uncle Brogan has all the blow up rafts checked on the regular. What good is a failsafe if it fails, right?

It takes longer to reach the pleasure craft waiting for us with my friends onboard than we expect and my arms feel like rubber when we finally do.

A hundred yards of paddling with oars is about my limit, but my friends couldn't risk dropping anchor any closer.

Twenty yards offshore and another eighty southeast of the mansion, there's no clear line of site to our backyard from this spot. Which means it won't trigger Uncle Brogan's security measures.

Aleks, who looks like an action-adventure hero but who wants to write scripts, helps me and my cousin into the boat.

Two inches taller than me with her brown hair pulled into a sleek ponytail, Goodwin hands us a couple of towels to dry the sea spray from our faces.

"It worked," Traci crows, holding out two glasses of champagne. "You two are the bomb!"

I shake out my arms before taking my glass. "Rowing on these choppy waters is harder than I remember."

"Drunk Shakespeare will be worth it." Carrie's signature giggle accompanies her words.

She's always smiling and is too sweet for showbusiness, but she's determined to break into television.

Like Aleks, though, she wants to write scripts. Not get in front of the camera even though she embodies the girl next door with her blond hair, trim figure and sunny attitude.

Traci has enough snark to make up for it. She's an actor, like me, but I have no doubt we'll see her on the silver screen. Goodwin too. She's third generation theater with more talent in her little finger than I have in my whole body.

We formed a posse freshman year and we're still besties.

Traci raises her glass. "Happy birthday, Rosy!"

Everyone else joins in the toast and a chorus of happy birthdays fills the air around me. Happiness fizzes through me with more bubbles than the champagne.

After a single sip, Goodwin puts her glass down. She has to pilot the borrowed boat back to dock. Her mom's sorority sister lives in one of the shoreline properties before the barrier islands to the east.

Once we arrive, all of us use the boathouse to change our clothes. The bay is too choppy to avoid salt spray and none of us wanted to arrive in Midtown looking like we just ran through a rain shower.

There's a stretch limo waiting for us in the drive, and I squeal. "You got us a limo!"

Yes, my family is richer than all the newly minted billionaires, but I get driven to school in a town car or an SUV. We haven't used limos in our family since my grandfather passed.

Uncle Brogan says they're ostentatious and don't give the right impression. I don't know what impression a mob boss wants to give that a limo doesn't, but this one is perfect for my birthday.

The interior is wild. With white leather seats, a drinks cabinet topped by a basin filled with canned pre-mixed drinks and pink LED lights along the ceiling, it's perfect for the trip into the city.

I grab a can with palm trees and an orange background that says Sex on the Beach and grin at Goodwin. I know this is her doing.

She smiles and winks. "I found all the fun drinks in cans. It's taken me months to get them all, and some are probably super gross—"

"Which is half the fun," I interrupt with a laugh.

We try the drinks and Goodwin is right. Some are awful. Some are pretty good and we're all feeling the alcohol by the time the limo pulls to a stop to let us out.

We're laughing and joking around while Kara shows the tickets on her phone so we can get in. We all get carded, including Kara.

I nudge her with my elbow. "Not such an old lady after all."

She grins and shakes her head, then leans down to whisper. "It's a good thing your fake ID is so good."

The guy who checks our IDs uses a UV light to confirm the state and public safety seals are on the driver's licenses.

I can't help looking around nervously and not because my fake ID is getting such close scrutiny. This is Cosa Nostra territory and there is a tiny chance we'll be recognized by someone on Miceli's payroll.

Not that I'm thinking about my gorgeous enemy tonight.

I'm so not.

Only being cautious.

That doesn't mean I'm looking forward to seeing him again on my actual birthday. Because no. Not.

The show is in the lounge area set up to look like an old library and we get to our seats without seeing any Cosa Nostra soldiers. Even if I wouldn't recognize their faces, I know a made man when I see one.

When the actors come out, they call for someone to come up and drink the first shot with the actor who's going to get five shots before trying to act his part in the play. My entire group erupts into shouts and points at me.

Kara's shrieking, "Let the birthday girl do it, let the birthday girl do it!"

The actor in charge of the shots makes a joke about Kara already having had her shot and I must want to catch up. Laughing I join the actors and after a lot of banter, take a shot with the actor chosen to play his part drunk.

It burns as it goes down and I confirm to the rest of the audience that this is real alcohol. My friends whoop and holler as I return to the table while the actor takes his four remaining shots.

The rest of the evening is kind of a blur but it's fun. By the time we're back in the limo, I'm watching my friends and listening to all the in-jokes we have with each other.

I cut a look to my cousin. Did she have friends like this before she got married?

Tilting her head, she looks at me. "What?"

"Was it like this for you before?"

She shakes her head. "I was still in high school. Dad would have had an aneurism if I got caught drinking."

I nod because I know that's true.

"But yeah, I had friends."

"What happened to them?"

"I keep in touch with a couple, but most of them didn't want anything to do with a nineteen-year-old mom. I couldn't exactly leave Fitz and go out partying."

"I'm sorry."

She grabs my hand and squeezes. "Don't. Neither of us made the world we live in, but we're both expected to keep it going."

Literally.

My choice in Uncle Brogan's study back in January means a night like tonight won't happen again. Not exactly this way. But seeing how much fun Kara had tonight, I'm determined that we'll find other ways to let loose.

Even if we have to bring along the nosy mafia bodyguards.

Things will change, but that's okay. We all grow up. And sometimes growing up means giving up things. I will give up my freedom for the sake of Fiona. Because Kara gave hers up for me.

But that doesn't mean I'm giving up living, no matter what my mafia husband-to-be thinks. And I'm going to make sure my cousin starts experiencing life again too.

Reality bites in the strict timing we have for our return, which means it's not that late when we get back to Long Island.

Neither of us wanted to try to navigate the raft tipsy, which means we have to be on the spot to sneak back in when Uncle Brogan and Mick return from Queens.

Our re-entry strategy isn't as foolproof as our exit. Because it's easier to ask for forgiveness than permission. If we get caught sneaking back in on the land side, the worst that happens is some yelling.

I've already got two more bodyguards than I need. What's Miceli going to do? Give me two more and make my extra security round the clock?

I don't have to find out because, by sheer luck, we manage to get our tipsy selves back onto the estate and into the house without being detected.

One of the guards is caught on his phone and Mick reads him the riot act while Uncle Brogan yells at the other guards for not noticing. Honestly, I don't think we would have made it through undetected without the distraction.

Sometimes Fate smiles on mob princesses who just want one night of normal fun. And tonight's that night.

Not like Portland when Fate was playing nasty tricks.

Fi wants to hear everything about our night and we happily spill it all.

Afterward, we finish watching a movie with her before raiding the kitchen for middle-of-the-night root beer floats. My favorite.

Fi insists on both me and Kara also drinking a full bottle of water before going to bed.

"Hangovers are caused by dehydration," she lectures.

We all end up sleeping together in my room, waking at some ridiculous hour to Mick pounding on my door looking for his wife. Kara lets him carry her out and I roll over to go back to sleep.

I don't think Fi even woke up.

All-in-all, it was a pretty perfect birthday, even if it had to happen a week early.

CHAPTER 19: MICELI

Catalina smiles up at me. "What do you think?"

I think it looks like a pink and gold balloon and confetti monster barfed all over Festa's VIP level.

"It's very pink," I say neutrally.

Not because I don't want my mother, who is standing on Catalina's left to lecture me. Or even because my brother will shoot me if I hurt his wife's feelings. In the arm. Probably.

But because my sister-in-law's pretty face has none of the pain-driven tension that has marred it so often since the surgery on her hip. Recovery and the physical rehabilitation of her hip under the watchful eye of my overprotective brother has been hard on Catalina.

When the hospital sent a male physical therapist, we very nearly had another body to disappear. I got that sorted without bloodshed or death. Go me.

Catalina is happy right now and it shows.

"And gold," she says happily. "Lucky for us that the black accents were already here as part of the regular décor."

One of my cousin Salvatore's high-end nightclubs, Festa's stark black and white simplicity is one of the reasons I like coming here. My one contribution to this party was suggesting the venue.

Festa's VIP area is the most secure party venue in New York. Especially if the entire floor is booked, which it is. By me.

Confetti, glitter and latex...not the fun kind but balloons...have transformed my favorite club into a backdrop for a new Barbie movie.

I didn't go to the first one and I'd rather not star in this one either.

My other contribution to this party: I'm paying for every damn piece of glitter.

"Lucky." A cavity is forming in one of my molars from the sweetness already.

Catalina laughs and lays her hand on my arm. "It's exactly what Róise wants."

"I'll take your word for it." I have to.

Catalina has spent more time with my future fiancée than I have in the weeks since the contracts were signed.

I've been busy overseeing an investigation into one of our older capos. Lorenzo Ricci is dirty, but I have to prove it before we can kill him.

I also had to fly to Portland to finalize details on a deal we're brokering between the Hades Brotherhood and one of our allies.

None of that is the reason I haven't texted Róise. After I texted her the first time and she figured out who it was, the harridan blocked my number.

Anything I want to say to her, I have to say through my own people. Because *they might as well be good for more than ruining my life.*

Her words, not mine.

Róise makes no secret of her antipathy toward our upcoming marriage, but she's going to have to come to terms with it. The contracts are signed and our copy is stored in the secret document safe room between Sev and Catalina's offices in the family penthouse.

The building could take a hit from one of those RPGs and it wouldn't destroy that room.

The marriage is happening.

But right now, my secret fiancée is pretending I don't exist. Not that Allessio and Zoey let me forget about Róise for a single minute.

One or the other sends me a picture of Róise's outfit before they leave the house. Not that they listen when I tell them to get her to change. All of her clothes seem to expose her midriff and every fucking outfit has some pink in it.

There's a message there. And it's not the *fuck you, Miceli* she intends it to be. Maybe it is, because every youthful outfit reminds me of the more than a decade between us. Of the virgin blood smearing my cock that night in Portland.

Because she wanted one night being a normal woman who got to choose who she gave her virginity to. And she did not want that man to be the mafia underboss she would have to marry.

She did not want it to be me.

She wasn't turning me down in Portland though, was she?

When she thought I was Ares, her god of war. And she was my Aphrodite, a woman I believed to be experienced.

I hope Fate got her laugh out of playing that joke on me.

"She loves pink," Catalina's words bust into my thoughts. "Trust me."

"She was wearing black when I met her." Once to seduce and once to sign our prenuptial contract.

Dressed for a funeral.

Catalina's brows draw together in confusion. "Really? She's always got something pink on when I see her."

"You might want to have a little chat with her about that." Mamma looks around the party décor with none of Catalina's enthusiasm. "It's one thing to have a signature color and another for it to be..."

This isn't about the color pink and we both know it. When we told my mother and Catalina about the planned alliance, mamma was appalled.

That's when I learned that forty years ago, her older brother was killed during a war over territory with the Irish mob. She has more in common with Róise than she knows.

Grandfather negotiated the current truce six months later. Too late for the uncle I never got to meet.

Mamma does not trust the Irish. Róise despises the Italian mafia. It's a match made in mafia war heaven.

If we want to stop the blood spilling every generation, this marriage alliance has to happen. Mamma knows it too.

"Lots of people like pink." I'm not one of them, but it's not my birthday party.

"She's not going to damage Miceli's rep by wearing pink," Catalina, who is decked out in lime green and yellow, gently chides mamma.

My mother smiles affectionately at the daughter-in-law she adores every bit as much as she does her own daughter. "If you say so, *cara*."

What are Róise's chances for the same affection? Zero to nil.

Everyone in my family adores my brother's wife. Catalina is different in a good way, nothing Sev expected and everything he needed.

I'm not expecting that result from my marriage. I don't want it either.

Seeing my brother with a heart of granite go soft over his wife is a great source of amusement, but it's not something that will happen to me.

And still for some reason, it really bothers me that Róise can't expect the same welcome Catalina received.

After one final look around the room, my sister-in-law says, "I put your gift for Róise on the table."

She bought a gift from me too? What does she think? That I can't be bothered to even buy my own gift for the secret fiancée? "What is it?"

"A pink cat bed."

"A cat bed?" That doesn't sound like much of a gift. "I didn't know she had a cat."

"She doesn't. There's a gold foiled coupon printed on thick pink stationary in the card."

Suspicious, I ask, "What's the coupon for?"

"A trip to the shelter to adopt a kitten."

"The fuck I'm going to the shelter..." My mother's look has me stopping mid-rant. "I apologize for the language, mamma."

But then I glare at Catalina. "You'd better be joking."

"Nope. It will be good for you."

"Róise told you she wants a cat?" I ask.

"No, but doesn't everyone?"

"A dog maybe." At least dogs can be trained and they're loyal.

"Oh no, are you a dog person?" Catalina asks.

"My brother is not an animal person," Sev says as he arrives.

"Your wife wants a cat," I inform him, knowing my brother is no more an animal person than I am.

And he will have a new feline companion for his wife by tomorrow if he believes me.

Like I said, he's gone for her.

Catalina's eyes narrow at me. She knows how Sev will respond too.

I dare her with my eyes to disagree. My sister-in-law said everyone wants a cat and *everyone* by definition includes her.

Besides if I'm going to be saddled with a furry nuisance eventually, assuming Róise will insist on bringing the animal with her after we marry, so is my brother.

Sev leans down and kisses the side of Catalina's neck. "You want a kitten, *mi dolce bellezza*?"

She shivers as he whispers something else in her ear.

Whatever my brother said has Catalina's eyes going unfocused as she says, "Mmm...hmm."

"That's enough you two. The guests are going to start arriving soon and the birthday girl even sooner."

"Where's the gift table?" I ask, determined to remove "my" present and replace it with the one I bought.

"No way. You didn't want anything to do with planning the party. You had your chance to give your input on the present and you said—"

"I know what I said," I interrupt.

"You gave me free reign and I know she's going to like it. Don't ruin it with your made man ego."

"Don't think that's a thing."

"It's a thing," Catalina assures me.

"My wife took the time to buy your fiancée a gift and you will give it to her." Sev's tone isn't or-I'll-kill-you-now, but it's close.

The synthesized four beat rock elevator chime is loud in the silence of the club.

Cazzo. That's probably Róise and her family now.

Maybe I can send Angelo to pick the cat out with her. The Angel of Death has a soft spot for animals.

The doors slide open revealing an older woman with bright orange-red hair, Róise, and the bodyguards I assigned her.

Róise's dress doesn't have pink accents. It *is* pink. From the hem of the flirty skirt that hits well above her knees to the tight, glittery bodice that cups and presents her perfect tits enticingly.

Her shoes aren't stilettos like the first night we met, but the silver strappy sandals add a couple of inches to her height. Her beautiful legs are bare and an image of her wrapping them around my waist while I pound into her flashes through my brain.

My cock stirs with immediate interest.

I count dead bodies to put my libido back to sleep.

Nestled in Róise's chin length burnished brown curls is a tiara made with some kind of pink gemstone, set in platinum. It could be white gold, but I would pick platinum if I were buying it for her.

Her necklace and earrings compliment the tiara and something primitive inside me rebels at the thought of another man, even her uncle, buying her jewelry.

Beside her, the older woman who barely reaches five feet, leans on a...glittery pink cane. They make pink canes? That glitter?

Other than the cane, the older woman's pale blue dress is every bit as understated and sophisticated as my mother's.

Róise's gaze travels around the club, going bright and a smile curves her lips as she takes in the decorations.

I guess pink isn't so bad.

Her eyes connect with mine and another jolt of arousal powerful enough to run the club lights zaps me deep in the balls.

Accidente. This woman.

With barely a pause, Róise's gaze moves on and warms when she spots Catalina beside me.

"Cat! It's fantastic," she cries as she heads toward my sister-in-law.

Cat? I mouth to Sev.

He shrugs, but his mouth sets in a firm line. He doesn't like other people giving Catalina nicknames.

I shove his shoulder with mine. "Your possessive bone is showing."

"Say that to me this time next year," he taunts right back. "Don't think I haven't noticed the way your eyes follow her whenever she's in the room."

"You've seen us together twice and tonight I haven't even spoken to her yet."

"Exactly."

I ignore my brother's taunt and put my hand out to Róise. "Happy birthday."

"Are you kidding me? You're going to shake her hand?" Catalina demands, disbelief pitching her voice an octave higher than usual.

"You'll have to do better than that if you want people to believe you two are dating," my brother offers. "At least kiss her on the cheek."

Róise looks horrified and takes a step back. "Not necessary."

She didn't mind kissing me in Portland.

"I don't agree." I step right into her personal space and cup her cheeks with both hands, preventing her an avenue of retreat. "Happy birthday, Róise."

She melted in my arms that night in Portland, her passion a fiery match for my own desire. No way has that combustible chemistry just disappeared.

No matter what she wants to believe.

Intent on proving a point, I lean down and press my lips to hers.

Her mouth is sweeter than the cotton candy pink décor and I can't hold back from sliding my tongue between her lips to chase that taste.

Róise moans, her hands gripping my wrists. Not to pull my hands from her face, but to hold them in place.

Triumph mixes with instant sexual urgency.

"It looks like the lovebirds are getting along," booms a voice from near the elevators.

Brogan Shaughnessy has arrived.

Like we would, and had, his people brought him and his family up the secure elevator in shifts.

Róise goes stiff at the sound of her uncle's voice and rips herself away from me, wiping at her lips. Shiny pink gloss smears on her hands.

Fucking candy cotton pink lip gloss.

Knowing it will be all over my lips too, I grab my handkerchief out of my pocket and hand it to her. "Do you mind?"

I'm pushing, rubbing in what we just did. The sparks of temper in her emerald eyes says she knows it too.

CHAPTER 20: RÓISE

Okay, one point to Miceli.

That kiss about knocked me off my feet. And he knows it too.

I take the handkerchief. "Thank you." After wiping off my lip gloss, I hand it back. "You might want to..." I let my voice trail off and point to my own lips and then nod to his.

He rubs it off, removing the evidence of our kiss and my body relaxes.

"Don De Luca, may I introduce my grandmother, Maeve Shaughnessy. *Mamo*, this is Severu, Aria and Catalina you already know, and Miceli De Luca." Introducing my intended last is deliberate.

Instead of looking mad, there's a glint of amusement in Miceli's eyes as he steps forward. "A pleasure to meet you, Mrs. Shaughnessy."

"Call me Maeve, young man. According to my son, we will be family soon enough."

Miceli agrees with an inclination of his head. "I would be honored to."

Why doesn't his charm come off smarmy? It should, but he sounds so darn sincere. *Mamo* is canny though and the smile she gives him doesn't reach her eyes.

She could navigate life at the Whitehouse if a mob boss ever got elected to president. It won't happen though. Not because it's impossible, but because the role is too public.

Syndicate heads don't spend their time in the public eye.

The elevator chimes again and soon my cousins and Kara's husband are being introduced to the De Lucas.

"Isn't the décor dreamy?" Fiona asks the group with a rapturous look around.

I have to cough to cover the laugh that wants to burst free. Both from my cousin's acting ability and the look on Miceli's face.

"He says it's very pink," Catalina says with an indulgent smile for her brother-in-law.

"I love it," I tell her. "It's perfect."

Catalina's smile widens. "I knew you would."

Does she know about Miceli's aversion to the color? I doubt it.

Talking about the women he doesn't take to bed isn't going to happen in front of his brother's wife.

From the way he dresses, you'd think he hates all the colors except black and dark gray. I don't know about that, but I do know he doesn't like pink.

He thinks it's too sweet and that I'm too young. Two facts I'm happy to exploit.

I know because my cousins and grandmother are like living with my own personal Google and gossip columnist.

Apparently, Miceli De Luca doesn't flirt with women dressed in pink, who have pink hair, or who wear cotton candy pink lip gloss. Like what I'm wearing now.

Was wearing before he kissed it off. Huh.

Speaking of, I tap Fiona's shoulder. "I need to refresh my..." I wave at my mouth. "Want to come with me?"

"I'm coming too," Kara says quickly. "I want to know how you lost your lip gloss between the time you came up in the elevator and we arrived."

Accessible by an elevator that requires a VIP keycard, this area of Festa is completely shut off from the rest of the club. From the tour I took with Catalina while planning the party, I know there are smaller rooms off the main area.

They're for private parties and patrons who want to use bottle service with their guests instead of ordering from the club's extensive drink menu.

We're not using them tonight and they've all been locked to stop potential sexcapades during my 21st while the alcohol flows freely.

Not that I plan on drinking much.

At least half the guests will be people I don't know from the Italian mafia. It's Miceli and my first public appearance together.

One big show for the audience of the New York underworld. It's weird though, right?

We had sex, but we've never been on a date.

Is his family hosting a party for my 21st considered a date? In our messed up world, it probably is.

Too bad he's not Mr. Romance and I'm not a blushing ingénue.

When we get to the ladies room, the *cailíní* and I automatically check to see if anyone else is in here before we start talking.

"Empty," Kara says after trying the handle on the final stall door and finding it unlocked.

Each stall is entirely walled off, with only a couple of inches above and below the black doors. Talk about an invitation to illicit sexy times. Or drug deals.

The bathroom fits the rest of the club's stark décor. The walls are white, while the doors and long counter with three sinks are black. Even the touchless faucets are black.

"No wonder Miceli picked this club for your party. He's surrounded by his favorite color," Fiona says.

Kara grins. "Maybe he wears red silk boxers."

He doesn't. Those are black too. And they're made of the same knit silk my favorite t-shirts are.

I don't say that. My cousins know about my act of rebellion in Portland, but not that Miceli is the man I had sex with. I was too complimentary of my one-night stand.

Now, I know he's Italian mafia, a freaking underboss who set two guard dogs on me that I can't shake. I don't want to compliment him on anything, especially his sense of humor and sexual prowess.

"Time to spill," Kara demands. "How did your lip gloss disappear?"

"He kissed me happy birthday," I grudgingly admit.

Fiona whistles. "Must have been some kiss."

Not wanting to dwell on how good of a kisser my not-quite-fiancé is, I dig in my small pink handbag.

I hand the keycard to Fiona. "This will open any of the private rooms. Use it when you need to get away from the crowd."

"Thank you, Rosy." Fiona hugs me tight. "I'm probably going to disappear as soon as the guests start arriving."

"We'll cover for you with dad, don't worry," Kara says. "*Mamo* will help."

Fiona nods. "She always does. I wish I wasn't like this."

"You are who you are, Fiona, and we love you exactly as you are," Kara says fiercely.

What we all witnessed and experienced eleven years ago affected each of us differently.

I hate mob life and the Italian mafia most of all. Funny, not funny, that I'm marrying into the very syndicate that killed my mom. Kara, who used to be the dare-devil rebel among us turned into a subdued rule follower who willingly married a stranger at eighteen.

The youngest at six, Fiona lost her trust in the world around her. She anticipates trouble all the time. Everywhere.

Therapy might help but Shaughnessy mob princesses don't see psychologists. Or therapists. Or counselors.

We soldier on.

Like my grandfather did eleven years ago when his life was under threat. Did he realize the danger he was putting the rest of us in?

After the shooting, our family never again traveled together to an event.

It happened outside the hotel where the wedding reception had been held. We'd left all together and were heading toward the limos parked in the waiting area.

It happened so fast, my memory is a blur. Loud pops. Red paint spraying everywhere. (Only later did I process that it was my mom's blood.) Mom falling to the steps in front of me. Dad dropping to his knee beside her, his gun out and pointed toward the car already speeding away.

I think he shot at it. I don't know.

My hip hurt. Later, I found out that I'd been struck by a chip of cement from the steps when one of the bullets hit them instead of vulnerable human bodies.

None of the mobsters were hit, but my mom died before the ambulance arrived and Fiona spent two weeks in the hospital. The bullet grazed her temple and knocked her unconscious.

She woke up thirteen days later and gone was the precocious six-year-old who never met a stranger and whose curiosity led her into constant mischief.

She had her first panic attack when they tried to make her go back to school.

"So, he kissed your lip gloss off and you're going to pretend it was nothing?" Kara teases, bringing me back into the present with a thump.

"It was nothing. He's a playboy. We all know that." Courtesy of *mamo's* intelligence network among the many syndicate wives she counts as friends.

Of course she hadn't got that tidbit from Aria De Luca. Aria is fiercely loyal to her children. But the wife of the Gambino don isn't nearly as charitable toward the De Luca men.

She thinks they're ruthless, cold-blooded killers.

The Gambino dona is not wrong.

But her husband is the same. Only according to her, none of the men in the other Five Families are as brutal as the De Luca's. She says there are rumors that Miceli's cousin murdered his fiancée for the mafia, that all the De Luca men would kill their own wives for the sake of the syndicate.

But if Salvatore was ever engaged, it never went public. And I don't see Severu killing his wife for the sake of anything, or anyone. He'd burn down New York first.

But what about Miceli?

Would he kill for me? Or kill me for expedience?

CHAPTER 21: MICELI

When Róise steps out of the bathroom with her cousins, early guests are starting to arrive.

She joins me near the elevators to welcome her friends and enemies. Such is the mafia life.

Sliding my hand around her waist, I anchor Róise to me. If I wasn't paying attention, I would have missed her quickly indrawn breath.

She still wants me. I still want her.

It should be a match made in syndicate heaven.

But I don't believe in fairytales. And if Róise does, she'll figure out pretty fucking fast that I'm nobody's idea of Prince Charming.

CHAPTER 22: RÓISE

My face hurts from smiling by the time most of the guests have arrived.

"That's enough." Miceli leads me away from the elevator, his arm still firmly in possession of my waist. "Any latecomers can find us."

"Don't you mean me?" It is my party after all.

"I'm the host. You're my girlfriend." His mouth twists on the last word.

My tummy tightens when he says it. "Your girlfriend? Really?"

"Get used to it. You'll be my fiancée soon enough."

"So romantic," I jeer.

"If you're looking for romance, you signed a contract with the wrong guy."

I believe him. Even that night in Portland, he wasn't romantic. Passionate and intense? Yes. Mr. Romance? Not even close.

"The fact we signed a contract says it all, doesn't it?" Even if Miceli didn't belong to a syndicate I despise, this kind of marriage is the last thing I want.

We veer toward the bar. "You know how this goes. You grew up in the mob."

"I grew up believing I would get to choose my own spouse." Or if I would marry at all.

He stops at the bar. "What do you want to drink?"

"I'll have my birthday cocktail," I tell the bartender.

Miceli orders a whiskey, neat.

A few seconds later, the bartender puts Miceli's rock glass on the bar and presents me with a pink concoction served with a maraschino cherry in a martini glass.

And it doesn't contain an ounce of alcohol. I can't afford to get drunk in this crowd.

The real celebration happened already anyway, and I got pleasantly tipsy then.

"More pink," Miceli mutters.

I smile. "It's good. Do you want to try it?"

I expect him to say he'll stick with his whiskey.

But he takes my glass and sips while I gape.

Snapping my mouth shut, I take my drink back. "Isn't it yummy?"

"So yummy you can't even taste the alcohol." He gives me a sardonic look.

"Because there isn't any."

"On your 21st birthday?"

I shrug, feeling no need to explain and move away from the bar, expecting Miceli to go off and do his own thing.

He doesn't. He follows me, his hand once again on my waist.

I try to step out of his hold, but his grip on my waist tightens.

"Do you mind?" I'm trying to hide my hostility from the partygoers around us, but it's getting harder by the second. "You don't need to act all possessive."

"I'm not acting."

That I believe. This man will keep what is his. But I'm not his. Not yet.

"Our relationship might be drowning in contracts, but you didn't buy me."

"Agreed."

I don't trust his easy agreement. "So, let me go."

"You drank that night in Portland."

"It was safer to drink there." No way am I going to admit to needing liquid courage to follow through on my plan to have sex for the first time.

"You thought it was safer to have your thought processes impaired when you were trolling for a stranger to have sex with than it is here among our families?" His tone is a mix of judgmental disbelief.

"Absolutely."

"You don't deny that is what you were doing?" he asks, something flickering in his dark eyes.

"Why should I? I did have sex with a stranger." Hard to deny that reality when he'd been the stranger in question.

"What I want to know is why?"

"Not your business." Besides, I already explained. If he didn't believe my explanation, that's his problem.

It's the only one he's getting from me.

"You planned to give your virginity to a man who was not me. That is my business."

"No, it is not. We hadn't signed contracts. I didn't even know you were the man I was supposed to marry. But you knew it was going to be me, didn't you?"

"Of course I knew, but I hadn't agreed to it yet."

"So, neither of us did anything wrong."

"You were a virgin."

"And you weren't. Your point?"

"My point is that if you had succeeded in fucking a stranger, I would have tracked him down and killed him."

"That's such a big double-standard, I'm surprised it fits in the club." I gulp down my drink, but it doesn't cool my anger even a little.

This guy makes other made men look like the evolved species.

Rather than reply, Miceli guides me onto the dance floor. Because this is the way my luck is running these days, it's a slow song.

He hands his now empty glass to a passing server and does the same to mine.

"I wasn't done with that."

"You can get another one. Slow dancing requires two hands." He flips me around and suddenly I'm in the same position I was in Portland.

Vulnerable with my back to his front, the music a soft, seductive thrum inside my body.

Everything in me rebels and I jerk around to face him, putting my hands on his shoulders to keep some distance between us.

It doesn't work. Miceli wraps me up securely, his hands pressed to the center and the small of my back. I'm not going anywhere.

He starts swaying to the music.

"Stop it," I hiss.

"Stop what? I'm dancing with my girlfriend."

"I'm not your girlfriend," I practically growl.

"That's not what all these people think."

"It's a business arrangement."

"It's a marriage."

"Not yet, it's not." I force myself not to squirm in his hold and draw the attention of our guests.

"It will be. You signed your life away, just like I did."

It shouldn't sting that he puts it that way. "Anyway, this boyfriend thing is already sold from you hosting my birthday party. Standing next to me to greet everyone shoved it in every face that might have been oblivious."

Can you say overkill?

"Do you like to dance?" he asks in a non sequitur.

"You know I do." Every minute of memory from that night galls me now, but I'm not going to pretend it didn't happen.

"From this point on, I am your only dance partner."

"I will, yeah." Translated for those without an Irish gran: *I definitely will not*. "If I want to dance with someone else, then I will."

Miceli shrugs. "Don't dance with anyone you don't want to see hurt. Or dead."

"Are you kidding me?" He doesn't sound like he's teasing.

"Men like me don't joke about violence."

That I believe. "You can't hurt someone for dancing with me."

"I can."

"Does that mean I get to kneecap every woman you dance with?" I demand incredulously.

Does he even hear himself?

"The only other women I will dance with are family."

I assume he means his family, but he could be referring to Kara and Fiona too. "I don't believe you."

"De Lucas don't break their marriage vows."

"Dancing isn't infidelity." I speak slowly, trying to get through his thick skull. "And *we are not married*."

"A wedding is just a formality. The deal is done."

The sound of steel bars slamming down clangs through my head. He means it. Regardless of when the wedding happens, as far as Miceli De Luca is concerned, we are committed to each other.

"We're not even engaged."

"It may be secret for now, but you are definitely my fiancée."

Secret? But real. That's definitely a different twist on our situation.

"Whatever. That doesn't mean you can go around pounding on other men for dancing with me. I assume women are safe from your murderous tendencies."

"If a woman hits on you, my cousin Nerissa will sort it."

"No. Just no. I don't want that kind of life." The walls are closing. Pretty soon I'll be locked in a box too small to even turn around.

"It's not a kind of life. It *is* your life and it's time you accept that. Do what I say and no one gets hurt." He thinks he's being reasonable.

His tone and expression aren't even a little upset, while my temper slips its leash and runs pell-mell through my body.

"That's not how it works in the real world," I grit out, not even trying to pretend to be the happy birthday girl anymore, much less this violent Neanderthal's girlfriend.

"It's how it works in our world."

"Yours maybe, not mine." I shove at his chest, hard.

"In my world any man who touches you dies. Remember that while you're pretending to live in a different one." Then he lets me go.

CHAPTER 23: MICELI

Róise storms through the crowd, ignoring the attempts of our guests to get her attention.

"You do realize this is supposed to be an alliance between our families, not the beginning of the next war, don't you?" Sev drawls in a mix of mockery and warning from behind me.

Still watching my angry secret fiancée, I don't turn to face my brother. "She doesn't want this marriage."

"Catalina didn't want to marry me either. We made it work." My brother's superior tone frays another strand on the last rope holding my temper in check.

"She is not Catalina." And I am not my brother.

He wanted Catalina from the beginning. I've questioned very few decisions my brother has made as don. The one to marry Catalina's younger sister?

Everyone but Sev knew that was a disaster waiting to happen.

"How would you know? You've spent no time with her since we formalized the alliance." There's nothing but censure in my brother's tone now.

"I've been busy." And she's not answering my calls.

But I'm not telling Sev that. I'm not some pathetic loser who can't keep a twenty-one-year-old in check. I've just been too busy to explain to her in person that her behavior is unacceptable.

Because your last explanation went over so well, she stormed off the dance floor. And the one before that ended up with her blocking your number.

Róise two. Miceli zero.

"Stop running, brother. You agreed to this alliance."

"I'm not the one who's running."

"Since when do you let your prey get away?" He lays a hand on my shoulder. "Listen brother, if you don't want this, I can find someone else, but you need to make that decision now."

"The fuck you are. The contracts are already signed and it's my blood on them," I grind out.

An older man grabs Róise's arm as she tries to go past him. I don't recognize him. He must have arrived after we stopped greeting guests at the elevator.

She makes a motion with her shoulder, wincing when he doesn't let go. He hurt her.

The last filament of thread holding my temper snaps.

It takes me seconds to get through the crowd, my knife in my hand when I reach them.

I press it against his neck under the guise of putting my arm around his shoulder. "Let her go."

Róise's eyes widen, but the relief there makes me press the blade into Gabriel Lion's neck. I keep my knives sharp. It would only take a little more exertion to cut right through to his carotid artery.

Her estranged grandfather's quick inhale tells me he knows it too.

I didn't recognize him from the back because I've only seen his picture, but there's no question who is stupid enough to lay hands on what is mine.

"Lean forward and you'll slit your own neck," I tell him conversationally.

He releases the birthday girl.

My knife stays right where it is. "Róise, tell him what I said would happen to anyone who touches you."

She closes her eyes, takes a breath, and lets it out before opening them again. The calm I see there surprises and impresses me.

"He's family."

"He's not my family," I deny.

"He's my grandfather." She sighs. "Maybe put the knife away before someone posts a picture of my boyfriend threatening my grandfather to their Instagram."

"Our guests know better." And for those who don't? There's a jammer blocking all cell phones and other devices while we are here.

"Don't talk about me like I'm not here, girl," Gabriel Lion, so called prophet and leader of the Armor of God militia, says dismissively. "Young man, you don't want to threaten me."

I lean down so he can't miss my next words. "I don't make idle threats. Grandfather, or not, if you touch Róise again, I will slit your throat after I cut off the offending hand."

Lion should appreciate the Biblical justice of that.

Shaughnessy arrives in a rush with his son-in-law before I can say more, both of them blocking the tableau from the rest of the room. "Put that knife away. That's her grandfather."

"Nothing to add?" I ask the finally silent old man.

"She's not worth making an enemy of me."

"*She* has a name," Róise says with a verbal eyeroll.

"It's Róise," I remind him helpfully. "Say it."

"She should have been called Rachel as I told her mother, not that heathen, foreign name."

Shaughnessy doesn't look offended, just resigned.

I raise my brows to him. "You let him talk like that?"

Róise is an Irish name and the asshole kissing my blade with his neck just equated it to being a heathen.

"Brother Gabriel is set in his ways. He doesn't mean anything by it."

"Bullshit. There's nothing wrong with Róise's name." It fits her even better than Aphrodite.

Being considered a heathen by this man is not exactly an insult, but if he said that about me, I'd cut out his tongue.

From what I know of the Armor of God, they consider anyone outside their insular cult to be damned.

I'm not a practicing Catholic. Religion is not my thing. I've seen too much to believe in a benevolent God watching over this world, but my mother is devout.

"Call her a heathen and maybe I'll set your tongue on fire before I cut it out."

"Miceli?" Sev moves to stand to my left, in perfect position to hinder the Irish mobsters.

"I am doing my best to save this man's life," I say righteously.

Sev nods. He turns cold eyes on Gabriel Lion. "You laid hands on one of ours."

"She's not yours," Lion rejects in a loud voice.

"You're not very good at playing polite guest, are you?" The desire to spill this man's blood grows.

"What did you think it meant when Miceli hosted her birthday party?" my brother asks.

"She is the fruit of my loins," the old man claims. "No boyfriend has more claim to her than me."

He's the second man in five minutes to deny the permanency of my claim on Róise and it pisses me off.

He's either incredibly stupid or stupidly arrogant.

"Remove your knife from my throat, boy."

Okay, so both.

"If you insist." My tone warns Sev, but everyone else relaxes.

Except Róise. She tenses, her eyes pleading with me. She believed me when I said I would damage or kill any man who touched her.

Depending on the depth of the offense. And my mood.

It's her birthday. Killing someone at her party would probably ruin it for her.

I slide my knife along Lion's throat, leaving a shallow, painful cut in the blade's wake. No point in wearing a knife that isn't nice and sharp.

He squeals like a pig, and I shove him toward Shaughnessy. "Get him out of here before he ruins the party decorations with his blood."

"What the fuck?" Shaughnessy's voice is filled with fury and offense, but he modulates it, so he doesn't draw more attention to us.

"Relax. He'll live. This time." I let the warning hang in the air between us. I put my arm out to Róise. "Come on, Aphrodite, you've got presents to open."

"You live up to our middle name, God of War. And that's not a compliment." She takes my arm though and I lead her away from Shaughnessy and Lion.

"Come on, gentlemen, you are making a spectacle of yourselves." That's my brother.

I know I've got a lecture coming later, but he will always have my back. And I will always have his. Which is why I am going to marry an Irish mob princess.

That and, the idea of another man claiming her makes me want to kill someone with fire.

CHAPTER 24: RÓISE

"Oh, wear the pink jumpsuit. Please, Rosy." Fiona presses her palms together and looks at me with puppy dog eyes from where she's sitting on my bed.

Miceli is taking me to the shelter to pick out a kitten. Miceli. Not his sister-in-law, which is who I assumed would actually accompany me when I opened the present at my birthday.

My fake boyfriend who will one day be my very real husband is not the type of man to give a coupon for a trip to an animal shelter as a gift. Did he even know the shelter exists before my birthday party?

I don't think so either.

"Come with us," I say, pulling the jumpsuit off the hanger in my walk-in closet. "You can wear something pink too."

"I don't know." Fiona chews on her thumbnail.

"You know you want to. There's a whole litter of kittens. You can get one too and they can play together."

My cousin's eyes cloud. "Until you move out."

"That's eons away." I strip out of the yoga pants and oversized black t-shirt I put on after my shower this morning. "We're not even officially engaged."

"I don't want to horn in on your date," Fiona tries again.

But I know my younger cousin wants to go. She loves animals and Uncle Brogan won't get mad if Miceli gets her a kitten from the shelter too.

I think.

If he does get angry, I'll tell him it was my idea.

"It's not a date." It's an obligation Catalina created when she got me the pale pink princess cat bed and slapped Miceli's name on the card.

"Pretty sure it is."

"I promise it's not." Even if it will be the first time the Italian underboss and I go anywhere together since signing the contracts.

He didn't even pick me up for my birthday party he was supposedly throwing for me.

"Come on." I give her my best lost kitten look. "It won't be crowded. You know how mob guys are. Miceli will have the shelter cleared before we get there."

"He's Cosa Nostra. Maybe they do things differently."

"Want me to find out?" I ask.

Allessio will know. I still have Miceli's number blocked on my phone. The underboss made the plans through his soldier. He didn't ask, but I couldn't give him a hard time about that because I blocked his number.

Besides Allessio and Zoey know my schedule better than I do now.

Fiona bites her lip and shakes her head at my offer. "What should I wear?"

I grin at her tacit agreement. "This."

I hand her the pink velour hoodie and pants I grabbed from my closet when I was getting my own outfit.

Fiona's eyes round in shock. "That's even more in your face than your jumpsuit."

I look at the two outfits critically. She's probably right. The velour ensemble is in your face, hot pink and my jumpsuit is rose pink.

"Do you want to wear the jumpsuit?"

"No." Fiona is decisive. "The velour is stretchy. I like stretchy."

"The jumpsuit is stretchy too." The French terry cotton has give to it, but it's definitely not as soft as the velour.

"I don't know how you stand wearing something you have to practically strip out of to go pee." Fiona gives an all over body shudder.

"You told me to wear it," I remind her.

"Because you like jumpsuits."

And she likes jackets with hoods she can pull over her head when she's feeling overwhelmed.

Fiona grabs the clothes and climbs off my bed. "I'm not wearing a pink t-shirt."

"If you did, it would probably make Miceli's eyes bleed," I weedle.

"Have you thought that your new penchant for pink could end up as good aversion therapy for him? By the time you get married, it's going to be his favorite color."

"That's assuming he associates it with something positive."

"You are the best thing that will ever happen to him," Fiona says with staunch loyalty and no empirical evidence to support it.

"You're prejudiced." Miceli liked me before he knew who I was.

More than liked. He wanted me so much he kept me up most of the night. My vagina was *sore* for three days after even with the witch hazel pads Kara suggested.

Worth it though.

I'll never forget that night. Because even if it was with Miceli, I didn't know it and he wasn't my enemy then. Sex will never be the same again.

How can it be? Now, I know who he is.

I ignore the loud clamor of protest from my ladybits.

The underboss is no more excited to get married than I am. If he was, this would not be the second time I'm seeing him since that day in his brother's office.

If he wanted to get around a blocked number, he would. That he hasn't says everything about how he regards our future.

A necessary evil.

He's possessive with the primal instincts of an alpha predator, but I'm not his one good thing.

His aversion to pink and my joy in needling him are both safe.

The look he gives me when I get downstairs is two parts horrified, one part disbelief.

Along with the jumpsuit, I'm wearing pink tennis shoes and a matching wrap style headband holding my curls back. It's a lot of pink.

Which I'm starting to like for more reasons than bedeviling Miceli.

Pink is a cheerful color and I find myself smiling more when I get dressed to go out.

"Hi, Miceli," Fiona says from behind me.

His gaze slides past me to take in my cousin. She's wearing an olive green t-shirt and beat up black Converse with the velour tracksuit.

"Hello, Fiona." Miceli's voice always gentles when he talks to my cousin. "I take it from the pink outfit that you are coming with us?"

"Why do you say that?" I ask.

"Am I wrong?" he counters.

"No."

"It's a good thing I brought the Beamer and not my McLaren."

"A McLaren Speedtail has three seats," Fiona says.

Miceli nods and smiles. "Which would leave no room for the kitten carrier and you. Besides, I never allow passengers in the seat to my right."

Security reasons, I bet, but I don't ask.

"I still want to know why you think Fiona wearing pink indicates she's coming with us. She likes pink."

"I'm sure you do too, but you wearing so much of it is a dig at me."

"That's pretty conceited." If true.

"Deny it."

"My styling choices are my business," I sidestep.

"That's what I thought. You didn't wear any pink in Portland, or that day in Sev's office." He makes it sound like an accusation.

"You two met in Portland?" Fiona asks before I can reply. "When? How?"

"Those are excellent questions, and your cousin can answer them all in the car," Miceli says.

My glare could singe paint but it doesn't even make Miceli blink. "I'm not answering any questions."

The look he gives me says, "Want to bet?"

From the look of rabid curiosity on Fiona's face, I don't like my odds.

"For your information, I was playing a part both in Portland and in Don De Luca's office—"

Miceli cuts me off. "Call him Severu." He opens the front passenger door for me.

"You call him Sev." I climb into the BMW, settling on the butter soft leather seat.

Miceli leans down, his face so close I can feel his breath and he winks. "My cousin and I do it to annoy him. Sev's never liked having his name shortened."

I don't have a response. I'm too busy trying not to close the distance between our mouths.

With a smirk, Miceli straightens, steps back and closes the door.

"I don't like when people call me Fifi either. Fi's okay, but Fifi sounds like a dog," my cousin offers from the backseat once Miceli is seated behind the wheel.

I wish I was in back with her, but I'm stuck in front with Mr. Tattletale De Luca. He didn't rat me out to my uncle, but he's obviously ready to tell Fiona everything.

It better not be everything. She's too young. Even I didn't tell her the details of that night. Most of them.

I might have mentioned Ares is impressively huge in the male anatomy department. *Oh, God. Please don't let her say anything about that.*

Yes, that was a prayer.

I'm not big on organized religion, but if I don't believe in God, how do I believe I will see my parents again one day?

I'm not giving that up. They're waiting for me wherever Heaven is and we'll be a family again.

But the priest who buried my dad said, "As a man sows, so does he reap."

Not comforting.

I've refused to go to mass with my family ever since.

But I still pray and right now feels like a good time to ask TPTB for help.

CHAPTER 25: MICELI

"Tell me if anyone does it again and I'll set them straight, Fi."

I don't tell the teenager that the shortened form of his name has become as close to a term of endearment as I'll ever use with my brother, the don.

"Tell your cousin how we met in Portland," I instruct Róise as I guide the car down the long driveway. Allessio and his team are in the car ahead of us and my usual security team is in the car behind us.

Once we are married, Róise will never go anywhere without two teams.

"We met at the club," Róise says shortly and then makes an obvious attempt to change the subject. "You mentioned a cat carrier. We'll have to buy one on the way to the shelter. I doubt they sell them."

"They provide cardboard carriers with a suggested donation, but we won't be using one."

"We're stopping at a pet store on the way?" Fiona asks, her tone a mix of excitement and uncertainty.

"I bought one already. It's in the trunk." Along with everything else the retired enforcer turned pet store owner that I consulted told me Róise would need.

Apparently, a cat bed is just the beginning.

"That was nice of you." Róise sounds suspicious.

What does she think? I'm going to hold the kitten supplies in ransom for a kiss?

Memories of her lips moving under mine are having a predictable effect on my libido. This woman gets to me like no other.

I want more than a kiss from my reluctant fiancée though.

Cazzo.

"I can be nice." When it benefits me.

Not needing to have a Long Island pet store cleared of customers while the security detail mans the perimeter like what will happen shortly at the shelter is definitely a benefit.

The fact the cat carrier is pink and a special order? That's just polite. It matches the cat bed.

"Okay, Rosy. Time to spill," Fiona says from the backseat.

"You're not putting the kittens in the trunk." Róise is not giving up.

She wants to avoid this conversation.

Which leads to the question why? What is she hiding? She must realize I'm not going to bring up the amazing sex at my hotel.

"We met at a club owned by the Greek mafia." Patience is not my strong suit.

It might not even be a suit in my closet.

"Nuovi Inizi is owned by the Greek mafia? Helios is connected?" The shocked whisper from the passenger seat is barely discernable.

But I hear it.

"You didn't know?" I ask.

"No."

"Miceli was *that* guy?" Fiona asks in clear disbelief. "Did you tell Kara and not me?"

Róise gasps and throws her hands over her face. "Did you have to tell her?"

Definitely. I definitely had to tell her cousin, especially if the knowledge is going to garner this kind of reaction.

"I was that guy," I agree.

Fiona's reply is a burst of loud laughter. "No way." More laughter and she hits the back of the seat. "You went three thousand miles..." Gasps and giggles. "And drugged your guards only to end up getting your cherry popped by the one man you were determined not to give your virginity to?"

Drugged her guards? What the actual fuck? She's more of a menace to her own safety than I thought. Not only did she give her detail the slip, but if she'd gotten in trouble, they were too incapacitated to help her.

"We'll talk about this later," I warn her.

When her innocent teenage cousin isn't listening to every word and my temper isn't so close to going nuclear.

"I can't wait," Róise mutters. Then she looks over her shoulder. "Kara doesn't know."

"She will in a minute," Fiona says.

"No, don't text her...crap!"

I'm guessing the text got sent.

"Serves you right for hiding that from me and Kara. We tell each other everything," Fiona says. "But why are you so mad about marrying the guy? According to you he's hung lik—"

"Fiona Moira Shaughnessy!" Róise's shout cuts her cousin's words off.

But there's no doubt what she was about to say. Hung like a horse. Not a bad description. I would like it better coming from Róise's mouth and not her younger cousin's though.

"I'm just saying..."

"Don't. Don't say. Don't speculate. Just...think about kittens."

"Um, yeah, kittens are exactly what I'm thinking about. I'm seventeen, not seven, Rosy."

"You're amazing and I love you, but can we please talk about something besides...besides..."

"Our sex life," I help out.

"Aargh!" That is Róise. "We don't have a sex life. We had a single night when we didn't know who the other person was."

"Eww...if you put it that way...just eww." Fiona's voice is soaked in disgust.

I smile. My job here is done.

The thought brings me up short. This is the way things used to be with me, Sev and Giulia, our sister. But that was ten years ago. None of us can indulge in that kind of byplay anymore.

Except, it looks like I *can* with my too young fiancée and her even younger cousin.

Managgia la miseria. Róise has been of legal age to drink for less than a week.

"Watch out, your face might freeze that way," Fiona teases me.

Me. Miceli De Luca. Genovese underboss and all around badass. Is being teased about the frown freezing on my face by a teenager.

What the hell is happening to my life?

Thirty minutes later as Róise cuddles the biggest *full size* cat I have ever seen, I ask myself that question again.

"That's a lot of cat. You might as well get a dog."

Róise covers the cat's ears. "Don't listen to him. He doesn't mean it. No dog could replace you."

"It has to be at least three feet long."

"She must have some Maine Coon in her mix," Róise says like that's a good thing. "Did you see how beautiful her babies are?"

Of course I have. Róise insisted on making me hold both of the kittens still left from the litter. Neither liked it any more than I did.

They must have sensed my antipathy. Or it was the scent of gun oil.

"Which of the kittens are you going to take?" I can hope that the off-spring will not match the mother in size.

The kittens are curled together in a ball near Fiona's knee. She's sitting cross legged on the floor, rhythmically petting a skeletally thin full size cat.

"Rambo likes you. He's usually really skittish. He survived getting hit by the ricochet from a shooting, but he doesn't like most people and we can't get him to eat." The look the shelter worker gives the cat is filled with sadness. "It's too bad."

"Why too bad?" Róise asks sharply.

"The I.V.s the vet has to give him to get some nutrients in him won't sustain Rambo forever."

Fiona looks up frowning. "Can I try?"

"If you want, but don't be surprised if he refuses the food. It's not personal. Rambo doesn't trust anybody."

The giant fluffball Róise was holding is now following her like a dog, as she walks over to her cousin.

She has gotten some dry cat food from somewhere and she drops the nuggets into Fiona's hand. "Try with this, Fi."

The pathetic looking animal sniffs suspiciously at the food before starting to eat. He finishes everything in Fiona's hand and meows for more.

The shelter worker comes back from wherever she disappeared to.

She offers a small bowl of what looks like gruel to the teenager. "Here. See if you can get him to eat this too. It's nutrient dense and better for his stomach right now."

Of course, the cat eats the gruel. Because the quest to adopt two kittens has morphed into the two mob princesses bonding with the two least likely cats in the whole damn shelter.

Cazzo.

There is no leaving the kittens to be adopted by someone else either.

"We can't leave them without their mother." Fiona looks at me like I suggested euthanizing them.

I appeal to Róise with logic. "They would leave their mother if we took them home, just like their brothers and sisters."

"It's not the same." Róise looks at the shelter worker. "We'll do the paperwork for all four cats."

Four cats? Is she kidding?

"There's plenty of room in the mansion for them all."

Róise's words remind me that the animals will be Shaughnessy's problem, not mine. My arguments against adopting four animals go up in smoke.

"We'll give one of the kittens to Fitz. Every child should have a pet," Fiona says firmly.

"Did you?" I ask.

"Before...I had lots of pets," she replies.

Before what?

"Fiona used to bring injured or abandoned animals into the mansion all the time." Róise's tone is wistful. "It drove my grandfather right around the bend."

"Not your uncle?"

Róise shrugs. "He didn't notice much of what we girls were up to back then."

"After Aunt Charity and Uncle Derry died, *mamo* was our only real parent." Fiona pets the now sleeping cat in her arms. "She still is."

I'm not surprised by the sentiment, but her willingness to share it is something else. Róise looks shocked by the younger girl's words.

Apparently, this openness is not the norm for the fragile young woman.

We end up getting two of the cardboard carriers and putting both kittens in one and Fiona's shooting survivor in the other.

"And where is the other kitten going?" I ask.

"*Mamo* of course," both say in unison.

So, the only cat I have to worry about living with is the fluffy monster sitting to heel at Róise's feet. Does the creature realize she is feline and not canine?

On the way back to the Shaughnessy family estate, Fiona holds her cat in her lap, the top of the carrier open while she talks to him in a low voice, the words indistinguishable, the entire time.

Róise's giant mama cat is in the pink carrier and napping like the oversized princess she is.

CHAPTER 26: RÓISE

"Och, look at you now," *Mamo* croons to the fluffy kitten she holds up close to her face.

Miceli presented Fitz with his kitten as a gift from the De Luca family. Somehow, he guessed we were worried about Mick or Uncle Brogan refusing to let our nephew keep the kitten and did the one thing that guaranteed that wouldn't happen. Refusing Miceli's gift would be an insult.

Miceli is Fitz's new superhero and Kara thinks the underboss walks on water.

"You'll be keeping Fiona's cat a wee secret for now," *Mamo* instructs. "My son takes news like this best in small doses and three new pets at once in the mansion is enough to start with."

We all agree because if Uncle Brogan gets a peek at Rambo in his current condition, he'll never let Fiona keep the traumatized cat.

My feet dragging, I return downstairs, Pusheen on my heels.

Miceli said he wants to talk. He said he would wait. However long it took.

He's determined to make a seven-course meal out of my Portland adventure.

But the first course in his office was enough for me. I've already got two new bodyguards. What more can he want?

He's in the living room where I left him, standing by the windows with a view of the bay. But he's too busy doing something on his phone to appreciate it.

He puts the phone away and looks up, his gorgeous face impassive. "That cat thinks she's a dog."

"Pusheen is a superior feline, that's all."

"Pusheen?"

"It means kitten."

Wonder of wonder. Getting the joke, his lips quirk to one side in a nearly there smile.

He offered me the gift of a rescue kitten. That is what Pusheen will forever be to me. My rescue kitten.

Nodding toward a chair, he says, "Sit."

"I'm not a dog." But I am the hostess here, a voice suspiciously like my grandmother's reminds me.

Which means I should have asked him to take a seat.

"Please." I indicate one of the long, pristinely white sofas facing each other across the twelve-foot square Turkish rug.

"After you," he insists.

Grumbling in my brain, I sit in an armchair several feet from either sofa. It makes up half of a seating group, with an occasional table between it and a matching armchair.

Pusheen saunters out of the room and heads up the stairs. Probably searching for her babies.

I feel abandoned though.

Ignoring my offer of a seat on one of the sofas, Miceli settles into the other chair.

My body responds instantly to his nearness. My ovaries have been singing songs by Nicki Minaj since he arrived and now there's a DJ doing a studio mix.

It's so unfair that he turns me on like this. He's the last man I should want. My mom's memory deserves better.

"You'd be more comfortable on the couch." The designer took all the large men in my family into consideration when placing it.

The armchairs are bone white French Provincial inspired wingback chairs made to accommodate shorter legs. Like mine.

His knees sticking up would be amusing on another man, but Miceli spreads his legs like he owns the place.

The bulge pressing against his suit pants makes my mouth water and I swallow.

"I assumed you wouldn't want this discussion overheard." He raises one sardonic brow.

I should have thought of that, but I was too busy trying to get physical distance between us, I ignored even more important issues of self-preservation. Namely, keeping my rebellion from my uncle's ears.

"You're right."

"You have to start thinking like an adult woman in our world and not a naïve student," he criticizes.

Stung, I snap my lips together on a nasty retort. That would only support his offensive claim about my supposed immaturity.

He was so different that night in Portland. Never once did he highlight the age difference between us.

Sex, the great equalizer.

There's no point in repeating my desire *not* to live in *our* world either. No one but my grandmother and cousins care.

I make a "go on then" gesture with my hand. He's the one that wants to talk. I'd rather be pretty much anywhere else.

"You have nothing to say?" he asks in an even tone that sends chills through me.

Is that his interrogation tone?

Well, I'm not responding to it. "Not really, no."

His eyes narrow, their dark depths reflecting glacial displeasure. "What the fuck did you think you were doing drugging your security detail that night?"

That's easy. "Taking the only chance I would ever have to enjoy a night of freedom before my life got hijacked by the unholy bargain you and my uncle made."

"Sev made the agreement," he corrects. Like it matters.

Newsflash: it doesn't. "With your full cooperation."

"As your uncle supposedly had yours."

"You know why."

He nods and waves it away. Like it doesn't matter.

Wrong again. "Blackmail is a bad foundation for a relationship, especially marriage. I might not have reached the lofty age of 33, but even I know that."

"You're showing your naivete again."

"No, I'm talking sense."

"Coercion is the basis for several alliances of long standing."

Could he sound any more superior? I don't think so.

"The alliance is one thing. Our marriage is another."

He shakes his head, like I'm oh, so annoying.

"There's nothing unholy about our bargain. Our marriage will be blessed by nothing less than an auxiliary bishop."

Nothing less than? The only position higher in the New York church hierarchy is the Cardinal-slash-Archbishop. And that's so not the point.

"It doesn't matter who blesses the union. It's based on an alliance between two criminal syndicates. That's pretty much the definition of unholy."

Miceli's eyes narrow. "Don't think you're going to sidetrack me with an argument."

"I wasn't trying to argue." But if discussing the sanctity of our upcoming marriage takes precedence over rehashing our recent past, I'm all for it.

And also, I don't like how quickly and easily Miceli sees through my attempts. Uncle Brogan has yet to realize how often the women in our family use his temper and willingness to argue as a diversion.

"Does your uncle fall for that look of innocence?"

What? Is he reading my mind now?

"Are you always such a drama king?" I ask, wide-eyed, sarcasm dripping from my voice.

"You're accusing me of being dramatic? You? The woman who just referred to her upcoming wedding as an *unholy bargain*, and not for the first time."

He remembers me saying that in Severu's office?

"It's not dramatic to speak the truth."

"Here's some truth for you, if you had gotten into trouble that night, you couldn't have called on your bodyguards *because you drugged them*."

"I researched the dose of Rohypnol to give each of them based on their size. They were never in any danger."

"You think I fucking care if your bodyguards died from their roofies?"

"Yes." Miceli can be merciless and a real jerk, but he's also a good leader who will put his life on the line for his men.

Kara felt the need to share those stories.

I don't like the way they make me feel toward him, but no way does he dismiss the lives of my uncle's men as unimportant. If we were at war? Yes.

But now we're in an alliance.

"The only thing I'm thinking about right now is what could have happened to you. You left yourself unprotected with no hope of backup."

I sigh. "You're right. I thought I was safe, but it was a risky thing to do."

"I'm right?" His eyes narrow. "Are you saying that to get me to shut up?"

"Do people do that a lot to you?" I ask with exaggerated wide eyes.

"No one does it twice." The look he gives me makes me shiver.

And it's not in fright.

"I know I took a risk doing what I did in Portland and I should never have drugged my guards. They trusted me and I took advantage of that."

"If a leader's men can't trust him, then he can't trust them to have his back."

"I'm not a mafia leader."

"You're the niece of the mob boss and you will be an underboss's wife soon enough. Our men, at least, will listen to you and look to you for certain things when I'm not around."

"What things?" I ask, intrigued despite myself.

"It depends on what role you choose to play in my life, but I need to know that you are safe and that means you don't circumvent security measures meant to protect you."

"I never did before and I won't again." I might have a little of my family's ruthlessness but the guilt afterward is all mine. "Your men are safe with me."

"Give me your word, or I have to warn them all not to take food or drink from you."

"I promise I will never drug one, or more of your people unless my life is threatened by them or something they are doing."

He stares at me. "You could have stopped at the not drugging part."

"But I can't vow not to protect myself."

"It's my job to protect you and my men will give their lives for you if they have to."

"Then there's nothing to worry about."

"You'll come to me if you're worried. You won't take matters into your own hands."

"But will you listen? It's easy to say my safety is your responsibility, but if I tell you something one of your people is doing and they say they are not, who are you going to believe?"

"Where is this coming from?"

I'm not telling him about my cousin's marriage. "It's a valid concern. You know I despise the Cosa Nostra and I'm sure there are plenty of them that despise the Irish. I know people died on both sides."

"So, you assume I won't trust you?" Miceli asks, his brows furrowed sexily.

The urge to reach out and smooth the lines between them is hard to resist. "Why would you?"

"Because I believe your behavior in Portland was aberrant."

"But why?" Why am I pushing him? Why does it matter?

"If you wanted to lose your virginity so bad, why not fuck one of the boys from school?"

"They're men, not boys. I'm in college not high school."

"Answer the question."

"Because I knew that if I had sex with someone locally, he would probably end up dead. Either at my uncle's hands, or yours."

"That is why I trust you. You're too smart not to have realized the risk you were taking, but you took it to protect the man you planned to have sex with."

"I thought it was worth it."

"Wasn't it?"

"You know it wasn't. I ended up having sex for the first time with the one man I was trying to avoid."

"It was still your choice. It will always be your choice, Róise."

His words hit me like a rogue counterweight slamming down from the stage grid. "What about the baby we're supposed to make?"

"That's not for a couple of years and I don't see you holding out that long."

Holding out because he won't force it.

Even if I have about as much chance of staying away from him as I do chocolate during my period, knowing he won't force it?

Snips away another vine of the poison ivy protecting my heart.

If I'm not careful, I'm going to fall for my enemy.

CHAPTER 27: MICELI

Being able to read people is the difference between life and death in my world.

But right now, I can't read the expression on Róise's face.

"That's good to know." Her tone says it's anything but.

Why? Because thinking the worst of me makes it easier for her to keep hating me. I may not be looking for a fairytale love story, but I'm also not looking for a wife who actively despises me.

It's time for Róise to let go of some of her resentments.

"Regardless of how either of us feels about it, our marriage *is* a way to end the hostilities." Her parents' deaths devastated her. "It's a way to help protect the children in both our syndicates from going through what you did when your mom died."

Her dad's death isn't on the Cosa Nostra, but I will find out who ordered the hit. I can't keep Róise safe if there's a potential threat out there I don't know about.

"Isn't the pursuit of peace holy?" I ask, when she remains silent.

She rolls her eyes. "We're back to that?"

"Yes." My future wife is not going to refer to our marriage as damned. I'm not a demon, even if some of my enemies think I am.

"At the cost of one life?" she asks sarcastically. "It's Biblical anyway."

"Two."

Oh, she doesn't like hearing that. Interesting. She can say she hates me all she wants but she doesn't want to marry a man who considers it a sacrifice.

Leaning back in her chair, she crosses her arms, unknowingly plumping her breasts upward and increasing the amount of cleavage on display.

She looks at me with accusation. "You could have refused."

How hard would it be to rip that pink jumpsuit right off her?

"My life is forfeit to the greater good of *la famiglia*. To refuse to do my duty would be a betrayal of my family and my don."

"I don't consider marrying a stranger a duty. It's the result of blackmail. Plain and simple."

That's the first hurdle we have to get over. "Yes, pressure was brought to bear, but women in mafia families are raised to believe it is their duty. Your cousins understand this. Why don't you?"

"How do you know my cousins believe that outdated garbage?"

"It's not garbage. We all have a role to play in keeping our families strong."

"You mean the syndicate."

"It's one and the same."

She huffs out an exasperated breath and jumps to her feet. "Let's go for a walk. If I have to listen to more lectures it can at least be in the spring sunshine."

I shrug, unwilling to argue over something so trivial and follow her to the French doors.

But when we get there, I stop her from going outside. "Let Allessio clear the area first."

"Are you kidding me? There's nothing out there but my backyard and the bay."

"A sniper in a boat—"

"Would be too unstable for accuracy. Alerting you to his intentions without a better chance of success would be stupid."

"Not all killers are smart." But she is. "Where did you learn that about the boat?"

"My dad. After my mom died, he told all of us girls because we didn't want to play outside anymore."

"And you believed him." It's not a question.

"I trusted him. But after he died, I looked it up because Fiona refused to leave the house at all. For a long time, the *only* place she would go was the backyard."

Allessio gives the all-clear signal and I open the door for Róise. "Does she see a therapist?"

Róise looks at me incredulously. "Don't tell me you let your people see therapists."

"If they need to."

"But what about…I mean how does that work when they can't talk about the stuff that probably bothers them the most?"

"There are several qualified mental health professionals in the Genovese Family." Most of their clients are not mafia though.

We allow it, but therapy is not popular and I don't know of a single soldier or high ranking made man who has been. But even my father understood that children deserve whatever kind of healthcare they need.

Carlotta is the first adult in the family I know of to attend therapy. Catalina goes now too. At Sev's insistence.

That is *not* something our father would have encouraged.

Róise is silent as we walk across the large lawn toward the water.

Finally, she speaks. "My father wasn't like Uncle Brogan, or my grandfather. Dad was the strongest and smartest man I ever knew, but he didn't see people as pawns in a criminal game of chess."

"Explain."

"Dad promised me when I was twelve that I would never be forced to marry someone for the sake of the mob."

That's unheard of. Her father was the oldest son and would have been the next boss if he hadn't died first.

His daughter should have been the first woman in the family promised in a political alliance. "Why?"

Why would he make the promise and why would he feel the need to?

"My grandfather and uncle signed a contract with the mob in Ireland for my sixteen-year-old cousin to marry a stranger. I had nightmares about it happening to me. Every night. Terrible dreams of being dragged up the aisle to marry a monster."

"Why did it terrify you so much? Mick Fitzgerald is a good man."

"He's a good mobster. A good father, but is he a good man?"

"You tell me."

"He could be. And that's not the point. I'd never met Mick. The monster was the marriage, not the man."

And now she's being faced with that monster, only it's marriage to me.

"So, your father promised not to force you into an alliance marriage?"

"He'd already refused on my behalf. That's why Kara was chosen." The guilt in Róise's tone causes a weird sensation in my chest.

That's where the nightmares came from.

Even without her dad telling her, Róise knew that as the daughter of the heir, she was the one that should have been promised in the alliance. Her tender age of twelve would have been no barrier.

Marriage arrangements are made at birth in some families. Her cousin was only eighteen when Kara married Mick Fitzgerald.

My sister finished college before entering her alliance marriage and no child of mine, whatever their gender, will be pushed into marriage before they're twenty-one.

"Dad didn't tell me that though," Róise continues. "I only learned it after his death. When I heard him arguing with my grandfather it was about any future marriages, not the one to Mick."

When had she heard? "Do you listen in on mob business often?"

If so, how is she still so innocent?

"It wasn't mob business. It was my life."

Another misdirect rather than answer and not accurate either. Her grandfather would have considered the marriage nothing but mob business at that point. She was too young for it to be anything else.

"Do I have to worry about you spying on me?" I turn from the view of the bay to face her.

"For my uncle?" she asks with insight I'm starting to realize should be expected. "No. For myself?" She shrugs.

"If both your father and grandfather promised you would not be used in a political alliance, why did your uncle force the matter?" Can Shaughnessy be trusted?

If he'll break a promise to family, he'll break them to us in a heartbeat.

"The promise from my grandfather was based on my father becoming the next boss."

"There was some doubt?" Derry Shaughnessy was the oldest and heavily involved in the mob's business at that point.

I've done my research.

"Dad loved my mom and he blamed grandfather for her death."

"Their marriage was arranged." Not sure why I feel the need to remind her of this.

We're not going to have a marriage like her parents. For one thing, no way in hell am I going to let her get shot like her mother.

Róise will have the same number of men in rotation as Catalina.

"Gabriel required a blood alliance before he would go into business with my grandfather."

She calls her grandmother *mamo*, an Irish term like grandma, but never refers to either grandfather with affection.

Róise sighs. "My mother believed marrying my dad was the best thing that had ever happened to her."

And then she was killed by a stray bullet meant for her father-in-law.

"So your dad threatened to do what? Walk away?"

"Sort of. He told grandfather that if he signed a contract on my behalf, my dad was going to take me to Ireland and fill the position one of his second cousins had been tapped for. Kara's marriage was an exchange, with one of the Shaughnessy men going to Ireland to marry the daughter of the mob boss in Dublin."

A proud man, her grandfather would have been livid at the idea of her father stepping down into a lower position and becoming a soldier for another boss. In Ireland, or elsewhere.

"When your dad didn't become mob boss like his father wanted him to, the promise was negated." Shaughnessy did not go back on his father's word.

"That's how my grandfather and uncle saw it. I guess this alliance was actually my grandfather's idea."

"But he didn't approach my father." I would know if he had.

"No, but he planted the seed in Uncle Brogan's brain for a strategic time."

Or when he had no choice but to offer up the alliance.

The cartel's plans for our territory wouldn't have succeeded even if war had broken out between the Irish and us. But there's no denying both syndicates will be stronger for the formalized connection.

And both would have suffered losses if we'd gone to war like the cartel wanted us to.

"It's done. Can you accept it?"

She looks away, not toward the water, but toward the trees that shield part of the backyard from the wind off the bay. "I don't have a choice."

"No, you don't." I could sugar coat it with some pink fairy dust, but that isn't going to help Róise come to terms with our reality.

Only truth can do that.

And maybe logic. "You were all raised with the knowledge that some kind of alliance marriage was in your future."

I'm sure of that. For fuck's sake, her own parents were an alliance marriage. As no doubt Brogan and his dead wife were as well.

"Knowing it's a possibility and being promised to a stranger at the age of sixteen and then shoved down the aisle at eighteen is not the same thing."

"Reality can't live up to fantasy."

"Spare me your platitudes." She spins to face me, her lovely features set in anger. "Yes, we knew what our future probably held, but we weren't raised in a bubble. We knew that wasn't normal."

Her hands gesticulate wildly. "That other women got to choose their husbands. Your sister got to go to college before getting married. Both our mothers were over twenty-one when they got married."

"There had to be a reason your grandfather insisted Kara marry when she was so young."

"He wanted heirs. Male heirs that carry his name. If my father had agreed, I would have been the one giving birth at nineteen."

"Your nephew's last name is Shaughnessy."

"Yes. He'll be the boss one day and he has no more choice about it than his mom had about getting married before she'd had her first kiss."

"She'd never kissed anyone at eighteen?" The mob might have some old world ideas about marriage, but we live in the present. "Don't most kids kiss in middle school?"

"Your sister had a chance to pop her kissing cherry before high school?" Róise asks with narrowed eyes.

"I honestly don't know." Giulia would never have told me or Sev if she had. Mamma probably knows.

"But if she had, it could never be more than a kiss."

It's starting to sink in how important it was to Róise to choose her first sex partner.

"I don't know what my sister got up to before the engagement was announced, and I don't want to, but there was no way she could marry a civilian. Neither can you."

"Why? Because we give birth to the next generation of mobsters?"

CHAPTER 28: RÓISE

Miceli's hand cups my nape, his thumb brushing up the column of my neck.

I try to suppress a shiver.

Not very well.

"Cold?" The masculine purr holds more satisfaction than concern. "Here."

He takes off his suit jacket and settles it over my shoulders, surrounding me with his scent. I can't get away from it. Or him.

Do I really want to?

I ignore the treacherous question prompted by my ovaries, but do I move away? No.

"My cousin Nerissa is adopted." Miceli's fingers are playing with the hair at my nape now. "We bring in recruits from outside the Genovese families every year."

"That's great and all." Who can blame me if my tone is a little breathless?

Miceli De Luca has magic fingers and I know what they can do to every part of my body. Even spots I thought no one would ever touch.

My sphincter tightens and it's not in fear of what might happen in the future.

"But our contract requires a baby to cement it. I'm sure your brother expects his wife to give him heirs." I'm proud of my ability to follow the train of conversation.

This guy is way too good at the sex stuff. I was pretty good at it too, that night in Portland.

"All that's true, but none of it is the primary reason my father contracted a marriage for my sister with a don's son."

"Then what was?" My feet are moving, but my focus is on the hand touching me.

Without Miceli's hold on me, I'd probably trip and fall flat on my face.

"Giulia will always have a target on her back because of the family she was born into. Her marriage to Raff keeps her safe."

"Did it ever occur to your dad to provide her with security instead?"

"I doubt it and I wouldn't consider that enough for my child either. It's not enough. Our connections protect us as much as our weapons. Giulia has two mafias watching over her. As my wife you will be one of the safest women in the world."

I believe him, but that's only part of the story, isn't it? "I wouldn't need protection if my family weren't part of the criminal underworld."

"You are born into the family you are born into," he says fatalistically. "Wishing won't change that, but refusing to accept it will make you bitter."

"I suppose you never doubted your place, or wished you could have a normal life." Cut Miceli open and he bleeds Cosa Nostra.

"By the time I knew the difference, I was already fiercely loyal to the Genovese."

"Brainwashed from infancy," I say flippantly.

"Taught a way of life." He pulls me even closer. "Our way."

Stopping, I turn in the embrace that now encircles me and look up into his handsome, serious face. "My dad promised he would make sure I had a different life. A normal life. Even if it meant changing my name and disappearing."

I'm not sure if I would have been any more willing to cut myself off from my family than I am now. What I do know is that once Uncle Brogan took over the family, my chances at a normal life went out the window.

I just didn't realize it until that day in his office when he gave me the ultimatum. Marry into the Italian mafia or stand back and watch while yet another cousin takes my place.

"You wouldn't have been able to disappear with your face in the spotlight." Miceli taps the tip of my nose teasingly, a whimsical twist to his lips. "Even a B Lister would get recognized by somebody connected. Or did you plan on being the world's worst actress?"

Miceli De Luca teasing? Ares was good at it, but I haven't seen this side of him since that night in Portland.

"The term is actor." My disapproving look doesn't reach my eyes and I know it. "And there is such a thing as plastic surgery."

My dad would have balked at that though, because I look so much like my mom.

Intense, dark eyes trap mine. "It would be a travesty to change a single feature on your face."

"Why are you being nice?" And why is my heart racing?

He cocks his head to one side. "Have I been mean?"

"You're an underboss; cruelty is your middle name."

"My job won't touch you. I am cruel. To my enemies. But you're not my enemy. You're going to be my wife."

"You were a jerk about Allessio and Zoey."

"And you were unreasonable."

I shake my head. He doesn't understand. I'm still waiting for the blowback at school. I know it's coming.

"If it makes you feel better, I'm not being nice. I'm being honest."

Like I told Miceli. I didn't grow up in a bubble. I've had guys hit on me. This isn't that. Oh, I'm pretty sure the underboss wants in my pants, but this isn't that.

What is it though? "I'm not all that."

"You know I think you're beautiful."

For a moment, that night hangs between us. His compliments whisper in the air around us.

My Aphrodite, you are so beautiful. Your name does not do you justice, it should be Helen.

The beauty that launched a thousand ships.

"It was the makeup and wig." This isn't false modesty.

The makeup artist has an amazing career ahead of her.

"No," he growls, the hand on the back of my neck tightening. "It was you."

When he says stuff like that and when my brain squints just right, I can forget he's Cosa Nostra.

Commence with the squinting, brain. My vajayjay wants some action.

My lips part without a command from my squinting brain and his eyes darken with instant lust.

I'm reaching up as his head comes down and our mouths come together like waves crashing against the rocks. He eats at my lips and I slide my tongue against his.

Jayzuz, Mary and Joseph.

That taste. Tingling lips. Electric sparks igniting a path to my clit by way of my nipples.

Clasping my hands behind his neck, I jump up. He grabs my bum and lifts so I can get my legs around him and hold on.

I tear my lips from his. "The boathouse."

We're only steps from it and privacy. Did my subconscious bring us here?

Maybe. Because the sexual feelings he woke in me back in February are a buzzing undercurrent along my nerve endings now. My cooch is contracting, wanting to be filled up by that big dick of his.

I've never had the chance to be sexually liberated and that night in Portland didn't change that. I ended up craving the one man I believed I would never see again, much less have.

Deprived of my mouth, Miceli trails his down my neck, latching on to a spot that turns those sparks into explosions.

"Privacy." My head drops back, giving him better access. "Naked."

That word does it.

We're moving like the starter pistol just went off at the Belmont.

He stops at the door to the boathouse and I gasp out the code for the electronic door lock.

Fumbling movement behind me. A muttered *cazzo* and then damn.

"Hurry up." I'm not helping, but I want this before the part of my brain that's not squinting starts throwing up roadblocks.

The door opens and we're inside the boathouse.

"Over there." I point to the area beyond the boat slips.

He bypasses the sofa, chairs and hammock that is perfect for reading in the summer with the bay doors open.

My back slams against the wall bringing back memories from our night together.

"You've got a thing for walls."

He lifts his head, eyes hazy with sexual need. "I've got a thing for you."

"This outfit isn't easy access," I point out.

Uncomprehending, he stares down at me, his body moving lewdly against the apex of my thighs.

"We need naked, unless you want to dry hump." I'm not averse.

I've never done that. It could be fun.

Miceli's head shakes in instant negation. "I want inside you."

"Condom?" Wow. Look at me being responsible.

"Birth control?" he counters.

"The pill." I've been taking it since a week after my uncle blackmailed me into the alliance deal.

"Don't need a condom."

I open my mouth to protest.

He kisses me then steps back with a groan. "I'm clean."

I believe him. But I'm not naïve. "Prove it."

Respect, not irritation, flares in his espresso gaze. He fishes in his suit jacket, his hands grazing both sides of my breasts.

"Can't remember which pocket your phone is in, old man?"

He grabs it with one hand and squeezes my boob with the other. "There it is."

Pulling it out, he uses the thumb on the hand holding it to get to where he wants while he keeps up that rhythmic kneading of my breast through my jumpsuit. No skin is touching skin, but my temperature is skyrocketing.

"All clear. See?"

I make myself read the test results. "The date is for two weeks ago."

He could have been with a dozen women since then.

"I haven't so much as slow danced with anyone since Portland." His teeth close gently on my earlobe. "Do we need a condom, Aphrodite?"

He's asking if I believe him. If I can trust him this much.

The truth hits me in the solar plexus. Yes, I trust him. "No." We don't need a condom.

CHAPTER 29: MICELI

"N o."

That single word resonates through every sinew of my being.

Róise still sees me as her enemy. She's still planning to divorce me some-day (never going to happen), but when I tell her I haven't touched another woman since Portland, she believes me.

Already hard enough to pound rocks, my cock presses insistently against the zipper on my slacks. My little head and big head are in full agreement.

He wants out. I want him inside her tight heat.

"How much do you like this jumpsuit?" My brain is figuring out scenarios for getting her back into the mansion unseen if I cut it off her.

I pull my knife out.

Her green eyes, dark with need, widen. "You are not cutting off my clothes."

The offer to cut a slit for access dies a quick death. I want to feast on every inch of her silky skin, but especially the honeyed depths between her legs.

I leave the knife out though.

Róise squirms against me. "Let me down."

Since I can't think of a way to get that jumpsuit off without releasing her, I do. Then I send a quick text to Allessio and Zoey

Miceli: *Do not let anyone near the boathouse until we come out.*

Both reply with an okay emoji.

When I look up Róise is already down to her panties, bra and socks. She scampers over to the seating area, her ass and tits jiggling.

She settles into a big white armchair and takes off her socks, but leaves her lingerie on. Her small feet come up to rest on the ottoman, her knees spread so I can see the wet spot on the crotch of her panties.

Reclining backward, she waves her hand at me. "Strip for me."

Her throaty voice goes straight to my balls.

She wants me to strip for her? "By the time I'm naked, you'll be panting for me."

"I already am."

Her breath *is* coming in little gasps, making her fleshy mounds rise and fall with each one.

I toe off my socks and know immediately why she kept hers on. The water friendly tile floor is cold as ice. But I'm hot enough to melt it. Ignoring the sting against the bottom of my feet, I unbuckle my belt and pull it from the loops, tossing it to land near her feet on the ottoman.

With a startled sound, she jumps. "Throwing things at me is not sexy."

"Everything about you is sexy."

A blush darkens her cheeks, but she snarks, "And that makes you want to throw things?"

"Just my belt." I have plans for it.

Unzipping my slacks, I let them fall to the floor. And then I wait. Her hungry gaze eats up my legs and she swallows, her fingers digging into the arms of the chair.

Only when those pretty green eyes lock on the tent in my black silk knit boxers do I start to slide the waistband over my straining erection.

When the head comes into view, she licks her lips.

I slide the waistband down a couple of inches, letting her see more of my engorged cock.

"You're teasing me," she pants.

"Isn't that what you wanted?"

Her eyes meet mine for a brief second before going straight back to my sex. "I thought it was."

Shoving my boxers the rest of the way off, I let my cock bob free. So hard, I can feel the pressure of the blood rushing through it, my dick sticks straight up.

Róise moans and shifts, like she's going to get up.

"Don't move." I grab myself, running my calloused hand up and down the aching shaft.

"Then you come here," she orders.

I smile. It's not a nice one. I'm not a nice man. "When I'm done."

"You only have your shirt left."

"Are you telling me you don't want to see the rest of me?" I won't believe her if she does.

Licking her lips, she shakes her head, nods, then shakes her head again.

Jacking myself slowly, I undo one button at a time on my shirt. When I get to the last one, it gapes. But it doesn't reveal much more skin because when I'm dressed for work, which is most of the time, I wear an undershirt.

"Take it off. Them. Take them off."

Her enthusiasm turns me on. "Slide your hand down your body and into your panties for me."

She sucks in a shocked breath, but one hand releases its death grip on the arm of the chair and starts the journey.

When she reaches the top of her panties, she runs her fingertip along the waistband, teasing us both.

"Be a good girl and do as I say."

Something flares hot in her eyes and her fingers dip beneath the pink lace. Her middle finger slides between her lips and she groans.

"That's good. Play with that little bud, but keep your eyes on me, Aphrodite."

The order is superfluous. Her gaze is glued to the hand stroking my dick. "Take them off, Ares. Please."

The please does it. I undo my cufflinks.

Plink. Plink. They hit the tile floor.

And then I shrug off my shirt and it follows them. I rip my undershirt over my head and watch her eyes dilate with pleasure at the sight of me.

Cazzo. This woman.

"Ares." My name is another plea.

Grabbing my knife, I stalk across the space between us. When I reach her, I lay the knife next to my belt and grab her ankles. Then I yank her toward me until her ass is on the edge of the ottoman.

She lets out a shocked cry.

Picking up the knife, I say, "Don't move."

"What are you going to do?"

"Make you feel good."

After a shaky breath, she nods.

Leaning down, I carefully slide the sharp blade of my knife between her hip and panties, flat side down. With a flick to the right, the lace rends. Then I do the other side.

After pulling the ruined underwear away from her, I lower myself to my knees. The hard tile against them gives me the dig of pain I need to maintain control of my cock.

I am not ready to come and I sure as hell am not doing it without being inside her. Not this time.

Her arousal perfumes the air around us. "Can you smell how excited you are, *mi dolce fiore*?"

"Yes," she moans. "What's *dolce fiore*?"

She forgot the *mi*, the most important of those three words. She is mine.

And her pronunciation needs a lot of work.

"My sweet flower, your perfume is all I want to smell." Leaning forward, I inhale and rub my nose along her slit.

Her pussy now has a small thatch of silky chestnut brown curls and I huff air over it, knowing how much sensation that can give a woman.

"Oh..." The word is long and drawn out. "That's so good. I thought..."

My tongue follows the path my nose has taken and her flavor bursts onto my tongue. "What did you think?"

"That it was more sensitive bare."

Her pussy?

"Let's find out." Pressing her thighs wide, I expose the flushed plump flesh of her inner lips and kiss them.

With my lips *and* tongue.

Her hands grip my hair and a litany of pleasure sounds fall from her sweet mouth.

I avoid her clit while lavishing attention all over her sensitive nether lips. Chasing more of her sweet honey, I spear my tongue into her channel, the tight flesh reminding me how innocent she is.

"Oh, Ares, yes...more...please..."

I give her more until she's begging *Ares* to let her come.

Lifting my head, I wait until she meets my eyes. "Miceli."

Call me Mars or Ares, I am the god of war, but she needs to acknowledge the man giving her pleasure is the Cosa Nostra underboss. The man she is going to marry.

Hazy eyes don't comprehend at first and then they focus, her mouth sliding into a slight frown.

Rubbing my thumbs up and down on either side of her swollen little bud, I lick her juices off my lips.

Her pupils dilate.

She likes that. My perfect bride-to-be revels in the earthy nature of sex.

But I need her to do it knowing exactly who she is getting her pleasure from. "Say, *please, Miceli* and I will give you the orgasm your body is screaming for."

"But you're Ares too."

"I am."

"So—"

"Say it." I will her to acknowledge me and who I am.

Her expression changes, her nose scrunching, her eyelids letting only a slit of her green irises show between them.

"What are you doing?"

"Helping my brain to squint."

What the fuck?

The beautiful features morph again, this time into a disconsolate frown. "I can't do it."

"You can't say my name?"

"I can't make my brain squint enough to forget you're a Cosa Nostra underboss."

"Good." Because that is what I am.

"But, it's easier if..." Her soft voice trails off.

I can guess what she was going to say though. It's easier to give herself to the stranger she met in a club than the man who is very much a part of her world. A part she has resented since her mom's death.

"I am not Bonanno."

"I know."

"If you want me to kill the man who shot your mother, I will." Supposing he's still alive.

"You can't do that."

"I can." I'll have to disappear the body because no way is the godfather going to sanction the hit.

"It's against your code."

"De Lucas protect our own."

"But..." She looks bewildered. "My grandfather forbade my father from going after her killer."

"Do you think he listened?" Will I be hunting a ghost?

Róise's eyes take on a faraway look and then she shakes her head. "No."

"Then he's already dead."

"Probably."

"I will find out."

"And kill him if he's alive?" she asks.

"Yes."

Instead of replying she laughs.

"What is funny?"

"This." She waves her hand indicating our naked bodies.

Almost naked. She's still wearing the pink lace bra that matches her now destroyed panties. It will be joining them soon enough.

After she asks *me* to let her come.

"I can't believe we're having this conversation like this," she adds. "It's absurd."

"No other way we can have it." I'm not putting my mouth back on her pussy until she acknowledges who I am.

"What does the tattoo on your arm mean?"

"You're so sure it means something?"

"Yes."

She's right. "The wolf is my father, but he is Sev too. And me. It is the savage nature inside us that protects our family."

CHAPTER 30: RÓISE

"The mafia you mean. *La famiglia.*"

He winces. "Your pronunciation is atrocious. The *famiglia* on my arm refers to the De Lucas not the Genovese."

Like the wolf represents him and the men in his family, not just made men. And not just him.

Miceli's right about my pronunciation. He gave different inflections to the syllables and the g was silent. I'd like to see him pronounce Irish without coaching.

"And the other word," I ask, putting my grievances aside.

"*Sempre* means always."

Family always.

But not his mafia family. "You said that your family and the mafia are the same."

"They are." He brushes his fingers along my inner thigh. "Except when they aren't."

I want to slam my legs together and trap his hand there. "And when that happens?"

"I kill any threat to my family, mafia alliances, or not."

"When we get married, will I be part of your family?" The words slip out of their own volition, but now I want an answer.

I need one.

"You already are."

"No, not yet. We're not even engaged." Not officially anyway. Can a contract make me family?

"You don't wear my ring. You don't carry my name, but make no mistake about it, *mi dolce fiore*. You are mine."

A thrill of pleasure goes through me at his words. Shouldn't that be revulsion? It's not though.

It's something way more dangerous to me. It feels like the first stirrings of an emotion I cannot feel for this man.

Love.

Lust is much safer. "I'm aching is what I am." I pause. "Miceli."

He doesn't even take time to gloat, but goes back to pleasuring me with his mouth. His finger slides inside me as he sucks my clitoris between his lips.

And just like that I'm back on the precipice, my body drawn taught as a bowstring.

I say the words he wants. "Please, Miceli. Make me come!"

The last is more an order than a plea, but that doesn't seem to bother him. His teeth scrape over my clitoris and he crooks his finger inside me, pressing against the bundle of nerves from the other side.

A two-ton blast of ecstasy detonates inside me and a scream tears from my throat as my soul leaves my body to float in delirium around us.

I'm just coming back to myself when I feel the cold steel of Miceli's knife at the top of my breast.

My eyes fly open. When did they close? During that cataclysm of pleasure, I guess.

"What are you doing?" I croak, my throat still raw from screaming.

"Yes, or no?" he asks without answering.

He wants to cut my bra off, just like my panties. Why is that sharp knife against my skin so exciting?

It should scare me, but I know deep into the soul that finally rejoined my body that Miceli will never physically harm me.

I nod.

"Say it."

"Yes." Might as well. With the panties destroyed, it's not a set anymore anyway.

The flat side of his knife blade slides up, lifts from my skin. Then he twists his wrist and pulls, cutting right through my bra strap.

"Don't move." He slides the knife over my collarbone and under the other strap.

Breathing shallowly, I don't so much as flicker an eyelash.

"Good girl." Another twist of his wrist and he's cut through the second strap.

A surge of pleasure pulses in my clitoris, my vaginal walls contracting in an involuntary spasm.

The knife slides over the slope of my breast taking the lace of my bra with it and revealing my breast. My hard nipple zings with electric current when the steel glides over it.

"You are such a good girl. So fucking perfect."

Those words fizz through my blood like an uncorked bottle of champagne.

He brushes the knife along my chest and over the curve of my other boob, using it to draw down the lace from that cup too. Then in a movement so quick, I feel the brush of air but don't see it, he cuts through the fabric connecting the cups.

The remains of the bra slips from my skin with a whisper of sound.

His hold on the knife shifts and suddenly it is pointing down at me. "Yes, or no?"

"Y—" I clear my throat. "Yes."

"Perfect."

He touches the tip of my nipple with the tip of his knife. Wetness gushes between my legs.

The sharp knife that cut my grandfather so easily doesn't cut me.

The hand that wielded the blade to leave a cut no deeper than a scratch on my grandfather's throat expertly wields it now. It touches me but does not bite into my skin. Does not draw blood.

He lays it on my chest, blade pointed toward my mons. Miceli doesn't have to tell me not to move.

He is showing as much trust in me not to hurt myself by doing so as I am that he will not hurt me with that wickedly sharp blade.

After bending to the side, he straightens and lifts his arm, his belt in his hand.

"Yes, or no?"

"What are you going to do with it?"

"Yes, or no?" he repeats.

I can say *no*. And he'll drop the belt. I'm as sure of that as I am my own unbearable excitement.

"Yes." It's barely a whisper, but he hears me.

He expertly binds my wrists with it. Did he learn that in the bedroom or on the job?

Does it matter?

The leather holds my wrists together without cutting into them.

He lifts them above my head and lays my bounds wrists on the chair. "Don't move them."

"If I do?"

"I'll remove the belt."

"And?" I prompt.

"And I'll keep doing what I'm doing, but your hands will be free." His gaze traps mine. "This is all about pleasure. For us both."

I nod my understanding.

"If you say *no*, I stop. If you say *stop*, I stop. If you say *off*, I take the belt off. If you say *get off*, I do."

"I don't want you to stop."

"Good." He picks up his knife and begins to run it over my body, leaving chills of excitement in its wake.

How can this feel so good?

After pushing my thighs as far apart as he can and since I am extremely limber, that's pretty far, he slides the flat of the blade over my labia. His pinky finger runs a parallel line between my inner lips, through the slick wetness.

I try to stay still, but my hips move restlessly. I can't help it.

The knife clatters as it lands on the tile.

There is no chance to feel the loss of it, or think I messed up. His big hands with fingers as delicate against my skin as his blade cover every inch of the path the knife took.

I thrust upward wanting more and almost cry when his hands leave my skin. But he picks me up, turning me over and putting me on my knees facing the back of the big armchair.

The sound of the ottoman moving barely registers in my fevered brain.

He bends me forward and arranges my limbs so my forearms rest on the back of the chair. My wrists are still bound.

"Miceli!" I cry, needing.

He rubs his hard length up and down the crack of my bottom. Is he going to…?

Am I ready for that?

"Do you want me inside you?"

There can only be one answer, even if I'm nervous about *where* exactly he's going to put that oversized dick.

He spreads my intimate flesh from behind and the head of his sex presses against my soaked entrance. Relief and disappointment both cause the sigh that gusts out of me.

Then he thrusts forward with his powerful hips, filling and stretching my tight channel. My vaginal walls squeeze and he grunts.

One hand comes around and hard fingers press against my clitoris.

It's so much sensation, my brain shorts out.

He thrusts in and out of me, keeping those amazing fingers against my sensitive nub. Ecstasy doesn't build, it coils tighter and tighter.

"Miceli, do something!" He has to end this terrible tension.

I can't take it anymore. I need to come.

He shifts behind me and then he's kneeling on the chair. He lifts my body so I'm sitting on his thighs, his knees bent under us. Then he wraps his arm around me like a vise, pulling my body up and flush with his.

He's completely surrounding me, controlling our movement.

His hips thrusting, he moves my body up and down with that viselike grip.

He's so deep, I don't think I can take him, but my body makes a liar of my fear.

My climax hits without warning, my body going rigid as every muscle contracts. He rubs my clit, forcing higher levels of pleasure until I scream and then the pressure is barely there.

That perfect control of sensation, giving it continuously but not too much pulls another powerful orgasm from me and then he's shouting and filling me with his hot semen.

My head flops back against his chest and we stay like that panting for a long time. Our mixed fluids drip out of me around him. Not as hard as he was, he's still inside me nevertheless.

My body tries to tell me it wants more, but my mind knows we have to stop.

I try to shift off of him but I don't get far.

"You need to take the belt off," I tell him.

He doesn't argue, but reaches around me and undoes the leather loops. He rubs my wrists before letting them go.

"We need to... I need to..." What? I need what? To go. "Go. Get up." Something.

Again, he doesn't try to talk me out of it, but carefully lifts me so he can slide out from under me. The loss of his body heat tells me he stepped away.

But then strong arms are sliding under my knees and tipping me back as he lifts me from the chair. I squeak.

Which I will deny later if he tries to bring it up.

"Bathroom?" he asks, his emotionless mask back in place.

I point. "I can walk."

"The tile is cold."

He carries me to the bathroom which is equipped with shower and towels for those hot summer days we decide to swim in the bay instead of the pool.

Miceli turns on the water and waits for it to heat the tiles before letting me down inside the shower stall.

His eyes focus between my legs. "You waxed your pussy so I wouldn't know what color your hair really was."

"I waxed my vulva because I wanted to." Because Kara told me it would enhance the sensations and I wanted to get everything I could out of my first time, my only time with someone not the man I was supposed to marry.

I didn't want that man to know who I really was, or what I really looked like though. So, in that way, Miceli is right.

Well, I just found out that it's every bit as hot and wonderful with hair down there than without. Even if it is different.

And my hope of staying anonymous to my one-night-stand is dead and gone.

"Which do you like better?" He licks his lips.

Oh, no. Not again. "We can't," I tell him.

He nods. "So, which one?"

"It hurts to get waxed."

"That's not what I asked."

"You want to know which I like better when we...you know?" How are our thoughts so in sync?

"Yes."

"Um, they're both good. When you lick and suck on my um...lips, when they're bare, it's..." I shiver under the hot streaming water. "But when you run your fingers over the tips of my hair..."

I'm getting wetter down there, aching for him again, still...whatever. "Which do you like better?"

"You taste better than anything I've put in my mouth either way."

Anything? "I read that people can be chemically compatible, so their taste and smell is really attractive to the other person."

He smiles. "I read that too."

"Um, so, yeah. It's probably chemicals."

"Good thing ours match."

I shrug and turn to face the wall, grabbing the loofah sponge. "I guess."

"Trust me, a lifetime with the same lover that smells wrong and tastes bitter is not what either of us wants."

"It's just science," I say more to myself than him.

"Biology," he agrees.

I lather the loofah and start washing my body.

He makes a strangled sound. "I'll get your clothes."

"Thank you."

Feelings pelt my insides while the water, at just the right temperature...no guy should be this perfect...pelts my skin. That was...it was...I shake my head.

Yeah. That.

Intense. Incredible. Not just science. Not by a long shot.

Imbued with trust. On both sides.

Dangerous.

That last one times a hundred.

When I first found out about this marriage deal, I was worried I couldn't love my Cosa Nostra husband. Now, I know that the really scary scenario is that I *could*.

Falling for the underboss would be a disaster. He'll never love me back. Not like my dad loved my mom.

Men like my dad are rare, in or out of the criminal underworld. I'm not risking vulnerability with a man programmed not to give into the tender emotions.

Miceli doesn't have to tell me that's how he was raised. I know it.

No matter how good he is in bed, or a chair...whatever. No matter how considerate and protective he can be, none of that equals love.

Not for a made man.

I find my clothes, such as they are, on the bench when I step out of the shower. There's a bathmat on the floor from the cupboard too.

Miceli again.

I dry off thoroughly everywhere. I have no panties to put on, so I have to get back into my jumpsuit without them. Or a bra.

It feels weird.

And also, kind of cool. Like it's something private just for me. Or me and Miceli.

He's not in the boathouse when I come out of the bathroom. His tie is laying neatly over the back of one of the chairs at the table though. And his knife is resting on the table beside the armchair that just witnessed so much activity.

There's a message there, but heck if I know what it is.

Or, he just forgot both?

CHAPTER 31: RÓISE

Before I can decide if I should head back up to the house, or stay and see if Miceli comes back, the door opens and he's there.

With a present in his hand.

Heat flares in his eyes when they land on me, but he banks it almost immediately. Like it was never there.

He crosses the room, grabs my wrist in a gentle grip and tugs me to the armchair. Where he sits down and pulls me into his lap.

"You're going to give me whiplash," I complain.

"Here." He thrusts the gift at me. "Open it."

"What is it?"

"Your birthday present."

"You already gave me one. The cats, the shelter, any of this ringing a bell?"

"Catalina bought and put that together." He doesn't sound even a little ashamed that his sister-in-law bought my birthday gift.

But then the present he's holding says maybe she didn't?

And in our world, it wouldn't be something to be embarrassed by.

I shift a little. It's weird sitting in his lap with no underwear on. Okay, sitting in his lap at all is odd, but the lack of panties adds to the oddness.

In a sexy way? Or in a *I really need to finish getting dressed* way?

Embarrassment warring with arousal says both.

"I knew you didn't pick out that pink cat bed." I try to scoot a little further back on his thighs so maybe my cooch isn't pressing down on his hard muscle.

I mean, it's not really. There's the French terrycloth between me and his leg. Not to mention his slacks. And my butt isn't exactly flat.

But it *feels* that way, okay?

"Stop squirming, or you'll never get to open your present."

"Why?"

The look he gives me.

"Oh." I do my best to stop moving. "What did you get me?"

"Open it and find out."

I slide my finger under the flap of the beautiful wrapping paper covered in roses. Portland is the City of Roses. Is there meaning to him choosing this wrapping paper?

No, of course not. That's too big of a stretch.

I get the present open without tearing the paper and pull it off the box before neatly folding it.

"I don't remember you being this careful on your birthday."

"That was for show. Not real."

"This is real."

I shrug, but don't disagree. "The paper is pretty too."

"Roses for when we first met."

Why did he have to say that?

Pretending I didn't hear, I open the box and peel back the layers of tissue paper to reveal a Barbie pink taser and a keychain with a pointy metal stylus on it.

"Um...thank you?"

"I figured if they're pink you won't mind keeping them on you."

"You want me to carry a taser?" Why? "I have bodyguards."

Two more than I want because of him. And even my dad didn't think I needed to carry a taser.

"You need to be able to protect yourself. If you don't know how to use the kubotan I'll teach you."

"What's a kubotan?"

"This." He lifts the keychain. "The sharp point will shatter glass that hasn't been reinforced to repel bullets. More effectively, hitting the right pressure points will incapacitate an attacker."

I examine the kubotan with interest. "Okay."

"It opens like this to become a knife." He twists the pointy end off, pulls and a thin sharp blade emerges.

"I'd probably cut myself." That's something my dad never tried to train me with.

"I'll teach you how to use it. How are your self-defense moves?"

"You're assuming I have some," I tease.

"Damn your uncle's Stone Age ideas about women. You need to learn self-defense."

He's right about my uncle, which is why he never trained my cousins. "My dad taught me, but I haven't had any more training since his death."

I try to keep up with the workouts, but my uncle's soldiers are forbidden from sparring with me.

"Will you teach me more?"

"I'll help, but you should have an ongoing instructor to work with a couple of times a week."

That sounds good, especially if my cousins join me, but this feels really domestic. "You're acting like a real fiancé."

And I'm not sure I like it.

"I told you. It's my job to protect you." He puts the kubotan down and picks up the taser. "My cousin has a guy who makes special cattle prods for him. He designed this and it will take down an assailant three times your size."

"Wow. Okay. Not asking why your cousin, who presumably lives in Manhattan like the rest of you De Lucas needs a cattle prod."

Miceli nods seriously. "Yeah, best not to ask." He prods the box. "There's one more thing inside."

Hoping the one more item is *not* a gun, even if that's the one weapon I'm trained to use, I dig through the tissue. Under the last layer, I find a phone.

It's pink.

I pick it up and turn it over. There's no manufacturer's logo. Instead there's a rose where the familiar apple usually is.

"It's shatterproof, waterproof and has satellite capability. The encryption is currently unbreakable."

"You sound like a salesman." The hand currently cupping my waist is distracting. "Why should I change my phone?"

"Because this one isn't monitored by your uncle."

"Just you."

He shrugs. "Part of keeping you safe."

"You don't need to read my messages to keep me safe."

"I won't. I would only use the full access function if you were in immediate danger."

"Why should I believe you?"

"Why not believe me?" It's a challenge.

And reminding him that he's Cosa Nostra is just going over the same ground again.

"I won't lie to you." The hand on my waist squeezes. "You won't always like the truth, or the answer I can't always tell you, but what I do tell you will be true."

He hasn't lied to me yet. Even when he told me his name was Ares, it wasn't a lie. It wasn't the whole truth, because although Mars and Ares are the Roman and Greek side of the same coin, Mars is still a different name.

But it wasn't a lie either.

"Changing phones is a pain." It's a weak argument and I know it.

"Everything is already loaded onto this one."

"I suppose Allessio stole my current phone to make that happen."

"Cloned it."

This man. "That's intrusive."

"If you say so."

I contemplate the phone.

"Put any finger on the screen to turn it on," Miceli urges me.

"That doesn't sound very secure."

"It's not touch activated. It only responds to your fingerprints. To access the phone, you need to hold it so the camera can capture your face. The phone uses a combination of facial recognition and a retinal eye scan to open."

"So, no sunglasses?"

"Just for the fraction of a second it takes for your retina to be scanned."

"Complicated."

"Give it a try."

I pick up the phone, my thumb pressing against the screen and it lights up. Then I lift it toward my face.

It opens to a screen set up almost identically to my current one.

There's an app I don't recognize. "What's this?"

"It's like social media, but it's a private app for my family."

I click into it. There's a newsfeed like I've seen on my friends' phones. It has pictures, and comments by different people in his family.

The latest picture is a little boy scowling at the camera. The caption says, "Like father, like son."

"That's my nephew, Neri."

"In Las Vegas?" His sister married the underboss to the Vegas Cosa Nostra.

"Yes. Tap the other feed."

I see what he means and do it. Suddenly the feed is filled with celebrity gossip and news out of Hollywood.

"You can personalize that with keywords and you'll get the most popular posts and videos curated from public social media. Your comments on them are only seen by the family but it allows you to stay current with the topics that interest you."

I can't believe he's serious. "You mean I can watch funny cat videos for hours if I want to?"

"If that's how you want to spend your time, but I think Pusheen might get jealous."

"She has too much self-confidence to be worried about video cats when she's here in person," I say loftily and then ask with little hope, of hearing a yes, "Could my cousins be on here?"

When Miceli nods, I throw my arms around his neck and kiss him.

After an interlude that leaves me breathless, he says, "We have a secure version of the app with limited access they can use."

"But my access is unlimited?" How am I any more trustworthy than Kara and Fiona as far as the De Lucas are concerned?

Is it because I put my bloody thumbprint on that contract in Don De Luca's office?

"All the features are accessible on your phone."

When he says I'm family already, Miceli really means that. Why does that make me feel warm and gooey inside?

CHAPTER 32: MICELI

Róise's eyes glow with eagerness.

Zoey is right. She says that the cousins all want access to social media, but it's strictly forbidden.

To be fair, no one high ranking in the Genovese Family, or related closely to them, is allowed to use social media either.

The PR team keeps accounts for the businesses and the fronts and even dummy accounts for our family. But nothing gets posted without their security approval. And it never gets posted by one of us.

Caution keeps us safe.

"Before the..." Róise breaks off. Shakes her head and then continues. "When she was a freshman in high school, Kara created a secret account and we all used it."

"I bet that didn't last long." It wouldn't have with our people.

"No, it didn't. Grandfather shouted the house down and accused our dads of spoiling us. We were all grounded from our phones, tablets and were supervised doing homework on our laptops for three months."

"Harsh." But no harsher than anything my own father would have done.

Or what Sev or I would do to convince our own children to stay safe.

"My cousins and I have a group text stream going throughout the day, but it's not the same." She touches the screen of the phone almost reverently. "You can't separate discussion threads in a text stream, and it takes forever to scroll back to something you want to see sometimes."

"My father had the family app developed when Giulia threatened to get a disposable phone so she could have a Facebook account. She was twelve."

I don't remember her being grounded. So maybe our father's reaction would have been different if he'd caught her using social media. He was always more lenient with Giulia than he could be with me or Sev.

"I can't believe you made this my profile picture."

The photo she's talking about is one Allessio took for his regular morning check-ins with me. Wearing shorts that show too much leg and an oversized lightweight sweater that slides off her shoulder, Róise is leaning forward revealing cleavage no one but me should see and she's blowing a kiss.

It was yet another attempt by her to poke the bear. Allessio paid the price for seeing what he should not have though and being on the other side of the camera lens when she blew that kiss.

The picture is cropped to her face and the hand blowing the kiss for her profile picture.

"Change it if you don't like it." But every time I see it, my cock throbs, as if our Aphrodite has those cotton candy lips pursed just for us.

"Why does Allessio bother taking the pictures? He never tries to talk me into changing my clothes."

"I know."

Róise laughs. "You sound so disgruntled. Maybe I'll let him keep taking them after all."

"I'm surprised you have so far," I admit.

"*Moma* says pick your battles. That wasn't one worth putting the energy into."

"Your grandmother is a wise woman." And both my dick and I are grateful.

"I don't think I want a picture of me blowing a kiss showing up on your family's phone screens when I interact with the app."

"Right now the privacy settings on your account only allow me to see you."

"But I can see them?" My mob princess sounds so shocked.

"Our marriage has no hope of succeeding if we don't trust each other." And I've figured out this woman has enough stubbornness to stop her from ever taking the first step toward that.

The family app seemed a good place to start with her. Sev knows she's on it and so do the rest of the family. They're not posting anything sensitive she can see until they trust her.

"Doesn't your mom have the app?"

I grimace. Of course, Róise zeroes in on the chink in the trust building armor. "She has her privacy setting so you can't see what she posts."

"Oh."

"It's going to take her time to trust you."

"If she gets there, maybe I'll be able to return the favor someday," Róise says with more honesty than she probably means to.

She looks down to her phone again and I settle her more securely on my lap, but her ass is not flush up against my rapidly hardening cock.

We don't have time for another round.

My dick does not care.

Róise gasps. "What...how...where did you get all these?"

She's found the album for her family.

Her Shaughnessy family. I don't think she'll miss not having any pictures of the Lions on there. Not after the way her grandfather acted at her birthday party.

"Your uncle gave Allessio and Zoey access to all the family photo albums, both physical and digital." There are pictures of her parents when they were children and later, after they married.

I created a separate album for their wedding and for all the pictures that have Róise with them. She's scrolling through those now, touching the screen off and on as if she can touch them through it.

"I didn't know if you'd want those to pop up every time you opened the album."

"You did this for me?" There's a catch in her voice and she swipes at the corner of one eye.

"Yes. Are they enough to make changing phones worth the hassle?" It sounds like I'm teasing, but that was the whole point of putting all that on the phone for her.

To make keeping it irresistible.

"You took all the hassle away." She stiffens and her eyes narrow. "This is a lot. Why is it so important to you I keep this phone?"

"For a starter, you can't block my number on it." Which is more important than it should be.

"Uh huh. I could have guessed that one. What else?"

"It tracks your location and dead zones are virtually nonexistent. A jammer can still affect it, but it's equipped to send out a distress signal via a secondary radio frequency if you trigger it."

"You're really worried about your family getting kidnapped, huh?" She goes back to scrolling on the phone, but she's thinking about it. "There are posts from your brother on here."

"You can't see anything he doesn't want you to." Why tell her that?

She lets out a breath and looks relieved. "That feels real. All this *I trust you even though our families were enemies like a minute ago* doesn't."

"I didn't say I trust you." I don't address the enemies comment.

I've already told her that the Shaughnessy and Genovese were never enemies. But neither were we friends. Rivals? Yes, that. But not enemies.

"No, you said you'd take steps to build trust and this is one of them."

"You keeping it is another."

She nods. "I get that."

"Open the home screen."

"Getting used to your bossiness is going to be as hard as trusting you."

"You like when I order you around."

"During sex. Yeah." Her lips twist with disgruntlement. "Not so much the rest of the time."

"It's a start." The way she trusts me during sex?

Is also a fucking turn on.

I point to an icon on the home screen. "That turns your phone into a listening device."

"Are you trying to pretend you won't have people listening in all of the time?" she asks with surprising insouciance.

I tell her the truth. "That takes way too much manpower." I put my hand up when she opens her mouth to speak. "Yes, I can toggle it on from my own devices, but you have my word I won't do it unless you are in danger."

"Imminent danger," she clarifies. "Mob families are always in danger."

She might be young, but she's not ignorant. "Imminent danger," I agree.

"And my cousins can use the app too?"

"A modified version, yes. If you want, we can install it on your grandmother's phone and even your uncle's. The app's privacy settings allow each of us to exclude them from all, or part of our activity as we choose."

She nods, like once again, that lack of complete trust is believable and makes sense to her. "I don't want Uncle Brogan on it. Or Mick."

"That won't bother Kara?" No way in hell would I allow Róise to be on an app like this without me on it too.

"Why should it? He's not part of our group texting now. And my uncle would only use it to compile information on your family."

Is she even aware of how she's protecting me...us, already? Róise won't betray her uncle to us, but she won't betray us to her uncle either.

There's a streak of loyalty running through her that's bone deep.

CHAPTER 33: RÓISE

I need a new mattress.

This one is too hard. Too soft. Something. I can't get comfortable.

I flip onto my back again, stretching my legs out. With an offended meow, Pusheen rises and saunters to the edge of the mattress.

"I'm sorry," I tell the cat.

She ignores me and jumps down to the floor. A second later I hear the rustle of something soft sliding across the floor. Sitting up, I try to see through the dark shadows.

It's Pusheen, pulling her cat bed. I can only make out the outline, but there's no mistaking what I'm seeing.

"Sheesh," I complain. "Are you a drama queen."

She doesn't stop until the bed is against the far wall. Well, that told me didn't it?

My new friend is fed up with all my tossing and turning for sure.

But I can't turn off my brain and it's this darn mattress's fault. Which might be a touch of self-delusion, but that's not all bad.

We all practice some level of self-delusion. Or so some claim.

I've read a lot of psychology books, trying to help Fiona. So has Kara. We compare notes. We're not experts, but Fiona can leave the mansion now and six years ago, right after my dad's death?

She couldn't leave her room. It's hard for her, but she never gives up pushing on the boundaries of her life. I wish I was as courageous.

If I was, maybe I would have taken *mamo's* offer to get me a new identity so I could disappear.

That's only one of the things that keeps playing wash, rinse, repeat in my brain. I choose to stay and that makes me complicit in this marriage deal.

Also, every time I close my eyes, I replay those hours in the boathouse.

Not the sex.

Okay, yes, the sex. But more the after sex. The birthday presents that mean too much.

A specially made taser I'm scared to touch. I mean, it's basically a mini cattle prod and I'm no cowgirl.

Do all ranches use cattle prods? I'll look it up. Later.

The kuboton isn't as scary, but Miceli's offer to teach me how to use it *is*. He wants to spend time with me.

Why? What does he get out of it?

Besides sex. He can get that anywhere.

If he does though, I'll use my new taser on his balls, but that's not the point.

What is the point?

Oh, right. The point is, this thing between us is supposed to be business. Business between enemies.

But that phone.

It's under my pillow, the outside of my pinky touching the edge of the case.

The thing is, Miceli De Luca is going to make me fall in love with him just being the kind of guy his family expects. The Cosa Nostra is different than the Shaughnessy mob.

Or maybe it's just the Genovese, but Miceli believes in fidelity. He insists I get more adept at protecting myself physically. For the sake of *my* safety. He gave me a phone with pictures of my parents on it.

Some I'd never seen.

What happens when I fall in love with the made man who can't love me back? And even if he could, which, come on...Miceli De Luca. But even if he *could*, he'll probably die a violent death before the baby I'm supposed to have even reaches adulthood.

Sooner or later, this life will take him away just like it took my mom and dad.

And what if I'm head-over-heels in love with him when that happens? It'll be the thing that finally breaks me.

I'd rather marry a man I feel nothing for than one who will tear my heart out of my chest when he leaves me.

I know what that feels like and the wall of prickly thorns around it is the only thing keeping my heart where it is.

If he destroys that wall, nothing will save me.

~ ~ ~

The next morning, I go through the motions of getting ready, rehearsing what I need to say to Uncle Brogan over and over again in my head.

I wait to talk to him until after breakfast and regret it when the food roils in my tummy like a boat on choppy water.

When I reach his office door, I stop and wipe my sweaty palms down the sides of my khaki camo cargo pants. Then, taking a deep breath and holding it, I knock on his office door.

"Come in." His tone is brusque, but not angry.

Okay, that's good. But his lack of anger probably won't last.

Letting the air finally escape my lungs, I turn the knob.

Uncle Brogan is sitting behind his desk, his laptop open and his cell phone on a stand beside it. He's working.

I should come back later.

No. If I don't talk to him now, I won't talk to him at all.

"Good morning, Róise."

"Good morning, Uncle Brogan." Ugh. My voice sounds like I swallowed a frog.

"I assume you're here for a reason..." he says leadingly after a minute of taut silence.

Stressed on my side. Impatient on his.

"Um, I've been thinking. I'm going through with this blood alliance thing, but can't I have a different groom?"

"What the hell are you talking about?" My uncle surges to his feet, all six-feet-two-inches vibrating with fury.

Right now, I wish his temper wasn't so easy to trigger. "I don't think marrying Miceli is a good idea."

"The fuck it isn't." Uncle Brogan doesn't even apologize for dropping the F-bomb in front of me. Not that I care, but usually he does. "Miceli De Luca is the underboss. There is no one as well placed to cement this alliance."

"Does it matter how high ranking my husband is? I mean, I don't think I'd make a very good underboss's wife. A regular soldier would be better." Someone not connected to the De Lucas too closely, so I don't have to see Miceli that often.

If ever.

My uncle takes a deep breath and then counts to ten in Irish. I know because even though he doesn't say the words out loud, he mouths them as he counts.

Then he smiles.

Uh oh. That's his convince the womenfolk with charm smile.

"You're young and it's natural to be a little nervous marrying a man as experienced and intimidating as Miceli De Luca, but it will be fine. You need to trust me on this, Róise. I know what's best for you."

"Like you knew what was best for Kara?" The minute I ask the question, I know I've made a tactical error.

Uncle Brogan doesn't like his decisions questioned, and he instantly gets his back up when you imply he's not father of the year. Is that even a thing? Really?

Father of the year? Who decides if it is?

Another thing to look up later.

Anyway, I just pushed two big red buttons when I was supposed to be convincing Uncle Brogan this change in groom was ultimately his idea.

Am I trying to sabotage myself?

"Your cousin is married to a good man and loves being a mother. Just like you will once you mature a little. Letting you attend college was a mistake."

Mob life. Take real life and set it back fifty to a hundred years in societal norms.

Forcing myself to ignore my uncle's awful statement, I continue to argue. "We're not even formally engaged. The groom could change now, and no one would even know."

"Your marriage to Miceli De Luca is going to happen. You signed that contract with your bloody thumbprint, just like I did. It's unbreakable." He gives me what I'm sure he thinks is a conciliatory smile.

All I see are shark's teeth ready to snap.

I shake my head in silent denial because my throat is too tight with anger to let the words out.

"Even if I could negotiate a different groom for you, I wouldn't. Miceli De Luca is the best option for you."

"You mean for the mob." I've lost the argument already, there's no reason to sugarcoat my responses. "And sending me to college is one of the few decent things you've done as my guardian!"

I spin on my heel and storm out of the office.

"Róise!" Uncle Brogan roars.

But I ignore him. If he wants to shout more 1950s chauvinist garbage at me, he'll have to do it after one of his guys drags me back into the office kicking and screaming.

Pusheen is waiting for me in the hall and pads along beside me as I stomp toward the stairs.

I couldn't have handled that confrontation worse if I'd tried. And I'm not sure I didn't. Subconsciously.

Which says what about me and my instincts for self-preservation?

Nothing good.

"Meow," Pusheen agrees mournfully.

CHAPTER 34: MICELI

Allessio's text tone chirps from somewhere to my left.

Rubbing my eyes, I look away from my laptop screen and fish my phone from the suitcoat hanging on the back of my office chair.

I have different alert noises assigned to certain people and groups.

It's efficient.

Yes, I changed Allessio's from the one designating my crew to something unique when he started guarding Róise. It's not so I don't miss a text.

It's information. I can choose to look, or not, depending on what I'm doing.

I wouldn't mind an in-person interruption from my fiancée though. Memories of her slamming into my office, breathing fire make my balls tighten.

Seeing a picture of her dressed for the day will have to suffice.

Even for me, sifting through data is tedious.

I'm not learning anything interesting right now, just a bunch of shit I already know about the Carusos and the Lucchese Family they lead.

Near dawn this morning, one of the cocktail waitresses from our club, Amuni, was attacked on her way to the train station.

This would be unfortunate, but not my problem if the attackers had not been connected.

Salvatore, capo over all our clubs and their money laundering, killed two of her attackers. He sent another to holding to interrogate later.

But we already know the attackers were part of another capo's crew. Not a Genovese capo, but Lucchese. The godfather's nephew's crew to be exact.

What the hell is Henry Caruso doing that his people are running amok in our territory? If this was a capo sanctioned hit and he didn't bother to clear it with Sev first, it could mean war between the Five Families.

Managgia la miseria! Relations between the Families is strained enough with the godfather's health the way it is.

And that fucking cowardly son-of-a-bitch in holding bit off his own tongue and choked to death on the blood. Either he was loyal as hell or too fucking afraid to face our method of questioning. I'm going with the latter.

Regardless, we're getting no answers there.

I swipe to open the text, expecting my morning update on my fiancée's wardrobe for the day.

Which I get.

But it's not the image I'm used to.

There's plenty of midriff showing and she looks as young as she always does. But there's no pink. Her camo cargo pants are drab green. Her high necked, long-sleeved top is tan and scrunched up so there's at least two inches between the hem and the waistband of the pants.

She's not posing and there are unhappy shadows in her green eyes.

What the hell is going on?

I text her directly.

Ares: *Where's the pink?*

I put myself in her phone as Ares and she's listed as Aphrodite in mine. As long as she knows Ares is me and I am him, I don't mind reminding her about Portland.

That I'm the only man she's ever had sex with. The only one she ever will.

Aphrodite: *Since you kissed the cotton candy lip gloss right off my lips at my birthday, I don't think it's having the effect I thought it would.*

I knew she was wearing pink to irritate me.

Ares: *I don't hate pink.*

Aphrodite: *Oh, really?*

Ares: *The women who wear pink are too innocent. They have stars in their eyes.*

So I don't fuck them. If a woman is wearing cotton candy lip gloss, she's too young and probably too innocent for me. It's simple math.

Math that got shot to hell with the woman on the other end of this text conversation.

Aphrodite: *You are ridiculous.*

Ares: *What's wrong?*

Aphrodite: *Nothing.*

Ares: *What happened?*

Aphrodite: *Seriously? You think I left the pink off because I'm suddenly jaded? The stars went out of my eyes a long time ago.*

Considering how much she and her cousins text, Róise uses almost no acronyms and her texts are long. Because she thinks I'm too old to know what the textspeak means?

Cazzo. I am not worrying that my arranged marriage fiancée thinks I'm too old. If anything, she's too young.

Ares: *I don't recognize you like this.*

She doesn't text back.

Ares: *Tell me what is wrong ~~and I'll fix it~~.*

I delete the last four words. What the fuck is wrong with *me*? I am not her knight in shining armor.

Still no answer.

I figure I pissed her off, but five minutes later, the alert tone I assigned to her number chimes.

I grab my phone and check the text.

It's a picture. She's wearing a baby pink top now and glaring at the camera like she wants to smack someone. Probably me.

I smile.

~ ~ ~

I'm not smiling several hours later as Salvatore and I dump the last of three dead bodies onto the drive behind our godfather's home.

They're wrapped neatly in industrial plastic cling wrap. Angelo insisted on installing a wrapping machine in the secret subbasement of the Oscuro Building. I'd seen a machine like it wrapping luggage at the airport, but never a human body.

I've got to admit it's efficient for those times we transport bodies instead of disappearing them in the chemical bath under The Box.

Wrapped up tight like they are, not a single molecule of their DNA is transferring to us or the trunk we transported them in.

We have two men with us, but it's me and Salvatore doing the heavy lifting. This is our responsibility. Our men stand at alert by the car.

I slam the trunk. "The woman something special to you?"

Not that she can be permanent. Like me, Salvatore will marry for the good of *la famiglia*. But he sounded plenty pissed at Pietro in the car on the way here because he drugged her.

"I want her."

"You want women. You have women. You don't kidnap and lock them up in your penthouse."

"I didn't kidnap her."

"Pietro was acting on your orders." I understand skirting the fine line, but facts are facts. "Aunt Ilaria will put salt in your coffee if she finds out."

Or worse. My aunt's every bit as intelligent as my mother. And devious. You do not want to get on the bad side of the women in my family.

Róise is going to fit right in.

"You amused at the idea of mamma salting my coffee?" Salvatore asks.

I shrug, not about to admit it was thinking about my too young fiancée that put the look on my face. "She's more likely to bring burned lasagna by for your dinner and sit there watching while you choke it down anyway."

My cousin grimaces. "Sounds about right."

One side of the double backdoor opens, cutting off our conversation.

CHAPTER 35: MICELI

The godfather lives in a 20,000 square foot mansion in Brooklyn. When he bought it back in the day, he also bought the surrounding houses.

He promptly tore them down before installing a high brick wall and planting fast growing arborvitaes that now tower twice the height of the wall.

He's the fucking godfather of the entire Cosa Nostra in America and probably the only man in New York who could get the planning permissions, but he got them.

And the house is as secluded as any can be in this borough. There is no line of site from the outside, unless you've got a drone. But he's got anti-drone technology installed by our people, so I know it works.

Someone could put cameras in the trees. Unlikely though. He's our godfather. Not only does he have powerful law enforcement on his payroll, but his property is continuously swept on a random schedule by quadrant for bugs and cameras.

Are we still taking a risk dumping bodies on the drive in the crowded borough of Brooklyn?

Yes. We're also making a statement.

The Genovese fear no one.

Two Lucchese soldiers come outside, weapons drawn, but pointing downward. I lean back against the car and pull out my phone, my thumb sliding over the screen to turn on the recording feature.

Then I open a game and start crushing candy.

"We're here to see Don Caruso." I don't bother to look at the two Lucchese men. "He knows why we're here."

Sev called the godfather and told him what happened and what to expect. My brother refused to talk terms over the phone and informed Don Caruso I am the Genovese representative in this matter.

Salvatore's phone rings. He curses, but doesn't answer. He doesn't greet the soldiers either.

Our silent stance is clear. We are waiting for the godfather.

This time Salvatore's phone buzzes. It's not on silent, but the buzz is low enough the two soldiers won't hear it unless they get closer to us.

The fucking phone is buzzing for the fifth time when the other door opens too. This time, four men come out walking abreast two-by-two, followed by Henry Caruso, that asshole.

Less than a minute later, the godfather comes out, surrounded by six more men.

The security team is overkill.

Our godfather has no reason to fear us. I'm loyal. Salvatore is loyal.

The whole fucking team has their guns drawn. Am I supposed to be intimidated?

I'm not. If they were going to start shooting, they'd have silencers attached.

Henry Caruso makes a movement with his hand and the guns are lifted to point at us. Another empty gesture but one I won't forget.

Would anyone really miss this guy if I disappeared him?

Our men stay on alert, but I don't signal them to draw their guns. A De Luca doesn't make empty gestures. If I tell my men to draw, my gun will be in my hand too and we shoot to kill.

Why in the hell is the godfather allowing his nephew to appear to take tactical point? *Appear* because I don't believe for a second those soldiers are shooting on anyone's orders but Don Caruso's.

I put my fist over my heart and bow my head. Slightly. The theatrics are pissing me off. Salvatore does the same, with the same small inclination of his head.

"Godfather," we say together.

"Miceli." Don Caruso shifts his gaze to my cousin. "Salvatore."

The phone buzzes again.

"Answer the damn thing." There's a reason my cousin isn't putting the phone on silent.

He wants to talk to whoever is calling. I want to make another point.

The godfather gives me a look of censure when my cousin obeys.

The harsh, "What?" that comes out of Salvatore's mouth doesn't surprise me.

The fact he talks for almost a minute does.

Maybe he's making a point too.

This, the dozen soldiers with their guns pointed at us. It's all bullshit and the only reason Henry is getting away with it is because we're on the godfather's property.

The men are not the show of strength he thinks they are though. They make him look weak. Our godfather too. If he has to protect himself from other Cosa Nostra, he's not certain of his hold on the mafia.

I look at the godfather, refusing to acknowledge the soldiers around us. He stares back stoically.

Salvatore's phone buzzes. Again.

The cocktail waitress has balls, I'll give her that.

My cousin says, "Excuse me, I need to take this."

Perfectly played. I approve.

A flash of respect shows on the godfather's face and he nods. Henry is turning red, his mouth working like he wants to say something.

"My mother sends her regards, godfather," I say into the silence. "She would like to visit soon."

Which is not true, but neither is it a lie. My mother *would* send her regards if she knew I was coming today and probably some of Emilia's panna cotta to tempt the godfather's appetite.

"Your mother is a good woman. Seeing her makes me miss my own Sophia, God rest her soul." He sighs. "Tell her to come for lunch on Saturday. Father John will join us."

The cardinal began as a priest in Don Caruso's family's church and is the only one to hear the godfather's confession for over fifty years.

"I'll tell her."

The godfather taps twice downward with his forefinger. His men lower their guns.

Henry slams his own gun against his thigh. "What the fu—"

"Silence," Don Caruso cuts him off, his tone sharp but his voice does not carry.

He has always been known as the don with a soft voice and ruthless nature, but this is different. His voice is almost weak.

Salvatore returns, his eyes reflecting satisfaction. The call went well then.

"You finished talking to your girlfriend?" I ask.

What else is he going to call a woman he kidnapped and has trapped in his apartment?

The godfather leans heavily on his cane but gives my cousin a harsh glare. "Maybe you want to explain to me how this is not an act of war on behalf of your don?"

Here we go.

The political jockeying I hate. And Sev knows it. I swear he sent me, instead of coming himself, because I ate the leftover cannoli from dinner last night.

Henry gloats like the man who knocked his opponent's knight from the chessboard but doesn't realize it's opened him up to lose his king.

Giamope.

How is this fool going to run the Lucchese Family? He can't even see two steps ahead.

Salvatore gives a brief rundown of what happened this morning. *In our fucking territory.*

"A cocktail waitress who shakes her ass for tips and doesn't even make your club extra money is hardly one of your own," the godfather dismisses.

Well, fuck.

Salvatore is attached to that cocktail waitress. To the point of taking her phone call in the middle of this pissing contest. I watch my cousin's hand twitch but he doesn't go for his gun.

I should be glad of my cousin's restraint. But maiming a few arrogant Lucchese soldiers stupid enough to draw on us would be fun.

However, killing our godfather's would start a war for sure.

"Amuni is one of our legit businesses," Salvatore grits out.

"Which makes this *puttana* even less one of your own," Henry sneers.

The man just can't help being a *giamope*.

My cousin takes a step toward the other capo. "Call my girlfriend a whore again and I will end you."

Henry can't meet Salvatore's eyes.

Codardo. And a spineless one.

"It is true then? The woman is your girlfriend." Don Caruso measures Salvatore with his gaze. "I had heard that is what you told the hospital, but I dismissed it as provocative gossip."

No surprise our godfather knows what's happening in the other boroughs. His intelligence network is legendary, but it's based on aging informants.

Sev's is already more efficient and pervasive. When he is godfather, he'll expand it.

"I thought Captain Playboy didn't do committed relationships." Henry can't stand being left out of the conversation.

Salvatore looks at Henry like the little pissant he is. "She is mine."

Well, fuck. Does my cousin realize he sounds just like Sev talking about Catalina? That's not *temporary until duty calls him to the altar* stuff.

Salvatore is showing signs of falling in love. If I didn't see it for myself, I wouldn't believe it, but he's hung up on this girl. My cousin's every bit as gone over this Bianca chick as Sev is over Catalina.

After what happened when Salvatore got made, I thought those emotions died alone along with the traitorous bitch he had to kill.

Fuck. Another De Luca brought to his knees by a woman.

That will never be me.

An image of kneeling to eat out Róise pussy flashes in my brain and I shove it away. After appreciating that pretty pink pussy for a few seconds.

That's sex. Not love.

Don Caruso chastises Salvatore for not protecting Bianca. No way is he transferring blame to us for his nephew's men acting without sanction in our territory.

"Only a fool doesn't protect what is important to him," Don Caruso criticizes.

Salvatore's eyes light with victory. "I'm glad you see it that way, Godfather, since I killed the three men who tried to harm her."

Henry about chokes on his own breath. He knows his uncle just hung him out to dry.

It's time to step in. I look directly into Don Caruso's eyes when I speak. "Regardless of their target, your capo's men were in *our* territory and they tried to kill someone without Severu's approval."

He's both don and godfather. Every action of a Lucchese soldier ultimately lays at his feet. And he knows it.

"Was it a hit?" Salvatore asks Henry.

The *giamope* pales, sweat gleaming on his forehead. "No."

Either he's scared shitless of being accused, or he's lying when he says *no*. Henry Caruso needs to be watched more closely.

His uncle sighs. "Does your don seek reparations?"

"Uncle—"

"Shut it," Don Caruso cuts his nephew off. "You need to control your men."

He glares at me next. "And your brother needs to prove his strength if he wants my support to take my place."

My shrug disguises the rage his words invoke.

"Severu's inclination is to wipe out your nephew and all his men in retaliation for this act of aggression. I thought you would be against it, but if you're sanctioning retribution..." I let my voice trail off with insolence I would not have shown this man a year ago.

Don Caruso swells with fury, but even that is muted in this sickly old man.

I would offer him nothing but respect, despite his physical weakness. But he made a huge mistake implying Sev doesn't have the ruthlessness to run the Genovese, much less the Cosa Nostra.

"My uncle said *reparations* not retribution," Henry splutters.

I ignore him like the pathetic buzzing fly he is and stare down our once powerful godfather.

"My nephew will pay a tithe to Severu for three months." Don Caruso looks with disgust on his nephew's dead men. "One for each man on his crew he could not control."

"Did you have to cut off their hands? It's going to upset their families," Henry whines.

"You're damn lucky we didn't chop them up into bite size pieces and dump them in the river."

I appreciate the imagery of Salvatore's words, but we don't dump bodies in the river. That's for old-timers and amateurs.

We've got a chemical bath under the floor of The Box that destroys bodies down to the molecular level.

"For the three months of the reparation tithe, we expect Lucchese soldiers to stay out of Manhattan," I warn Don Caruso. "Any found in our territory will not be returning for a proper burial, or otherwise, regardless of their reason for being there."

Don Caruso shakes his head. "We have always had good relations between our families."

Yeah, no.

The Five Families fight like siblings and sometimes we draw blood.

But I give the godfather the words he needs to hear. "And that will continue if there is no further aggression."

I'm not offering anything more than that. Sev will protect his family at all costs, and if that means wiping out another Family, he'll do it. And I'll be standing beside him, doing what I was born to do.

Be Mars. The god of war.

CHAPTER 36: RÓISE

*F*riday

A new cat bed identical to the first one, but the size of a midsize dog bed is waiting in my bedroom when I come in after classes.

Pusheen is lounging in it like the queen she is. There's an envelope with my name written in a slashing, heavy hand on my bed.

The card inside is solid white, embossed with a coat of arms I'm going to ask about later. There's a single line written in a bold scrawl.

A more fitting bed for our cat.

He didn't sign it, but there's no doubt in my mind who wrote it and provided the more appropriately sized cat bed for Pusheen. My fake boyfriend and secret fiancé, Miceli De Luca.

Still unsettled by what happened in the boathouse, I text him a quick thank you. I'm relieved when his return text is only two word.

Ares: *You're welcome.*

I'm *not* disappointed he doesn't say anything else.

There's another card on my desk. I almost never get mail. Who does? But the number of birthday cards that have been delivered the past two weeks is kind of staggering.

My friends don't do snail mail, so most are from people trying to impress my uncle. This must be another one, although the envelope is thin, cheap paper. *Not impressive.*

There's no return address, but the postmark is Pennsylvania.

Revulsion sends goosebumps down my arms. The only people I know of from Pennsylvania are my mom's blood relatives.

Not her family.

They don't deserve that title, but they do share her blood.

If I wanted a distraction from checking my phone again and/or texting Miceli, this is definitely working.

Slipping my finger under the flap, I tear it open and a note slips out.

My eyes go to the signature first. Hope. My grandmother, Hope Lion. I've only spoken to her a handful of times in my life and that's fine by me. She lives in total subservience to my grandfather and did nothing to protect my mom from Gabriel.

Dear Róise,

Your uncle has held Brother Gabriel off for three years, but now that you are twenty-one, you must have a care.

Have a care? What does that even mean?

Do not leave the house without your bodyguard, the note goes on. *Ever. My sister didn't want you anywhere near this life, but if Brother Gabriel has his way, you'll be as trapped as any of us.*

Trapped? Us?

This isn't from my grandmother. It's from my Aunt Hope, my mom's younger sister. And she says that Uncle Brogan has been holding Gabriel off since I was eighteen.

Any urge I have to thank my uncle is obliterated by the fact he used the threat of marriage to one of Gabriel's sycophants as leverage to force me into the contract with Miceli.

My aunt doesn't need to worry about me going anywhere without body-guards though. Miceli has taken care of that.

That twinge of warmth I'm feeling is probably an allergic reaction to something. Not affection or gratitude toward Miceli De Luca for his vigilance on my behalf.

I'm in bed later, online buddy-bingeing a show with Kara and Fiona when my new phone rings. I send a message through the group watching app.

Rosy: *Miceli is calling. Be offline for a few.*

Then I swipe to answer. "Is this important? Because I'm group watching a show with my cousins."

"Hello, Róise. It has been a busy day, productive if not pleasant, thank you."

He's not here to see me roll my eyes. "Hello, Miceli. I'm busy."

I don't want to know what *productive if not pleasant* means.

"Are you okay?" I ask before I know the words are coming out of my mouth.

Well, great. I just said I didn't want to know. And like everyone else in my life sometimes, I'm not listening to me.

"Yes. Others are not so fortunate."

"Sometimes, you sound so formal."

"I wasn't allowed to use contractions until I learned to communicate without them."

"Really? Isn't that weird?"

"Not in my family."

"I always heard the Italian mafia is more stuck up than other organized crime families, but that's something else."

"Stuck up implies we think we are superior because of how we talk."

"Don't you?"

"No."

"But you do think you're better than everybody else."

"Not everybody."

I laugh. I can't help it. "You're so stuck on yourself."

"Our syndicate puts more time into training new recruits than others and children born into the mafia are trained from birth for their role."

"You've never had a time you didn't know you'd be underboss one day?" I know the answer.

He already said, but it's hitting me harder right now for some reason.

"No."

"Our child will be just as trapped." But not as trapped as the children born into the AOG.

My aunt's warning is on my brain because her concern came through the short note, but so did her hopelessness.

"It's not a trap, *mi dolce fiore*. It's a privilege."

Of course, Miceli would say that. "What if he or she doesn't want that privilege?"

And also, why do I love that he calls me his sweet flower? Is it a play on my name? I feel like it is. The words he said the first time he used it play over in my brain when I should be thinking about other things.

Your perfume is all I want to smell.

Even now, my core gives a throb and my thighs clench at the memory.

"Not all people born to a mafia family are meant for the mafia life." He says it like everyone knows that.

But that's sure not how my family sees it. Not even *moma*.

"That's not an answer."

"There are children every generation who walk away from the life. If our child is one of them, we will respect that choice." Miceli doesn't *sound* like he's lying.

"Will you still love him or her? If they don't want to be part of this world?" Like my dad loved me?

"Love is not a word I use, but my children will always know they are part of the De Luca family, whether or not they are part of *la famiglia*."

Love is not a word I use. What does that even mean? I figured he isn't going to fall in love with his wife, right? But his children? He'll love them, won't he?

"You love your family, don't you?"

"My family knows I will kill for them and die to protect them."

Okay, yeah. In this world, that's one definition of love, I guess. But even when it comes to his family, he's not going to use the dreaded L-word.

I sit up and rub my chest. "You're giving me heartburn."

"Stop eating so much crap on campus and you'll be fine."

I don't bother asking how he knows my preference for tacos, pizza and smoothies. Allessio is a born tattletale and Zoey probably is too.

"I don't eat crap." I eat the food that I never even tasted before going to college.

And it's yummy.

"Tell that to your heartburn."

The pain in my chest didn't originate in my stomach, but I'm not admitting that to either of us. "What do you want? You called for a reason, right?"

"I am checking up on our cat."

"Our cat?" The big ball of fur chooses this moment to jump onto my lap, knocking my tablet over.

Like she knows Miceli is on the phone.

I pet the Maine Coon and her deep purr rumbles over my thighs. "Since when did you become Pusheen's other human?"

"When we adopted her."

"I adopted her, not us."

"Really? Because I signed the paperwork just like you did."

"No..." Did he? "Why would you?"

"Why wouldn't I?"

"You don't want a cat."

"I don't particularly want a wife either, but I've got both now."

I don't particularly want a wife. Sheesh. Talk about being blunt.

"Well, I don't want a husband either and newsflash, we aren't married yet."

"Not conventionally no."

"We are not having this discussion again. Until we say our vows in front of family, friends and enemies, we are *not* married."

"Just remember who you belong to and the semantics don't matter."

"Semantics do matter. And ditto." Why did I say that?

He already promised not to cheat. Why harp on the issue? But then why is he?

It's kind of an issue with him, isn't it?

As if I'd deliberately put someone in his crosshairs. When he says he'll kill a man for touching me, Miceli is speaking his own deadly truth.

"Pusheen is fine."

"So, she didn't jump from the top of a display cabinet in the hall and knock over one of your uncle's guards?"

Allessio or Zoey must have told him about that. "She's a lot more playful than I expected."

"He didn't hurt her in retaliation." It's not a question.

I still reassure him fast. "No. He was a good sport even though he ended up with a few scratches."

"As one of the family bodyguards, he's going to have to learn to watch out for cat antics now." Miceli sounds really pleased by that.

"Troy isn't a bodyguard."

"Then what the fuck was he doing in the hallway outside yours and Fiona's bedroom?"

"You drop the F-bomb a lot for a man taught to speak like he's royalty, or something."

"Not around my mother and that's not important. Answer my question. What was this Troy doing in that hallway?"

"How should I know. He's one of my uncle's men. They don't answer to me."

"None of his men that are not part of the security detail should be in the halls leading to family bedrooms." He says it like it's a rule.

"Is that how you do it in the Cosa Nostra?" I ask without a lot of interest.

My uncle's men are always around. I don't leave my room in my pajamas and I always wait to change into my swimsuit until I'm down at the pool or the dock.

It is what it is.

"It's how it should be done there too."

Judgy much? "Says you."

"Think about it, Róise. He wasn't there to see you." Miceli's tone is implying something nefarious.

"He was probably delivering a message for my uncle."

"That should only be done through your security detail," Miceli says bossily.

"I guess my uncle doesn't agree." But I am thinking like he ordered...darn him, and I send a text to the chat window on the show that's been playing silently this whole time.

Róise: *Fiona, do you know why Troy was in the hall today?*

Fiona: *No. But I wish the men would stay away from our rooms.*

Kara: *It's worse around ours. Mick has his crew in and out of our rooms at all hours. I never know who's going to be there when I come out of the bedroom.*

Fiona and my rooms might have less space, but we have more privacy than Kara.

I have a regular bedroom suite with a giant walk-in closet/dressing room and full bathroom. So does Fiona, but Kara and Mick have a set of rooms set up like an apartment. *Moma* does too.

The only people she invites into her space are us girls and Fitz.

I doubt Uncle Brogan and Mick even notice.

"Go watch your movie," he says abruptly.

Okay, then. "You do remember you are the one who called me? And it's a show. We're bingeing episodes."

"Which one?" he asks, like he didn't just basically tell me to hang up.

So, I tell him the title and what it's about in excruciating detail. After all, he asked.

Am I smiling with malice?

Maybe a little.

Saturday

A huge basket of cat treats and toys from Miceli arrives the next day for Pusheen.

I text him a picture of our...*my* cat hugging the stuffed mouse that smells like catnip. Her long front legs are wrapped around it like a baby.

Ares: *Tell her there's more where that came from if she keeps attacking soldiers coming into the family wing.*

Aphrodite: *You are obsessed about that.*

He has my name as Aphrodite in our text stream, but it's Róise everywhere else. Which means it's some kind of special tech mojo.

That I want him to share with me so that I can:

1. Change his name to Bossy Know it All.

2. Change my name for my cousins to Rosy.

Sunday
Ares: *How is our cat? I want proof of life.*
I take a picture of Pusheen stretched across the chair in the boathouse. Yes, *that* chair.

Fiona says the water is soothing for Rambo, so we're in the boathouse with the bay doors open.

My cousin is cuddling her cat in the hammock while I finish a paper on my laptop at the table. Kara and Fitz are building Legos at the other end.

"Who put that smile on your face?" Kara asks, sounding bemused. Then she frowns. "You're not dating someone at college are you?"

"What? No! If I was willing to date someone local, I wouldn't have planned that whole fiasco in Portland."

"Was it a fiasco?" Kara asks, sounding wistful.

Fitz jumps up and runs toward the main coon. "Let's play, Pusheen."

My cat lifts her head and surveys my nephew regally. And then without warning, she springs, landing two feet beyond him. He turns and tears after her, yelling like the exuberant five-year-old he is.

"He's happy," I say.

"Mick wants to send him to a military academy next year for school. I told him no."

"Good."

"I don't think Portland was the fiasco you believe it was." There's a far off look in Kara's hazel eyes. "I was terrified the day of my wedding."

"I would have been too. You were only eighteen."

"I'd never been kissed, or had a climax that didn't come from my own fingers."

"The nuns would be scandalized," I tease.

She attended the Catholic private school with all the other mob children. So did Fiona until the shooting.

"You know it." Kara grins at me, but then her pretty face turns serious again. "You've had sex with Miceli and now you know he won't hurt you in bed."

Horror grips my insides. "Has Mick hurt you?"

"No. That's one area I have no complaints, but I didn't know what it would be like beforehand. I was so scared. *Mamo* offered to get rid of him if he hurt me." She shrugs. "But no one could stop my wedding night happening."

"Except your dad."

Mamo had offered to kill Kara's husband if he abused her? I'm not surprised. Our grandmother has more steel in her than my uncle's weapons store.

Kara sighs. "Dad has always put the mob first, you know that."

We share a commiserating look and then both our gazes go to Fiona, talking in low tones with her rescue cat.

"Thank you for making him promise to give her the freedom your dad would have given you."

"She's the only leverage he had to convince me to agree to the blood alliance and he knew it."

"He'll keep his word because if he doesn't, the Genovese mafia will stop trusting him."

Kara is right. I extracted that promise from my uncle privately and it has nothing to do with Miceli's mafia.

But it's my uncle's desire for a strong alliance with them that will force him to keep the promise he made to me.

CHAPTER 37: RÓISE

*M*onday

"Are you really part of the mafia?" The question is hissed from one of my classmates sitting behind me during our Art and Community Engagement class.

You only have to take one class in this designation, but this is my third one. I've already taken a class on tactics and another on activism. I took that one my freshman year.

Because I see acting as more than a way to get famous. In fact, that was never my goal. My goal was to live out the lives of other characters for other people to enjoy.

Now, my goal is to graduate and hope that as an underboss's wife, I can volunteer in theater program for underserved youth. Or something.

I ignore the question because I don't know the guy who asked it. I mean, I know his name. It's Boaz. And I've seen him around, but he's not a friend.

I don't owe him anything, much less an explanation of whatever he thought he found on Google.

It has been a few weeks since my security detail increased by two and started following me around campus.

At first, when my friends asked what was up with that, I said I had a new overzealous head of security and they accepted it. Enough students at the school come from family with some level of personal security, it wasn't too big a deal.

I joked about preparing for the day I was famous enough to need this all the time and my friends laughed.

I thought I dodged the bullet that hit me so hard in middle school. After spending the rest of grade school and my first two years of middle school in anonymity, one of my classmate's parents dropped the bomb to their kid.

My dad was part of the Irish mob.

Which meant, I was part of the Irish mob. Suddenly, my friends were crossing the hall not to walk beside me, and kids were asking questions that made me sick to my stomach.

Did my dad kill people? Had I ever killed anyone? One of my former friends lost her phone and rumors I'd stolen it went through the school like wildfire.

At the request of the school administration, I did distance learning for the last two months of my 8th grade year. I was asked not to attend graduation.

The next year, I started high school in a different Burrough, using my middle name as my last name.

"I know a girl who went to middle school with you," Boaz says in a whisper loud enough to be heard by other students around us. "She says your uncle is the head of Irish organized crime in New York."

My face heats as other students around us hear his words and stare at me, waiting for a response.

They're going to be waiting a long time. Like forever.

The professor comes in and starts talking, but the whispering behind me doesn't stop. At least now it's not directed at me, but the classmates around us.

Finally, our professor, a gray haired woman who looks like Gloria Steinem, demands to know what all the chatter is about.

"We've got a real mobster in our classroom," Boaz replies promptly.

"Oh really?" The professor rolls her eyes. "And who might that be?"

She's that kind of teacher. She faces stuff head on and then gets us back on track. She's one of the profs who takes time to dispel urban myths around our profession especially.

She always has a few well-chosen words of logic and instructions to read a certain book, or visit a website with multiple sources (that don't all refer back to each other for god's sake – her words, not mine).

What will she say now? Maybe she'll just tell the jerk to mind his own business.

"Róise Aisling. Only her last name isn't Aisling, it's Shaughnessy and her uncle is a bigwig in organized crime."

"I see. Is that the reason for your increased security over the last month?" the professor asks me, without bothering to ask if it's true, or not.

I mean it is, but also, Aisling *is* my name. Just my middle name. And I planned to use it instead of Shaughnessy for my career. Lots of actors use stage names.

Why not start early?

Unwilling to lie to her face, I stare at my professor without speaking.

Giving a brisk nod, the professor says, "Róise, please stay after class. I would like a word with you. Now, getting back to..."

But I don't hear the rest of her words. All I hear, over and over again in my head is, *I would like a word with you*. If anyone had any doubts about what Boaz said, she just gave it legitimacy.

My skin grows clammy, and I want to throw up.

Because I know what's coming.

And it's not understanding with a promise to talk to the other students at the next class. Not that it would matter.

Everyone at the university will know about my family's mob ties by tomorrow, if not sooner. Nobody gossips with more drama than theater people.

And finding out that I'm connected is too juicy not to serve up.

The day only gets worse. I don't even try to eat lunch in the dining hall. I don't want to answer a bunch of intrusive questions that I'll have to lie my way through.

No matter what they think they know, confirming my family's criminal connections would be a betrayal. I can't deny I'm a Shaughnessy, but I also can't talk about what that really means.

I can't correct the impression that Uncle Brogan is the head of Irish organized crime without explaining about mobs and how we're different from the Cosa Nostra and other mafias because we don't have a godfather.

We're more like the bratva, but I'm sure not going to explain that either.

So, I drown myself in tacos at a Mexican restaurant far enough away from campus there won't be any other students there.

Allessio and Zoey eat at a separate table. Like that makes any difference now.

But it's protocol.

Like following me around.

A student with a note from the dean is standing outside the door of my afternoon class. It's handwritten and signed in dark black ink.

I sigh and follow the other student, who keeps giving me curious looks over his shoulder. At least he doesn't ask.

The dean's secretary thanks and dismisses the other student before taking me into the dean's office.

Dean Howell is sitting behind his desk and he doesn't get up.

He looks a little like an aging Tom Hanks, and usually has a watered down version of that actor's affable smile and manner.

His expression is stern now though. "Some disturbing information has come to my attention."

"Yes?" I ask.

Don't give anything away. Keep the family's secrets. Don't cry.

"It appears you enrolled under a false name, Ms. Shaughnessy."

"It's not false. My middle name is Aisling." And if they'd done a rudimentary background check on me, instead of accepting the transcripts from my high school and test scores with that name on them, they'd know that.

But that's what I counted on when I enrolled. After what happened in middle school, my dad had falsified records and bribed school administrators to enroll me in high school under the name Róise Aisling.

Uncle Brogan wouldn't have done it for me for college though, so I was glad I already had the supporting documentation for my application three years ago. I even used my school I.D. for the picture identification required for the file.

Only, just like middle school, my real identity has come to light, and I don't have my dad here to help smooth it away.

Miceli De Luca is already causing big, unpleasant changes in my life and we're not even married yet.

CHAPTER 38: MICELI

*M*onday

Sev texts and tells me to meet him in his office at home before dinner.

I'm in one of the visitor chairs, sipping on a scotch when he comes in. Late, his hair tousled, and not wearing a tie, he looks like he just rolled out of bed and threw a suit on.

He probably did.

The man is addicted to his wife.

"You might want to comb your hair before dinner, or mamma will comment."

Sev pivots toward the attached bathroom. "Pour me one of those. I'll be right back."

He comes out looking more put together, hair combed, tie in place. "There's a lot going on right now, but Catalina needs my time too."

"Sure," I agree without any conviction.

Sev shakes his head. "Talk to me again after you marry that feisty Irish rose."

Róise is back to ignoring my calls and texts.

"I don't think there's any risk of her *needing* my time after we're married." She'd rather pretend I don't exist at all.

"That's going to have to happen this summer instead of next."

My brows furrow. "Why?"

As underboss with every intention of training my future nephew to take over my role someday, when I marry doesn't matter.

Maybe he wants to use the wedding as a chance to shore up support with the other dons.

"Because when I become godfather, I'm stepping down as Don of the Genovese."

His words kick the air out of my lungs and I stare at him in shock for long seconds of silence. "But..."

"The godfather being the don of a family divides his time and loyalty. Don Caruso's waste of space nephew wouldn't be a capo if another Lucchese ran that Family."

"Much less in line to be the next don," I agree with disgust.

Sev's expression shows the same feeling. "He's putting bloodlines ahead of what's best for the mafia."

"Are you saying you'll do different?" I know that's how we were raised, but Sev is not our father.

"I won't have to," Sev says with firm conviction. "You being the next don is good for the Genovese and the Cosa Nostra."

"I'm the underboss. I was raised to wage war, not lead."

"Bullshit. You were raised by the same father as I was. You were tutored in the same political and battle tactics as I was."

"But Sev, I'm not you." That's one truth he cannot refute.

In some ways he's harsher, in other ways I am. Would those differences really be good for our mafia?

"Right after papà died, Aunt Ilaria took me aside. I think she knew I was having doubts."

I'd seen those doubts too, but then one day they disappeared and Sev stepped up like I knew he would. I stepped with him, my gun pointed at anyone who wanted to come for my brother.

"What did she say to you?"

"What I'm about to say to you. You were born to be my underboss, my god of war, but that isn't all you were born for." Sev's expression reminds me more of our father right now than it ever has.

"She told me I couldn't take hold of the future without taking hold of the present. You can't either."

"But my future was being underboss."

"No, your future was to become the next Genovese don. You will have your own sons to train, both to be don and underboss."

"I might have daughters." Which doesn't mean one can't follow in my footsteps, but unlike a son, she would have more options from infancy.

"You know sex is determined by the chromosomes passed down by the father. The men in our family have fathered exactly two women in the past five generations. And one of them was born over a hundred years ago."

Papa was so shocked when Giulia was born, he had a DNA test done on her. Mamma never knew, but Sev and I found the medical report confirming paternity when we went through the files in the document safe room after he died.

Of course, we never told either of them.

I wonder if Catalina has found the test results? If she has, she hasn't said a word either.

"Our father planned for this. He expected me to be the next godfather and he counseled me to pass the mantle of Don of the Genovese onto you."

"He never said anything to me." Neither did Sev.

"He would have."

But he died and any chance to advise his younger son on a different path than the one I was on disappeared.

"You'll be an excellent don, Miceli, but you're two years younger than me."

"Three years older than when you became don."

"And you remember the unrest with the older capos. My marriage to Catalina was necessary. You need to marry Róise before you wear the ring."

"A family connection to the Shaughnessy mob is something none of the other dons who will challenge to be godfather can bring to the table."

Sev nods. "It is an alliance that is good for the entire Cosa Nostra, not only the Genovese."

That explains my brother's insistence on the blood alliance. He gave me a choice about being the groom, but I know my duty.

Does Róise know hers?

~ ~ ~

"Róise said she's busy and won't be able to make dinner on Friday." Catalina grimaces at the asparagus on her plate and shoves it to the edge with her fork.

Weird. It's one of her favorite vegetables, which is why we have it at least twice a week. The cooks adore her.

Mamma dabs at her mouth with her napkin and then smooths it over her lap again. "That's for the best, isn't it? It's a family dinner after all."

"Róise is family, mamma. She's going to be my wife." This thing about my mother's uncle runs deeper than I thought.

Aria De Luca knows her duty. She was an excellent don's wife and fulfills her role as don's mother just as effectively.

Besides, she's a lot kinder than I will ever be. The acceptance and compassion she offered Catalina when she married Sev is severely lacking with Róise though.

"We need to plan the wedding for this summer," Sev says, his tone final. "I'll call Brogan about it after dinner."

"This summer?" Catalina asks, eyes wide.

"It's already May. The earliest we could possibly plan a wedding befitting your brother is the end of September." Our mother's tone is every bit as firm as Sev's.

My brother frowns. "You planned my wedding in three months."

"Yes, but I am certain Mr. Shaughnessy will insist on the wedding taking place at St. Patrick's Cathedral. It is an old and prestigious church located in Manhattan with strong ties to the Irish community."

Making it the best venue to respect the affiliation of both syndicates. That's the mother I know, thinking of all the angles.

"So? Our wedding was in a cathedral." Sev is not looking at mamma, his eyes are fixed with concern on Catalina's pale face. "Are you well, *mi dolce bellezza?*"

My sister-in-law smiles wanly. "Just a little tired."

"I haven't overtaxed you with social engagements have I?" my mom asks worriedly.

Catalina shakes her head, grimaces and takes a quick sip of water. "No. Really. I'll go to bed early."

Sev leaps to his feet all plans for my wedding forgotten. "You'll go to bed *now.*"

Catalina's protests are interspersed with laughter as he carries her from the room.

Mamma and I breathe out identical sighs of relief. That low tone of Sev's and his wife's amusement means she's not really sick.

Maybe tired means, I want to fuck my husband now. That's fine by me.

Mamma looks at me, her beautiful face troubled. "I am sorry, Miceli. I want to be a good mother-in-law to your wife, but I can't forget what her family did to mine. Once I get to know her better, I'm sure..." Her voice trails off like she's not convinced of her own words, so she doesn't finish the sentence.

Is this what I have to fight with Róise?

A prejudice buried so deeply even a woman as reasonable as my mother can't dispel it.

"You know that a Cosa Nostra killed her mother. Róise believes her father's killer was also one of us."

Mammo looks outraged. "We aren't the Bonannos."

Her words are echoes of the ones I said to Róise and now her retort comes back in my own voice. "We are all Cosa Nostra."

"Which makes it even less likely she's marrying you with good intentions." My mom will come around eventually.

She's a good person. Better than me. But the past holds on hard sometimes and clearly that moment is not now.

"Her intentions are to protect her younger cousin from having to be the sacrificial lamb."

"Marrying you is no sacrifice, *mio figlio*."

If I move Róise into a home where the matriarch distrusts her and despises her family it will be.

Which means Róise and I won't be living here after we are married.

CHAPTER 39: RÓISE

*S**till Monday*

Not wanting to take my bad mood out on my family, I turn down Kara's offer to go for an after dinner coffee and Fiona's offer to watch *All About Eve* with me for the dozenth time.

When *mamo* asks me to read to her while she does her cross stitch, I tell her I have a headache and need to get some fresh air.

My grandmother loves her audiobooks and she lets me read to her, using different character voices to practice getting into different characters quickly. But I'm sure it's a lot more fun for me than it is for her.

My extemporaneous reading, with my stops and starts and stumbles isn't the same as listening to a smoothly polished audiobook.

They're all being wonderful, but they don't deserve for the gray cloud hanging over my head to start raining on them.

I'm not just sad. I'm angry. At that stupid jerk, Boaz for blabbing my business to the whole class. At the dean for telling me to stay home for a few days while the board gets together to discuss *the problem I present*. At my professor for going to him in the first place.

And at Miceli damn De Luca, underboss from hell, who put the whole thing in motion with his extra vigilant bodyguards.

Out here, I can cry where no one can see. Tears are a weakness we're not supposed to give into. But I can't always control mine. Even Fiona is better at keeping the waterworks from starting.

She'll huddle in a ball of shivering anxiety and not shed a single tear.

It's not right, but even *mamo* ascribes to the axiom, *mob princesses don't cry*.

"What are you doing walking out here alone? I'm going to fucking kill Allessio." Miceli's voice interrupts my solitude.

Swiping roughly at my cheeks, I croak out, "Allessio and Zoey are off the clock. I don't need a security detail in my own backyard."

And what the heck is Miceli doing here?

"How often do you come out here alone like this? Do Kara and Fiona do it too? Does Kara let Fitz play out here without security?"

I spin around and glare at the source of one of the worst days of my life. "What's it to you? Contrary to what you think, Miceli, you are *not* king of the world. You're not even his little brother."

The underboss's brows draw together as he studies me. "What's wrong with you?"

"Something has to be wrong with me to ignore your texts for a day? Come on, how controlling are you?"

"You were crying. God-fucking-damn-it! I told that insensitive son-of-a-bitch to let me break the news to you."

"You knew I was going to get kicked out of school? How? The dean wouldn't call you." So far as anyone knows, I'm still just the girlfriend and that's hardly common knowledge among normal people.

And as far as I know, even Uncle Brogan doesn't know about my *temporary* suspension.

"You got kicked out of school? What the hell happened today?"

"What I told you would happen!" My fingers curl so tightly, my nails dig into the palms of my hands. "I told you," I say again, this time my voice filled with defeat.

He reaches for me and I rear back, unable to bear his touch right now.

Dropping his arm, his hand fists at his side. "Tell me what happened."

So, I tell him, ending with, "I'm on unofficial suspension until they decide what to *do about me.*"

"I will speak to your dean," Miceli says grimly.

"What? No." I shake my head in vehement denial. "That's all I need, for them to find out I'm not only the niece of a known mobster, but the fiancée of one as well."

"We keep a lower profile than the Irish. As far as your dean is concerned, I'm part of a powerful and *generous* multibillion-dollar family empire."

"You are not bribing the university with a donation to let me continue taking classes." Enough people are using me for gain, I'm not letting the dean be added to that list. "I've done nothing wrong. They have no right to do this."

"Your uncle won't allow you to pursue legal recourse," Miceli says with certainty.

I blow out an angry, frustrated breath. "I know."

I could pretend that I believe that since I'm an adult, I can do what I want. But I know that's not true. So does the underboss watching me so stoically.

"That doesn't mean I'm going to let the dean profit from treating me like crap." A minute ago, I felt helpless. Now, I don't. "And *he* doesn't know I won't sue. I'm an actor. I can be pretty convincing."

"Never make a threat you aren't willing to back up," Miceli says.

"Yeah, that might work in the mafia, but normal people make threats they don't plan to carry out all the time."

Miceli looks out over the dark water. Not like he's admiring the view, but like he's watching for something. *Looking* for something.

"If a sniper isn't going to shoot from a swaying boat in the middle of the day, he's sure not going to try at night," I point out.

Is there a reason Miceli is extra worried about someone trying to kill him?

"First, while shooting from a rocking boat might increase the difficulty of the shot, it wouldn't make it impossible. Second, it's not someone trying to kill you that I'm concerned about."

"Me? Why me? You're the target, not me." Of the fictitious sniper in the boat that is nowhere to be seen anywhere near us in the water.

"Divers could come out of the water and kidnap you, one of your cousins, or your nephew before anyone in the house even knows you are gone."

"First," I copy him. "There *are* perimeter guards. Second, when there's a risk to our security, we don't come back here."

"You are always at risk. Any of you would be leverage against Brogan. And now you are leverage against me." He says the last like that's an even bigger deal.

"You're ruining everything else in my life, do you have to ruin this too?" The back yard isn't just a safe space for Fiona.

All of us enjoy the relative freedom of being out here. Especially when the constraints of life in a mob family get too tight. Like today.

Besides, we're never really alone. Not even here. There are guards that patrol the perimeter of the estate and I know Ollie is somewhere in the trees watching over me.

Close enough to guard me, but far enough away to give me what privacy he can.

"How have I ruined your life, Róise?" Miceli's tone implies he thinks I'm being dramatic.

Again.

My feeling of helplessness in the face of my hijacked life boils over. "I wasn't going to be a mob wife. I was going to pick my husband, if I got married at all. I was going to have a normal life with friends that carry phones, not weapons. I was going to be an actor!"

Part of what hurts so much right now is the realization that even if I fight the dean and win about returning to college, I'll never be able to use my degree.

Not even if I divorce Miceli, which in my heart of hearts I know will never happen. Not if he keeps the promises he's made to me.

But even if I did, for the safety of the child I've agreed to have, I'll never be able to pursue a career on stage, or in Hollywood. Or anywhere else I will be in the public eye and risk putting my child (and Miceli) there too.

"Life changes for all of us." He doesn't look or sound dismissive. More pensive.

"Oh, yeah, how has it changed for you? According to you, you always expected to marry for the sake of the mafia."

He looks at me for a long, silent moment before going back to his vigilant observation of the dark bay waters. "Severu is making a bid for godfather when Don Caruso dies."

"I care about this why?"

"It's the reason we have to cement our alliance publicly right now."

"What difference does the title make? He's already a don."

"Like ancient Rome, the mafia has a *re*. A king. We call him godfather. He rules over the Cosa Nostra in the United States. Once he is elected by vote of all the dons, he is godfather until he dies."

Do syndicate men ever think they have enough power?

"What if he's a bad godfather?" I ask, my curiosity pushing aside some of my bad mood.

Miceli shrugs. "What if a king fucks up his country?"

"They get away with it," I say a little bitterly.

The Irish mob doesn't have the same kind of structure as the Italian mafia, but Uncle Brogan has no checks on his power.

He's the boss over the Shaughnessy family in New York and no one can challenge that. Not without bloodshed.

But Uncle Brogan's authority doesn't extend beyond our territory even if his influence does through alliances.

There is no King of the Irish Mob.

Miceli shrugs again. "Or they get assassinated."

"That's hardly a reliable check on his authority. Even good kings get assassinated."

And whether they were good depends on who wrote the history, right? That's almost never the general population who live under the tyranny of monarchy. People like me, whose lives get stolen by the powers that be.

Maybe I could be a history teacher and change that. You know, teach good little mafia girls and boys about the real history of *la famiglia*.

Shoving away the fanciful thought that is also silly because I don't *know* that history, I ask, "So, the godfather is the king. What does that make the dons? Princes?"

"If you are referring to Roman princes."

"Why do they have to be Roman? And please don't tell me it's because of Italian superiority."

"Roman princes ruled over their own fiefdoms."

"This sound like feudalism."

"You wouldn't be the first woman to say that the mafia is stuck in the Middle Ages," Miceli drawls sarcastically.

"Oh, joy. Every modern woman's dream is to end up married into a Medieval culture setting equality back centuries."

"It's not that bad, but our leadership structure *is* feudal."

"The dons rule over their own territories. Like my uncle."

"Yes."

"And the capos?"

"The *capo dei capi* operate under the authority of their don. They have a second-in-command and no one except the don outranks them."

"What about you? You're the underboss. And Big Sal is the *consigliere*."

"Your accent is improving."

"I'm learning Italian on Duo Lingo." I'm not living with a bunch of people who speak a language I don't understand.

"I am equal to the capos in rank, unless I am speaking on behalf of Sev. Then I carry the authority of his position."

"A prince's prince," I quip.

"In a way. If we go to war, as my brother's right arm, I also have the authority to conscript soldiers from the capos if I need them."

"It really is like a medieval kingdom."

"The capos and soldiers pay tithe to the organization from the businesses financed and built by it."

"You can't tell me that the De Lucas need tithes from their mafia."

"We don't," he agrees. "We put the money into an account used to support widows and children of our soldiers."

"You mean for the men who die for the mafia?" That's kind of cool.

Do we have something like that in the mob? I could ask Uncle Brogan, but would he tell me. I bet *mamo* knows though.

Miceli shrugs. "Or who die from a heart attack, or getting hit by a car."

"What? Really?" That's...more than I expect from a criminal organization.

"We take care of our own."

"Are all mafias like yours?"

Miceli shrugs again. Like it doesn't matter. Like the only thing that matters is how the Genovese do things.

For him it probably is.

CHAPTER 40: MICELI

Róise is calmer than when I first arrived.

That's going to change when I give her my news. There won't be any sex in the boathouse today. I'll be lucky if I leave without her trying to tase me.

She's so pissed about what happened at college today. When she finds out this is her last year, it won't be the dean in her crosshairs.

It will be me.

"I've been looking into your father's death." This is not what I came here to tell her, but maybe knowing I'm keeping my word about identifying her dad's killer will help sooth the blow to come.

"What about my mom's murderer? You vowed to kill him." She frowns at me accusingly.

Okay, we'll deal with that first. "The Bonanno soldier whose stray bullet robbed your mom of her life died of a heart attack while visiting her grave in remorse on the one-year anniversary of her death. He was twenty-nine."

"My dad?"

I nod. "In the week that followed your mother's shooting, while your grandfather was trying to negotiate peace, your father waged a one-man war, killing over two dozen Bonanno soldiers."

"Against my grandfather's orders?"

"The order to stop didn't come until after the Bonanno don sued for peace, offering concessions your grandfather wanted." The old man had been ruthless, willing to capitalize on his son's grief-stricken rage.

"But mom's killer wasn't dead yet."

"No. Your dad is a legend among the Bonanno Family. They still tell the story of how he kidnapped and tortured the soldier for three days."

"But he let him go?"

"With a promise of more pain to come and eventually a death the soldier would not see coming. The last year of his life, that soldier lived in constant fear of your father taking him again." Derry Shaughnessy's torture techniques came out of a playbook as effective as ours.

"Good." The satisfaction in the single word shows how much of her father's blood runs through my fiancée's veins. "And the Bonanno don didn't investigate a twenty-nine-year-old man having a heart attack on the grave of a woman he killed?"

"He wasn't willing to risk the truce he'd reached with the Shaughnessy Mob." The don should have offered his soldier over as restitution, but the mob boss didn't ask for that. "No one doubted that Derry Shaughnessy was responsible."

"Is that why they killed him?"

"The Bonanno don swore a blood oath to your grandfather that he had not ordered the hit."

"He could have been lying. A blood oath is only as trustworthy as the man offering it."

"He offered his own grandson in restitution if any proof could be found linking the Bonanno to Derry's death."

"What a horrible thing to do!" For a moment, she's the innocent twenty-year-old I met that night in Portland. "Even if he wasn't guilty, someone could have manufactured evidence to get rid of one of his heirs."

Okay, not so innocent. "It convinced your grandfather."

"He never said. He let us believe it was another flare up with the Bonanno Family."

"I don't know why he did that."

"He was devastated by my dad's death, nearly comatose with grief at losing his oldest son. But he was still the boss." She sighs with a world weariness that does not belong on my feisty wife-to-be. "He would rather we believed it was the wrong syndicate than admit he had no idea who had killed his son. I always assumed he didn't go to war with the Bonannos because of his own failing health."

"It was no secret that your grandfather had serious health issues at the end. Whoever killed your dad wasn't targeting your grandfather," I voice the only theory that makes sense. "They shot who they meant to."

"Because they didn't want my dad to become the next boss?" she asks, quickly drawing the same conclusion I did.

"Yes."

"But why? My dad's death wasn't going to weaken the mob. My uncle was ready to step into his shoes." A look of horror comes over her features. "You don't think it was Uncle Brogan?"

"No." But if it was, I will kill him slowly for all the grief his ambition caused my woman.

She shakes her head. "No. Even Uncle Brogan has to draw the line somewhere."

It's not a ringing endorsement of her uncle's familial loyalty, but I agree with her. I don't believe the older man's honor would allow him to order a hit on his brother.

"What if it *was* bad aim again?" She looks sick. "What if my grandfather took out the hit on himself so he would die a legend, not a sick old man?"

Unfortunately, from what I know of the deceased mob boss, it's not a farfetched theory.

"I'm not ruling anyone out. Including the Bonannos until I find the sniper who shot your father and make him tell me who ordered the hit."

Once I find her father's killer and dispatch him to hell, Róise will see that I can be trusted. That I'm not the enemy.

"It could be a her."

"Yes." Some of the deadliest snipers are women, but they are a tiny percentage of a small population.

"Dad was always there when I needed him." She hugs herself. "Until they took him away from me."

"Sev needs the alliance between us and your mob to go public."

Róise sighs. "Time to make the engagement official."

If only it was that easy. "Yes, and when we do, we will be announcing our upcoming wedding."

"Okay." She stares out over the water, but she's not looking for potential threats.

Brogan must have security measures against attacks from the waterfront that Róise doesn't know about. He would not allow his daughters and niece into the backyard without a full security team otherwise.

Even if he would, he would not risk his grandson and heir.

Nevertheless, until I know what they are and if improvements need to be made, Allessio is going to have to increase his team. There will be no time my fiancée is not guarded by my people, whether she is at home, or not.

"We will be getting married in September."

"That will make *mamo* happy. More than a year is plenty of time to plan a wedding. Even a traditional Irish one." The words are agreeable, but Róise's face is wearing the same troubled expression as when I arrived.

Her assessment shows a naivete toward wedding planning I have no intention of dispelling. She's still struggling with our upcoming marriage.

But mamma took two years to plan Giulia's wedding and lamented only having three months for Severu's more than once.

Even so, Maeve doesn't have the year her granddaughter believes she does. "Four months, but my mother will help with the planning."

"No. That's not right! The contract says June 30th of next year. I thought you were generously giving me an extra couple of months not trying to take away the little time of freedom I have left."

"It says *no later than June 30th*, but there is no language stating the wedding can't happen earlier."

Her glower would make a godfather proud. "Except your bride refusing to show up."

"This is necessary, Róise. We would not be pushing the date forward if it were not."

"But the engagement is enough." Her gaze fills with appeal, like she can't imagine anything worse than moving our wedding forward. "Once it's announced, everyone will know our alliance is familial."

"Engagements are broken all the time," I dismiss.

"And marriages end in divorce."

"Not as often in our world and no one outside the five of us know about that clause in our contract."

Not that she'll be exercising it. Dons do not divorce.

Not that I would ever have let my Aphrodite go as an underboss either.

But as a don? It is unthinkable.

She's lying to herself if she doesn't acknowledge that.

CHAPTER 41: RÓISE

*T*uesday

"Just to be clear, Dean Howell, you are saying it's okay for me to attend classes tomorrow?" I ask after his stammering apology over the phone.

"Yes! Yes. Definitely."

Okay, that's *definite*.

"What changed your mind?" I ask suspiciously.

"I didn't change my mind." Gaslighting, it's not just for politicians anymore. "I wanted to ensure your safety on campus."

Yeah, so not what he said yesterday. "And now you're sure I'm safe?"

"Yes, of course."

"What exactly is going to ensure it?" I push, not ready to let it go.

"Well...um...your security detail..."

"Has been with me for weeks."

"And well, your professors have been encouraged to curtail any gossip about you during class."

Huh. This has my almost fiancé's bloody thumbprint all over it.

Does he think getting me back into school for the last week of classes makes up for losing my senior year and my degree?

Not that we talked about that last night. But there's no way I'm attending classes in person as an underboss's wife. Catalina takes online classes, but I don't know how I can do my senior year that way.

I barely got any sleep last night, trying to figure out a way and I still don't have any answers.

But if Miceli donated a single penny to the school to make this phone call happen, I'm going to empty Pusheen's litter box onto the driver's seat of his McLaren Speedtail.

"Thanks for letting me know, Dean Howell."

"So, you'll be back tomorrow?"

This sounds more like threats than bribery, but even Miceli isn't going to threaten the dean with physical violence.

Is he?

"I'll be there." This might be my last week at college.

If it is, I'm going to make sure I get every minute out of it.

Wednesday

"Okay, spill. You grew up in the mob?" Carrie drops her plate with a BLT and fries onto the table and sits down in the booth across from me. "I thought you might be secret royalty, but the mob?"

"I can neither confirm or deny." Taking a bite of nachos, I watch for the others.

Traci is on her way over with her favorite Mediterranean salad, but Aleks is in line for a protein smoothie and Goodwin is waiting for her plate of Kung Pao Chicken.

"Come on." Carrie makes a gimme gesture with her hand. "Tell me something."

"In some circles, I'm considered a princess if that makes you feel better." I scarf down another chip loaded with cheese, taco meat and a slice of jalapeno.

Carrie's eyes round. "You mean mob princess is really a thing?"

"I'm not saying *I* have any syndicate connections, but it's a thing."

"Oh, girl. What the actual fuck?" Traci slides into the booth next to Carrie, stealing a fry from her plate. "Where were you yesterday?"

Carrie returns the favor, grabbing a cucumber slice from Traci's bowl.

"In light of the rumors circulating about me the dean thought I should stay home for a day." I'd thought indefinitely, but he'd personally called me late yesterday afternoon to apologize for the supposed misunderstanding.

"That douche-canoe!" Traci points her fork in the general direction of the administrative building.

Carrie's blonde head leans forward and she whispers, "Did your uncle threaten him?"

I roll my eyes. "Not likely. You know I wouldn't even be here if my dad hadn't set the tuition money aside for me."

Uncle Brogan has never attended a single one of my performances and my friends know it.

"What did I miss?" Aleks slides into the booth beside me.

He's been buffing up and I have to scoot over so as not to get squished by his broad shoulders.

"Nothing," I mutter.

"Our girl is a mob princess. She's connected." Carrie makes air-quotes when she says *connected*.

Goodwin puts her plate down before dragging a chair from a nearby table and positioning it at the end of the table. "Connected to what?"

"I never said that," I protest.

Traci wiggles her eyebrows. "The mob."

"Oh, that." Goodwin shrugs. "That's not new, right?"

I nearly spit out my bite of nachos. "What do you mean? You knew?"

"Well, sure. I mean, it makes sense you use a different last name here, but we've all met your cousins and grandmother. Maeve Shaughnessy was married to the mob boss back in the day."

Tracy picks the perfect bite of her salad, balancing lettuce, feta, a single olive slice and a bit of cucumber on her fork. "How do you know all this?"

"My dad got his start with backing from Fergal Shaughnessy."

Goodwin is a legacy. Her dad's famous for his smooth baritone and has two platinum albums. Her great-aunt made it big in British theater. Goodwin is a good singer too, but she prefers stage direction.

"Just because my grandfather bankrolled your dad starting his career doesn't make him a mobster."

"You said you could neither confirm, nor deny," Carrie says.

Traci's dark red faux-hawk bobs in vehement agreement. "That's practically an admission."

"Correct." Aleks sucks at the straw in his protein shake. "Your family convinced the college administration to let you come back?"

"Hey...you know about the dean suspending her? Why didn't you tell us?" Traci demands.

Goodwin stirs rice into her Kung Pao Chicken. "Of course he knew, his boyfriend has work study in the dean's office."

"Why didn't you say?" Carrie asks.

Aleks pushes his empty smoothie cup away. "I was going to tell you in Script Analysis, but she was back."

"Fair," Traci says.

Goodwin bumps Aleks's shoulder. "You're forgiven, but I'm not sure what for."

Carrie laughs and then explains.

Goodwin shakes her head. "What a tool."

I'm not sure if she's talking about Boaz or the dean.

"I think we should put a steaming pile of dog shit in the dean's car, though." Traci munches another one of Carrie's fries.

It's so close to my plan for Miceli if he paid off the college to let me return, I raise my fist for a bump. "Great minds."

"Right on," Traci bumps my fist.

"The fuck was he thinking?" Aleks demands.

Carrie's face forms a rare frown. "Can you believe Boaz?"

"You should get one of your uncle's friends to give him a beat down," Goodwin mumbles around a bite of Chinese food.

"Unnecessary," Aleks says complacently.

Alarmed, I ask, "What did you do?"

"Yeah, what did you do, Aleks ?" Traci asks with relish.

Aleks shrugs. "He'll think twice about messing with one of us. That's all I'm saying."

"He's in my Stage Management and Direction class. Which he sucks at." Goodwin looks around the table, like she can't find something and I put the extra bottle of water I bought in front of her.

She smiles. "Thanks. Anyway, Boaz left in the middle of class, moaning and clutching his stomach. I thought he ate something bad for breakfast."

"Oh, you put an emetic in his protein smoothie, didn't you?" Traci grins.

Boaz works out at the same time as Aleks on Tuesday and Thursdays. He's always trying to beat Aleks's reps, but yeah, good luck with that. Aleks is a beast.

"He made Rosy miss a day of classes. Only fair he missed one too."

I've got great friends. Knowing they'll do their senior year without me makes me want to cry.

"You guys, promise we'll always be friends , no matter where we end up," I say impulsively.

"Promise, " Traci says.

Aleks nods once . "'Course ."

"You bet." Carrie says.

Goodwin salutes me with her bottle of water. "Always."

Can underboss's wives have friends in the theater?

This one will, I promise myself.

CHAPTER 42: RÓISE

I don't bother to knock on Uncle Brogan's office door this time. I'm a little surprised when the knob turns easily in my hand.

That should mean he's not in a meeting at least. Well, not a meeting in person anyway. He's on the phone when I come in.

Looking up Uncle Brogan glares when he sees me. The look I give him back is not friendly.

I'm so done with being treated like what I want doesn't matter. He made a promise to me and he's going to keep it.

I am not quitting school to marry Miceli. I don't care if I use my degree, or not. I am getting it. This is my last connection with my parents, with the life *they* wanted for me.

They put the money in that account for my education, ensuring I got full, legal access when I turned eighteen. Uncle Brogan is not a trustee on the account. No one related to the mob is.

Along with the money, mom and dad left a letter telling me to get the education I wanted and to pursue my dreams. Whatever they were. A letter they wrote together before my mom died when I was ten.

Marrying a mafia underboss isn't my dream, but getting my degree is.

That marriage might put my other dreams out of reach, but not this one. Not unless I let it. And I won't.

Uncle Brogan puts his phone down on his desk. "In busy Róise. If you need to talk to me, I'll see you at dinner."

"This won't take long."

He makes an impatient gesture with his hand. "Go on, then."

"I'm not getting married in September."

"Not this again. The wedding is going to happen. You gave your word, Róise."

"To marry the underboss, but I didn't agree to quit college. In fact, I made finishing my degree a contingency of my agreement." I swallow, my throat tight.

"Things change. We all have to make concessions."

I don't roll my eyes. This is too serious. I don't ask what concessions he's making either. I'm not going to let him sidetrack me.

"If you don't keep your promise on this one, I have no reason to believe you'll live up to your word on the other two and therefore no reason to go through with the marriage at all."

After a mostly sleepless night figuring out what to say that might influence my uncle, I practiced what to say and how to say it in my room.

Pusheen was not impressed with my rehearsal and abandoned me over an hour ago to prowl through the house. She's probably visiting Fitz.

He's the only male who Pusheen deigns to acknowledge.

Uncle Brogan surges to his feet. "Now, listen here, young lady, I know what's best for you and for this family."

"Wrong. You know what's best for the mob and for your powerbase. If you want me to marry Miceli, then I finish school."

"You can do your senior year online like the don's wife."

Kara is getting an online degree too. But my cousin signed up for her online courses at NYU without telling either her husband or her father.

"I can't take an improv class online."

"Then take a different class."

Like it's that easy. "No. I need that class to graduate."

"I'm sure we can get the administration to find a different class for you."

"I'm not a child looking for a crayon you can fob off with another color. I'm finishing school." I'm not backing down on this.

Because what I said earlier is true. If I can't trust Uncle Brogan to keep his word on this, I can't trust him, or Miceli, about the other things.

Two years of birth control.

Fiona not being pushed into marriage for the sake of the mob.

If I can't be certain he'll keep his word about Fiona, what is the point of going through with the marriage at all? Much less having a child that will tie me to a mafia underboss for the rest of my life.

Ignore that little voice saying Miceli might be the point all on his own. I am.

"I have no problem announcing the engagement," I offer. "But there's no reason the marriage has to happen so soon."

Uncle Brogan narrows his eyes thoughtfully. "I would have thought the engagement would suffice as well, but Severu De Luca is adamant."

That's what Miceli said. And I don't care.

"Then you be adamant right back." I can't believe I'm saying this to my uncle. "What is more important to you? Keeping the mafia don happy or keeping your word as a mob boss?"

That night in Portland was supposed to be my last good thing for me, but it turned out to be a prelude to my future. I'm not giving up the last thing that is mine.

The one thing I'm sure my parents would be proud of me for doing.

CHAPTER 43: MICELI

Thursday

Salvatore brings his kidnapped waitress to the family dinner. As a deterrent against Catalina's matchmaking, it's pretty effective. Especially with the way the two of them keep sneaking heated looks at each other.

Catalina doesn't throw her sister in my cousin's path once before we leave to meet in Sev's office.

Uncle Sal follows his son into the room and I bring up the rear.

My brother leans against the front of his desk. "Everything still going smoothly with the bar properties?"

Salvatore's tone is filled with smug satisfaction when he gives the breakdown to my brother. He deserves that smugness. One of the bars is in Manhattan and allowing any other mafia to own it would put us in a weaker position.

The two that are in other boroughs will give my brother leverage in his bid for godfather.

"No interference from Stellar Holdings?" Sev asks.

Henry Caruso and his cousin in the Lombardi Mafia up in Boston tried to buy the properties out from under us. It didn't work, but Henry is going to have to be dealt with sooner than later.

He cannot be the next Lucchese don, no matter what his uncle wants.

Salvatore reassures Sev that the man who sold the bars won't be a problem and therefore neither will Henry Caruso or his Lombardi cousin.

I ask about the jammer blocking texts and calls from them to the man who owned the bars.

Juniper tried to double cross us to get more money for the properties from the Lombardis, but we don't play fair.

Now, the bars are in Salvatore's name. Sev has his leverage and we have two additional properties outside Manhattan and one in it for laundering money.

Salvatore says, "Now that the paperwork is filed it is set to self-delete once he sets his device to charge."

"I'm surprised Matthew hasn't sent people to check on him." I would in his place.

"No reason to. The GPS on the woman's phone still registers at the house and the false GPS signal Domenico's people set up for Juniper's phone does too."

Which is smart on Salvatore's part, but not an excuse for Lombard's inaction. "It's still sloppy."

My cousin's expression says he agrees.

"Lorenzo called me." Sev looks at Salvatore and not me when he says this.

But I'm the one overseeing the investigation into that rat.

Our cousin crosses his arms, looking belligerent.

"He says you were very disrespectful when he came to Amuni," Uncle Sal throws his oar into the water.

Family dynamic in the mafia is always a juggling act. Uncle Sal is the consigliere. His son is a capo. They're equals in terms of rank, but they are also father and son.

It was easier for me and Sev because our father was the don. When we got made we each vowed to submit to his authority as our don.

Salvatore and Uncle Sal exchange some words.

"He's lucky I did not kill him. If he tries to touch her again, I will slit his throat," my cousin finally says, anger making his voice rough.

I don't even try to hold back my cynical laugh. "It's Severu all over again. No woman is going to turn me into a Neanderthal like you two."

Sev isn't impressed. "Good luck with that. You share my DNA."

"But not your obsession for your wife." My brother's feelings for Catalina have nothing to do with DNA.

We are both our father's sons.

"If you did, I would have to kill you," he replies in a conversational tone that I do not mistake for one that lacks conviction.

Sev will kill any man who touches his wife, including me.

Still, my lips twist wryly. "You know what I mean, brother. I will never obsess over a woman like you do Catalina."

Not even a certain Irish mob princess whose pussy tastes like the honey of the gods.

"*Never* is a dangerous word you could end up eating." Severu gives me a big-brother look.

A don would not concern himself with such trivial things. But my brother? Yes.

I shake my head though.

I'm not worried. I'm marrying for the sake of the mafia, not for my own sake. That's no recipe for love.

Even if I thought I was capable of feeling that emotion. Lust is another matter.

Salvatore raises his hand palm out toward his dad. "Do not tell me you would do any differently if he tried to maul mamma."

"Oh, how the mighty have fallen," I say with mocking pity.

Uncle Sal is not amused. "Are you saying this nobody, this outsider you have known less than two weeks, is your woman? Monica worked for you for six months before you were serious enough about her to ask Enzo's permission to tell her the truth about your role in *la famiglia*."

We all wait in silence for my cousin's response. Pretty sure my uncle is expecting a different one than me though. I don't know what Sev thinks.

"She is mine." Salvatore's words don't surprise me.

But I'm the only one.

Sev gives our cousin a narrow eyed stare. "Are you saying you are not open to being the husband in the alliance deal with Shaughnessy?"

What the fuck?

No one is marrying Róise Shaughnessy but me. It's my bloody fingerprint next to hers on that contract.

"I'm the sacrificial lamb in that scenario," I remind my brother in a hard voice. "The deal is done."

The look Sev gives me is not friendly. "You two fight like cats and dogs. Maybe Salvatore won't piss her off so easily."

What the fuck is he talking about? Róise was disappointed when I told her about moving the wedding forward, but she wasn't pissed off. Her fury was reserved for her dean.

Who will not make the mistake of believing he can disrespect her again.

"She is my fiancée." My hands curl into fists and I have to slam a lid on the desire to drive both into my brother's smug face.

"I am not marrying her," Salvatore inserts with utter conviction.

The blunt words, if not the sentiment, surprise me. My brother could see that kind of adamant refusal as disloyalty.

Not that he does. The surprise on the *stronzo del cazzo's* face morphs to satisfaction almost instantly. He nods at my cousin in silent permission to pursue Bianca.

The look he gives me doesn't have any of that approval. "Figure your shit out with Róise then. This marriage is supposed to cement an alliance, not start a war."

Salvatore leaves. No doubt to go find his new obsession.

"Severu—" Uncle Sal starts to say.

My brother puts his hand up. "No, Uncle Sal. I don't want to hear it. If you can't see the way Salvatore looks at Bianca, I can. She's good for him."

I have to agree. I see more of the cousin that I knew when we were younger than I have in two decades.

"Marrying her does nothing for *la famiglia*," Uncle Sal says.

"No, but it would do a lot for your son. He's a good, loyal man. He deserves to be happy. And you know Aunt Ilaria agrees with me."

Uncle Sal lets out a long-suffering sigh. "My wife sometimes allows sentiment to overcome good sense."

"I'll be sure and tell her you said so," I say with a shark's grin.

Uncle Sal just rolls his eyes. "You can't get me in any more trouble than I am already. I haven't been friendly to my son's girlfriend and according to my wife, that is equal to a cardinal sin."

I'm not surprised Aunt Ilaria has taken such a shine to Bianca Gemelli. Salvatore's housekeeper is my aunt's best friend and Rosa has adopted Bianca right under her protective wing.

I wait for our uncle to leave before rounding on Sev. "What the hell was that?"

Without answering, Sev walks over to his drinks cabinet and pulls out the whiskey. Pouring himself a glass, he asks with a raised eyebrow if I want one too.

I jerk my head in the affirmative.

After handing me my glass and taking a sip of his own whiskey, he looks me straight in the eye. "We have to present a united, *strong* front in the face of Henry's bid for power."

"Agreed." It's more imperative now than ever to go public with our mob alliance.

Sev frowns. "Brogan called me earlier. Róise refuses to move up the wedding date."

"She didn't say anything about..." I let my voice trail off because that's not true.

Okay, yeah. She said she wasn't going to agree to it. But only once. And she didn't bring it up again.

I left Long Island believing Róise was onboard with the new plan.

Or not really caring either way?

Because I assumed having Brogan's agreement was what really mattered. I'd gone to tell her myself about the change out of courtesy, not because I was looking for her approval.

"*Cazzo,*" I mutter.

Sev just looks at me.

"She was mad at the dean, and I fixed that problem." Believing I was doing her a favor.

Managgia la miseria.

Tripped up by my own arrogance. Because I didn't fucking ask. Róise said she wasn't going to walk down the aisle and I dismissed that as her go to reaction.

Stubborn refusal.

My brother throws back the rest of his whiskey. "Apparently she was mad at you."

"You think?"

"Yep."

"That was rhetorical," I say sourly.

"Brogan said that she came to him asking for a different groom last Friday." My brother drops this bomb without inflection.

"No fucking way."

"I thought you smoothed things over after her birthday." I hate the look of disappointment in my brother's eyes.

I don't let my family down. Ever.

"They were. We had hella good sex and she loved the birthday presents I gave her." Why would she ask her uncle for a different groom?

It makes no sense.

"Sex doesn't fix everything."

"Did you get that wisdom from Catalina or *Cosmo*?"

"My wife has mentioned it a time, or two."

Or ten, I bet. "Listen, Sev, Róise and I texted back and forth all week. She wasn't looking to get out of our contract."

"She's doesn't want to break the contract."

"Just marry some other guy. That will happen over my dead body," I warn my brother.

It looks like my secret fiancée and I need to have a talk.

~ ~ ~

When I see the three empty spots at the dining room table, I decide to mess with my cousin. Smiling at my aunt, I sit in one of the empty chairs near her clearly meant for the couple.

Pretending not to hear my aunt's hissed, "That's Salvatore's chair," I pour myself a glass of wine from one of the decanters in the center of the table.

I haven't even taken a sip when my cousin pulls out the chair next to me for Bianca.

"Where is Nerissa?" she asks.

My aunt gives me a disapproving frown. "She's working tonight." Her tone is nothing but sweet for the pretty redhead though.

I have to admit Salvatore has good taste, but green eyes are the only ones I want to look into this close up. Doesn't matter. Messing with my cousin is the goal, not his girlfriend.

I'm ready for the punch when it comes so I don't flinch, but *cazzo*, my cousin's punch carries some power.

"Move, Miceli, this is my seat," he growls like some damn Neanderthal.

I go to take a sip of my wine. "Catalina didn't assign seats tonight."

Salvatore grabs the glass and marches around the table. He's lucky the stem on my wineglass doesn't break when he slams it down on the table. "I'm assigning them. Move your ass."

Aunt Ilaria gasps. "Salvatore, you cannot speak to the don's underboss that way."

"That's rich coming from you." I'm not sure who the glare is for, but I get that I'm not the only one on Salvatore's list right now.

I wonder what Aunt Ilaria did to earn his ire. It wasn't criticizing Bianca. My aunt likes the enigmatic younger woman too much.

Catalina smiles at me. She's used to my warped humor. "Miceli, come and sit by me. I want you here when me and Severu make our announcement."

Ah, they are finally going to share their news. Not that I'm supposed to know what it is, but hello? We live in the same damn space. What else is going to cause her to turn up her nose and go green over her favorite foods?

"Have you got a bun in the oven, *cara?*" I ask, sitting beside her.

"Don't call my wife endearments," Sev orders. Then both joy and utter determination take over the irritation in his face. "We're expecting the next little De Luca around Christmas."

I know what that determination is about. Sev is going to make sure his family is safe if he has to burn down hell to do it. Becoming godfather and making powerful alliances are a given.

I pull my sister-in-law into a tight hug. "Congratulations. The baby couldn't ask for a better mom."

Then I stand up and grab my brother. "I'm happy for you brother. You have my word that I will lay down my life for your child."

Sev gives a jerky nod of acknowledgement to my vow.

He insists we all drink sparkling juice rather than champagne so Catalina can share completely in the toast.

My brother, the scariest don in New York is a sentimental sap for this woman.

There's nothing sappy about him when we learn Don Caruso has had another stroke. Mamma's lunch with the godfather isn't going to happen.

The margins in our timeline for our plans just disappeared too. The next weeks are going to be crazy busy and fraught with danger.

"Send out a message," he orders me. "Security is on yellow alert for the foreseeable future."

I nod and start typing out a text that will go to all the capos and their seconds. Then I start making calls. Just like Salvatore.

We have people to put in place and mafia leaders to sway toward Severu for godfather.

CHAPTER 44: RÓISE

Trailed by my security detail, Traci and I walk through the Quad after a special guest lecture. None of the others are attending the Saturday bonus series on obscure plays but we geek out over the same things.

We discuss the similarities and differences in comedic timing between now and when Bartholomew Fair was written in the seventeenth century as we walk, reaching the parking area before we know it.

"Who's that?" Traci asks, pointing to a guy leaning against a sleek, black motorcycle . "It looks like he's watching us."

A guy? More like *the* guy. "Uh, that's Miceli."

"Miceli who? Is this a date?" she asks eagerly.

A date? Probably not. Not with that forbidding expression giving the underboss's features a demonic air.

Shoot. I knew Uncle Brogan would tell on me to the De Lucas eventually, but I expected him to try to change my mind at least once more before he did it.

"He's uh..." What do I say?

If I pretend he's just a friend, when the engagement is announced, Traci will think I lied to her.

Traci's eyes narrow distrustfully. "He looks scary intense."

"He's my boyfriend," I blurt out.

And I'm not scared. Those goosebumps are because of the chilly spring air. I should have worn a thicker jacket.

Traci stops and drags me to a halt with her. "You have a boyfriend? Since when?"

"We've been together since February." Miceli's voice sends more not-scared shivers through me.

"What's wrong with you that she's hidden you from her friends?" Traci is always blunt.

Even with mafia underbosses, I guess. Not that she knows what Miceli is, and I don't plan on telling her.

Wearing head-to-toe black leather and scuffed boots, with a dark five o'clock shadow, he looks more like a biker than a billionaire mafia under-boss.

"I asked her to. Our families didn't want the media getting hold of the story before we were ready."

Traci gasps. "You're in the mob too?"

"Traci!" I yelp.

Jayzuz, Mary and Joseph. All we need now is for Miceli to decide my friends are a security risk.

"Worse than that, I'm the COO of Oscuro Enterprises." He winks at Traci.

I stifle the groan that wants out. "What are you doing here?"

"Taking you home. Get on."

"That?" It's not my finest moment.

But I've never ridden on a motorcycle. Just another one of the things for-bidden to a mob princess. I doubt mafia princesses get any more freedom than me and my cousins though. So, this is a calculated move on Miceli's part.

He's already figured out how much I crave things forbidden.

I want to ride on the back of that motorcycle so much my teeth ache. Even if it means putting my arms around Miceli's strong torso.

Maybe even more so because of that little detail.

How many chances will I get to ride it?

I doubt an underboss's wife is encouraged to do something so carefree.

"Here." He holds up a soft pink leather jacket and I slide my arms into it without hesitation.

It fits perfectly, even when it's zipped.

"Have fun!" Traci says as a classic Mustang rumbles into the parking lot. "That's my ride."

We hug.

"See you Monday," she says.

"Stay out of trouble," I yell as she walks away.

But I don't think my friend is the one who needs that warning.

The black helmet fits just as perfectly as the leather jacket. Either he got it for me or the other women he's given rides to have a head the same size as mine.

I don't like the thought, but I ask him about it anyway. "How many women have you had on the back of this bike?"

"None." He puts on his own helmet, dropping the visor and becoming a mysterious stranger.

No one would recognize him now, except maybe me. I know the shape and muscular contours of his body intimately.

Like a lot of other women.

But none of them are going to marry him, are they?

Even knowing exactly who he is and what he is to me, something deep inside gives a shudder of atavistic fear acknowledging that this man is dangerous.

He mounts the bike and puts his hand out to help me climb on behind him. My inner thighs grip his hips and I'm really glad I'm wearing jeans today.

With a grip on both of my thighs, he yanks me forward until I'm pressed indecently close to him. I don't try to scoot back, but lean forward and wrap my arms tightly around his middle.

"Good girl."

The shivers that go through me when he says those two words have nothing to do with fear.

The bike engine purrs to life and Miceli takes off, wind whooshing past us at even the sedate pace of the parking lot. The security detail pulls out behind us and I'll eat Fitz's Play-Doh if Miceli is sticking to the speed limit.

I figure out pretty fast that he's not taking me straight home when he takes the turn toward Brooklyn instead of back through Nassau County.

The wind whips around us now and I'm glad for both my jacket and helmet. The deep purr of the bike's engine and the hum between my legs causes a feeling I do not expect.

How am I getting turned on right now?

OK, yeah that might be a dumb question. This man is my sexual kryptonite. But who knew that riding behind him on the back of a motorcycle would be so erotic?

My vaginal walls clamp and wetness gushes into my panties. And my nipples? They are so freaking hard, they ache. I hug him tighter, not caring if he realizes it's not to stay on.

The one thing between us that doesn't feel wrong, that doesn't feel like it's about the mafia or the mob, is the way our bodies react to each other.

Sex. Really good, out of this world sex.

CHAPTER 45: RÓISE

We slow down only a little to cross the Brooklyn Bridge and a little more when we enter Lower Manhattan.

Two turns on the surface streets and I'm confused, pretty sure that neither the Oscuro Building nor the De Luca's family home are this way.

Where is he taking me?

Fifteen minutes later, we pull up in front of a building I've never been to. Not that I spend a lot of time in the City, but I know where I've been and this isn't it.

The shiny glass exterior isn't anything like the Art Deco façade on the building where the De Luca's family home takes up the top two floors and rooftop. It doesn't tower nearly as high as the Oscuro building either.

Only when we park in the underground garage, do I realize our security details aren't with us.

I pull off my helmet. "Where are the bodyguards?"

"They stopped following us as soon as we crossed the bridge." Miceli shoves the fingerless leather gloves he'd been wearing into the helmet and leaves it on the seat.

I let him take mine and put it beside the other one. "I didn't notice."

Ollie is probably calling my uncle right now to tell him about Miceli dismissing the team. Not that it will do my bodyguard any good. If I've learned anything about Miceli, it's that he does what he wants.

The parking bay we are in is cut off from the rest of the garage by cement walls and a garage door that is lowering back into place. Miceli taps something on his phone and a red light above the door starts to blink.

This is a serious level of security. Whoever we're going to see must be someone important in the mafia.

Is he taking me to meet the godfather?

No. Not dressed like this.

The Italian mafia is way more formal about stuff like that than the Irish mob, or so my uncle insists. Uncle Brogan isn't exactly casual though.

Anyway, I don't know why we're here. I don't know what we're doing. What I do know is that if I ask, Miceli probably won't tell me. So, I'm not giving him the satisfaction.

"You told me you were taking me home." That's not a question. It's an observation.

I follow him toward the far wall.

"I will. After."

After what? Sex? Even though it makes no sense he's brought me to this high-security, undisclosed location (How James Bond does that sound?) for that, my thighs press together in hopeful anticipation.

My ovaries scream yes, yes, yes! But my brain is all, no, no, no. Do not let Miceli De Luca sex you up until you'll agree to anything he asks.

It's too real a possibility with this man.

Miceli presses something on the wall and it slides back to reveal a stainless steal elevator door. He steps up to a biometric eye scanner and lets it do its thing.

The doors open revealing a small elevator with enough room for maybe six people. This building has at least ten floors. No way is this elevator adequate. There are no floor designations, just another biometric scanner, confirming the suspicion formed when I saw the size.

It's a private elevator.

To where though?

Miceli's hand settles on my lower back and he presses slightly so I step onto the elevator. The ride is short, but with no stops that could mean we're on the top floor or the second.

I'm guessing the top. The De Luca's are penthouse kind of people. I'm sure their friends and associates are too.

The door slides open with a whoosh directly into a large, open space.

The scent of linseed oil and turpentine teases my senses. Lights come on, and a second later, the soft whir of an invisible fan fills the air around us.

There's enough light from the floor to ceiling windows, the extra illumination isn't really necessary but maybe the owner likes really brightly lit spaces?

Unframed paintings hang gallery style on the wall to the left.

Is this some kind of private art gallery?

No. Not a gallery, a painter's studio.

Empty canvases stand, stacked against the wall on the bare wood floor. To the right, there's a kitchen with butcher block countertops.

Instead of dishes on the open shelves, there are jars smeared with paint, some filled with paint brushes. On this side of the island there are two art supply cabinets with lots of wide shallow drawers tucked under the breakfast bar.

Devoid of couches or chairs, there is only an artist stool and three easels. All sit on top of paint splotched drop cloths and have other, smaller cloths covering the canvases sitting on them.

We are standing in a private studio for an individual who does not expect to entertain.

"Who are we here to see?" I ask.

Miceli looks at me for a long silent moment. "Not a who. A what. This is my studio."

To stunned to speak, I stare back at him, my mouth hanging ajar. Attractive? I doubt it. But seriously?

The underboss has a studio? He's an artist?

"My father brought me here the first time when I was ten."

"That was kind of him." Surprisingly so for a ruthless don like his dad. "I mean, if you're an artist."

I'm still having trouble wrapping my mind around the idea that my underboss fiancé...*almost* fiancé...is an artist.

"I started drawing before I learned to read. My father trained me to only draw on paper. Eventually." Miceli shakes his head, like he's dispelling an unpleasant memory. "He couldn't get me to stop sketching all together though."

"Why would he want to?"

"To protect me."

From what? The drawing police? "I don't understand."

"When I was ten, he realized two things about me." Miceli stops talking, lost in his memories?

Is he going to make me ask what they are. Well, I will. I don't mind being nosy. "Two things?"

This time my underboss shakes his whole upper body and then nods. "First, I'm talented."

There's no arrogance in his voice. It's not smug like it usually is when he's right about something. It's just matter fact, maybe a little sad.

Two questions fight for supremacy in my brain. The first, can I see? The second, what was the second thing?

I decide to find out what that is first. "So, what else did he discover about you?"

"I have a weakness that could be exploited if anyone else found out about it. As much as he wished I didn't have it, my father understood the obsession."

"He did?" The studio says *yes*, but Miceli's belief his painting is a weakness says *no*.

"This was my father's space before it became mine. We shared it until his death."

I look around me. Having a hard time picturing the merciless don I heard about while I was growing up as an artist. And maybe that's the point. The reason both he and Miceli felt the need to hide that side of themselves.

Sensitivity is not considered a strength for a made man, especially one in a position of leadership. Having an artist's soul? Also, not a benefit.

Is my heart cracking right down the center at the thought of Miceli hiding this part of himself behind the extreme security this place has? Yes.

"Not even my mother knows about this place." Miceli looks at me like he's willing me to understand the silent message in his gaze.

I don't. What is he trying to tell me? Why does it matter that he hasn't told anyone else in his family?

Then the truth crashes down on me like a falling brick. His dad never told his mom. Not about himself or their son. *But Miceli is telling me.* I'm in on the secret.

The walls erected around my heart against this man are shuddering from the direct hits they're taking.

"Why is being an artist so bad you have to hide it even from your mom and siblings?"

"It's an obsession. I cannot stop drawing. Or painting. Neither could my father. Anything with that strong of a hold on you is a weakness."

Hearing those words is painful because isn't love like an obsession?

Even if my heart falls beneath the onslaught of this man, his heart will always remain aloof.

He has one obsession, he'll never let himself have another.

"I don't see how an enemy could exploit your need to create. It's not like it's going to stop you from doing what you have to do to further the interests of your mafia."

I should know. I'm one of those things he has to do.

"People believe artists are sentimental. Emotional. That they are more susceptible to allowing their emotions to control them."

"There is no way anyone would ever believe that of you," I assure him.

"Maybe. Maybe not. But I am taking no chances. I am the underboss."

"Ares, the God of war. You are your brother's right arm. The one that holds the weapon." But that night in Portland, Ares was my lover.

Because Ares and Miceli *are* the same guy. Does he realize that?

"Just like my father, my brother is capable of doing whatever he has to keep our enemies under us. But until now it has been my job to do that for him." He pauses and then adds, "In most cases."

I wonder what those exceptions are. Will Miceli ever trust me enough to tell me? The trust he's showing tonight blows me away.

Is his trust and lust and commitment enough when I feel my heart filling with that obsession we all know is love?

Something else he said snags my attention. "What do you mean until now?"

After almost a minute of silence, during which he stares at me with every bit of mesmerizing intensity his dark eyes are capable of, something shifts in his gaze like he's made a decision.

My breath is stuck in my chest while I wait for him to act on it.

"There is a reason the marriage has to happen now," he says.

Ugh. That's what he said before. Nothing new there. The anticipation buoying me up pops like a birthday balloon filled with too much helium.

Did he bring me here and tell me his secret to soften me up?

It's not going to work. Not about this.

"I am not giving up my education. I do not care if I get to use it," I inform him when he opens his mouth to say something else. "You all made that promise."

Him, the don, and my uncle. My dad made the same one years ago and even dead, he did his best to keep it. I'm not budging.

"I signed that contract contingent on me finishing my degree. How do I trust any of you to keep your word if you break it about this?"

CHAPTER 46: MICELI

Róise's words hit me with the power of a blow from my brother's closed fist.

I'm showing her my trust in an attempt to gain hers without acknowledging the one thing I have to do for her to consider me trustworthy.

Keep the fucking vows I make to her.

Neither Sev, nor I, questioned my future wife quitting school. To us, it was a given. A necessary sacrifice for the good of our family. After all, what does she need with a Fine Arts degree she can't use?

But it's not about the practical use of her degree, is it? It's about my fiancée's ability to trust my word when I give it.

Cazzo. There is only one reply I can give and maintain my honor.

"Then you finish your degree." Even if it means sending a dozen security guards with her every day.

"How is that going to work?"

I like the question because she's not assuming it's going to be easy. I don't like it because of the distrust I see in her eyes when she asks. Like she doesn't believe I'll follow through.

Why should she? I almost broke my promise to her already. I don't apologize because what's the point of *I'm sorry*?

It's just words. Actions speak the language that can be believed.

"Are there any courses you can take online?" I start a mental list of what needs to be in place before she returns to college in the fall.

"Uncle Brogan just assumed that if I was going to go to school after we married, I could take all of my classes online." Her pretty lips twist in a grimace. "It doesn't work that way with my degree."

Controlling the urge to grab her and fuck her senseless that's been riding me tighter than her body against my back on the way here, I ask, "Are you saying there aren't any?"

"No. There are two. "

She's looked into it. Good. She's not unreasonable. I knew that the day she put her bloody thumbprint next to mine on the alliance contract.

For whatever reason, she wants to get a degree for a career she can never have. But she's willing to figure out how to make that happen within the framework of our world.

More importantly Róise wants assurance that I will keep my word to her.

I will in every way but one.

She's not divorcing me. Ever.

But that's not something we're going to discuss right now. Because in reality, it will never be an issue and letting a hypothetical derail her trust in me would be stupid.

Which I am not.

This woman is fiercely loyal to her family, her love for them so deep, she's sacrificing her own freedom for the sake of her younger cousin.

No way is she ever going to relegate herself to the role of half-time parent.

I know it and one day she will allow herself to know it too. Considering how stubborn she is, that will be sometime after the birth of our third child.

Right now, she needs the idea of divorce to not feel trapped by the marriage that will be permanent for both of us.

"If you can do any of your schoolwork, study groups, etc. away from campus, that needs to be arranged too."

"You mean like my senior project? That actually requires time in a developmental studio."

"I'll have one installed in our home."

"Uh, that's overkill for something I will never use again. But I'll find a studio to rent that will be easier to secure than a college campus."

"There's no such thing as overkill to keep you safe." If I were her uncle, there would be underwater security on the shoreline twenty-four, seven.

"You are only going to get worse about my security detail after we get married," she says morosely. "Aren't you?"

"Do you really need to ask?"

She shakes her head. "Yeah, no. Anyway, I'll ask my senior project group to meet at your place, but if they don't want to go into the City, we can find someplace on Long Island that meets your security requirements."

"It will be *our* place." For some reason, it's important she acknowledges that.

Her shrug is not the agreement I'm looking for.

"We'll make it work," I vow.

"By make it work, you mean..."

"You'll have a security detail of eight people if not twelve." Getting the college to accommodate that kind of entourage will require offering the bribe she's so opposed to.

Róise's mouth opens closes, opens again, and closes again with a snap. Finally, she burst out, "Why so many?"

"Because a don's wife has to be protected. You will become a target the minute our engagement is announced, but it will only get worse once I become don." She'll be vulnerable to attack in a way she never would as the wife of an underboss.

Róise goes through the sequence of opening her mouth and closing it several times again, shaking her head and nodding by turns in between.

"Don's wife?" she squeaks, a note of hysteria creeping into her voice.

"When my brother becomes godfather, I will become the Don of the Genovese."

"But I thought Don Caruso...that he was both the don and the godfather."

"He is. But Sev believes that a godfather needs to represent more than one family. As a don, even the godfather will have a preference for one family over another. "

"You can't tell me your brother won't always have a preference for the Genovese."

"We are his family, but his time and energy will be focused on the Cosa Nostra as a whole and not the Genovese Family."

"You'll be the don?" she asks as if she cannot believe the words.

"Yes."

She frowns, crossing her arms. "My uncle didn't say anything about this."

"That's because he does not know. No one knows. Except maybe Catalina." Sev doesn't keep secrets from his wife.

Róise's arms drop to her sides, her expression filling with confusion. "Why are you telling me?"

Good question. Since she already all but agreed to the earlier wedding if she got to finish school, I didn't have to tell her about what's going to happen and risk her revealing our plans to her uncle before we're ready.

"Remember when I said the trust starts somewhere" I look around the studio significantly and back to the woman I am going to marry. "This is where it starts for me."

"You trust me not to tell anyone, not even my cousins, about your studio *and* the future plans you and Don De Luca have."

"Yes." I want this woman to be my wife, not a glorified mistress with a ring on her finger.

I don't want love but I do want a partnership. For that to happen, I have to be able to trust her. And this is a good test to see if the loyalty she gives so fiercely to her family will extend to me.

"I still don't see why you're so adamant about moving the wedding forward. The engagement is as good as marriage to guarantee the blood alliance until I give birth to our first child. That won't be for at least almost three years after we get married."

We agreed that she could have two years of birth control after the marriage. My assumption she would be willing to chuck that requirement was as shortsighted as believing she'd quit college without protest.

Róise might be over ten years younger than me, but she's got a will of iron and a sense of fair play to match it.

"To solidify my place with *la famiglia* as their don, I need to show the stability of marriage and provide an heir." Otherwise, I risk one of the Genovese capos making a play to take my place.

It damn near happened to Sev and he was my father's chosen heir. Fucking Lorenzo Ricci. He won't be an issue very soon, but he's not the only man from my father's generation who doesn't want a boss twenty years younger than him.

"But—" Róise is back to looking at me like I'm the devil's minion.

"I am not going to fuck with your birth control," I promise her. "If you choose to stick to the terms of the contract, that's your decision. But your safety and mine will increase after you give birth to our first child."

I'm not going to sugarcoat it. She deserves the truth.

"But why? I don't understand how having a child will make you safer."

"Sev faced a lot of pushback when he became don, even after my father had made it clear he expected Sev to take his place one day. Only part of that pushback was the fact he was young. The rest came from the instability his lack of a wife and heir gave to the future of the Genovese Family."

"But he's not even forty! He has plenty of time to have children."

"The first one is on his way. My sister-in-law is pregnant." And the timing is excellent for Severu's bid for godfather.

If a don needs to show the stability of a family, a godfather even more so.

"You're seriously telling me the capos might not accept you as don if you're not married?"

"That is one fear, yes. But there is also the very real consideration that at the age of 33, if I do not have an hier soon, I will be unable to train him adequately to take over as don before my death."

"Sheesh, morbid much?" She turns from me and walks toward the kitchen, taking off her jacket as she goes.

When she reaches the island, she tosses her jacket on top and then hops up to sit with her legs dangling in front of my paint chests. "What if our child doesn't want to be a don? What if our first child is a girl? What if she *does* want to be dona?"

"I have already said that if our child chooses a different path, I will do my best to help them on it, and if our first child is a girl the same applies. If she's anywhere near as strong-willed as her mother, she'll convince the Genovese to accept her claim to the role when the time comes."

"Okay, let me get this straight." Róise leans back on her elbows, her stance fucking provocative. "The alliance is for Don De Luca to become the godfather? But the marriage happening now is to smooth the path for you to become don?"

"Yes."

"And if I agree to moving the wedding date forward, I will still finish my degree?"

"Yes."

"Okay. Can I see your art?" Her legs kick back and forth negligently, never quite hitting my paint chests with her heels.

Shrugging out of my own leather jacket, I prowl toward her. "Are you sure that's what you want right now? To see my art?"

"Why? Do you have something else in mind?"

"Stripping those jeans from your sexy legs and eating out that fine pussy."

Her pupils dilate with desire. "You promise I get to see the paintings after?"

"Yes." It's an easy promise to make.

When I brought her here, I knew that meant sharing my art with Róise.

Right now, there's something else I want to share with her. My hard dick.

CHAPTER 47: RÓISE

Miceli walks toward me with a gaze so intense, my core clenches. I've wanted him since I got on the back of that motorcycle. And right now, the only thing I can think of is having him.

When he reaches me, he yanks my tennis shoes off while I'm busy undoing my jeans. But he takes over and pulls those off too.

Goosebumps form along my thighs. From the climate controlled air? Or the desire crashing through me? Yeah, probably that.

Picking up my jacket, he creates a pillow for my head. "Lie back."

When he uses that tone, my insides turn to molten lava.

"No kiss even?" I tease though, not wanting to be too easy.

"I'm going to kiss you, *dolce fiore*. My mouth moving all over the delicious, plump lips on that hot pussy."

Hot is right. And wet. The crotch of my panties is soaked. Even I can smell how turned on I am. He's standing right there.

Of course, he smells it too.

Not that he seems to mind.

I lay back, my head tilted just enough I can see the absorbed expression on his face as he looks at me there. When I feel the smooth flat blade of his knife slide under the hem of my panties, more moisture gushes from my inner core.

Jayzuz, Mary and Joseph, why does this turn me on so much?

Smooth metal sliding across my skin and a whisper of sound before the fabric rends apart. That obsessive gaze unwavering, he drags the flat of his knife across my cotton covered mons to my other hip.

With a twist of his wrist, he does the same thing on that side of my panties.

Then he bunches up the front panel of cotton in his fist, and pulls upward, dragging it over my already swollen clit.

"If you're going to keep slicing up my panties, I'm going to run out." I croak.

"You think that's a deterrent? The thought of you walking around without panties makes my dick hard enough to drill rock." Hot air puffs over my excited flesh.

He's right there. His mouth is so close, and I want it.

When I'm with Miceli, I feel like the sexiest woman alive. This man, who has so much more experience than I do, wants me. His sweet flower. His good girl. Oh, man, do I love when he calls me that.

Not because of the contract. Not because of the alliance. The way his mouth devours my intimate flesh...that is 100%, pure desire.

I grab his hair and shove my hips upward wanting more of that mouth, more of that tongue. Every thought coalesces into one, the need to come.

Then he takes his mouth away and I cry out in dismay.

He looms over me, and his hand comes down in a sweeping arc, the blade of his knife pointed toward me.

I don't move. I know he will not hurt me. With a thunk, the knife is embedded in the wood above my head.

He guides my hand toward the hilt of the blade and wraps my fingers around it. "Take it. Hold it tight with both hands."

I do as he says, one hand wrapped around the other.

"Good girl."

The praise shivers through me.

"If you pull, it will come loose and if you aren't very careful, stopping your own momentum won't be an option before you cut me. So be a good girl and don't move."

"I could just let go."

"But you won't."

He's right. I won't. And if I forget and bring my hands down, that sharp knife could cut him. Because I lose my ability to think when he touches me.

This is more effective than any restraint he could put me in. I will never risk doing him harm.

How does he know that though?

Does he realize I'm falling in love with him?

Yes, I realize I'm already there. But self-delusion is still my friend.

His talented, hot mouth returns to the apex of my thighs and his tongue slides over my clitoris in one hard swipe. My thoughts scatter and I am once again a mass of nerve endings on the brink of bliss.

Big fingers invade my tight channel pushing, rubbing, and causing explosions of excitement along my nerve endings. While his mouth gives my labia and clit one filthy kiss after another, he drives my pleasure higher and higher.

Miceli slides his fingers in and out of me one slow glide at a time, my slick wetness squelching against his fingers.

The sound only adds to the intense sexual heat burning me from the inside out. He pulls his wet fingers out of my core, sliding his big middle finger down and pressing the tip against my tight sphincter.

Rubbing the natural lubricant of my own wetness around, he builds my nervous anticipation to a fever pitch before pressing his fingertip inside.

Ecstasy detonates with the power of an exploding rocket from the single, tiny invasion. I scream, my hands clutching the hilt of his knife so tightly it's going to leave imprints in my palms.

Miceli brings me down slowly but keeps me on the edge, never allowing my pleasure to dissipate completely. His fingertip wiggles and stretches my tight backdoor.

Then he stands, his lips and face covered in five o'clock shadow glistening with my essence. Only then do I realize he's still fully dressed except for his leather jacket.

A wave of arousal rolls through me. Because apparently I am that woman. The one who is turned on by knives sliding over my skin, being told what to do (during sex only, but that's pretty obvious, yeah?) and having my lover fully clothed while he pleasures my body.

Miceli licks my juices off his lips. "I want your ass my little love goddess."

Everything inside me goes taut. "You're too big."

"I'll get you ready."

He doesn't say anything else. Just waits for me. For my answer. His gaze challenges me and asks a question.

One I have to answer once and for all, or how do I walk down the aisle toward this man in September, or any time?

Do I trust him?

With my body? Absolutely.

With my heart? Absolutely not.

But he's not asking for my heart right now. He's wants my body in a very specific way. A way I would never have expected to desire too.

But I do. A lot. "Yes, okay, I want this."

Without hesitation, his finger pushes in past the first knuckle. The sensation is different. There's a stinging where my sensitive skin stretches around that finger. But it feels good too. More than good.

Amazing.

It's like that first time in Portland, but different. This time he knows I have never had sex like this before. Something in his expression says that matters to him. I don't know why. Not sure the why is important.

I want him in every physical way. I want his heart, but if I can never have that, I want to own every bit of his physical pleasure. Every memory he has of a sexual position. Of any kind of ecstasy.

I want that memory to be dominated by our times together.

Yes, I am possessive.

I guess I have more of my father's blood in me than even I realized. Because the thought of killing any woman stupid enough to touch this man doesn't sicken me. It fills me with satisfaction.

He shoves my shirt up over my torso and past my bra, exposing the cotton cups. Yes, I *am* wearing cotton. I didn't expect to see him tonight, did I?

I smile at him, taunting. "You can't cut it off like you did my underwear. I've got your knife."

His deep, rich laugh washes over me as suddenly another knife appears in his hand.

"I'm a mafia underboss, *mi dolce fiore*. The day I carry only one knife is the day I'm ready to die."

"There's that morbid streak again." The words come out in a half-breath as I pant with excitement.

He destroys my bra just like he did my underwear and all I am is turned on.

I lose track of time as he touches me everywhere. Playing with my nipples and then sucking on them before nipping at my breasts. Barely touching my clitoris, sliding his fingers over my vulva, but never giving me enough stimulation to draw another climax out of me.

I exist on the precipice of ultimate pleasure, but never go over.

He draws his finger out and wets it with more of my juices running like a river down my crack from my over stimulated lady bits. This time when he puts his finger inside me it's thicker. Bigger.

No, it's *two* fingers. He scissors them. Shards of pleasure mix with twinges of pain. But the pain only makes the pleasure bigger. I writhe against his hand, craving more.

I want this so much.

How does this feel so good?

What is he doing to me?

His eyes burn into me, his gaze possessive and predatory.

Oh...oh *fuck*... It's so tight. It's so much.

Now it's three fingers. Oh...I...oh...I cry out, the sound animalistic.

Miceli kisses me, shoving his tongue inside my mouth.

I suck on it, wanting more of him no matter how I get it. All of the pleasure. Those tiny sparks of pain morphing into something so big I don't know how I'm going to hold it inside of me.

It's too much.

It's not enough!

I can't get enough air. I don't care. I need more, but my body is trapped.

And then it all stops. His fingers pull out of me and he steps back.

I scream my frustration. "I was so close!" I yell.

"Not without me," he says darkly. "When you come this time, I will be inside your tight, virgin ass."

"Then put your dick in!" I don't want to talk about it.

I want to do it.

"Can't do that with my clothes on." He's laughing at me.

I glare back. "Unzip and pull him out."

But he doesn't. He starts with his shirt, undoing one button at a time.

Screw this! Planning to help him get out of his clothes, I let go of the knife. *I mean to let go of the knife*, but my fingers refuse to let go.

His admonishment to be his good girl and hold on rings through my fevered brain.

He sees my inner war and the smile he gives me sends atavistic chills down my spine. "Good girl."

"Say it in Italian," I order. Why? I don't know.

"Mi brava ragazza."

That's why. It sounds so much more intimate, like only I have ever been *his* good girl.

My thighs spread obscenely wide, I undulate my hips in invitation.

Eyes nearly black with lust, Miceli rips the rest of his clothes off.

He bends down but not to touch me. I hear a cabinet door opening. Then something else. My thoughts splinter as he rubs something smooth and viscous around my sphincter.

What is that? Over the scent of our combined arousal, I smell it. Linseed oil. He's coating me with it, rubbing it into my tender, stretched flesh.

Jayzuz, Mary, and Joseph! What is this man doing to me?

His fingers slide in and out of me with no impediment. My back channel is slick with the oil. Those three fingers stretch me again and I know his sex is going to stretch me even further.

And I want it.

Now. Now. Now.

But he's drawing it out, pushing my pleasure to a fever pitch. Again!

My head turns side to side on my makeshift pillow and my hands grip that freaking knife so tight.

Then he's there, the big, blunt tip pressing against my entrance. "You ready?"

"Yes!" I scream. "Please, fuck me now!"

CHAPTER 48: MICELI

There is that word.

Fuck.

When she says it, I know my innocent fiancée is ready for me to fill her with my cock.

When I took her virginity in Portland, I didn't know the gift she was giving me.

Tonight, I do.

Not every woman likes this, but *mi dolce fiore* does. She's panting for it.

If Róise doesn't come on my cock without me even touching her clitoris, I'll throw my favorite knife into a landfill.

Stretching her body, I pull her ass right to the edge of the island counter and arrange her legs so her feet are flat on my torso.

Then I grab her thighs and press against that oiled and stretched opening. "Push out."

She does and my head pops inside her. She screams and I stop.

If her glare were a weapon, I would be dead. "Do not stop," she says, enunciating each word. "Fuck me."

It's one order I am willing to obey. I thrust deep into her tight channel. So hot, it feels like I'm pushing into liquid fire.

Cazzo.

So fucking good. Who knew the sweetly innocent woman who wore cotton candy lip gloss to her 21st birthday would respond so perfectly to my darkest cravings?

Pulling back slowly, I know the sensation of my retreating cock will excite every one of numerous nerve endings along the tight passage. Her moans tell me she is enjoying this every bit as much as I am.

Her gorgeous green eyes are open, her pupils blown with pleasure. She stares at me as if she has to see me in order to hold her to reality.

I let her see in my eyes the truth we both know. She is mine. Fucking mine. From now until forever.

We signed it in blood.

Her moans grow more frequent, her cries, more desperate, and I increase my pace. Pistoning deep inside her with every forward thrust.

Her tits jiggle, the hard little points flushed with blood. Her knuckles are white around the handle of my knife. And suddenly I know what else I want.

I stop moving and pick up the knife I laid aside after cutting off her bra. She watches me unblinking, her mouth parted, her lips and tongue and invitation.

"You are mine." I prick my thumb and let the blood well. "I will protect you. I will protect our children. I will never betray you."

I press my bloody thumb against her left breast right over her heart, leaving a smeared print on her perfect, smooth skin.

She releases the knife above her head with one hand and offers it to me. "You are mine. I will protect you. I will protect our children. I will never betray you."

This fucking woman. She is so perfect for me. So fucking perfect, period.

I prick the tip of her thumb and she waits until there is a large drop before pressing it against my left chest. Over *my* heart.

"I promise, Miceli."

There are no marriage vows that will bind us more tightly than the words we have just spoken with my dick in her ass, and our bloody thumbprints on each other's bodies.

I begin to move again. Slowly this time. This is more than sex. More than sharing two explosive orgasms.

This is connection.

My heart beats heavily under her bloody thumbprint.

Róise pulls my thumb to her mouth, sucking the blood off and sending powerful currents of pleasure straight to my dick.

My balls draw tight and I have to grit my teeth against coming. But I'm not ready. Because *she's* not ready.

Her eyes filled with an emotion I refuse to name, Róise offers her thumb.

Bending, I lower my head to take it into my mouth. The sweet copper flavor of her life's essence bursts over my tongue. Sucking and licking, I treat that sweet digit like the erogenous zone I know it can be.

Her eyes go half-mast and my body speeds up until I'm pounding into her like an animal. She urges me on the whole way, moaning and trying to meet my thrusts with the little movement I've allowed her body.

And then, she goes rigid, her eyes unfocused her mouth open on a silent scream. Her ass muscles choke my dick so tight if I wasn't hard as a pike, I wouldn't be able to move.

I fuck her through her climax wondering if the pleasure just might kill me. This time when my nuts grow tight with that burning sensation that says I'm about to come, I thrust harder and deeper.

I erupt inside her, coming so hard, it hurts, but it's a pain I never want to end.

Words I have never said sit on the tip of my tongue and I clamp my mouth shut.

We belong to each other, but the organ beating in my chest does not have a corresponding entity in my soul.

Love is a weakness and I have spent my lifetime controlling mine. Hiding them.

~ ~ ~

Afterward, we shower and I find her a paint splattered T-shirt to wear.

Like usual when I'm here since my father's death, I'm naked. Paint smears on my clothes would be hard to explain. If I felt the need to explain myself.

But *I like* creating naked. In those hours I am not a De Luca made man. Not the Genovese underboss. I am simply Miceli, the core of myself. The core no one alive has seen until now.

Why did I bring her here? I'm not Sev. I don't think Róise needs access to all my secrets. But I've given it to her.

Cazzo.

What's done is done. But this is as far as it goes.

We can enjoy each other's bodies, but that doesn't mean getting our hooks into each other's souls.

"Are you going to show me your art now?" Róise asks walking toward one of the easels.

There's a little hitch in her step.

I'm beside her in a second, grabbing her shoulders and turning her so I can see her face. "Are you alright?"

Against her loud protests, I meticulously checked her ass for tears and/or blood in the shower. She was swollen but not torn.

"More than." She grins and then winces. "But it will be a few days before we can do that again."

"More like a few weeks."

"Says you."

"Says me."

"Listen here, Mr. Big Shot Underboss, I let you boss me around during sex, but you don't get to boss me around *about* it. If I say my body is ready in a few days. It's ready."

I don't argue. But I'm not fucking her ass until I'm sure she's up to it.

To change the subject, I pull the cloth off of the painting on the center easel. "This is what I'm working on now."

Well, one of them.

She gasps. "This is what you paint? How would anyone looking at this think painting weakens you?"

I look at the burned-out hull of a car with the skeletons of long dead occupants still inside it on a torn up stretch of pavement. The crumbling skyscrapers in the background are set against a darkening sky.

"What did you expect me to paint?" I ask.

"Not this scene of destruction. It looks like the end of the world."

Her words please me. "That's what it's supposed to look like."

Róise looks more closely at the painting and then at me, her eyes narrowed.

"What?"

"The covers on the books of one of my favorite series have pictures like this. I bought the first one because of the cover."

I didn't expect to reveal another secret so soon. "I didn't figure you for a reader of post-apocalyptic fiction."

"What do you think I read?"

"Romance? Books on acting?"

She laughs. "I read those too. The books on acting mostly for class."

"That series seems a little depressing for you." I point to the painting with the thumb I drew blood from while we were fucking.

Not that there's any significance in that. It's just the easiest hand to use.

"Not really. It reminds me that no matter how bad the world seems sometimes, it's not that. We're not post-apocalyptic. We haven't completely destroyed ourselves and I don't believe we will."

"Philosophical thought for twenty-one-year-old." I don't comment on her youthful naivete because I'm not sure her hopeful outlook is about her age.

I think at *her* core, Róise harbors hope in a way I never did.

Tugging at the hem of my t-shirt she's wearing, she wanders to the next easel. "Isn't college when you're supposed to be your most philosophical?"

Her modesty after screaming for me to fuck her in the ass is as much of a turn on as her sexual daring. I ignore the pulse of blood in my semi-erect cock.

I'm always aroused when I'm with her. I'm not about to act on it again. Her body needs rest.

"What's this one?" Róise starts to lift the edge of the cloth covering the largest canvas in the room.

My hand jerks out of its own volition to stop her, but then I let it drop. This painting is a secret she already shares with me.

"Not a post-apocalyptic scene."

"Is it another book cover?" she asks, pausing with her hand on the cloth.

"Look and find out."

She flips the cover over the back of the painting and then makes a choked sound of surprise.

A platinum blonde lies in the center of a hotel bed. Her body flushed with pleasure her thighs spread obscenely, her pretty pink, perfect pussy on display. It's my memory of the woman I thought I would never have again.

The one I am going to marry.

"It's me." Her voice comes out in an awed whisper.

"Yes. "

She bites her lower lip. "But not really."

"Yes, really," I disagree. "Every centimeter of that woman is you. That wig doesn't matter. The make up..."

I let my voice trail off. But her eyes are wide, and I know she knows. She looks at me.

She looks back to the painting. "You left off the makeup. That's me. That's my face."

"I know, I painted it," I say sardonically.

"Don't be a jerk."

Even her fucking bluntness is intoxicating.

"I started it the day after I got back," I admit. "I couldn't get the face right until after we signed the contract."

She reaches as if she is going to touch, but she doesn't.

"It's still wet to the touch." It would be surface dry by now, but I keep coming back to it. Or I did, until I started the other painting on the last covered easel.

"What are you going to do with this?" She bites that sweet lip again. And looks up at me through her lashes.

"I was going to keep it here before I knew you are she and she is you." As a reminder of a night I will always treasure.

That's one piece of sentimental idiocy, I'm not about to tell her.

"Now, what are you going to do?"

"Hang it in our marital bedroom," I tease.

She looks properly horrified. "What if someone sees it? It's too explicit to hang on our bedroom wall. When the maid cleans, she'll see it."

She's starting to spiral, twisting the hem of the t-shirt until her thighs are exposed nearly to her pussy. Which I'm positive is not her intention.

"I'll keep it here. A secret for you and me to enjoy."

"To enjoy?" she squeaks.

"Oh yes, I think we both get pleasure from seeing you like that."

She doesn't deny it, but she does look away and points to the only easel with a covered painting on it still. "What about that one?"

I don't say anything. Róise takes my silence for permission and moves to uncover the last of my current projects. This time there is no sound at all from her.

She simply stares at the portrait in silence.

It's her. Of course. Her face surrounded by bouncy brown curls with hints of red and her shoulders. The background and edges around her are whorls and splashes of all the shades of pink that remind me of *mi dolce fiore*.

The dark, almost purple pink of her pussy when aroused. The soft pink of her lips. The darker raspberry shade of her nipples. The cotton candy pink of her birthday lip gloss.

Hot pink. Rose pink. So many pinks and all of them her.

"I look...it's..." her voice fades without her saying what *it* is.

"You," I finish for her. "And it will hang on the wall of our living room when it's done."

For everyone and my mother to see my obsession.

Fuck.

"So the engagement is official?" Róise asks.

Not what I expected to hear, but I'll go with it. "Not quite."

I walk naked over to my trousers and pull out the small velvet box. There's no logo from a famous jeweler. It's the ring first De Luca who came to America gave to his wife.

I want Róise to feel like she is part of not only our family but of our family's legacy here in New York. She might have been born an Irish mob princess, but now she is Cosa Nostra. Róise will be the mother of another generation of De Lucas who serve the Genovese family.

The next Genovese don.

I open the box and pull out the ring. It's not the biggest diamond in our family's collection of heirlooms. However, the oval center stone surrounded by small diamonds in the delicate Victorian setting is a pink sapphire.

She followed me and is standing near when I turn. She looks down at my closed fist.

"Give me your hand."

Without hesitation, she lifts the small appendage toward me and I slide the ring on her finger. The fit is perfect. It should be. I had it sized for her.

"It's beautiful," she breathes. "Is this a family heirloom? Only, it's antique gold. Like *moma's* ring from her great grandmother. Vintage gold is darker sometimes, with more of a copper tint."

I kiss her to stop the babble.

She kisses back until my cock is a pulsing column between us. I pull back, reminding myself once was enough.

Not that it ever is with this woman.

"It's from the first De Luca matriarch to make her home in New York a century ago. She came from Sicily to marry my ancestor."

"Wow." She holds her hand out in front of her, examining the ring. "You De Lucas have been doing this marriage of convenience thing for a long time."

"Pretty sure the Shaughnessy's have to." The ring isn't holding my attention, but her bare legs sure are.

"You're right about that." She sighs and drops her arm. "What next?"

"There will be a press release accompanied by a press conference."

She makes a face of distaste.

"We both need to be there for pictures and to answer questions," I inform her.

Her brows draw together in suspicion, like I'm one of the reporters she apparently doesn't want to deal with. "What kind of questions?"

"Whatever questions reporters who report on society stuff ask I guess." This really isn't my thing. But it is necessary.

"They're going to want to know how we met. They're going to ask about our age difference. They'll want to know if our families are friends. Those society reporters can be really invasive."

"It's a good thing we have an easy meet-cute to tell them."

"You know what a cute is?" Her face reflects her surprise.

I don't live under a rock. "I've heard the term," I say dryly.

"What are we going to say? That we met in a club?" She doesn't sound thrilled by this. "That I let you pick me up?"

"Don't sound so horrified. That's what happened."

"Trust my one and only one-night-stand to make it into the papers."

"No one is going to know it was supposed to be a single night of sex. We're getting married, remember?"

"Right." She's back to twisting the hem of the t-shirt she's wearing. "Let's not mention it was a club in Portland though."

"That could cause more trouble with your uncle than either of us wants to deal with right now," I agree.

She gives me a disbelieving look. "Somehow I don't think you care about trouble for my uncle."

"I care if it causes you stress." It is my job to protect her after all.

Even from censure from her family.

Róise blows out an exasperated breath. "Could you just act like an ass for a while? I think I need you not to be so perfect right now."

I'm far from perfect, but with her permission to be a selfish ass, I swoop down and carry her to the only bedroom with a bed in it. It's only a single, but we don't need a king sized mattress to fuck each other's brains out.

CHAPTER 49: RÓISE

Miceli waits to pull out his asshole routine until after we've had sex twice more.

Once with him pounding my vagina into submission and another in the shower, where he rubs us both off with his hardon pressed against my clit and my legs wrapped tightly around him.

I finish pulling my jeans on over my naked nether regions. I have a feeling riding back to Long Island on the back of Miceli's bike is going to be a whole new experience for me.

"I trust you won't be going to your uncle and asking for a different groom again." Miceli slips into his black leather jacket and his stoic under-boss persona all in one go.

"He told you about that?" I ask, feeling kind of bad. "You never said anything."

"Neither did you."

"Because Uncle Brogan refused to even consider it."

"You want to marry someone else? Another De Luca? Maybe you've seen my cousin and you think he's more your style. Or you think the wife of a capo can be a movie star."

"Uh, I don't even know who you are talking about. And I'm wearing your ring, so I don't know *why* we're talking about it either."

"I'm just confirming that this time, you're going to follow through on your promise."

"I'm not the one who tried to back out of their promise," I deny hotly.

Man, when he goes for jerk status, he goes all in.

"Then we're in agreement."

"Yes."

"You are going to marry me at the end of September."

"Yes!"

"Good."

"If you're looking to win the award for least romantic proposal ever, you've got it in the bag," I snark.

"We're not a romance."

"You can say that again."

The ride home on the back of his bike is pure torture. In more than one way.

I limp inside the mansion without saying goodbye.

For a little while there, when he was sharing his secrets and making love to me like I mattered to him, I thought maybe it's okay to fall in love with my convenient fiancée.

But all of that was just to convince me to go ahead with the early wedding.

That sex wasn't making love. It was about getting my compliance.

Angry and not ready to see anyone else, I sneak into the morning room. It's a small room with big windows that my mom used to love. Hardly anybody uses it anymore. Except me.

Already angry with Miceli, when I remember my questions about how he cleared the way for me to return to college, I call him.

Maybe he'll answer my call and crash doing it. Cold dread washes over me and my knees buckle.

I'm about to press end call when I hear his voice. "What?"

"Are you still riding your motorcycle?"

"It would be a miracle if I wasn't. I'm not even off the island yet."

"You should not answer the phone when you are driving, but especially riding a bike."

"Then why did you call?"

"I'm hanging up now," I say instead of answering.

"Relax. I have a speaker and mic in my helmet. What do you want, Róise?"

"The dean called me himself on Tuesday and asked me to come back to classes. Did you bribe him?" I demand.

"You said you didn't want the college to benefit from your pain," he says almost patiently.

"I don't." I shift on the comfy sofa, so I'm sitting on my hip, not my butt. That's better.

"I used a stick, not a carrot."

"You threatened him?" I ask, not sure how I feel about that.

Okay, I am sure. I like it. And that makes me what? Not the woman I thought I was, that's for sure.

"Not with violence but something far worse. Losing their federal accreditation."

"You could do that?" This should not turn me on.

Especially after his asshole behavior before bringing me home. And also, I *should* be sickened by the threat.

I'm not. If I was wearing panties, they'd be getting damp.

"I am a Cosa Nostra underboss."

Which says it all, I guess. "Well, thank you," I say grudgingly. "If I had to miss the last week of school, I would have been really bummed."

I've only got a year of anything resembling normal life left before that word won't even have a passing acquaintance with my life.

CHAPTER 50: MICELI

We are not a Romance.

But if we aren't, what are we? Because the woman who just climbed off my bike and walked into her home without saying a word to me, is more than just a means to an end.

That twenty-one-year-old college student makes me feel things I thought I could no longer feel. The heart that I would swear had atrophied in my soul, is beating again.

Black it might be. Stained with sin. But it beats.

Róise is more than my sweet flower. She is sensuality wrapped in innocence. She is a conscience I thought long dead. She is a smile when everything around me is pain and destruction.

She is a hope. My hope.

I swore I would never fall for a woman like my brother and my cousin.

But only a weak man denies the truth when it stares him in the face.

Róise doesn't just give me her body, she sparks tendrils of expectation for the future. New eyes to look at the world, even this dark one we were both born into.

She is not my light, because that implies she could be turned off.

She is everything good that infuses the center of my being.

And she thinks I'm an asshole.

Which? Is the truth.

But she will learn to love this asshole. Because I will not be in this obsession alone.

CHAPTER 51: RÓISE

I review the same page of notes for the fifth time and none of it sinks into my brain.

I can't sit still. Honestly, sitting at all right now is not in the cards. I'm lying on my side on the bed with my tablet propped up so I can study for my Performance Theory final.

Only, very little studying is getting done. Every time I shift, I feel the movement in my stretched sphincter muscles and something decadent flutters deep in my belly.

Flashes of what happened in Miceli's studio keep interrupting the words on the screen.

A loud pounding on my door startles me and I sit up, accidentally putting my hand down on Pusheen's tail.

I don't think I hurt her, but she yowls and leaps from the bed in protest.

Before I can even call out to ask who it is, because that is *not* the knock of one of my cousins, or grandmother, the doorknob starts to turn.

Screeching, I jump to my feet a lot like Pusheen, but I'm diving for a robe to cover the stretchy tanktop that barely reaches my thighs. I'm not wearing underwear.

I'm halfway into the robe when Miceli bursts into the room looking around like he thinks I've got someone in here with me.

"What are you doing?"

His eyes lock on the half of my body still exposed and lust he makes no effort to hide kindles in their depths.

What the heck? "What are you doing here?" I amend my first question.

But really, I'd settle for an answer to either.

"You cannot entertain visitors dressed like that," he says in full bossy mode.

I let the robe slide right back off and put my hands on my hips? "I *can't*? Only it looks like I can."

"I am different. You can entertain me naked, but not if you don't want to mess the sheets up on that princess bed of yours."

"It's not a princess bed." There's no canopy. So what if pink is an accent color in my room?

I like it a lot, but I wear it a lot more since finding out about my contract fiancé's aversion to the color.

His eyes are focused on the apex of my thighs. "Shift just a little and I'll see the soft curls on your pussy."

"What? No! Anyone could walk in." I put a hand up to stop him even though he hasn't moved a single inch since bursting into the room.

"My point exactly, *mi dolce fiore*. And if this anyone is a person not related to you by blood, I will gouge their eyes out with my favorite dagger before I bury it in their heart."

I want to think he's exaggerating, but that look on his handsome, unhinged face says he's not. "Then you'd better shut the door."

He steps back without shifting his gaze away from me and slams the door.

"Make some more noise, why don't you? You're tough and all, but I don't see you winning if *mamo* catches you in here."

"I like your grandmother."

That should not make me smile. I shouldn't care that the jerk I'm going to marry likes the woman I adore, but it does. "She's likable."

Miceli shakes his head like he's coming out of a daze. "Put your robe on, please, Aphrodite. Neither one of us wants to find out what your grandmother would do to me if she walked in on me living out the fantasy in my head."

"You haven't called me that in a while." I bend down and retrieve the robe, muscles unused to the activity we indulge in earlier twinging.

"It's a fitting name for you." There's something strange in his voice.

"Not sure how a guy who doesn't do love thinks the Goddess of Love is a good name for me."

"You love lots of people." His eyes shift away from me.

If it was anyone else, I'd think he was trying to avoid my gaze. But it's Miceli. He's probably cataloguing every tiny splash of pink in the room.

"I'm not sure about lots, but I love my family." Even my uncle, who I don't always like.

I'm not sure if I love Mick. Are you required to love your cousin-in-law? I'm pretty sure not. If I am, I might be in trouble.

All of my resentment for Kara having to get married so young coalesced on him and it's never shifted. Kind of like how I resent Miceli for being the other half of our forced union.

Which isn't fair and I'm not even sure I resent the marriage anymore. How do I resent being forced to marry the man I'm pretty much head over heels in love with?

Even if he *is* a Grade A jerk sometimes.

I tie the belt on the robe as he thrusts a bag toward me. "There's an Epsom salt mix in one of the jars. Put two capfuls in the water and soak for at least thirty minutes. Afterward, rub some of the cream in the smaller jar on your asshole. It will help."

"You went and got me stuff to help my aching uh...muscles?" My face is flaming red, but my heart squeezes.

This man.

"You were sore and then you had to ride nearly an hour on the back of my bike." He shrugs. "It's no big deal."

Him taking the time to find the stuff in that bag and bring it here is a very big deal. We might not be a romance, but he treats me like I'm important.

More than just the uterus guaranteeing the blood alliance between our families.

"Have you had dinner?" We didn't eat the whole time we were in his studio "I was starving when I got home."

"Did you eat?" he asks immediately.

"I had some crackers and cheese. I wasn't up to sitting down to dinner with the family. Luckily Uncle Brogan wasn't there tonight." It's the one meal he insists we eat as a family.

And when he's there, he expects the rest of us to be too.

"Do you want tacos?"

"Do you have everything you learned about me memorized?"

"I don't forget important facts."

"Me liking tacos is one of them?"

"Yes." His tone dares me to ask why.

Yeah, no. I'm not sure I want the answer. It might be something along the theme of *we're not romance*. Like it's about keeping me healthy to carry his baby, or something equally infuriating.

I don't want *mamo* to walk in on me clobbering him anymore than I do her catching us in bed together. Just no.

"If I say I want tacos, are you going to run out and get some?"

He shakes his head slowly. "I'll order one of your uncle's men to do it."

"Can you do that? Order my uncle's men around?"

"Men in our world know who I am and if they know what's good for them, they do what I tell them."

"I just bet. I'm not one of my uncle's men though."

"No, you are most definitely not."

"We don't need to order out for tacos. There'll be leftovers from dinner in the kitchen."

"And your housekeeper doesn't mind you scrounging around in her refrigerator?"

"Nah. Does yours?"

"We have two cooks besides a housekeeper and none of them would take kindly to me messing up the kitchen."

"What do you do when you're hungry between meals?"

"Call one of the staff."

"*Mamo* would say that's taking on airs. No offense."

"None taken."

"Anyway, the trick is probably not to leave a mess behind after you snack. *Mamo* would still rap my knuckles with a wooden spoon if I did that."

Miceli's not about to show shock at *mamo's* methods of discipline. He was raised by a don to be a soldier. His corporal punishment would have been far worse.

"I don't want you to hurt our children," I blurt out. And when did child become plural?

"I won't."

"I mean the training. It's barbaric."

"How would you know? Fitz is too young for the type of training you're talking about."

"Yeah, if Mick tries to train Fitz at any age with some of the things *mamo* warned us girls about, Kara will turn mama-bear and maul him to death. I'm pretty sure."

"Ah, so your grandmother told you. I will teach our children to fight and the only time I will strike one is dummy strikes during that training."

"Your father didn't strike you?" That surprises me.

Miceli's face shuts down. "I didn't say that. He was a good father and he trained me and my brother the way he'd been taught."

"But you're not going to follow in his footsteps?"

"Not in certain respects, no. Neither will Sev."

"Wow. That's good to hear." Like really, really.

It would be a real bummer to have to poison the man I love. But yeah, there are things my grandfather did to train my dad and uncle that I would have dosed his coffee with rat poison for.

Miceli lets me feed him leftovers, watching every move I make in the kitchen. It's weird. Because the lust is banked and he just seems...happy maybe?

Like I said. Weird.

After bossing me around some more about taking a bath and treating my bottom and vagina...seriously? I'm supposed to use the tiny tube of cream there. Anyway, after all the instructions, and a kiss that pretty much blows my mind, Miceli leaves.

And somehow, not one of my family interrupts us.

After that *very* weird night, I spend the next day studying for my finals.

All of my tests are on Wednesday and Thursday, which gives me Monday and Tuesday for study groups on campus.

~ ~ ~

Fiona finds me in my room on Sunday. She wants to talk about her eighteenth birthday.

"Dad's already got this big bash planned and I'm going to hate it. You know I'll be hiding for most of it."

"Tell him you don't want the party. It's your birthday." And Fiona isn't exaggerating. She'll last about thirty minutes with the crowd and then she'll disappear.

Uncle Brogan doesn't even yell about it anymore, but he doesn't stop forcing her to attend events either.

"You know it's not that easy. Since when has our birthday ever belonged to us and not to the mob?" Fiona sounds more jaded than I've ever heard her.

I don't have an answer for her. It's not just Uncle Brogan. My dad allowed my birthday and his own to be used as events for networking with his criminal buddies.

But mom and dad also started the tradition of me celebrating my birthday separately and privately with friends and really close family, i.e. my cousins.

"Whatever networking even your dad plans for the day of, we can have a private celebration just you and me and Kara," I promise.

"And Zoey. I want her to be there too."

My first reaction is to say no way. But this is Fiona's birthday. And she's going to be eighteen. Old enough to date the nineteen-year-old. If Fiona wants to date a mafia soldier, that's her choice.

I just hope she doesn't end up with her heart broken. "Okay, and Zoey."

Fiona smiles. "I want to do like you did on your 21st."

"You mean sneak out?" Where would my cousin want to go?

"Yes."

"You don't want to go into the City do you?" I ask.

She bites her lip and shakes her head. "I want to go for a bike ride on the trails at Caumsett."

"Uncle Brogan won't refuse for you to do that."

"But I want to sneak out. You and Kara had so much fun doing it."

I get it. I really do. We *did* have fun. The risk of getting caught added to the excitement that night.

And Fiona wants to experience that. If it doesn't backfire, it could build back some of the confidence in her that the shooting the day of my mom's death ripped away.

"Okay, Operation Sneak Out the Birthday Girl is a go, but Zoey can't come."

"What? Why?"

"It's literally Zoey's job to tell on us. Well, me anyway."

With the increased security Miceli has in place, it's going to be hard enough for me to get out of the house without one of his assigned shadows. There is no more *off time* for my mafia guards. Just a bigger detail with a guard on hand even when I'm at home.

"She wouldn't tell."

"Maybe." I'm not convinced, but Fiona could be right. "Do you want to put her in the position of being punished if we're discovered though?"

"No." Fiona's lip wobbles. "It's not fair. We can't do anything fun without this stupid mob life ruining it."

Hard to argue that with someone who spent two weeks in a coma as collateral damage to this life. "We *can* do fun things. And we will. Listen, let me try to figure this out. If I can come up with a fool proof plan, we can invite her without worrying."

A plan like telling Miceli and letting Fiona think she's sneaking out when Zoey is actually there as a bodyguard? Yes, it's sneaky, but sometimes sneaky is the only way to get what you need out of this mob life.

CHAPTER 52: MICELI

The phone calls start at three in the morning and they don't stop.

The guy I planted in Lorenzo Ricci's crew has evidence of the capo skimming money from the profits of our drug trade going back decades. The rat has been stealing from *la famiglia* almost as long as he's been a capo.

Stronzo del cazzo.

That makes two men my father trusted fucking liars. We owe it to papà's memory to make Lorenzo's death painful and prolonged.

We can't bring him in immediately because we need to know how deep this corruption runs. Who are his accomplices? Where is the money he stole?

Torture can accomplish a lot, but it has its limits. A man who knows he is going to die has little incentive to tell the truth about where he hid his money. Especially if he has an accomplice he wants to leave that money to.

The next phone call is from my brother and I answer while I'm shaving. I use a straight razor which is silent and efficient.

"Did you get my text about Ricci?"

"Yes, but that's not why I'm calling. I agree that your guy on the inside needs more time to get all the information we want."

I grunt my approval.

"I need you to go to Boston."

The fucking Lombardi don. Salvatore was right that this land deal is good for *la famiglia* but dealing with the fallout from Matthew Lombard trying to steal it out from under us is a pain in my ass.

"You want reparations." It's not a guess. I know my brother.

"Yes. Matthew Lombard has to relinquish any position of authority within the Lombardi mafia and never be allowed in a position to influence Cosa Nostra business again."

It's a merciful alternative. Killing him would net the same result. Sev is good at diplomacy. Letting the don's nephew live will put the don in our debt.

He'll back Sev as the next godfather in compensation.

"I don't like Boston." And I don't want to leave town right now.

The thought of leaving Róise with a potential target on her back makes the back of my neck itch. There's no identifiable specific threat, or I'd refuse my don's order for the first time, but I still don't like it.

We're on yellow alert, like all the Cosa Nostra should be. Some aren't, but that's on them.

"She'll be okay," my brother says in uncanny response to my thoughts, not my words. "We haven't made the official announcement. Right now, she's just your girlfriend."

"She's more than that."

Silence meets my growl.

"I want extra guards on her while I'm gone." I wipe the extra shaving soap off my face before patting my cheeks with aftershave. "A stealth team or I'll never hear the end of it."

"I'll get Angelo on it."

"He can coordinate with Allessio." Angelo is our top assassin, but his crew have all trained for covert ops with Niccolo's team.

I'm on the jet, readying for takeoff, when I try to call Róise. My call goes to voicemail.

I leave a short message. "Our PR firm will be contacting you to get information for the press release and arrange the press conference with you."

I end the call before I can say something dumb, like *call me back*. I don't need her to call me back. I've got too many people calling me as it is.

Even if Róise's voice is the only one I want to hear.

The third time images of *mi dolce fiore* spread across my bed interrupt my thoughts, I have to consciously lock them away in the vault I put my drive to paint in when I am not in my studio.

If I don't, I'm no good to Sev and right now my brother needs me.

We have only months if not weeks to solidify his place as the next godfather. If we want the transition to happen without bloodshed or creating a schism in the Cosa Nostra, we need to spend every minute of that time convincing the other Cosa Nostra mafias to back him.

The godfather is not always a unanimous vote. There have been times the Cosa Nostra has been split. Not that anyone on the outside ever knew that. But division among the families is not good for any of us. It is our job to keep our people safe.

And we have enough enemies from without. We don't need our own Cosa Nostra brothers gunning for us.

I want to get the business in Boston handled as fast as possible so I can get back to New York and Róise. But I can't do that if I'm mooning over her either.

For the first time I truly understand what is driving Sev. Why he wants to be the godfather so badly.

It's not for the sake of the Cosa Nostra, even if there isn't another man alive who could handle the role as well. It's to ensure the safety of Catalina and their unborn child. And the children yet to come.

Because now I know I will do anything to protect Róise. Including becoming the don. You protect from a position of power and there is no more powerful position in the Cosa Nostra except the one my brother will hold.

CHAPTER 53: RÓISE

Miceli tries to call me when I'm in one of my study groups.

I don't answer and he doesn't call back, but he does leave a voicemail.

Listening to it before the next study session, I grimace. Yeah, that's definitely not romance.

I'm dumping you on some random public relations person to handle our engagement announcement.

That's the gist anyway.

I get a bunch of calls from a number I don't recognize during the next study group. After three of my friends give me dirty looks, I put my phone on DND and focus on the material we're going over.

The group runs over and when I take the do not disturb off, there's a long string of notifications telling me I have four missed calls, three texts and a video message. All in less than two-and-a-half hours.

None of them are from Miceli.

I start from the oldest and make my way up. They are all from the same person. Giovanna Ricci, Communication Specialist with Oscuro Public Relations.

She uses the entire title with every voicemail she leaves. The texts are basic and all say the same thing.

AR: *This is Giovanna Ricci with the PR division of Oscuro Enterprises. Miceli De Luca gave me your name. Please return my call immediately.*

Immediately. Not *at your earliest convenience* or *when you get a chance.*

Her peremptory tone puts my back up and when I watch the video message I dislike her even more. She's gorgeous with a perfect figure and perfect hair.

I'm assuming about the figure because I can only see her torso, shoulders and head, but she's got the phone camera set far enough away, I also get to see part of her desk and what I'm sure is supposed to be an impressive office.

She cinches her place in my list of least favorite people when she mentions that she and Miceli are old friends.

Why do I need to know that?

And by friends does she mean fuck buddies? Because I'm not putting anything past this pushy woman.

I don't think Miceli will be happy when I tell him how difficult I'm finding it to get ahold of you, Róise.

Did I give her permission to call me by my first name? No, I did not.

And also, is that supposed to be a threat? I play the video for my friends while we slurp down caffeinated beverages to sustain us for the final study session of the day.

At least this one is for the class we're all taking so we'll be in it together.

"That's definitely a threat." Goodwin sips her iced mocha. "What a bitch."

Carrie winces at the b-word. "Maybe she's just frustrated. I bet he forgot to tell her it's finals week for you."

Did I mention that it's finals week to Miceli? Allessio probably did, right? "Regardless, I have a life that does not revolve around the mafia."

"Pretty sure they all think that's what your life is now," Traci quips.

I contemplate my Cherry Dr. Pepper morosely. "I have to call her back, don't I?"

They unanimously agree on the answer to *that question*. Yes. I have to call her back.

"Be the bigger person," Aleks advises.

Carrie nods in agreement.

"Fuck that. Tell her where she can put her stalker behavior." Traci slams back her five-shot espresso.

"I'm on Team Traci with this one," Goodwin says, making the rest of us laugh.

We call her Goodwin because her first name is Tracy and it's confusing in conversation. She's used to being called Goodwin from her time in amateur theater, which she started at the tender age of ten.

I text my stalker.

Róise: *I will call you in two hours, after my study session.*

Maybe if I give her some info on why I'm busy, she'll back off a little.

No such luck. My phone starts ringing about two seconds after I send the text. Same number. Yes, I check.

If I'm hoping Miceli will call, that's my business.

Annoyed at myself for hoping he'll call and the PR lady for being so impatient, I turn my phone all the way off. Which is not as easy as it used to be.

But I am determined.

After the study session I turn it back on, telling myself that I am *not* hoping there will be a missed call or text from my mafia lover. Good thing, because if I had been hoping, I would be disappointed.

There are however, several more from Giovanna Ricci.

I don't bother listening to the voicemails or reading the texts this time, but find a quiet place to sit down. Settling onto the prop sofa in the back of one of the improv classrooms, I call her.

She picks up on the fourth ring. Mind games? Really?

"Hello, Róise, it's good of you to finally return my many messages and phone calls."

"I prefer Miss Shaughnessy since we are strangers, Ms. Ricci." I may not play the part of mob princess often, but I know my lines. "As to your aggressively excessive phone calls and texts, I would suggest seeing a therapist for your compulsive behavior, but my guess is that you're just rude."

Along with her anxiety, social and agoraphobias, Fiona has a mild case of OCD. She would never hound someone the way this woman has been doing to me all day.

"Not returning my phone calls makes you the rude one and that's what I told Miceli when I finally called him practically in tears of frustration."

> 1. If this woman ever cries with genuine emotion, I'll drink the next noxious protein smoothie Aleks suggests.

> 2. Miceli had time to talk to my stalker, but not me?

"I'm sure the underboss was impressed by your inability to deal with the job he gave you without any handholding. Oh, wait...you called him. My bad."

Her silence tells me that maybe my fiancé wasn't all that excited to receive her phone call. Question is, would he even pick up for me?

"We've gotten off on the wrong foot, Ro—Miss Shaughnessy," she stresses my name. "My name is—"

"Giovanna Ricci," I cut her off. "I got that from your epic number of texts and messages."

"You do realize you are marrying into the Genovese Family? I am one of the capo's daughters. You should be cultivating my friendship, but maybe you are too young to realize that."

Wow. This woman reminds me of the popular girls in high school and she's making comments about *my* age?

"I'm marrying into the don's family. I'm pretty sure Catalina and Aria will smooth my way better than you ever could."

Her laughter is ugly. "If Aria De Luca didn't hate the Irish, maybe."

Okay, I've had enough. "If you've got something to say or ask about my upcoming wedding, say or ask it."

"I have several questions."

What follows is a barrage of inane inquiries, like *What is your favorite color? Who's your favorite singer? Please don't tell me Taylor Swift.*

Of course, I tell her I'm a Swiftie. And I'm not even lying to get on Ms. Ricci's nerves. That it succeeds in doing that, I take as a win. Go me.

"What do you like to do in your spare time? We'll definitely leave any reference to RPGs out of it."

Is she proud of herself for knowing the acronym for role playing games? I'm an actor, of course I've played some. Almost all of my friends have created at least one character for a Dungeons and Dragons session.

However, I prefer scripted acting and since starting college, I haven't had time for playing any games.

"I'm a student," I remind her. "I don't have time for hobbies right now. I'm lucky if I get a chance to read a book that isn't on my curriculum."

Or to watch a movie or a show that isn't part of one of my classes. That night I binge watched a TV series with my cousins was the first time in three months I got to do something like that.

And I still had to write a paper on it for one of my classes to justify the time.

"Good. I'll put down reading, shall I? Do you do any volunteering?"

"What part of my last answer would make you think I have time for that?" Some students do, I'm sure, but then they don't have the additional social responsibilities that come with being a mob princess.

Most of the time, I cover for Fiona, which increases my responsibilities, but it's totally worth it.

As the conversation progresses, Ms. Ricci talks to me like I'm a teenager, not a twenty-one-year-old woman.

"The age gap is going to be hard to spin," she says, like she's doing me a favor figuring out how to do that.

Unimpressed, I say, "Miceli is only twelve years older than me."

As of my birthday.

He might think I'm too young. And this PR person definitely thinks I'm too young, but in the mob, women get married younger with a bigger age gap to their groom. My grandmother was twenty years younger than my grandfather.

The mafia is the same. Even I know that. So, why is Giovanna Ricci pretending she doesn't?

She continues with her silly questions about surface things, and then talks at me like I have no say in when the engagement gets announced or when the press conference is supposed to happen.

"Keep in mind that my last final ends at 3 PM on Thursday," I inform her. "My calendar is pretty clear after that."

"I will text your security detail with the particulars once they are firmed up," she replies, not acknowledging my words, like she's ignored so many other things I've said during this phone call.

What was the point of that call, much less the communication specialist's dozens of calls, texts and messages to get ahold of me?

To make me mad? Because that's the one goal she succeeded in accomplishing.

I text Miceli.

Mi Dolce Fiore: ...

What the heck? He changed my name in our text stream. Is that significant?

Aphrodite is the Goddess of Love. He doesn't do love. Maybe he prefers thinking of me in other terms.

I can't exactly be offended by my sweet flower though. It's a play on my name and well, I like that he always includes the possessive *mi*.

Mi Dolce Fiore: *I don't like your PR lady.*

Ares: *Giovanna can be a little intense, but she's good at her job.*

Mi Dolce Fiore: *You think? She didn't listen to anything I said. I'm pretty sure she's going to make it all up when she creates my bio.*

Ares: *Don't worry about it. Do you need to ask or tell me anything important?*

Because the fact I intensely dislike the person in charge of handling the public relations for our engagement isn't that?

I guess I won't ask him about being *old friends* with her. He probably thinks stuff like that isn't important either.

Ares: *Róise?*

Mi Dolce Fiore: *I have nothing important to add.*

I tuck my phone in my bag and go looking for Allessio and Zoey. Unsurprisingly, I don't have to go far. They're waiting outside the door to the classroom where I left them after Allessio cleared the room.

~ ~ ~

There have been no texts from Miceli since yesterday. Looks like he didn't have anything *important* to say to me. Like, *goodnight.* Or to ask. Like, *how are you?*

I wouldn't dream of texting him anything so trivial either.

I put my phone on DND as soon as we reach campus and for the next two days, I only take it out of do not disturb at night before bed.

Not that I get any calls. Or texts.

CHAPTER 54: MICELI

My already piss poor mood sours even further when I see whose
calling me.

Brogan Shaughnessy.

What the hell does he want?

Róise is the only Shaughnessy I want to talk to tonight, but that's not
going to happen.

After dinner with the Boston don, I have a conference call with one of
our legitimate business partners in Melbourne and our marketing team.

My fiancée will be asleep by the time I'm done and I'm not going to wake
her.

According to Allessio, Róise's burning the midnight oil studying. She
needs her rest.

I want to fly home tonight, but I have a breakfast meeting with some
Massachusetts politicians in the morning. Lombardi set it after agreeing
to back Sev's election to godfather.

Tapping to answer, I say, "You have two minutes."

"You need to announce the engagement ASAP."

Why doesn't he know the interview to do exactly that is tomorrow?
Giovanna should have told him. Yes, we agreed our PR would handle the
engagement, but she should have liaised with the mob's people.

Did she not understand that?

"It's happening tomorrow."

"Good." There's too much relief in Shaughnessy's voice for my liking.

"Why?" Is Róise threatening to back out?

Not going to happen.

Cazzo. I need to be in New York.

"Her grandfather wants Róise to marry one of his lieutenants."

What the fuck? Gabriel Lion's lieutenants are in the same generation as he is. The twelve-year age gap between us is nothing compared to the obscene decades between her and any of her grandfather's top men.

"She's mine." Age differences be damned. That's all that matters.

"Yes," Brogan agrees readily. "But Gabriel has wanted Róise returned to the AOG since her father's death."

"She can't be returned to something she was never a part of to begin with."

"Once the engagement is announced, he'll back off," Brogan assures me. "He respects the sanctity of marriage."

An engagement is not a wedding, but that will happen soon enough. No one is taking Róise away from me.

Anyone who tries will learn how hot a god of war's wrath burns.

"I'll increase security on Róise for the time being just in case, though." That does not sound like a man confident of his own assurances.

"Unnecessary. I have it covered." I didn't inform Brogan about the stealth team I assigned to her when I left New York.

If they can't evade detection by his people, they aren't doing their jobs right.

"You're a possessive bastard. She's still my niece."

"That contract we all signed in blood says she is *mine* and I will take care of her."

CHAPTER 55: RÓISE

Thursday morning, I'm eating what Fiona considers brain food (homemade, high fiber, high protein granola) and Ollie is on his second cup of coffee when Allessio and Zoey arrive.

"You're not finished with breakfast?" Allessio asks.

"My first final isn't until ten." I slather a piece of toast with butter while Fiona and Zoey make googly eyes at each other.

"Where are your clothes for the interview? Zoey can put the garment bag in the car while you finish eating." Allessio sits down and pours himself a cup of coffee.

No longer on the list of people I dislike, he and Zoey eat breakfast here as often as they don't. As nosy, mafia bodyguards go, they're not too bad.

Even Ollie has warmed to them. Not that you can tell by his current frown. "What interview? I wasn't apprised of any events today."

"You weren't?" Allessio's brow furrows. "We're handling security, but you still should have been told."

Never mind Ollie not knowing about it. No one told me either. This has miss high-and-mighty, otherwise known as Giovanna Ricci, written all over it.

"We'll have to leave the campus by noon if you want time to stop back by the house to grab clothes on our way into the city," Allessio's warns me.

Like I'm going to leave campus before my last final.

"Yeah, I don't know anything about an interview." And it can be rescheduled as far as I'm concerned. "But that's not happening."

My first final ends at 11:30 AM but my second one starts at 1 PM and has a two-hour window to finish.

The shock in Allessio's eyes is too candid to be feigned. "Giovanna didn't arrange it with you?" He swears in Italian. "I assumed you got your finals moved and took at least one of them yesterday."

"No. And no."

"The interview's in Manhattan at 2:30," Zoey says earnestly. "Miceli is flying back this morning to be there for it."

If Miceli plans to be there, this must be the formal engagement announcement. Only Giovanna told me it would be done with a press conference.

"I told that..." I don't say the word I'm thinking. "I told her I had finals until three o'clock today."

Allessio looks pissed, whether at me for my stubborn refusal to bow out of my last final or the super-b for instigating this situation, I don't know.

Wait. Miceli is out of town? Maybe out of country? That could explain the radio silence.

"Flying back from where?" I ask.

"Boston."

So, no. Boston is only an hour's flight away and in the same time zone. My bad mood escalates and I take a deep breath.

I am not bombing my last two finals because of stress over the Italian mafia, or any of its members.

"Let's be real clear here, Allessio. I will be on campus from 9:30 AM until 3 PM at the minimum."

His eyes widen and he pales a little.

"What's the big deal?" I demand crankily. "We can reschedule."

"I don't think so. It's an interview with..." He names a very popular media personality.

So, I can't be an actor, but we can court publicity for this? I know it's not the same thing, but my give-a-darn broke about the time Allessio mentioned that bitch's plans.

Yes, I said it. And I meant it.

Giovanna Ricci is not my friend and if she doesn't watch out, I'm going to put capsaicin in her eyeshadow.

I am my father's daughter after all.

CHAPTER 56: MICELI

The jet hasn't even touched down and I'm getting texts from Giovanna and Allessio.

PR Giovanna: *Róise refuses to be there for the interview.*

What the actual fuck?

Allessio: *Róise can't leave campus before three o'clock.*

Why the hell not?

Too tired for this bullshit, I go straight to the source. I call Róise but my call goes to voicemail.

Damn it to hell. I asked her if she had anything important to say when we were texting (in the middle of a negotiation with the Lombardi don) and she said no.

Her refusal to show up for the interview to announce our engagement is pretty important.

I text her.

Ares: *Call me when you get this.*

I give her the time it takes to deplane and text again.

Ares: *Don't ignore me, Róise. This is important.*

She does not reply by the time I'm driving back toward the City. Once I am don, I'll have to use a security detail like Sev does.

All the damn time. I intend to enjoy my freedom to drive my McLaren while I have it.

I use the hands free option to text my recalcitrant fiancée again.

Ares: *You need to be at the hotel by 1:30. This is not negotiable.*

We're doing the interview in a suite at the Ritz-Carlton – Central Park. No one else needs to know the significance, but Róise does.

I thought it would make her smile.

Guess I was fucking wrong.

She hasn't called me by the time I reach the Oscuro building. So, I send one more text.

As an afterthought, I add another text because plans have had to change.

Ares: *We need to talk about living arrangements.*

Thirty minutes later when there is still no reply, I text again.

Ares: *You are being immature and stubborn. Sometimes you are more trouble than your worth.*

Which is a fucking lie, but I don't like being ignored by her. I want to see her. I need to see her. If she comes into Manhattan early, we can have lunch together before the interview.

Or spend our time doing something else.

Clearly, that is not happening.

I should have taken her with me to Boston.

The knowledge she might have refused to go sends my already foul mood plummeting.

This obsession is only getting worse.

When my brother and cousin figure out how bad it is, and they will, they are going to laugh their asses off.

CHAPTER 57: RÓISE

I finish my first final feeling pretty great. I know I aced it.

But when I check my texts, that sense of accomplishment gets shoved aside for anger.

I don't know what he means we need to talk about where we're going to live after we're married. Did he put that in there to try to get me to answer his texts in the middle of an exam.

Newsflash: it's a nonstarter. We've got nearly four months before I move in with him and there's no surprises waiting in the wings. The whole family, except his sister who lives in Vegas, reside in the top two floors of the De Luca's apartment building.

The last text makes me clench my hands in anger.

I'm more trouble than I'm worth? Really?

I told Giovanna about my finals schedule. She's the one who screwed up. Not me.

She could've scheduled this any other time, but she did this on purpose. Apparently, I'm on her list of people she doesn't like too.

Pulling up my shopping app, I put capsaicin in my cart.

I don't bother to text Miceli back, but I do tell Allessio that I am not leaving this campus before my last final exam is finished.

"And if it was so important to you all that I be there, someone could have told me before this morning." I give both him and Zoey the stink eye.

"Giovanna made it sound like you were already on board with the interview," Zoey says, way more worried about what I think of her than Allessio.

She wants to date my cousin.

"Giovanna is a bitch," I pronounce firmly. "I don't know what her problem with me is, but she has one."

"Um..." Zoey looks guilty.

"Spill," I demand.

But it's not Zoey who answers. It's Allessio. "As the daughter of a high ranking capo, Giovanna thinks she should be the underboss's wife."

"Plus she's got it bad for Miceli."

"And that's who he chose to put in charge of the publicity around our engagement?" Are all men that stupid, or just arrogant ones like my fiancé?

"She's always nice to him." Zoey rolls her eyes. "Too nice."

"Okay, so now I know that she's going to do her best to make me look bad. That doesn't change how today is going down."

"I never thought it would," Allessio says, approval tinging his voice. "I assume she didn't forward the press release to you either?"

"She sure didn't."

"I'll send it before we leave campus. But don't think about it or anything but the stuff you need to remember for this last test. I know you studied your ass off for it. Pardon my language."

My smile for Allessio is brilliant.

My phone rings and I'm still smiling when I look down to see it's Miceli.

I'm tempted to ignore the call, but I am *not* stubborn and immature. Okay, maybe stubborn, but I am not childish. You show me a mob princess who is a child past the age of ten and I'll start believing in miracles.

I tap to accept the call. "You have ten minutes. Talk fast Miceli."

I'm eating lunch so I don't go into my last final on an empty stomach.

"You need to be at the Ritz-Carlton at 1:30. "

The interview is at the Ritz? The hotel where we made l—had sex for the first time? Well, not the exact same one, but the one here in New York.

Whose idea was that?

"I can't. If I'd gotten a heads up, I might have been able to take my final early." That's not a given, but I'm betting Miceli's threat still has some leftover weight to carry. "Giovanna didn't bother to tell me and she implied to Allessio and Zoey that she had, so they didn't either."

"She didn't tell you about the interview? I find that hard to believe. She's one of our best communication specialists."

"Who also wants to be Mrs. De Luca, or so I'm told. I don't know why. So far, the job isn't turning out to be a lot of fun for me."

"Fuck."

"Yeah, no. That's not happening either."

Am I lying to myself? Maybe. Sometimes self-delusion is our only friend.

"Damn it. Róise, I thought you knew. You have a final?"

"Yes. My last final of the year," I say very slowly for the underbosses in the room. "Finishes at 3 PM. If I get done early, I will leave early. If I don't, you will see me when you see me because traffic."

"You get cranky when you have finals, huh?"

As opposed to cranky being the default, like with him? "I have worked really hard to earn straight As since I started college. Except that A- from the professor who doesn't believe in the concept of perfection. I'm never taking another one of his classes, I'll tell you that."

Realizing I'm straying from the subject, I get myself back on track. "I know my degree does not matter to you or my uncle, but it matters to me because it is a gift from my mom and dad. And I will not waste it. So yeah, I'm a little stressed about these finals. There's been a lot going on in my life, which you should know."

Because he's at the center of most of it. I can't believe I word-vomited all that.

"You're going to do great." There's not a hint of humor in Miceli's tone now. "You are fucking smart. I'll see you after your final."

"I need to get my clothes, unless you want me showing up in my sweats and Converse?" Test taking requires comfort.

"The helicopter will be waiting for you at the helipad near your uncle's mansion."

It's a private helipad used only by the estates in our neighborhood. Uncle Brogan would prefer to have his own, but *moma* won't hear of having half the lawn torn up for it. When he suggested putting one on the roof, she put salt in his bread pudding.

For a month.

I don't get my ideas for retribution from a stranger. Neither did my dad.

"Okay, I'll be there."

"See you soon, and Róise..."

"What?"

"Don't wear too much pink."

Suddenly, I feel an urgent need to wear the pinkest outfit in my closet.

CHAPTER 58: MICELI

On my way to the helipad, I call Giovanna and fire her. Not just as our PR rep, but from the company.

I don't know what kind of games she's playing, but they stop now.

She's still squawking when I hang up and call her boss. I explain the situation in a few short sentences. Primarily that if she doesn't fix what Giovanna fucked up and get the interview moved out an hour, heads will roll.

Being a member of *la famiglia*, she knows I'm not using a euphemism.

I'm waiting with the helicopter when Róise arrives. If I had gone to the mansion, we would not have made it out of her bedroom for at least twenty-four hours.

The wind ruffles her shiny brown curls, the sun glinting off the natural red highlights. Her gorgeous body is encased in a 1950s inspired taffeta dress. Pink of course. A matching bow is holding her chin length curls back from her face.

I smile. She scowls in return and fuck do I want to kiss that frown right off her lips. I wanted her to wear pink, because she is everything I think of when I see the color.

Innocent. Hopeful. Emotional. Her youth isn't something that bothers me now because this woman will keep me feeling young for the rest of our lives.

But if I asked her to wear pink, she would've worn black.

Her contrariness and resistance to authority is only one of the many reasons she is so vital to me.

Unwilling to wait for her to come to me, I stride across the helipad and pull her right into my arms, laying a kiss on those luscious lips that lasts until the rotor blades start whirring.

"That's our cue. Come on, Aphrodite, lets get you inside before the wind from the rotors sends your skirts over your head."

"You wish."

I really do, but I lift her into the helicopter before that can happen.

Once we are inside, she tries to sit on the bench across from me. Not happening.

I pick her up and put her down next to me. "I prefer to face forward when flying."

She opens her mouth to say something. Argue probably. But it just hangs open as Allessio climbs into the helicopter carrying Pusheen's pink cat carrier.

He buckles it in the seat between him and Zoey and the soldier-in-training closes the door.

"What is my cat doing here?"

"Pusheen is part of our family. Naturally, we'll want her in some of the pictures."

"What if she doesn't like to fly?" Róise asks worriedly, squinting to see Pusheen inside the carrier.

The cat is cuddled up with one of her catnip toys.

"She's fine. She's too formidable a beast to be bothered by something as inconsequential as a helicopter ride."

"Is that a catnip toy?" Róise asks.

I nod. "She likes them."

"I can't believe you're drugging my cat."

"I'm not drugging her." But I do have a hypodermic with a sedative in it on the off chance Pusheen didn't take to flying with her usual Queen of the World approach.

"Whatever. Why did you come?" Now, she's squinting at me like she's trying to read my thoughts. "Did you have a meeting with my uncle?"

"No."

"I don't understand."

"I haven't seen you in four days."

"So?"

Deflated ego, thy name is Róise. "So, I wanted to."

"Why?"

"How did your exam go?" I ask rather than answer a question I'm not ready to answer.

She wouldn't believe me if I did because she's not ready for the words either.

"Really well."

"You aced it." It's not a guess.

If Róise puts her mind to something, she will accomplish it.

"I hope so."

"You studied hard enough," Zoey pipes up. "Makes me glad that my job didn't require college. School is not my thing."

"It requires intelligence and skill to make it through the training program you're on. Allessio says you are doing well."

Zoey beams. "Thank you, boss."

"Don't thank me for the truth. It's not always so palatable."

"Don't ruin it by being a jerk now," Róise admonishes me.

"Telling the truth does not make me an asshole."

"I didn't call you that. I called you a jerk and yeah, sometimes telling the truth makes you nothing *but* an asshole." She grins, inviting me to share her joke.

I cup her nape and kiss her. Again.

She melts into me without hesitation and it takes all my formidable willpower to pull my mouth from hers.

I glance down at her feet. "I like the tennis shoes."

"I've got heels in my bag." She looks around, her expression turning panicked. "Where's my bag?"

Zoey holds up a tote bag stenciled in glittery pink with *Actors do it in character.*

"Oh, good. Thanks, Zoey." Róise smiles at the soldier and then looks at Allessio. "Did you send the press release to me? I can read it now."

Oh, this should be interesting.

Allessio nods and Róise fishes her phone out of the bag before tucking it on the seat beside her.

The first screech comes about a minute later. "Six kids? I'm homeschooling them? I'll kill her."

"I'd prefer you didn't. Especially since that's in there because I was punch drunk tired when I answered her questions. It made me facetious."

"Facetious? More like ridiculous and completely out of touch with reality," she says sarcastically. "Giovanna didn't ask *me* about children. Really, I know you think she is, but you're pet PR person is not very good at her job."

My pet PR person? Is Róise jealous? My dick likes the thought that she might be. Very much.

"It's no longer her job, so that tracks."

"You fired her?" Róise stares at me, her green eyes wide. "From handling the engagement, right?"

"From Oscuro Enterprises. She'll be lucky to get a job in Public Relations anywhere in New York."

"You blackballed her?" The shock in Róise's tone makes me smile.

I shake my head. "I didn't have to. Her boss is throwing her under the bus as we speak. She had to arrange the schedule shift on the interview. Our media personality is not amused."

"I did tell Ms. Ricci about my exams. On the phone and then when I thought she wasn't listening, I emailed her."

"I believe you. I don't care what her personal feelings are, when I give an order, I expect it to be carried out."

"Have you slept with her?" she asks, her words rushing together.

"Not for lack of trying on her part, but no," I say dryly.

"Is that why you fired her?" my fiancée asks. "She was coming on to you?"

"Giovanna fucked up. There's no place for her under my leadership."

"Are you that unforgiving with everyone?" Róise licks her lips, her head cocked in question.

My eyes follow the tempting pink tip of her tongue as it goes back into her mouth. Mine wants to follow it. "No."

"Why this time?"

"She tried to embarrass and hurt you." And that I will not stand.

CHAPTER 59: RÓISE

The interview goes a lot easier than I expect. Mostly because instead of his usual stoic underboss routine, Miceli acts like a human being with feelings.

Which we both know is a lie, but he's a better actor than I gave him credit for. A little too good.

When we sit down, he gently but firmly moves Pusheen to the cushion on my other side. Somehow, I'm sitting in the center of the couch and his big body is taking up the space beside me.

He pets Pusheen and tells her she's a good cat. Who is this man?

Pusheen gives him a regal look, lays her head and forepaws on my lap and promptly falls asleep. She's not at all impressed with the celebrity interviewer.

Miceli rests one long arm negligently along the back of the sofa, surrounding me with his presence and doing a pretty good job of looking like a doting fiancé. His fingers trail over the bare skin of my shoulder, sending a constant stream of sensation along my nerve endings I'm trying hard to ignore.

With spectacular failure.

I should have worn a dress with a high neck and long sleeves. Not that it would have done any good. Having the underboss this close interrupts normal programming in my brain, even when we're not touching.

"Pusheen is our rescue kitten," Miceli says, answering a question.

"That's a pretty big kitten."

I reach down to pet Pusheen and my hand tangles with Miceli's.

He grins. "Róise connected to her immediately, so we knew we were taking her home."

Leaning down, he kisses my temple and I want to clobber him. My heart is having a hard time not believing the man-in-love-with-his-fiancée schtick.

And that makes me cranky.

"You make our relationship sound like the romance of the century," I whisper accusingly when our interviewer consults with one of the producers about moving to another location in the suite for the rest of the interview.

"Would you rather I pretended not to like you?" he teases.

Teases!

I look around to make sure the other people in the suite are still occupied with each other. "Did you get a personality transplant in Boston?"

He laughs, like I'm joking.

The interviewer and the producer choose that moment to return to us.

Miceli gives them both a measured look. "We're fine where we are."

We stay where we are. Of course. And I think maybe an alien *didn't* take over Miceli's body.

"Thanks for taking the time to meet with me," the interviewer finally says. "This is going to be a great piece. Spring romance. My viewers are going to love it."

I recognize wrap up words when I hear them and I perk up until I remember we still have the photo shoot to get through.

The photographer took several photos during the interview but wants more, and the De Lucas want formal engagement photos to go out with the press release.

The woman who interviewed us got her copy early minus the line about the six children I'm supposedly homeschooling. It's going out to all the other news outlets tomorrow morning.

A billionaire getting married is newsworthy. Even when most of the world doesn't know he's a Cosa Nostra underboss.

The Cosa Nostra are way better at flying under the radar than our mob, but then Shaughnessys have been part of the criminal underworld for generations. The De Lucas have too, but they didn't take over leadership until the 1980s, when the Cosa Nostra went into stealth mode.

Well, as stealthy as any criminal organization that settles their disputes with death and destruction can be.

Huh. Maybe teaching mafia history to Cosa Nostra kids isn't such a far-fetched idea after all. *Moma* could do it for sure.

"Did I lie?" he asks with a eyebrow raised mockingly.

Thinking back over the questions and our answers, I have to admit none were a lie. Except one. "You said you knew I was the one for you the first time you saw me."

"I did."

"If you'll remember, that was a one-night stand and neither of us planned to see the other again."

"That night, I knew you were the one I wanted in my bed. And after the amazing sex, I wished you could be the one on the other side of the contract."

Can I believe him? But why lie? It doesn't change anything.

Except how I feel. Darn it.

It's way too easy to look at him adoringly while the photographer gets the necessary traditional poses. And when he insists our cat be included because we aren't having kids for a while, that adoration turns a little too real.

"You two ready to have some fun?" she asks.

I shrug, but Miceli says, "Sure."

Who is this man and where is my taciturn and grumpy underboss fiancé?

"I love the 1950s look." She grins at me. "Coupled with Miceli's dark suit, you two look like a couple right out of the 20th century."

I'm not sure *what* to say to that. "Um, thank you?"

"Pick her up, like you're going to carry her over the threshold."

Miceli doesn't wait to be told twice. He bends and puts one arm under my knees and the other behind my back before lifting.

The photographer puts her camera up to her eye and starts taking pictures. "Okay, now twirl her around. Make those crinolines fly."

He adjust his hold slightly and then starts spinning. And my skirts do fly.

"How are you feeling?" he asks in a whisper, as he spins me around and smiles down at me adoringly.

There should be a warning sign on this man. Because my heart? Is finding it way too easy to believe what it sees. Even if our brain knows he's putting all of this on for the sake of the mafia.

"I'm fine." What else can I say?

The truth? That I missed him like crazy the last four days and being in his arms feels like coming home?

"How's your ass?"

I gasp and stare at him wide-eyed.

"Yes, just like that! You look like he just proposed to you," the photographer crows.

I guess that's better than her knowing he just asked if my butthole is still sore. Or close enough.

"It's fine," I hiss. "I'm fine," I repeat, a whole different meaning in those two words right now.

"That's good to hear," he purrs.

Jayzuz, Mary and Joseph, my ovaries just fainted. "If you were that worried about me, you could've called earlier this week."

"I have been in meetings from 6 AM until midnight every day."

That schedule is bonkers. "Are you serious?"

"Yes."

Looking closer than I have since finding him waiting with the helicopter because looking at him makes me want things. Not just sex things either.

Emotions he'll never give me.

Anyway, I see the lines of strain and exhaustion on his face now and my chest aches.

"Is it always like this?" I mean, am I going to be married to a ghost? "Do you work like this all the time?"

"You know there are no set hours for men in my position. But right now, things are particularly volatile and it's my job to either burn down my enemies or throw water on the fires that are burning." "

Like a superhero not averse to killing his enemies. My vajayjay swoons. "I'm sorry. You look tired."

"Good to know."

"You know what I mean."

He doesn't answer because the photographer is telling us it's time to try another pose.

Miceli stops spinning and I realize the photographer is standing on the top rung of the step ladder she used to set up the taller lights and reflectors.

She hops down. "These are going to be great. Now, sit in that armchair with Róise in your lap."

Miceli settles into the chair she indicated with my butt right on his thighs. There's something pressing into me through the layers of my skirt and underskirts that's harder than the bulging muscles of his thighs.

He's turned on. Because he's holding me?

"Let's spread your skirts." The photographer messes with my dress. "That's good, but maybe a little leg showing?"

She artfully pushes the fabric up and tells Miceli to grab and hold it. He does, his fingertips sliding up my naked skin under the cover of my crinoline.

He makes a sound that makes my core pulse with need. "You're wearing thigh highs," he growls low for only me to hear.

"Perfect. Don't move. Don't change a single thing. Especially your expressions." The photographer is back on the stepstool, getting a bird's eye view of us.

Normally I would protest how much of my cleavage will show from that angle, but right now if a single word comes out of my mouth, it isn't going to be about the pictures.

We spend another hour taking photos and by the end, I never want to see the opposite side of a camera lens again. Maybe because I want to see Miceli naked so badly.

Pusheen jumps down from the couch where she's been napping since her part in the photo shoot ends. She saunters over to us and rubs along Miceli's ankles and then mine.

Lulled by her innocent behavior, I notice her bunched back legs too late.

"Watch out," I yell as my cat leaps halfway across the room to land on the back of one of the photographer's assistants.

The man goes crashing down to the ground, expensive equipment landing around him like the debris from a four-car pileup. Pusheen's back end swishes as she walks away, no concern for the mess she left behind.

Miceli calls for Allessio to put Pusheen in her carrier, but he doesn't apologize for my cat's tendency to knock down unsuspecting persons and he won't let me either.

"We do not apologize for Pusheen exhibiting her nature."

However he pays more than double for any damages and thanks the photographer for her efforts. With a hand low on my back, his fingers over the top swell of my butt, he guides me out of the suite.

My heart pounds so hard, I can feel it knocking against my breastbone.

Once we're in the back of what is no doubt an armor plated SUV, I ask, "What now?"

"Allessio will take Pusheen home and see her settled. We have reservations at Bar Pitti in thirty minutes."

"It's early for dinner in the City, isn't it?" I don't mind eating at six, but I expect Miceli to prefer later.

My thighs clench at the look he gives me. "I have plans for after."

"Can't wait."

He growls in response. "Don't tempt me or we aren't going to make it to dinner."

"I'm down for that." My stomach decides to take that moment to gurgle loudly.

"First, I feed you. Then I fuck you."

"You're so crude."

"And you love it."

I do. Almost as much as I love him.

When we get to the restaurant, the smells coming from inside make my stomach rumble again.

Ignoring the other people waiting in a line near the host stand, Miceli steps right up to it. "Miceli De Luca."

That's all he says. His name. But the man nods quickly and says, "Your party is this way."

As we go by the host stand, someone says, "We don't take reservations." I don't hear any more of the conversation though.

The maître 'd seats us at a table on the terrace near the red velvet rope separating it from the sidewalk and leaves.

The table is set for two. "I thought he said our party was already here?"

Miceli shrugs and looks at the menu.

"I just heard that waiter tell the person calling they don't take reservations," I lean forward to whisper to Miceli.

He glances up briefly to meet my eyes. "They don't."

"But you said we had a reservation. You gave that guy your name."

"We do."

"You're not making any sense."

"When I call for a table in a Manhattan restaurant, one gets set aside for me."

"It must be nice to be king."

"Right now, I am the prince and it has its perks."

But he will be king. Once Severu De Luca becomes the next godfather, my fiancé will become a don. King of New York.

I have to stifle a giggle at the thought.

Irish mobsters don't think in terms of royalty. Boss is more than a title, it's a position and it comes with power and influence.

But my uncle is right. The Italian mafia is more formal than we are.

My pasta is being set down in front of me when a commotion behind me catches my attention.

I turn to look and gasp. "That's..."

I don't say the name of the celebrity aloud but I can't help staring.

"Yes, it is. Now, turn back around and eat your food, Róise."

Suitably chastised for my gauche behavior, I do as Miceli said. I know better than to rubberneck, don't I? How many times has my family been gawked at when we eat in public?

Uncle Brogan might not be a king, but he's as notorious as any member of the Royal Family. And we are by association.

Miceli's expression isn't judgy though. He's smiling at me. "Do you want to meet her?"

I shake my head. "Not really." The truth is, I'd rather be here, alone at the table with him.

Which makes me a lot less brainy than my grade point average implies.

CHAPTER 60: RÓISE

"What are we doing here?" The barrier rises and the driver pulls the SUV into the underground parking garage for the Oscuro building.

I'm not totally against sex in his office. I've dreamed about it often enough since telling him off about my new bodyguards. But it seems a little weird to come here just for that purpose.

Miceli looks up from his phone. He's been focused on it the entire drive.

I interrupted him once and he turned an almost demonic expression on me. "I'm holding on by a thread, *mi dolce fiero*. Do not talk to me. Don't even breath in my direction if you don't want me to fuck you right here."

"What do you me—"

He puts up his hand. "This SUV has a bulletproof divider that can be raised, but no visual barrier to the front seat."

Unwilling to give the two men in the front seat a show, I zipped my lips.

Now Miceli looks at me like he doesn't understand the question. Then he shakes his head as if clearing it. "The penthouse."

"There's a penthouse in this building. Like one you live in, not a giant office suite." But then if they had one of those, that would be where Miceli and his brother's offices were located, wouldn't it?

"Yes."

Seeing the no doubt bewildered look on my face, he says, "It's not uncommon for a company like ours to have at least one floor of apartments for business use."

I'm not sure I want to know what kind of business needs an apartment, so I don't ask.

"We put our clients up in the smaller apartments, or executives from sister corporations here for training, etc."

"And the penthouse?"

"Is mine."

I'd ask what he means by that but again, I can guess and it's no more pleasant than my last one. I don't say anything as Miceli leads me to another elevator with biometric access.

This one has buttons. Not enough to cover all the floors in the building, but a few. They aren't numbered though.

I guess you have to know where you are going.

The elevator opens onto a foyer with double doors to the right. The doors require more eye scanning to get in. But once I hear the click of the lock, Miceli doesn't open the door. He has me step forward and let the system scan my eye.

I also have to put my hand against a black panel for a full handprint scan. "That will open the door from the inside, but not out here."

"I have to scan my hand to open the door?"

"It's just a security measure."

"Have I told you that you're a little excessive when it comes to that?"

The corner of his mouth tilts. "On at least one memorable occasion."

"As long as you know."

"There is no such thing as too much security when it comes to keeping you safe." His dark gaze traps mine with serious intent.

Fanning myself, I ask, "Is it warm up here? Maybe you should turn down the heat."

"No chance." Both brows raise suggestively.

Jayzuz, Mary and Joseph. This man is lethal.

Once we step through the double doors, they shut with a whoosh behind us.

Miceli points to the left. "I'll show you the rest of the penthouse later." Then he points to the right. "The bedrooms are this way."

Bedrooms as in plural? How many does he need to sex up his women?

Reminding myself that no matter what happened before, I'm the only woman in his life now, I follow him through the double doors.

Another hallway? How big is this place? There are a set of double doors in front of us and four more doors to our left, with another set of double doors at the end of the hall.

Six bedrooms, or is one of them an office? What would he need an office for when he's entertaining women? What would he need with extra bedrooms?

This place has even taller ceilings than the executive office floor. At least fifteen feet, but it could be twenty.

And the two outer walls are made up of windows that go all the way from the floor to that soaring ceiling. I can see a terrace beyond the windows, so there must be a door in them, but I can't see it.

"You like the view?" Miceli lays his hands on my shoulders and pulls my back flush to his front.

Desire wars with awe. "I feel like I should be able to see my house from here. How tall are these ceilings?"

"Eighteen feet."

"Right in the middle."

"The middle of what?" The pads of his thumbs run up the back of my neck on either side of my spine, leaving sparks of sensation in their wake.

"I guessed fifteen or twenty feet."

"You've got a good eye for space."

"I've helped build a lot of stage sets." Why are we talking about measurements?

He husks out a laugh. "You asked."

And I asked that last internal thought out loud too. "I'm just full of questions tonight."

"I'd rather you were full of me."

My body sizzles with sexual energy.

His lips on my neck scattering my thoughts, I fling myself into sensation.

There's something we haven't done. Something I've never done. But I want to.

Breaking the kiss, I drop to my knees in front of my fiancé and put my hands on his belt.

I look up at him through my lashes And I smile in a way I hope is enticing. "I want to taste you."

Heat flares in his eyes. "There's no way I'm going to turn that offer down."

"I'm glad." Because I really want this.

I undo the buckle on his belt and slide it out of the loops on his slacks. Letting it drop to the floor. Then I undo the fastening and zipper before pushing his pants down.

His big erection strains against his boxers, and I take a deep breath, inhaling the scent of his sex and excitement. It turns me on, like some kind of combustible chemical reaction.

I'm the fuel. He's the oxide.

Together, we burn.

Taking a breath for courage (because his erection does not get any less intimidating on acquaintance), I pull the waistband of his boxers away from his body. I force myself to go slow, sliding the fabric down over the impressively hard penis pressing against his flat stomach.

"Beautiful," I breathe.

Darker than his normal skin tone and flushed with blood, veins pop along the imposing length. Why did so many ancient sculptors downplay the artistic merit of this part of anatomy?

His laughter is choked. "My cock is not beautiful. Your pussy on the other hand..."

I huff warm air over the tip, and he doesn't finish his thought. How badly do I want to taste the pearl of precum beaded on the slit?

"You're so big," His girth makes my mouth water even though I have no idea if I can stretch my lips wide enough to take him, or not. "I can't believe I fit this in my vajayjay, much less my back door."

"Your body was made for mine." He gently removes the headband from my hair and tosses it away so he can run his fingers through my curls. "I'm going to fit right down that tight little throat of yours too."

My vagina pulses with want, but I say, "I'm not sure if I'm ready to deep throat on my first time."

"Don't underestimate yourself." He winks down at me. Then grows serious. "But my perfect Aphrodite, I'll take what I can get even if it's you licking my head like a lollipop."

That sound like fun, so I lick right over his slit, the taste of his pre-cum sweeter than I expect. I thought guys jizz was supposed to be bitter.

More pearly liquid seeps out and I lap it up like Pusheen with a saucer of cream.

Gripping that big erection with both hands, I squeeze. Cliché, I know, but my fingers don't touch. It amazes me I can take this big piece of meat inside of my body.

His groan goes through me like a caress.

I like this. I like it a lot.

I suckle the tip until he snarls for me to *do something*. He doesn't say what, just *do something* in that deep, growly voice of his.

So, I do something, sucking him in as far as I can. He hits the back of my throat and I suck harder.

I don't have much of a gag reflex which my cousins have always envied when it came to taking pills and brushing our teeth, etc., but now I'm *really* happy for it.

I can suck more of him into my mouth, but I'm not sure about swallowing him into my throat. If I do, I'm not going to gag, but will I be able to breath?

His hips jerk a little, but he doesn't try to shove forward. Stretching my lips as wide as I can, I revel in the sensation. They sting a little and my jaw sort of aches.

And I like that too. Will I like him in my throat? My hands squeeze involuntarily at the thought and he groans. Loudly.

He likes that.

I do it again, but this time I push them down to his root before pulling them all the way back to meet my mouth on his dick.

Am I masturbating him? Milking him? I need a sex dictionary. Preferably with diagrams. Maybe I can find one at my favorite online UBS. Used bookstores have the coolest books on subjects you wouldn't expect.

Anyway, I don't know what you call what I'm doing, but it feels good to do and it's making Miceli make all sorts of sex noises. His legs are even shaking a little.

A sense of power rushes through me. I can do this to this man. Me. Róise Shaughnessy.

And nobody else ever gets to touch him like this again. No one except me. My thighs press together hard and I moan. Because that feels good too.

I suck harder and he hits the back of my throat again, this time a little harder. "Swallow me. It will work. Trust me."

I don't know if I would be willing to try except, he sounds so desperate. And I like that almost as much as his taste.

The next time he hits the back of my throat, I swallow hard and he goes down my throat. Just like that. Wow.

I keep swallowing and a litany of curses falls down on my head. Some in Italian. Some English. Some are shouts and others an agonized whisper.

Fucking good! *Sì, cazzo!* So goddamn delicious. *Sei mio.* So fucking perfect!

This man is out of his mind and it's all for me. All because of me.

"Show me your tits, Aphrodite. Let me see them."

I have to let go of him to reach around my back for the zipper. He pulls back so he's not in my throat and I suck in a deep breath as I unzip the curve hugging bodice.

It's so form fitting, it doesn't need a bra, so the girls swing free when I pull my arms out and let the bodice drop around my waist.

"Oh, fuck! Be a good girl and squeeze them for me. Pinch those hard little nipples."

I don't hesitate. I know how good breast play can feel. Even before we had sex the first time, I explored the way touching my chest made me feel and discovered that direct line of pleasure between them and my clit. My nipples especially.

I play with my breasts until we're both moaning and saliva starts to drool out of the corners of my mouth. Uncaring, I shove my head forward, demanding more of him and he gives it.

Swallowing him down my throat, I'm so turned on, I shove one hand under my skirt and between my legs. Diving right into my underwear, I rub circles around my clit.

He's so deep, there's no way I can breathe, and knowing he has control of that sends me over the edge. I rub my hand furiously against my bundle of nerves, forcing the pleasure to a nearly intolerable peak.

His sex blocks the sound of my scream, but he must feel something in my throat because he starts to come.

I swallow and I swallow, but when he pulls back to let me breathe, there's still more and some comes dribbling out the side of my mouth.

CHAPTER 61: MICELI

This fucking woman.

Sex with her is like bathing my soul, something I thought impossible. Bending down, I lift her up and kiss lips swollen from stretching around my cock. Róise returns the kiss, holding nothing back.

Like every single time we touch.

She offers the beauty of her soul along with her body and that sweet, dirty sensuality. I lick my seed from around her lips and she moans.

Fucking moans.

No other woman matches me like this one. Age and innocence don't matter because at her core, she is a deliciously sensual creature.

And yet so pure, her soul shines like a beacon in the darkness of our world.

I rip her dress getting it off her and she doesn't yell. She laughs.

She's not laughing when I plunge my hard cock, that never softened after coming, deep into her perfect, tight pussy.

No, she's moaning and writhing and meeting me thrust for thrust.

It's my turn to play with her tits and fuck if I don't get lost touching her until she screams in my ear. "Move, Miceli. Fuck me like you mean it."

Ah, the word that only comes out of her mouth when she's so far gone in her need, she can't help herself.

Twining my fingers with hers, I push them down onto the bed on either side of her head. Our gazes lock and I let mine show words locked too deep inside my broken soul to find voice.

Driving my cock as deep as it will go, I heave above her. Lungs bellowing and heart pounding, I push us both toward another catastrophic climax.

For one long perfect moment, we are joined so completely, the essence of who we are mixes and we are one.

Afterward, I hold her tight, brushing my hand up and down her naked back and pretend not to notice the hot moisture dripping from her eyes to my chest.

Her tears express the profound connection of our lovemaking that I have no words for.

That she allows herself to cry in my presence is both an honor and a gift. I lost my ability to cry before I learned to read, but Róise was taught not to cry in front of others, like my sister Giulia was.

"I can't believe you're still wearing the top half of your suit." Her giggle is a little waterlogged. "Take it off. I want to feel your skin. All of it."

"That's an order I don't mind taking." I sit up and start stripping out of my suit jacket, askew tie and rumpled shirt.

She watches me like I'm putting a show on for her. "I'll remember that."

"Just remember, I expect reciprocity. Reaching out, I tug one of her sweat damp curls.

"Like that's a problem. Keeping my clothes on around you is the bigger challenge."

"We fit."

She nods. "Way more than I thought was possible."

"Just think, you could have ended up married to Jed."

"You know about that?" she asks. "Only my uncle would even consider marrying me off to a man Gabriel picked out."

"You would never let that happen." And I'm not so sure her uncle did consider it.

The way he talks about Gabriel's disgusting plan doesn't indicate a man who sees it as a viable alternative for his niece.

Regardless, a woman as resourceful as Róise would have disappeared before marrying the man closer to her grandfather's age than her father's.

The fact she's here means she sees me as a better alternative, but that's not saying much.

"My dad hated Gabriel. He would never have considered allowing me to marry into that cult."

"Why?"

I wait to see if she'll tell me and I feel like I won an all-in hand of poker when she starts talking.

"Gabriel Lion is a chauvinist, misogynist piece of crap who believed in the whole spare the rod, spoil the child thing. My mom would have married a gorilla to get away from him, but she fell in love with my dad."

"He was a good man." I didn't know him personally, but I knew Derry Shaughnessy's reputation.

"The best." Her face fills with regret. "He promised my mom he would stop doing business with the AOG once he became boss. He never got the chance."

"Your dad was going to cut ties with Gabriel's cult?" This is news to me.

"Yes. Even after mom died, he intended to keep his promise to her. He was honorable like that."

He'd also been a vicious fighter and brilliant strategist. "Did Gabriel know?" I wonder out loud.

Róise shrugs, lost in old melancholy.

But the thoughts shooting through my brain with rapid fire logic energize me. "I haven't been able to find any information, not even a rumor about a hit being taken out on your dad."

Not within the Five Families, or any of the other syndicates in New York.

"You're still investigating?"

"I promised I would."

"But I thought you had mafia stuff you were doing for your brother."

"I do." As well as my many commitments as COO of Oscuro Enterprises.

"Thank you." She presses a soft kiss to my chest.

That tiny expression of appreciation goes through me like a stiletto, touching something I could swear is nothing more than cold ashes. The remnants of a soul incinerated by a lifetime of damning choices.

"The Shaughnessy mob has a lot of enemies." Róise's swollen, pretty lips twist in a grimace. "They're not all Italian."

I squeeze her in reprimand. "With our marriage none of those enemies are Italian."

"Yeah, yeah, yeah. I get it. The powerful Genovese will keep the rest of the Cosa Nostra at bay." Her sass is back in full force.

And I lov—like it. A lot.

"I've looked into the likely candidates. No one took responsibility."

"They wouldn't would they?" she asks, her brows drawn together.

"They would, at least among their own circles. Someone would know something. Even if it was your Grandfather Shaughnessy taking a hit out on himself anonymously, there would be a whisper of it somewhere." At the very least, speculation on who might have done it.

But there's nothing.

"Are you saying you have contacts in all those circles?"

"Pretty much, yeah."

"Oh." She looks impressed despite herself.

I want to smile, but the topic is too serious.

"If it wasn't an enemy, but someone who didn't want anyone to know they had your dad killed because doing so would make an enemy out of an ally..."

I stop talking, letting her draw her own conclusions.

The narrowing of her eyes says she's reached one. "You think it was my grandfather, Gabriel Lion."

Got it in one, my smart fiancée. "If he knew your dad's intention to stop doing business with the AOG once he became boss, it's almost a certainty."

And he doesn't have to outsource a hit. He has his own people for it.

She doesn't look shocked or disbelieving.

"I'll find the answer," I promise her.

She nods, swallowing back emotion.

I want to tell her not to do that, not to hide her feelings. To cry again if she needs to. The words stick in my throat though, just like so many others I forgot how to speak.

"I spent so many years, hating the Cosa Nostra, and I probably would have anyway because of my mom. But we're not enemies. Not anymore."

"I'm glad you finally realize that."

"Pretty sure I realized it a while ago or we wouldn't be sitting here naked."

"There's such a thing as hate-sex."

"Well, I'm not into that."

"Good." I bring her hand to my mouth and kiss her palm. "I'm not either."

The only sex I'm into now, is sex with her.

Her lips set in a firm line. "If that hypocrite had my dad killed, I am going to cut his throat and enjoy watching him bleed out."

"Blood thirsty."

"I have some of my dad in me. I figured that out a while ago."

I believe her, but it's the best parts of the man. Not the ability to kill. "As much as I appreciate the sentiment, leave the killing to me. I'm trained for it."

"You promised to train me," she reminds me.

"We'll start this week. But I'm training you in self-defense. It's not the same thing."

"So you say. "

"I do. Trust me, *mi dolce fiore*, killing isn't as easy for someone like you." And there's no way her father taught her aggression fighting techniques. "No matter how much you hate the person you are taking out."

"As opposed to someone like you? What do you think you have that I don't?"

I kiss her hand again and close her fingers around it to hold my affection as I want no one else to do. "It's not what I have, but what I don't have."

"I know you have a conscience. Your actions with me show it. When you realize you screwed up, you backed down. You're keeping your word. And it's not just about being trustworthy in the criminal underworld. You care about keeping your vows."

"Yes. I do. But, I don't have a soul anymore. Or if I do have one it is so black you can't see it. One more killing won't make a difference in the opaqueness."

"You have a soul," she says earnestly. "I feel it every time we touch because our souls connect. If yours was as black as you think it is, that connection wouldn't feel as beautiful as it does."

"If there is any beauty in my soul, it's because of you."

Her beautiful eyes glisten with moisture. She smacks my arm. "Don't say stuff like that."

"I will speak the truth..."

"And shame the devil?"

"I am the devil and I feel no shame for the goodness you bring into my life."

With an inarticulate cry, Róise throws herself at me, kissing me with hot and irresistible passion.

CHAPTER 62: RÓISE

I wake up needing to pee and hungry.

After Round 4, or was it Round 5? Does mutual masturbation count as a round? Anyway, at some point we stopped sexing and fell asleep.

From the sound of his breathing and the leashed power tension in his body, I know Miceli is already awake. The fact he's sitting up against the headboard with my body tucked into his side is a dead giveaway too.

Yawning, I lift my head.

He's on his tablet, a pair of glasses perched on his nose.

"You wear glasses?" I scramble to my knees to get a better look.

Bare chest. Treasure trail disappearing under the blankets resting across his hips. The *Family Always* snarling wolf tattoo on the heavily muscled arm.

Mmm. So sexy.

"When my eyes are tired." He taps on the screen and then swipes up. "They're blue light blockers with a small magnification."

"I like them."

His gaze lifts from the tablet to meet mine. "Yeah?"

Scuttling backward, I shake my head. "Get that look off your face. I need to pee. And I'm hungry."

"If you'd eaten your dinner... "

"I wasn't hungry then." Thoughts of Miceli's plans for later had strangled my appetite.

"Not for food anyway." His voice is heavy with innuendo.

Which I force myself to ignore, scooting off the mattress to stand beside it. "I need a shower before we do anything else in that bed."

Sex is way messier than I expected. And I kind of love it.

But right now, I smell a little too earthy. So, shower. I'd kill for a bath though.

Not literally. Maybe.

He points his thumb toward a set of double doors. "Bathroom. The kitchen is through the door in the hall. It's fully stocked."

"Closet?" I ask.

I plan to steal one of his shirts for after my shower. I love the scene in romance novels when the FMC goes around naked except for her lover's shirt.

We aren't romance.

Maybe to him we're not, but I can live my side of this relationship any way I want. And right now, I want one of his shirts.

He waves toward a third set of double doors on the other side of the room. The first one, we came through when we got here.

I pad over unembarrassed by my jiggling flesh, mostly because he watches me like a hungry wolf.

When I open the door to the closet, a light comes on.

"I have to say I enjoy this automatic light thing you've got going on. I'm going to talk to Uncle Brogan about installing some in the mansi..." I lose my words as my brain processes what my eyes are seeing.

First, this room is off the charts. It's almost as big as my bedroom. (And hello, mansion...my bedroom is not small.)

One side is suit jackets, slacks dress shirts, you know...guy clothes. Whatever.

But what has my attention riveted and words stuck in my throat like I just swallowed cement is the other side.

It is filled with my clothes. Not clothes for a woman in my size. And not a few items from my closet. But if my entire freaking closet isn't hanging up here, I don't know my own wardrobe.

I rush to the island in the center and yank open one of the drawers on "my" side of the closet.

You guessed it, my underwear. I open another one. Those are my socks. open another one. Those are my T-shirts. Crap! All of my clothes are in here.

"Miceli!" There may be a slightly hysterical note in my voice.

I blame the clothes snatcher. Have I been adult-napped? Lured in with fantastic, earthy sex instead of sweet candy?

Spinning around, I'm ready to charge back through the door when I'm stopped short by the sight of him lounging in the doorway.

His shoulder leaning against the jamb, His expression is calm. Maybe even a little smug. Definitely not underboss stoic.

I wave my arms wildly around. "What are all of my clothes doing here?"

"Not how did they get here?" He sounds almost teasing.

But underbosses don't tease. So, what is that weird look on his face?

"No. The how is pretty easy to figure out. You have your minions and a devil's bargain with my uncle. The why is what I am trying to understand. I don't live here."

"You do now."

"No. I don't. I would have remembered agreeing to moving in with you. And there was never a discussion about that." I would remember.

No matter how intensely I studied for my final exams.

"Sev discussed it with your uncle."

My fiancé has to know those words are like waving a red flag in front of a bull.

Make that an already enraged bull.

My temper erupts like a cracked gas line jarred one too many times.

And I scream.

Not recognizable words. Just a sound. A long, furious shriek that hurts my throat. And I don't care.

He winces like maybe I hurt his ears.

Good.

He's not leaning against the jamb like he doesn't have another care in the world now.

Double good.

In fact, he looks worried.

Triple good.

Miceli puts his hand up. "Calm down *mi dolce fiore*. You knew you were going to move in with me eventually."

"Are you kidding me with this?! You already moved up the wedding date. At least then you had the intelligence to talk to me about it, even if you didn't listen the first time I said no."

"I won't make that mistake again. "

What mistake is he talking about?

Talking to me about what he's planning to do or not ignoring me when I say no?

I don't bother to ask. I'm so freaking angry right now, I can barely get words past the tightness in my throat "I don't want to move in here."

"You already have."

"No."

He takes a step toward me, and I take a step back. He puts both hands up in a stopping gesture or maybe a *look I'm not dangerous* gesture, but we both know that's a lie.

"It is too high risk for you to remain at the mansion. Both for you and your cousins."

I don't ask why my cousins because I understand collateral damage better than anybody.

"It's a volatile environment in *la famiglia* right now. Some high ranking men in the Cosa Nostra don't want Sev to be the next godfather. I'm his right hand and you're leverage against me in the wrong hands."

"Which you could have tried explaining before you moved all my clothes in here." I can only be leverage if I matter to him, right?

But is it because of the blood alliance and my healthy uterus, or because *I* matter? And how are these needy thoughts making it through the haze of rage in my brain?

I know they say love is the strongest emotion, but stronger than my fury?

"Where's Pusheen?" I ask angrily while he tries to come up with a reason for acting like an asshole.

Yes, I said it. Jerk isn't strong enough for my feelings about his actions.

"I didn't see *her* stuff in the bedroom."

"She has her own room, which she seems to like a lot more than you like yours," he tries to joke.

"Don't." I shake my head. "This is not funny, Miceli. Why didn't you talk to me?"

"Your uncle told Sev about the Jed situation while I was in Boston. My brother and I were already worried about your safety. He ordered me to bring you under our protection."

"What part of protection is taking me out to a very public restaurant?" I demand, not buying his explanation for a minute.

"We had a security force of twelve of my best men around us, including two snipers, watching rooftops and windows."

I can't process that. Or this...this closet filled with my clothes. My cat having her own room. None of it.

"I want Pusheen in my room."

"Our room."

My only answer is a glare.

"I'll move her stuff while you're in the shower, but she might appreciate having her own space."

"We'll get another cat bed so she can decide," I push out between clenched teeth.

"Good idea."

Ignoring his approval, which I do not need, I grab one of his shirts. It's a silk tuxedo shirt and probably cost as much as the dress he tore getting off me earlier.

"I'm taking a shower. Stay out of the bathroom."

He steps out of my way and I march past him, careful so our bodies don't touch. He raises his arm, like he's going to stop me.

"Don't touch me."

"Fuck, Róise, I didn't mean to hurt you."

"Telling me my uncle knew before I did was deliberate."

"No! It was..." He stares at me like his words are as trapped as mine were a minute ago. "A mistake."

The two words sound like they came through ground glass to get past his vocal cords.

"What was? Telling my uncle first or telling me he knew first?" This time I want clarification.

"Both. I meant to talk to you before we fucked, but I couldn't tell you at dinner. I couldn't explain the reasons where I could be overheard."

"You could have talked to me on the drive back." Unless he didn't trust his own driver and bodyguard to hear the discussion.

"No, I couldn't." The passion that's always an undercurrent between us flares in his dark gaze. "I told you, it took every ounce of my self-control not to fuck you in the SUV."

"I'm pretty sure the argument we would have had would have cooled your jets."

"And I'm positive it would have only made me want you more." His erection growing between us is undeniable proof of his words.

"Sheesh, Miceli! Sex doesn't solve everything. I'm not sure it solves anything."

He gets the weirdest expression on his face when I say that.

"I should have controlled my need for you long enough to tell you what was going on. I'm sorry I didn't."

"You're sorry?" That's not a word I've ever heard from the men in my family.

Not my grandfather for sure, but not my uncle either and not even my dad.

"Yes. I used to think the words were useless, but you deserve to hear them. I'm not sorry I moved you in. It had to be done."

That's the Miceli I know...and yes, love, darn it!

"I am very sorry you were hurt by the way I did it though."

Heaven help me for being a fool, but I believe him.

CHAPTER 63: MICELI

Róise doesn't respond to my apology, but something inside me settles after saying the words. Maybe they have power after all.

Not that I believe an apology without actions to back it up is worth the air it took to utter the words, but saying the words and then proving their sincerity with actions? Róise deserves it all.

Which is why I text one of my men to get us another cat bed for Pusheen and move the current one into our bedroom.

Our cat does not like being woken for the transfer and swipes her claws lightly across my forearm to let me know. I take the shallow scratches as a win.

I'm finishing up a plate of street tacos for Róise when she walks into the room. She's wearing my shirt, the top three buttons undone. On her shorter frame that leaves the entire valley between her breasts exposed.

The hem hits her mid-thigh, but the white silk is all but transparent, her pink nipples and areolas easy to make out. The only thing that adds a tiny bit of modesty is the pleating down the middle that is more opaque over her pussy.

She looks at the plate greedily. "Are those for me?"

"Yes." I almost ask if that's for me, meaning her body, but I know the discussion we started in the closet isn't over.

This time, I'm not letting my libido derail me.

Róise takes the plate and wanders into the living room. This part of the penthouse is total open concept. So the living room, dining room and kitchen are all in one big space. There's a sunroom off the kitchen with a smaller table that opens onto the terrace.

I usually do what Róise is and eat on one of the sofas, if I'm not eating standing up by the sink.

Her gaze is fixed on the spectacular view out the window. "What is this place?"

"It's my apartment." I sit down beside her and steal one of her tacos.

"Hey, those are mine. You said."

"Didn't your parents teach you to share?" I tease.

I know my girl. She's not eating six street tacos in one sitting. Four maybe. But not six.

"Fine, you can have two," she says like she's making a big concession.

Did I call it, or what? "Thank you, *mi dolce fiore*. Your generosity touches me deeply."

With a defiant look, she takes a bite of taco and chews aggressively. "I thought you lived with your family at the De Luca building?"

"I do. But sometimes I need my space.

"You mean so you can screw around with women?"

"I don't bring sex partners into my private spaces. The family can be too much sometimes, so, I come here. I also crash here on the nights I work too late to go home." What used to be my home.

Now, this penthouse, with Róise and Pusheen living here, is my home.

"It's a pretty big space for a crash pad or to get away from your family." She looks around pointedly. "Besides, I thought that's what your studio was for."

"I only go to my studio a couple of times a month. Going there isn't about getting away from the family home. It's about giving vent to my secret passion."

Forcing myself to stay away as much as I do has helped me develop an iron will, that this woman decimates with a single touch.

"It must be awful to feel like you have to hide your need to create." Her emerald green eyes are filled with compassion and sorrow.

For me.

Has anyone ever looked at me like that? No. Not even my mother.

"It has made me stronger."

"Or more of a jerk. The jury is out on that one."

"Maybe both," I freely admit. Being an asshole can be useful in my position.

Both as COO of Oscuro Enterprises and as the Genovese underboss.

The wry twist of her lips acknowledges the truth of my statement. But then she sighs. "Even if I never use my degree as an actor, I can still do things that will give that side of my creativity an outlet."

"Like what?" Maybe I can make her finding those outlets easier.

"*Mamo* lets me read aloud to her doing the different characters in the book. It's fun. For me anyway. I think she prefers her favorite narrators, but she never says so."

An idea starts to form, but I don't voice it. "I like your grandmother. Would she be open to coming to visit a few days a month?"

I don't want to take Róise from her family, but our life will be in Manhattan.

"Maybe." She chews on her lower lip as she looks around. "I know you say this is your apartment, but it sure doesn't look like anyone lives here."

I try to see the main living area through her eyes. I don't have any artwork up because even putting up paintings recommended by the interior designer feels like showing too much of myself.

"We used the same interior designer as we did for the executive offices."

"That explains the office feel with all the glass and chrome."

"There's wood too." Alder to be exact.

"Yeah, I can see her attachment to Scandinavian design, but she misses the *hygge* by a mile because there's no coziness here."

"I like that it's not cluttered."

"But there are no touches that makes it feel like a home. Nothing that reveals you at all. Except maybe the wood accents. They're they same wood as your easels, aren't they?"

"You noticed that?" I feel exposed, but having Róise's eyes on the me I kept hidden feels good.

Not vulnerable. Not weak.

"Yes, but even with the wood, this place is soulless. Yours, or not, no one lives here."

Soulless? That *is* me, but it's not her.

"Make any changes you want. Redesign the whole apartment. Make it a home."

She swallows. Something I said touched her emotions. "I can add some personal touches, but it's hardly worth redesigning the whole place for a temporary living situation."

"Our living together is not temporary." Sev could become godfather tomorrow and I wouldn't let Róise move back in with her uncle.

She is mine, damn it.

"That's not what I meant. But this isn't our permanent home, right? We'll be moving into the De Luca apartment building with your family at some point."

"No. This is our home."

CHAPTER 64: RÓISE

I look around with new eyes, because *this is our home*.

But the fresh perspective doesn't change what I see.

A soulless space devoid of family. "I don't mind moving in with your family. There are less De Lucas living there than Shaughnessys in the Long Island house."

For once, the memories of living there with even more family don't hurt as much.

But Miceli shakes his head in denial. "It's a bad security decision to have the godfather and the don of the most powerful of the Five Families living in the same building."

"But the Godfather right now *is* a don." Which means both the don and godfather live in the same house.

"We don't do things the way other families do them. That's why I will be don when Sev steps up to be godfather."

I think their separation of duties is smart, and maybe their decision not to live together is too.

But does that mean we have to live *here*? "What about getting a house on Long Island? With the helicopter, you could get here faster than driving from the De Luca apartment building to Oscuro."

He's shaking his head again and I hastily add, "Not in one of the boroughs of course."

That would cause all sorts of problems.

"*Mi dolce fiore*, the don of the Genovese has to live in Genovese territory. And that is Manhattan."

"But this isn't even an apartment building. It's an office building."

"That's a benefit, not a detriment. Most offices are empty by seven p.m. and with the private elevator we'll have the kind of privacy that could only be achieved by having a standalone house."

"I don't want that kind of privacy. I've lived my entire life surrounded by other people. I don't want to live on the top floor of an office building."

"We'll get to see more of each other when home is only an elevator ride away." Every time he says the words home, some emotion I can't read passes through his dark gaze.

Okay, that's a fair point. Given the choice between seeing more of Miceli, or less, I choose more. But an office building?

The idea of living here with no family around makes it hard to breathe.

"I can't live here, Miceli."

"We don't have a choice right now."

Does that mean we might in the future? Hope sparks to life inside me, but it's not enough. "But my cousins," I try to explain so he'll get it. "I had four months to get used to leaving them."

"Sometimes just ripping the Band-Aid off is best. "

"That might work with Band-Aids and waxing my pubes, but this isn't that. People with actual emotions take time to adjust to emotional changes. You and your brother can't just rip me away from my cousins, from my whole life and think that's okay."

"I'm not ripping you away from anyone. You can see them when you like."

"So I can leave right now and go visit my cousins?"

"You know you can't. Don't be childish."

"Let's get one thing straight, Mr. Made Man, every time you get frustrated with me or angry or whatever the heck is going on here, you do not get to accuse me of being childish. I may be twelve-and-a-half years younger than you, but from where I am standing, I am the one with the emotional maturity. You are the one with stunted growth in that department. "

It's a lot to say in one go and I feel kind of bad saying it, but if we're going to build a relationship that works, it starts with both trust and honesty. He's been working on the trust. I'm working on the honesty.

And communication.

Yeah, he's got a ways to go on that one.

He doesn't reply.

"Nothing to say?"

"I'm mulling it over. You might be right."

The admission disarms most of my residual anger and that makes me mad all over again. What is with this guy?

Love and hormones have a lot to answer for. I'm just saying.

"I need a say about the important decisions in our life," I add when the silence stretches and stretches.

"You can decorate this place any way you want. Make it our home."

That is not an answer. "Seriously? Could you be any more of a chauvinist? What if I don't want to decorate this place?"

And no amount of interior design can fix the basic flaw of the apartment's isolation.

When I tell him that, he says. "We have barracks two floors down for the single soldiers on our elite teams."

"Barracks?" I practically screech. "That is no better than offices. It's not like I'm going to spend time with mafia soldiers chatting over coffee. Or watching movies."

"You sure as fuck won't!"

"Are you being deliberately obtuse?"

"You're not going to be isolated, Róise. You can have your friends over. Your cousins can come to stay. Your grandmother too. They just won't live here with us."

Which is exactly the problem. "I'm going to do this whole place up in every shade of pink I can find."

He laughs. Not a chuckle, but a freaking belly laugh.

He's so different like this, I sit entranced watching him until he grabs me and kisses me like he can't get enough of me.

I'm dazed when he lifts his mouth from mine. "Make it as pink as you want, as long as you are the one doing it."

"You better watch out or I'm going to think you like me."

A lot.

Does he? I never had the high school crushes my friends did. It just wasn't an option in my situation. I couldn't bring boys to the Shaughnessy mansion because I was going to school as Rosy Aisling.

For my own safety, I couldn't socialize a lot away from home either. So, yeah, I'm attached to my cousins. Sue me.

But these giddy feelings inside of me this up and down, this uncertainty...it feels like that. Miceli and I are going to be married for goodness sake, and I am wondering if he likes me.

If he *doesn't* like me, we're both in a world of trouble.

Which I know is a complete about face for me. Because yeah, I started this whole thing sort of despising him.

I love him now though.

"I more than like you, *mi dolce fiore*. You make me believe in my own soul again." His kiss almost obliterates mine.

That sounds like love.

Will the underboss learn to love me, after all? Stranger things have happened, right?

CHAPTER 65: MICELI

Róise is on the back of my motorcycle, her body pressed tightly to mine. It's the last trip we'll make to the studio until the yellow alert level is over.

This trip is too important to put off though. I've taken precautions. Keeping Róise safe means sharing my secret with four of my most trusted men.

One of them is the man I plan to make my underboss when I become don, Allessio. Not only do I trust him like family, he has the intelligence and animal instinct to do what must be done.

He came up with the route and strategy for getting me and Róise safely to the studio.

The trip goes without incident and the security detail peels away in the parking garage to take up guard positions outside the private access.

I haven't told the team what I do in this building, but telling them I come here is an exercise in trust. As I told Róise, it has to start somewhere and a don has to trust more things to his men than the underboss.

I stop the bike and climb off before helping my fiancée. After checking the guard positions, I close the door and arm the alarm on it. Then I divest both me and Róise of our helmets and leather jackets before taking her by the hand and leading her to the access panel.

Sev gave Catalina access to the secret archives of our family's history in the New York Cosa Nostra and to the safe in his office. But Róise doesn't care about information, family, heirlooms, or money.

I'm here to give her something a lot harder for me to offer: access to what is left of my heart. I hope she can hear the message in my actions, because I'm still struggling to come up with the words.

"I'm glad we're here. You need this space, Miceli."

I grunt. Not as much as I need the woman at my side.

"Thank you for bringing me."

"I want you with me." Always, but that's not practical.

I understand why my brother has changed his schedule and where he works so much since marrying Catalina though. I said I'd never be as gone on a woman as my brother and cousin, but the truth is? I'm worse.

No way can either of them be as obsessed as I am with my Aphrodite. Having Róise an elevator ride away is fucking intoxicating.

And when things are trying to go to shit, knowing she's there in the penthouse brings me peace.

I access the panel and explain to her how to do it. "Now stand still and try not to blink."

The retinal scanner takes a map of her retina's blood vessels.

When it's done, Róise blinks up at me, her eyes soft. "I think your painting is an important part of you and I hate that you hide it from everyone who loves you."

My lips twist too, but it's not a smile. "I don't think the world is ready for a don who is also an artist.

"I think the world, including the world we live in, can surprise you. Look at how well Uncle Brogan is doing with the calf's eyes that Zoey and Fi keep making at each other."

The older man does surprise me with his acceptance of his youngest daughter's choice in partners. But Róise told me that one of the conditions of her agreeing to marry me is that Fiona will never be forced into an arranged marriage.

Perhaps not being able to see his daughter as a mob asset allows Brogan to be more accepting of Fiona's choices.

"Those two are so into each other it's like walking into an electric field when you stand between them." *Me dolce fiore* fans herself. "Everyone is going to be relieved when Fi turns eighteen, and they can start dating."

I grunt again. It's a useful expression with my woman. She comments on things I don't have any interest in. Like her youngest cousin's dating life. If I say I'm not interested, it hurts Róise's feelings.

If I grunt she assumes agreement and keeps talking. I like the sound of her voice, so It's a win-win.

"Speaking of Fi..." My fiancée stops talking, a cagey expression on her face I don't like.

"Speaking of your cousin?" I give the little troublemaker a look meant to intimidate as the elevator doors open.

Of course, she just smiles back and steps onto the elevator. There is not one iota of fear of me in her clear green eyes, and I cannot regret it. That doesn't mean I'm leaving this elevator before she gives me the answers I'm looking for.

I press the emergency stop. Recognizing my print, the elevator halts.

"What did you do? We're not moving."

"I'm aware." I lean back against the wall. "You did say you are going to work on my communication."

"What does that have to with..." She realizes the trap.

I smile. "Lead by example."

She rolls her eyes, but starts talking. "Fi wants to sneak away for her 18th birthday celebration."

"She wants to sneak away from the big ball? Doesn't she always find a quiet room to hole up in at parties? What's different about this time?"

After making an appearance, the guest of honor is not necessary at these events because the real reason for them is the chance for syndicate players to gather without drawing scrutiny.

"Nothing. We've already got the room she'll retreat to planned out. She wants to have a private birthday celebration with me, Kara, and Zoey. But she wants it to be..."

"What does she want it to be?" I prompt when Róise doesn't finish the sentence.

Why do I feel like my feisty fiancé has something to do with whatever scheme her cousin is trying to cook up?

"Well, you see for my 21st birthday..." She looks at me. "Can I tell you something in confidence?"

"What do you mean by confidence?" I'm not sure I have any limitations on what I will do for her.

Keeping her secrets is a pretty easy ask, but I won't allow her to put herself in harm's way. I guess that's my limitation.

"I need you not to tell my uncle. Because other people are involved. Adults. And we all have a right to privacy."

I warn her, "I can't allow you, or anyone else in your family, to be put at risk."

"No one is going to be put at risk and there is no risk in regard to past actions because they are over." She looks up at me with sweet innocence.

Which I know is a lie. What the hell has my fiancé been up to? "Talk."

With a disgruntled look, she does. "I wasn't thrilled about spending my 21st birthday having a fake party with a bunch of cronies of my uncle and you guys."

"What did you do about that?" I ask with genuine curiosity.

"My friends and I got together and watched Drunk Shakespeare."

"I'm surprised your uncle allowed that. It would be a difficult venue to secure "

"Well..." She looks up at me through her eyelashes, which is far too effective. "He didn't exactly know about it."

Understanding is making my gut tight. "Are you telling me that you snuck out?"

Did she hear a single word I said that day in my office when we argued over her new security detail? Said detail is in so much fucking trouble.

"I know that look on your face and knock it off. At that time, I didn't have guards assigned to me when I was at home. They didn't know about my plans. Neither did Ollie. No one knew about it and they never found out either."

She sounds proud of herself.

"How?" I'm not relaxed against the wall anymore, but looming over my unrepentant fiancée.

"Everybody thought the three of us were in the theater room for a movie night."

"But you weren't?" How the hell did they get out of the mansion without being seen?

She tells me.

And I am equal parts, impressed, and furious. "You paddled on a blowup raft to a boat in the dark on the bay? Those waters are choppy. You could have capsized."

My throat muscles are straining with the effort it takes not to yell.

"It was amazing. You should've seen Kara, she was so like 007, except she said she was Salt. I felt like a superspy though."

She thought she was 007? Was she carrying a gun? "Do me a favor and explain this *amazing* escape in tiny detail for me."

The rest of the telling is no less hair-raising than their trip in the boat. "Your uncle's men could have shot you thinking you were intruders," I grind out.

"Oh, no. We timed it right and Kara's hacks worked perfectly."

"What if they didn't?"

"Then the alarms would have blared and we would have yanked off our hoodies so they knew it was us."

"What if there had been a trigger-happy guard on duty?"

"There wasn't. Or if there was it didn't matter because nobody saw us, okay?"

So not okay, but I want the whole story, so I don't say anything.

"Kara was careful not to shut anything down long enough for our enemies to get onto the grounds and sneak up on the guards, or into the mansion undetected."

"I am so glad you were worried about the *armed* soldiers." Can she hear the sarcasm in my tone?

Her grimace says she definitely does. "It wasn't that bad. We had it all planned out. We got to the boat. My friends took us to another house further up the shoreline. We changed into clothes for our night out in the

City and it was wonderful. The perfect night before losing my freedom. Or at least that's how I saw it."

How does she see it now?

Am I her jailer? Or the man she wants to spend the rest of her life with?

"I think that's the problem though. We told Fi all about it. And now she wants a night like that for her 18th."

"You have to be twenty-one to get into Drunk Shakespeare. It's in a bar."

"A lounge."

"The distinction does not matter to me. Your cousin is only turning eighteen." Another thought hits me. "*You* weren't twenty-one yet. "

She rolls her eyes at me.

Rolls. Her. Eyes.

"I wasn't twenty-one when I got in at Nuovi Inizi either. I have a very good fake ID."

"Which you have now destroyed?" I ask with little hope.

"Well, no." She looks up at me appealingly. "It's a keepsake now. A memento of my 21st birthday and the first night I met you."

I don't have anything to say to that, so I say nothing but neither do I demand that she destroy the fake ID.

"Kara and I aren't stupid, Miceli. We wouldn't do the same thing now, not with the threat level as high as it is. But at that time, neither of us had any reason to believe we were in danger."

She starts counting facts off on her fingers, like that makes them more convincing. "No one saw us leave. No one knew we were going to Drunk Shakespeare. My friends bought the tickets. And they were sworn to secrecy."

"You trust these friends to keep secrets like that?" I'm not judging her.

I am asking if she really believes she can trust the four students she spends most of her time with on campus. Of course, I know who they are. I know everything about my fiancée.

Except that she has a stronger predilection for sneaking out than I believed. The self-defense classes start tomorrow and she's sharpening her gun skills.

Róise looks at me, her expression as serious as I have ever seen it. "Yes, my friends, Aleks, Carrie, Traci, and Goodwin are as trustworthy as any human beings on this earth."

"Okay then. None of my investigations into their background contradict your assessment." Time to get this conversation back to the present plans. "If not drunk Shakespeare, what does your cousin want to do?"

"She's agoraphobic, yeah? So, it's not going to be to go to some crowded bar to watch actors do improv."

Róise has me there. I shouldn't have guessed that particular thing. "What *does* Fiona want to do?"

"To go bike riding at Caumsett Park."

I wait for her to add something else to this big secret birthday getaway and when she doesn't, I stare at her with incomprehension. "Why does this have to be a secret? "

"The most important element of the bike ride for Fiona is the sneaking away part." Her eyes beg me to understand.

I don't, but that doesn't mean I won't help her. "This is not the first time I haven't understood what is motivating a Shaughnessy woman. Go on."

"If we told Uncle Brogan that Fi wants to go on a bike ride, he wouldn't deny her. He's not a monster. But he would send a bunch of soldiers with us and it wouldn't be the same at all."

"What do you need from me?" Does she want me to help them sneak away from their security?

Because that's definitely not happening, even if I accompanied them. Not with the threat level where it's at right now.

I want you to tell Zoey that it's okay for her to pretend to sneak away with us. And I was really hoping that you would send that awesome security detail that I can never spot when we're out on our dates to protect us, so there's no question of safety."

I shouldn't be surprised by the maturity of this beautiful woman. But her solution to her cousin's desire is both compassionate and intelligent. Róise is not going to put herself or her cousins at risk.

However, she's determined to give Fiona an experience like the one she had for her recent birthday. Which will be giving me nightmares for months.

"Done." I press my finger to the button to get the elevator moving again. "You figure out how to make it seem like it's the great escape. And I will make sure that you have a security detail on you at all times."

CHAPTER 66: RÓISE

That was so much easier than I expected, but I knew I needed to talk to Miceli about what Fi wants.

Trust goes two ways. He has been giving me proof of his trust all along. Today was my chance to show that I trust him too.

And it paid off.

When we get up to the studio, I'm surprised to see what looks like a super comfy, oversized chair in one corner of the studio. It's pink. Definitely for me.

Of course, the first thing we use it for isn't me watching him paint. But to reenact our first lovemaking session in the boathouse.

After a quick shower, I pull on Miceli's discarded shirt. He paints naked. Yum!

I tear myself away from the eye candy to go to the bedroom where all of the finished canvases are stored.

You can tell the difference in painting style between Miceli and his father at a glance. While my fiancé paints wildly imaginative, if sometimes morbid fantasy covers for books, his father painted portraits.

The only portraits I've seen from Miceli are the two he did of me.

Every painting I pull out on his father's side of the storage room is a portrait of some member of the De Luca family.

You can tell the ones from when he had just started painting, and those from when he was older, but one thing that is common among all of them is the love you can feel of the artist for the subjects of the paintings.

There is one portrait, almost life-size of Aria that brings tears to my eyes. She is painted as a beautiful, ethereal being, almost angelic. That the painter worshipped her is clear in every stroke of paint.

"I always wanted to show that to my mom, but this was my father's secret, and I didn't have the right to expose it."

I turn to face Miceli, making no effort to hide my tears. "Your father is dead. Your mom is still alive. Do you really think he would want you to withhold all of this from the people that loved him and that he so obviously loved. "

"A promise is a promise."

"But was your promise for after death?" Did his father really swear him to posthumous secrecy?

Miceli stares at me for a very long time before saying, "It was never actually spoken out loud."

"So, you're going on the assumption of what you thought he wanted you to promise him that you never actually did." That's not a vow. "It's not a promise when you didn't actually make it."

"He was so adamant about me hiding my weakness –"

"Being an artist is not a weakness," I break in. "Your dad was afraid to express his emotions but he had them. All of you would've been happier if he had told you the things in his heart while he was alive."

When Miceli doesn't disagree, I go on. "Now you have the chance to show your mother the depth of the love your father had for her and your brother how proud he was of him. They're like love letters written for each of you."

The conflict in Miceli's expression hurts my heart. "I can't make you share these with them. But I will tell you that if it were me and there was something out there from my dad, no matter what it was, that let me feel his love one more time, I would want it."

My fiancé sighs. "You're right, but showing them the paintings means telling them about me."

"Would that be such a bad thing?"

"It might be. Sev could decide that I'm not strong enough to be Don of the Genovese."

"I don't think your brother's that's stupid."

Miceli's smile is sardonic, but something is flickering in his eyes. Hope? "I'll think about it."

"While you're thinking about it, consider this: are you going to teach our children that their gifts make them weak? Because I won't support that."

I am going to hang at least one piece of Miceli's artwork in all of the rooms of our penthouse.

If that means his family cannot come to visit, so be it. Because he said to make it into a home and the only way that happens is if both our hearts are in the design.

His heart is in his paintings.

~ ~ ~

The following weeks are a dream I don't want to wake up from.

The self-defense classes start the day after Miceli gives me access to the studio. He spends an hour every day teaching me. Despite my former training, there's nothing easy about learning the skills he wants to teach me.

But he flies my cousins in by helicopter twice a week to join us and that helps make up for the sore muscles and bruises.

He assigns Zoey to teach them three more times a week.

He cares about my family and their safety. That means a lot to me.

Fiona's special "secret" 18th birthday celebration goes off with without a hitch. She absolutely loves the cloak and dagger of sneaking off the property and the bike ride is so much fun.

She calls me late that night to tell me she had her first kiss. And it was wonderful.

Kara texts me fifteen minutes later.

Kara: *I told Zoey that if she broke Fi's heart, I would cut hers out of her chest.*

Rosy: *I'll help.*

You can take the girl out of the mob, but you can't take the mob out of the girl.

Remembering that would have saved me a lot of heartache grieving my lost dreams.

Moma comes to stay for two days a week and helps me with the interior design update. Miceli makes sure he's there to have at least one meal with her and she adores him.

I haven't lost my family at all.

There's also a bunch of construction happening two floors down. I've asked what it is, but Miceli keeps telling me it's a project for the office building. Only I'm pretty sure this isn't about an increase in office space, especially since they're tearing down offices on those floors.

We go out on public dates once or twice a week. So do Severu and Catalina. Though we never meet up.

Miceli says it's our way of showing the city that the De Lucas are not afraid.

That doesn't mean he's like my grandfather and putting me at risk. Oh, no. Whenever we are out those snipers he told me about are always there. The stealth security detail is always there too. Miceli said it's the same for Severu and Catalina.

My fiancé works from his home office as often as he can. Which is the desk in one of the spare bedrooms.

One of the first things I'm going to fix in this apartment, that's really a giant six bedroom hotel suite, is his home office.

Even the terrace outside has no personality. I have an entire container garden of bright foliage and mini trees arriving soon to make it more welcoming.

I'm having fun making Miceli think I'm using pink everywhere. *Moma* said I always had a streak of mischief in me.

She is not wrong.

I keep pink swatches of fabric out all the time along with paint cards. But underneath I have the real stuff.

I'm updating all the furniture to warmer items. I like Scandinavian design too, but I'm adding the throw pillow and blanket throws that give coziness to a room. Even one as big as our great room.

The sunroom off the kitchen reminds me of my mom's favorite room in the mansion. She called it the morning room so I'm calling this one, the morning room too. It's my domain and I've already changed the furniture.

Instead of a glass top table with four leather chairs, there is now a wicker dinette set with a matching chair and ottoman in one corner.

There's one other change I'm making right away. The far bedroom at the end of the hall is the only other room, besides the primary bedroom, with a corner view and two walls of windows.

It's perfect for an artist's studio, but I have no idea how Miceli's going to respond to it when it's done. I hope he'll use it because I want his heart here.

Not in another building.

The table is covered with my design samples right now and it makes me happy to see them because I finally get why we're really living here.

It's to protect me, but not from our enemies. Miceli's mom hasn't accepted me yet and he doesn't want her distrust and lack of welcome to hurt my feelings.

CHAPTER 67: MICELI

As a capo, it is not often my cousin Salvatore's job to interrogate our enemies. But this is a special circumstance.

Lorenzo Ricci didn't just steal from our mafia, he put Salvatore's woman at risk. He also betrayed his don. My brother.

I am still underboss, so his punishment is my responsibility for the embezzlement and the treason. I let Salvatore get his anger out in the interrogation though.

His specially designed cattle prod is impressive. I might need to get me one of those. Flipping my knife over in my hand I shake my head.

It hasn't let me down yet.

I use it to cut the straps on the ball gag in Lorenzo's mouth before I yank it out and throw it away.

I slap the traitorous capo. "Start singing cuckoo before I feel the need to get involved because I'll cut your balls out of your nut sac and feed them to you."

It's a messy way to get information, but it works.

"Her dad was my bookkeeper," Lorenzo sputters out fast. "He stole from me," he whines. "I didn't want her around *la famiglia*."

"Wrong answer." My cousin shocks the other capo in the thigh.

Lorenzo screams like a stuck pig, begging Salvatore to stop. What follows is the typical back and forth with a man who hasn't figured out he's dead yet.

The only thing left to determine is how much he's going to hurt before it happens.

When Lorenzo starts whining again about his former bookkeeper stealing from him, I'm too disgusted to stay silent. "You stole from *la famiglia*. From your don and the men in your crew."

I don't like his reply so I punch him in the kidney.

"What were Lucchese hit men doing in Manhattan and why did they attack Bianca?" my cousin asks, showing he suspects the same thing I do.

The fuck that attack was random. It was a hit. Which Henry Caruso agreed to execute in another Family's territory.

Lorenzo confirms the hit seconds later.

"Did you tell Caruso you had our don's approval for the hit?" Salvatore asks with some more not so gentle persuasion.

"Yes. He wouldn't send his men otherwise."

I shake my head. That doesn't track. "He would have checked."

Henry Caruso is an idiot, but he doesn't have a death wish.

"He wanted to be godfather. I gave him a way."

Lorenzo is behind the attempt to buy the bars out from under us? That I didn't see coming.

Salvatore isn't happy either and he looks ready to zap the guy with enough juice to bring on a heart attack.

I grab him to stop him. "Information first then retribution."

That information fills me with rage. Two of our former consigliere's men are rats for Lorenzo. One is already out of commission. Uncle Sal cut out his tongue for blabbing to a woman he was dating about the Cosa Nostra.

But the other? Is a man we all thought we could trust. Uncle Sal even kept him on his crew. Turns out he's Lorenzo's half-brother. How did we not know that?

"I actually liked that asshole," I complain. "Now I have to torture and kill him."

Salvatore's face twists with disbelief. "You did not like that blabbermouth."

Miceli shrugs. "Okay, like is too strong a word, but I didn't object when Uncle Sal brought him onto his crew when he became consigliere."

"None of us did." Salvatore sounds as pissed as I am.

Do we have other spies in our ranks? Is Róise safe? Are my family?

"You sold out your don and tried to have an innocent woman killed for what, you traitorous prick?" My fury and disdain drip from every word. "Our don had you under investigation already."

Lorenzo is back to looking wild eyed. Maybe he's finally figuring out that he won't be breathing when he leaves here. "No."

"His guy found your duplicate books and your hidden accounts." Salvatore sounds about as impressed with Lorenzo's stealth as I am.

I give the man who betrayed his made man vow a look of contempt. "All of them."

Lorenzo's moan is music to my ears.

The money will go to the soldiers and their families that weren't complicit to make up for working under such a huge, steaming pile of shit all this time.

After we've extracted all the information necessary, Salvatore leaves.

"Now, it's just you and me, Lorenzo. You betrayed my brother. You betrayed my father. You betrayed your vow as a made man!" I shout the last.

And then I begin meting out the punishment that level of betrayal deserves.

CHAPTER 68: RÓISE

I laugh out loud at the post Fiona put up on the family social media app.

Rambo has started living up to his name. He's taken over for Pusheen and is jumping on the soldiers' heads from high perches.

The latest picture Fiona posted shows the cat sitting on the face of a soldier knocked flat on his back. It must have been quite a jump.

This isn't the only picture Fiona posted of Rambo's new pastime. I scroll through giggling.

Everyone has posted comments on them. Everyone but Aria.

Enough is enough. Miceli says that trust has to start somewhere. Maybe if I start trusting his mom, she'll learn she can trust me.

It worked for Miceli with me, didn't it?

I scroll through my contacts and tap on Aria's phone number, calling before I have a chance to chicken out.

When Aria answers, I don't waste time on pleasantries. *Moma* wouldn't be happy, but sometimes polite behavior just gets in the way.

"We need to talk, Aria. Can you come over today?" I don't identify myself.

She has my number even if she doesn't want to use it.

"I'm not sure I have an opening in my schedule," is her stiff reply.

Refusing to be daunted by her cool demeanor, I ask, "When would be a good time?"

"Well... " The sound of a sigh over the line. "Yes, in fact this afternoon is available. What time would you like me to come over?"

"Would 4 o'clock work?"

"Yes. I'll be there."

I rush around getting things ready, making sure I have both Italian and Irish pastries on hand to go with the coffee. I deliberately mix them on the plate, so it's not like Irish on one side and Italian on the other.

Will she notice the subtle message?

Aria arrives promptly at 4 o'clock and I show her into the living room. She does not have access to the penthouse and I have to let her up.

Miceli did that. Did he know I would invite his mom over one day and need that extra reminder that this is *my* home?

I pour her coffee and she asks about plans for the wedding. I tell her the things *moma* and I have discussed. It's probably not anything Aria doesn't already know.

Moma is keeping her in the loop and asking for Aria's opinion on things she thinks will matter to the former don's wife.

So, really this is just stalling.

"Here's the thing, Aria," I dive in bluntly. "I know you lost someone to hostilities between the Bonanno Family and the Shaughnessy mob."

"It was my brother. My baby brother." Old grief creases the fine lines of her face. "He had just gotten made and then he was gone."

"I am truly sorry for your loss."

Aria nods. "Thank you. I know you lost your mother to another flare up between the families many years later."

"She was gunned down in front of me." I don't sugarcoat it.

There's no point. Aria knows what happened.

"Can you imagine how hard it was for me to even contemplate this marriage with your son."

"Better than most. But all the strife, the conflict, it's because of you stubborn Irish."

I could blow up, but that wouldn't accomplish anything. Build trust, I remind myself.

Aria wrings her hands. "I'm sorry. I shouldn't have said that."

"Maybe not, but hiding behind manners isn't going to solve the issue between us."

"It's just...I'll never understand why your family won't sell those properties to the Bonannos." Aria snaps her mouth shut.

Like she's said too much. Like I don't know exactly what the source of the tension between the two syndicates is.

"If my uncle asked your son to sell the De Luca apartment building to him because it is technically in our territory, would you expect Severu to do it?"

"Of course not. We have over a century of history there."

"How old do you think the Queens properties are?"

Aria puts her cup down without taking the drink she planned to. "I don't know."

"The first of the Shaughnessy clan came over in 1869. More of the clan emigrated over the next decade. They weren't alone, other clans like them came too."

"Like them in what way?" Aria sounds curious in spite of herself.

"They were not law-abiding citizens. They flouted the laws and what they saw as the tyranny of the wealthy back in Ireland. They did the same when they came to America, forming mobs, some still connected to those in the Old Country ."

"Are you trying to point out we have a similar history?" Aria asks.

"Yes. The warehouse the Bonanno don wants so badly is on the first tract of land my ancestors purchased in New York."

"So you're saying sentimentality keeps them from selling the warehouse?"

"No. Necessity. Not many years after they bought the land that the warehouse is on, they purchased the land to build an apartment building where they could all live. Which they did. They added a second apartment building a couple of years later."

"How interesting," Aria says, but her eyes are glazing over.

"I'm not a great storyteller, unless it's someone else's story written down for me," I admit. "The point is that they had three buildings, not far from each other in the middle of Queens."

"What are you trying to say?"

It's all about the Bunker. Telling Aria about it is a risk, but like Miceli says, trust has to start somewhere.

"The agreement between the Cosa Nostra and our family to operate different major criminal enterprises in New York is supposed to keep peace between the syndicates."

"I am aware of that." Aria sounds a little snippy and I like her more for it.

The perfect persona she presents to the world isn't the woman in the portraits her husband painted.

"I don't know what happened when your brother died, but twelve years ago, the Bonanno don decided he wanted to get into the weapons trade and he wanted our warehouse to store them."

"I didn't know that."

"And what your former don didn't know was that even if my grandfather had been willing to allow him to horn in on the weapons trade, he would never sell *any* of the properties in Queens."

"But why?" she asks in a voice laced with old anguish.

"Because those buildings are connected by a warren of tunnels and storage rooms impervious to being spied on and in over one-hundred years, have never been found and raided by the FEDs."

Aria's eyes widen in understanding. "Those properties aren't just a piece of Shaughnessy history, but that's where you store the things that are most important to your mob."

"People are the most important thing to any mob, or mafia. You can't build an empire on things, only with people. But you're right, we can't sell those buildings without giving those spaces up and they *are* important."

"I can't believe you're telling me this. What if I pass the information on to the Bonanno don?"

"You won't," I say with conviction. "You have too much integrity."

"You can't know that."

I can because she raised Miceli. "Your son told me once that trust has to start somewhere. And he trusted me with something very important to him."

"Is that how you reconciled yourself to your coming marriage?"

"It's part of it." A big part. I couldn't love Miceli if I didn't trust him.

"One of the things he trusted me with is the family social media app."

"I know."

"If you never unblock me from your feed, I'm okay with that, Aria. I can promise I'll never betray Miceli or my new family, but that's all I can do. Is promise."

Aria nods. "It should be enough."

But I don't agree. "You know how you said that you understand better than anybody how hard it was for me to agree to marry into the Italian mafia and give birth to a child that would become one of them?"

She nods again.

"Well, I understand better than anybody too how hard it is for you to accept me. So, let's just start by getting to know each other, okay?"

"You know a lot about your family's business..." She lets her voice trail off. I smile.

"For a woman?" I ask. "*Mamo* says women in the underworld have to hoard information."

"My daughter-in-law would agree with her."

"Catalina *is* pretty great."

"She likes you too."

"I'm glad." One day maybe Aria will be able to say the same thing.

"Miceli says that if I spend time with you, I won't be able to help but like you," Aria takes a bite of one of the Irish soda bread cookies. "My son is a wiser man than I give him credit for."

CHAPTER 69: MICELI

The smell of disinfectant mixes with lavender and eucalyptus.

They are trying to make it not smell like a sick man's room, but there's no way. The odor of impending death is here.

You just have to look at the shrunken figure on the bed to know that his time is close.

I wait for Sev to speak, watching as he and the Godfather measure each other with their eyes.

Finally, Don Caruso says, "So, you have come to pay your final respects. You're a good Don, Severu. You will make a fine godfather."

"So you have said. But have you said it to others?" Sev asks, his tone hard.

"I have, yes. Not only to the don's amidst the Five Families, but to all the dons of the Cosa Nostra as they have come to pay their respects. I have made it clear to each of them that you are my choice to succeed me. For what it is worth, you have my support." He waves with a feeble arm indicating his state in the bed. "For what it is worth."

"It is worth a great deal to me," Sev says, sincerity ringing in his tone. "To have a man I admire so much believe in my strength and capability to lead the Cosa Nostra into the future."

"I am glad to hear this, my son. You have been a good and loyal friend and don from the day you took over from your father. You have brought the Genovese into the present and now you must do this for the rest of the Cosa Nostra."

"There are many that will fight me on this." Sev doesn't sound like he's worried.

He's just telling the godfather that he knows how difficult the task is before him.

"None so much as my idiotic nephew."

"He conspired with his cousin to purchase land in the Five Family territories by another Cosa Nostra family." I say this with all the contempt I feel for Henry Caruso's betrayal.

The godfather seems to sink deeper into the bed. "I have heard rumors of these things. I had hoped they were not true."

"I have brought documents to show you," I say. "If you need proof, we have a lot of it."

Including a recording of Lorenzo's *testimony* during interrogation.

Sev says nothing.

He and the godfather lock eyes once again.

It's the godfather who looks away. "I do not need to see these evidences. A De Luca does not lie. "

"The same could be said of a Caruso if Enrico Caruso no longer walked this earth." Severu says the words firmly.

It is clear he is not asking permission, but telling the godfather of our plans.

Nevertheless, the godfather nods and puts his hand out.

Sev walks forward. The godfather raises his trembling hand a few more inches and my brother takes it, bending over and pressing his forehead to the godfather's ring.

"The death of Enrico Caruso at the hands of the De Luca family within the Genevese mafia is sanctioned by me." The Godfather begins to cough.

It is not the cough of a common cold or the flu, but the death rattle of a powerful man on the verge of his own demise.

Don Caruso looks to his lieutenant, a man nearly as old as he is. "Send the message to all of the Cosa Nostra. I have sanctioned the death of Enrico Caruso, no longer recognized by *la famiglia*, no longer recognized by me."

The man nods his head and leaves the room.

This is more than Sev or I expected when we came.

We thought we would have to strong arm the godfather into accepting that he needed to name a different capo as his heir.

But he is a man of honor, and his nephew has betrayed the Cosa Nostra.

Sev straightens. "I look forward to meeting the man who will be the next don of the great Lucchese family."

"I will introduce him to the rest of the capos tonight." The Godfather knows how eminent his death is and is determined to impose his will one last time.

For the good of *la famiglia*.

The call comes in the early hours of the morning.

I snag my phone without jostling Róise's sleeping form. I exhausted her with lovemaking last night.

I crave her body all the time, but after finding out how she reached out to mamma, I had to show her the depth of my feelings again.

"Sev," I say into the phone.

"Caruso had another stroke. He's on life support."

"Why?"

"He gave instructions to do it and assigned me power of attorney to decide when to turn them off."

"Giving you time to finish gathering support."

"Yes."

"We're close."

"We are," my brother agrees. "Salvatore wants to kill Henry Caruso because he sanctioned the hit on Bianca."

"It is not his place. You are the don whose territory was defiled and I am your right arm. Besides, he already killed the men who touched her."

"Would that be enough for you?"

No. It would not. "I'll rock, paper, scissors him for it."

"Whatever works, but the man dies soon."

"Agreed."

I put the phone down and shift back down to lie beside Róise.

She nuzzles sleepily into my neck. "Who was that?"

"Sev. The godfather is on life support."

Róise sits up like someone hit her with one of Salvatore's cattle prods. "What? The godfather is dead?"

"Not yet, but he will be. Sev will turn off life support when the time is right."

"Why your brother and not a member of the godfather's family?"

"He's giving us time to shore up Sev's bid for godfather."

Róise yawns and flops bonelessly down onto my chest. My arms come around her automatically.

"If only the rest of the world realized how much politics is involved in organized crime." She's snoring lightly before I can answer.

~ ~ ~

I win the rock, paper, scissors, but Henry Caruso has done a runner.

I'm tracking him down, but for all his stupid decisions, he has the instincts of a prey animal to hide.

At least this time I know no one in our organization nabbed him up already.

Not like Salvatore did with Lorenzo before bringing him to The Box.

Feeling the way I do about Róise, I understand my cousin's irrational behavior, but that doesn't make me any less annoyed with him.

Which is why I call him at three o'clock in the morning to ask if he has Henry Caruso sitting somewhere on ice.

He tells me to fuck off and hangs up.

I call again to ask if he's *sure*. He sends my call to voicemail. Which means he's awake. That's all I want.

If I have to be awake looking for the piece of shit, Henry, he can be awake regretting pulling that stunt with Lorenzo.

CHAPTER 70: RÓISE

On one of the hottest days in July, Miceli asks me to meet him in his office.

Thinking it probably has something to do with the wedding, (which is pretty much dominating all my conversations with *moma* and my cousins right now) I wear summer weight cargo pants cropped to capri length and a short-sleeved top that exposes my midriff.

So far, no one has tried to tell me I have to dress like an old lady to be an underboss's wife. And honestly, if they did? I'd ignore them.

Because the way I dress drives Miceli wild. And just as important, but not as exciting, my style works for me.

Miceli isn't alone when I enter his office. An elegant woman who could be thirty or fifty (I'm not great at guessing ages.) is sitting in one of the armchairs, a cup of coffee in her hand.

My fiancé's eyes warm when they land on me. "Róise." Placing his hand on my back, he guides me to a chair near the other woman. "This is..."

And he introduces me to an agent from the freaking oldest talent agency in the United States. Not only the oldest, but one of the biggest.

I stare at him. "I don't understand. I thought—"

"She's here to discuss career opportunities for voice actors."

"Voice actors." My voice loses volume and I have to clear my throat before repeating the words. "*Voice actors.*"

Sheesh, why didn't *I* think of that? It's not like I haven't taken any classes on voice acting. It's just...I was so busy fighting against the change in my life, what I thought I could do pretty much shrank to volunteering in a youth theater program and reading aloud to my grandmother.

"I could be an audiobook narrator," I say with excitement.

"Among other things," the agent says. "And you can do it anonymously under your stage name."

For the next hour we discuss what those things are.

When she's ready to leave, she gives me her card. "Contact me after you graduate. We'll discuss particulars and get you signed up with the agency."

She makes it sound easy, when I know it's not. No one just gets signed on with this agency. Heck, getting to talk to an agent with her weight is about as likely as meeting a unicorn in Central Park.

A real one. Not a person or horse in costume. That's not unlikely at all in New York.

Dazed, I nod.

And then she's gone.

I throw myself at Miceli. "Thank you!"

"I want you to be happy, Róise."

Sudden emotion chokes my throat. "I am happy. With you."

Miceli's reaction to my words leaves us sweaty and messy.

Draped half over him, I trace a heart on his chest. His hand lands over mine and holds it in the center of the invisible heart.

I didn't think I could luck out and have what my parents did, but I'm starting to think that I should buy a LOTTO ticket.

~ ~ ~

That night, Miceli tells me he wants to put a tracker on me. "All the women and children in our family are fitted with them."

"Is that why you got me the meeting with the agent, to make me compliant?" I ask suspiciously, not impressed by the *everyone else is doing it* line.

"If I wanted to make you compliant, I would drug you." *Like you did your guards* lies silent in the air between us. "I want your permission."

"And if I refuse to give it?"

"Don't."

"Do you have a tracker implanted on you?" Fair is fair, right?

"Do you really think having a record of where I go would be smart?"

I narrow my eyes at him, but he's got a point. "I guess not."

"This is for your safety and my sanity, *me dolce fiore*."

"No fair pulling out the Italian endearments," I grumble, but we all know I'm getting the tracker.

Which I do.

After three orgasms and gelato from my favorite shop on Long Island.

CHAPTER 71: MICELI

"What the fuck does this mean?" I bend over Brogan's desk and indicate the text I received from him the night before.

BS: *Keep a close eye on our girl. GL still wants her to marry his lieutenant.*

"What it says. Róise's grandfather is one of those old-school guys who thinks the fruit of his loins as he calls it, belongs to him." Brogan sounds fed up with the man.

My feelings are more violent. "That doesn't sound old school. It sounds psychotic."

"Whatever you call it, once the wedding happens, he won't be a problem anymore."

"You said the engagement would take care of it." Not that I trusted that it would.

But there has to be a reason Brogan is more worried now than he was right after we announced the engagement.

"I thought it would."

"But it didn't."

Brogan sighs and shakes his head. "He called yesterday demanding I get her away from you and turn her over to him."

Someone just signed his own death warrant.

"And you said?"

"That he could go fuck himself. What the fecking hell do you think I would say?" Brogan's voice rises with his ire.

"There has to be a reason he believes you would do what he's demanding."

"Other than sheer, pig-headed arrogance? The man sees women as property. I wouldn't put it past him to try to nab her himself." Brogan runs a hand over his face. "But once the wedding is done, he'll back off. His religion sees marriage vows as sacrosanct and doesn't acknowledge the legality of divorce."

"The fuck are you talking about? My woman is at risk for being kidnapped and this is the first I'm hearing of it?" He sure as hell didn't mention the possibility when he told me about the reprehensible old man's pipe dreams to marry my woman off to one of his buddies.

"I didn't think that was a legitimate threat before this. I was wrong." Brogan's admission comes from between clenched teeth.

He doesn't like admitting he's wrong? It's better than being dead if he didn't admit it and something happened to Róise.

"Your family is on yellow alert and that should be sufficient, but I wanted you to know about the escalation in Gabriel's demands. And the fact my alliance with him is on shaky ground right now."

I immediately text my team and Sev to tell them about this complication. If Shaughnessy's alliance with the AOG is shaky, then ours is now nonexistent. Our alert status is pushing toward red.

Cazzo.

I promised Róise dinner out, but until I've taken care of this threat, her security status is going red regardless of what Sev decides to do.

If I lose Róise, I will turn the world into rubble around me. I don't know when it happened, but *my dolce fiore* is the most important person in my life.

I would survive losing anyone else. But not her.

Managgia la miserisa! I love her.

Unaware of my disturbing inner revelations, Brogan sighs. "His phone calls and texts have been getting more strident. The engagement should have taken care of the problem. Who is stupid enough to believe they can go against your mafia and win?"

"Gabriel Lion apparently."

"There's something wrong with him. Like I said he's got this –"

"Psychotic belief that Róise is his property." She is my woman, but Róise Aisling Shaughnessy is nobody's property.

"Apparently, he promised her to Jed a long time ago. But I didn't know that."

That tracks with the things I've found out about Derry's death, once I started looking in the right places.

"Did Gabriel know your brother planned to cut ties with the AOG when he became boss?" I ask.

"What does it matter? That was six years ago."

"Did he know?" I demand.

Brogan waves at one of the chairs in front of his desk. "Sit down."

I ignore the invitation and wait for an answer to my question.

"Yes," he finally says. "My father told him. He had some idea that if Gabriel apologized to Derry and made a pretense of remorse for how he treated his daughter Charity, business could go on as usual."

"You don't sound like you believe that was possible."

"My brother despised Gabriel and thought compromise was for the weak."

"Why the fuck haven't you investigated the AOG for your brother's death?" I know he hasn't because he would have found what I did and already killed the son-of-a-bitch.

Brogan Shaughnessy is ruthlessly mercenary, but his loyalty to his family and mob is unbreakable.

Pain too acute to deny crosses Brogan's features "It wasn't the AOG."

"It wasn't the fucking Bonannos." Brogan has to know that too because again, if he blamed the mafia, he would have been waging war the past six years, not building bridges.

"I know that."

"Then why not investigate the AOG? They had the most to gain by Derry's death." Except the man in front of me.

I know it wasn't him, unless he was in on it with Gabriel.

He must see the suspicion on my face. "It wasn't me. I loved my brother and I have always been loyal to this mob."

I don't say anything. Silence is a better form of interrogation than questions with a certain type of man.

Either he'll tell me, or he won't.

"I was going to take this with me to my grave," he says after a long beat. "But I know it wasn't Gabriel. Or me."

"You sound certain." Of something entirely incorrect.

"Trust me, I would much rather believe Gabriel Lion ordered the hit than live with the truth."

"And that truth is?" What lie has he accepted as fact?

"My father took the hit out on himself. He wanted to go out in a blaze of glory. And it ended up costing him his oldest son. It broke him."

"Why do you think that?" Yes, Róise and I floated that idea, but why would his own son be so sure of it?

"He told me, at the end... Da said it was all his fault."

"And you took that to mean he'd taken out a hit on himself that went wrong?"

Brogan stares at me. "What else could it mean?"

"I don't know, maybe that he realized if he hadn't told Gabrieal about Derry's plans to cut ties with the AOG, or had cut ties himself, the bastard wouldn't have had a reason to kill your brother."

"If my da had wanted me to cut ties with the AOG, he would have told me. And if he believed Gabriel was responsible for Derry's death, he would have."

"You sure about that? What would you have done if your dad told you the hitter was AOG?"

"Gone to war." No hesitation.

I nod. "Maybe he thought losing one son was enough."

The AOG are paranoid religious fanatics, but they are also a formidable force made up of military trained soldiers. Would the Shaughnessy mob have won that war?

Without a doubt, but not without casualties.

"Your father made peace with the Bonanno don only weeks after your sister-in-law's death," I point out.

"He did what he thought was best for the mob."

I shrug. "Sometimes what's best for the syndicate isn't what's best for your family."

It's a tightrope we all have to walk.

"You're one-thousand times better an option for my niece than that fucker Jed. And you are strong enough to protect her from the AOG."

Brogan's words show defensiveness about his decision to offer his niece for the blood alliance. They also indicate that he might have been thinking of Róise and her safety as much as growing his powerbase when he offered the alliance to Sev.

"I am," I agree.

He sighs. "I will open an investigation into Derry's death. I should have done it six years ago."

But he'd believed his father was responsible.

"There's no need." I tap twice on my phone. "Look at the attachments I just sent you."

One is the statement for Jed's bank account. It shows five $9,999 deposits (staying under the mandatory reporting limit) each a month apart starting the day Derry died. The payee is the AOG. Taken independently, that money could be payment for anything.

But the other attachments condemn Jed.

"That parking garage has line of site for a competent sniper to where your brother and grandfather exited the building on the day of Derry's death."

"Let me guess," Brogan says, fury deepening his tone. "Jed is a trained sniper."

"He racked up one of the top scores for kill shots during Desert Storm. Those videos show Jed driving into and out of the parking garage on the day of Derry's death. He'd been there twice before."

"Recon."

I nod. "He paid a toll on I-80 shortly before receiving a speeding ticket on his way back to the AOG compound. The timing fits for the shooting."

Brogan's face twists with agony only another made man with family who have died at the hands of our enemies can understand. "You're telling me ..."

"That Gabriel had your brother murdered so your mob would continue to do business with him."

Rage replaces pain on the older man's features. "That's when Gabriel promised Róise to Jed. I'm going to kill him."

"No. That is my privilege. Gabriel and Jed are threats to Róise and she is mine to protect."

"He had my fucking brother killed. He's mine."

"Are you saying you want to be part of the operation?" I'm not offering more than that and it will be my hand that ends Gabriel Lion's life.

Brogan nods grudging agreement. "I knew you were the right man for Róise."

"Are you saying you set up the blood alliance for the sake of your niece?" Supposing is one thing.

Knowing another. And if it is true. Róise deserves to know.

"I have alliances with mobs all over this country and Europe. I have alliances on every continent with other syndicates. So, no I didn't need this alliance. But I wanted my niece protected."

"And it didn't hurt that you probably figured my brother was going to be godfather one day."

He doesn't attempt to deny it. "There is that."

I respect him more for not pretending his intentions were entirely altruistic.

"Does Róise know about Gabriel killing her dad?" he asks.

"Yes." No way would I tell her uncle before telling my fiancée.

Her temper flashes hot and big when she's riled. And while that can be fun, hurting her isn't. Being the last to know who killed her father would do that.

"She's probably down at the boathouse telling Kara and Fiona everything." Brogan grimaces. "Once my mother finds out..."

He just shakes his head morosely, not finishing the thought.

"How many underwater guards do you have on duty?" I ask over my shoulder, heading toward the door.

Even if the number is half a dozen, I'm not comfortable with Róise hanging out in the boathouse without me right now.

Hell, probably never. It's just too damned exposed.

"None. I told you we don't need them. I ran tests on our sonar's detection levels and nothing is getting past it. Even if it could, it would take a plasma torch to get through the net."

Which Róise and Kara paddled right over in their dinghy.

My gut twists. If the sonar had alerted to the women during their great escape, they wouldn't have gotten away.

No one can approach the boathouse during the day in a dinghy without being seen. Not with the men Brogan has patrolling that part of the property and watching water.

My men make four more sets of eyes. With Brogan's security, it should be enough, but my gut is screaming it's not.

I send a text, instructing my men to converge on the boathouse and pull up Róise's tracker just because.

Relief surges through me at the steady dot located at the boathouse. She's going to be pissed when they crash the party with her cousins, but better safe than sorry.

I'm halfway to the boathouse when I hear a scream. I start to run.

CHAPTER 72: RÓISE

All the bay doors are open in the boathouse. Fitz is dangling his feet in the water and we're all hot. Even with the doors open, the breeze isn't enough to compensate for the hot summer temperatures.

I just finished telling my cousins that Gabriel had my dad killed. They're furious, but every time I mention Miceli's name, Kara gives me a concerned look.

"You're in love with your fiancé, aren't you?" she asks.

"If I am, don't you think he's the first person that should know that?"

"Why shouldn't she love him?" Fiona plops down next to Fitz and drops her feet into the water. "Loving your partner is a good thing isn't it?"

"When they love you back, it's the best thing. But when they don't, it's..." She looks at Fitz, gives a little shake to her head and finishes. "Not."

"Well, I think he loves her too. You saw the pictures from their engagement announcement. He's got moony eyes."

"What's moony eyes?" Fitz asks, suddenly tuning into our conversation.

"Like this." Fiona makes her eyes really wide and adoring.

"You look funny, Aunt Fi."

Fiona tickles Fitz and he tickles her back.

Under the sound of their feet splashing, Kara asks, "Are you planning to tell him?"

"I don't know." I might as well have just said I loved him to begin with.

Because how is that not an admission?

"Why not tell him?" Fiona asks. "Isn't it better to share your feelings with each other?"

"Are you and Zoey sharing feelings?" I ask because I don't have an answer and I don't think Kara wants to give one.

Fiona blushes, but the happiness on her face makes both Kara and I smile.

"We're taking things slowly, but I really like her." Fiona's eyes go a little dreamy.

Moony eyes.

"I'm glad you found each other." Kara bends down to hug her sister. "She seems just as into you as you are into her, but remember, you're both still very young."

"You were only eighteen when you married Mick."

"I know." Kara doesn't say anything else but there is a world of emotion in those two words.

What that emotion is, only Kara knows. As much as we share with each other, what she feels about her husband is one area we don't go.

And maybe that is as much of an admission as me saying I don't know if I'll tell Miceli about my feelings.

"He got me an appointment with an agent," I tell my cousins.

Bored with our talk, Fitz gets up and returns to his play cars. Doing a pretty good job of imitating the different street noises, he drives them over the obstacle course he and his mom created with pillows and other stuff on hand in the boathouse.

"I thought you couldn't get famous if you were going to be a mobster's wife?" Fiona looks at me with confusion. "Did dad change his mind?"

"It wouldn't matter either way." I'm not seeking recognition for the sake of my family, both old and new, not because my uncle says not to. "It's for voice acting though."

"Oh, wow, that's a great idea!" Fiona grins at me. "You'll make it big in animation and no one will ever know who you are."

"I don't really care if I make it big." I never have. "I just want to act."

Fiona nods, fanning herself. "I think we should go for a swim. Anyone with me?"

"Me! Me! Me!" Fitz yells.

"Okay, buddy. Go change into your swim trunks." Kara turns to me and hugs me tight. "You're really lucky that Miceli cares about your dreams."

Kara is doing her degree online and in secret from both Uncle Brogan and her husband, Mick. I'm pretty sure neither man cares if she finds a fulfilling career.

But I know Uncle Brogan loves her. And sometimes Mick looks at Kara with the kind of yearning that a lot of actors would offer up their first child to be able to emulate.

She never seems to notice though.

Everyone changes into their swimsuit, except me. Miceli is taking me to dinner after this and I don't want to get my hair wet. I sit on the dock and ask myself if I'm as oblivious as Kara.

Does Miceli have feelings for me?

I have one of the pictures from the interview announcing our engagement as the background on my phone. Not because I put it there. But because he did.

It's the one where Miceli is petting Pusheen while his other arm is tight around my shoulders. The look on both our faces is either Oscar worthy acting...or real.

And those two floors in the Oscuro building *are* being redesigned as apartments for Miceli's top enforcers. Some are dorm style apartments; others are set up for families.

So, we'll have neighbors. *Because I want them.*

Of course, Miceli is taking it one step further. So that I will feel like I'm living in a community, not an office building, one of the lower floors is also being renovated with a gym even though there's already a full facility one for employees.

This floor will only be accessible to residents and in addition to the gym, it will have a pool, a recreation room and a limited menu café.

It's a lot, but he's doing it because he doesn't want me to miss my family. *Because he wants me to be happy.*

If Miceli De Luca doesn't love me, he definitely cares about me. A lot.

But it kind of feels like love.

Water splashes my legs and I look down, expecting to see Fitz or one of my cousins.

It's not them. Arms covered in black neoprene rise out of the water, reaching for me. I scream and kick out with one foot, aiming at the black apparition's head.

I make contact and his head goes back, but hands like manacles lock around my ankles. A bullet hits the dock, sending splinters flying.

I hear a rage filled roar as I'm yanked under the water.

Shutting my mouth, I expel air through my nose as I thrash, trying to get away from the man...no, *men*...attacking me.

One of them grabs my feet and then something hard and thin tightens around my ankles. I keep fighting, but the water makes it hard and it's three against one.

Assholes!

They get zip cuffs over my hands, scraping my knuckles in the process and then yank them tight. Now, I'm squirming like an eel. My chest hurts with the need to suck in air.

But there is no air. It's water.

Then an opaque diver's mask is shoved over my face, turning everything around me black. A mouthpiece jams into my mouth and unable to stop myself, I suck in.

But it's oxygen, not water that fills my mouth and lungs.

The next few minutes are a blur of water rushing by much faster than any human could swim. Are we being towed by a boat?

CHAPTER 73: MICELI

Later, I will realize this all happened in a few seconds, but in the present, everything happens in excruciating slow motion.

Men in black diving gear have my woman. She's fighting, but there are three fucking assailants in the water that is supposed to be safe.

A gunshot rings out and the dock near Róise explodes.

"Hold fire," I shout as loud as I can.

Some idiot is going to kill my fiancée in his attempt to rescue her. If that happens, I will cut off his hands and feed him to the sharks.

Terror I have never felt before runs through my veins like corrosive acid.

My men converge on the water.

Too late.

I know, it's too late.

But I don't order them not to dive. I'm almost there.

Allessio pops up to the surface and shakes his head. An enraged shout erupts from my throat, but I force myself not to dive into the bay.

I know what he's going to say before he says it.

"They had DPV's boss," Allessio shouts from the water. "No way to catch them."

"She's got an oxygen tank," the other man who went into the water shouts.

Like that's supposed to make me feel better.

The two soldiers who were furthest away, patrolling the north and south perimeters, reach me.

"With me," I bark before pivoting and sprinting to the boathouse.

Brogan has a speedboat as well as a yacht.

I type in the code I saw Róise use and open the door. Ollie and one of Brogan's other men are already untying the speedboat from its mooring. I jump on board. My men are right behind me, crowding one of Brogan's guys out. But Ollie manages to get on board too.

"Is this thing equipped with sonar?" I don't bother looking at my phone for Róise's location.

Deep water is one of nature's signal blockers.

"No. The yacht is, but that would take too long to get in the water."

"Let's go."

Ollie's body is rigid with the need for action, but he says, "Waiting for the boss."

I make the choice easy for him.

Pulling my gun, I point at his head. "Get this fucking boat moving."

I don't bother to threaten to shoot him. If he isn't smart enough to figure out I will, Ollie shouldn't be the one driving in pursuit.

Róise's bodyguard shows the smarts I expect and pushes the throttle forward, pulling slowly out of the boathouse.

As soon as we clear the mooring, he asks, "Which way?"

Straining my eyes to see even the smallest ripple to indicate the DPVs' progress, I see nothing.

Dannazione!

We have no fucking way to know which way they went. Three yachts are out in the bay. Any one of them could be the destination.

Or those *fottuto stronzos* could be planning to use the DPVs to get all the way across the bay. It would be dangerous, but that doesn't mean they won't try it.

Most likely, they have a helicopter waiting and plan to surface under the cover of another boathouse. But that could be anywhere along the shore in either direction.

I think about the man my gut tells me is responsible for this kidnapping. What would Gabriel Lion do? And I have no fucking clue.

If it were me, I would get to shore as quickly as possible and head for a helipad.

I call Brogan.

He answers on the first ring. "You left without me, you son of a bitch. That's my niece out there."

"She is my woman." My fucking beating heart. "Yacht or helicopter? Which are Gabriel's people likely to use?"

"If Gabriel planned the op, they'll rely on reaching the shore undetected and use a vehicle."

"No fucking way. These men are not that stupid."

"Gabriel doesn't have a yacht or a helicopter. He's got a jet he's really proud of, but that requires filing a flight plan."

"A helicopter doesn't."

"The AOG are all about self-sufficiency. He's not going to borrow a helicopter from an ally."

Trusting Brogan's take on this, I tap Ollie's shoulder. "Head southeast."

The man opens the throttle and we sail across the water. Even if they're using the fastest DPVs on the market, Róise's kidnappers are going to max out at about 9 mph. The speedboat can go ten times that on calm water.

The problem isn't catching up, but overshooting them.

There's the mumble of another voice near Brogan and then he says, "They cut through the net."

That tells me something. These guys are professional. Not that I expected anything else from the military trained AOG.

It tells me something else too. Brogan has a fucking rat working for him. Someone ignored the alarms that would have been set off by the sonar at the three-man team's approach.

"Put the men you have stationed on sonar watch duty on lockdown," I order.

We'll question them after. After I get my fiancée back and gut the men who tried to take her.

"Already done. You can sit in on the interrogation."

Ignoring his oblique order to stay out of it, I say, "They have a plan for getting across Long Island without pursuit."

What that fucking plan is, I don't know. Except they are bound to ditch Róise's phone. Good thing I don't have to rely on the phone's tracker.

They could have a signal jammer, but that also stops them from communicating with their backup.

"Keep in mind, they might be military trained, but they're also arrogant as hell," Brogan says. "They believe in their supremacy over everyone that isn't part of their cult. That can translate into stupid mistakes."

"I'm not relying on someone else's mistakes to get *mi dolce fiore* back. I will find her."

"I'm putting the house on lockdown. Do you want your two men to stay here or to come after you? We can provide them with dry clothing and weapons."

Their guns went swimming with them. We use weapons unlikely to be affected by submersion, but when it comes to Róise's protection, I'm not settling for unlikely.

"Get them weapons and tell them to head southeast along the shoreline." I have to go on my instinct with the direction they are taking her. "Have the other two vehicles from our envoy delivered to the helipad."

"Will do."

I hang up without saying another word.

My gut says Róise's kidnappers are heading back toward New York, with a plan to drive straight through to Pennsylvania. If they are as determinedly self-sufficient and arrogant as Brogan says they are, that's their only option.

I will get Róise back, no matter what it takes. But I do not want her to fucking leave this island with those assholes.

After instructing Ollie to slow down for a visual inspection of every boathouse we encounter, I call Sev.

"That son of a bitch, Gabriel took Róise."

"How many people do you need and where do you want me to send them?"

"Send the cargo helo. It will carry ten with a full arsenal. They can land on the helipad near Brogan's place. Two of our vehicles will be waiting."

"Done."

"Tell the helicopter pilot to remain on standby. Brogan says Gabriel doesn't have a helicopter, but I'm not taking any chances."

"I'll get Catalina and Domenico's team looking into potential access to one."

"Good. There are three yachts in the nearby vicinity, get our smaller passenger helo in the air to do recon on them."

"Done. Are you sure it's Gabriel?"

"Brogan told me that Gabriel demanded he get Róise away from me and turn her over to him."

"And they call me a psychopath."

"It's almost a requirement for the job. But that guy makes the rest of us psychopaths look bad."

"We'll get her back." There's no doubt in Sev's tone.

"We will and then I'm going to kill Gabriel and Jed."

"Agreed. We don't leave threats to our family free to come after us again."

CHAPTER 74: RÓISE

I don't know how long we go through the water. At one point we stop and a hand gropes at me. I struggle wildly. What are they doing? Hard fingers slide into my pocket and then drag out my phone.

A second later, we start moving again.

Ha. These guys aren't nearly as smart as they think they are. I'm engaged to a psychotically possessive and protective mafia underboss who will be able to track my location. Because I let him put that darn tracker in me.

My thigh was sore for three days after. But now? Totally worth it.

Unfortunately, Miceli probably has a better idea of where I am than I do. I can't see anything through the blackened diver's mask.

But I'm pretty sure I know where we are headed. Pennsylvania.

There's only one person I can think of that would want to kidnap me. My grandfather.

The colossal asshole believes that women are property and that makes me his to do with however he wants.

Like using me to pay off one of his lieutenants for killing my own freakin father.

Ass. Hole.

We begin to slow down and then stop. One of my captors drags me out of the water and throws me onto a hard surface.

Something thunks as it lands beside me and I decide I'm on wooden decking of some kind. There are two more thunks and then the sound of clothing being peeled from wet bodies.

I spit out the mouthpiece. "Don't touch me!"

"We're not going to rape you," one of the men says, his derisive tone not comforting.

"You belong to Brother Jed. We don't touch another man's property." This voice is making an attempt at soothing.

Maybe because I'm squirming, trying to find the edge of the dock so I can throw myself back in the water. "I'm nobody's property!"

"Jed will train that willfulness out of you. Your desire will be for your husband, and he will rule over you." This voice is different than the other two.

A little older maybe? Also, that's fanaticism in his tone, not condescension.

"Strong men don't need to subjugate women." I make sure my voice drips with the stuff.

"Pick her up," Man 3 says. "We need to go."

I increase my efforts to worm my way across the decking. There's open air under my head when I'm jerked upwards and thrown over a hard shoulder.

Oof. The air whooshes out of me as his shoulder digs painfully into my diaphragm.

I squirm as hard as I can and beat on his back with my bound hands. *Never let them take you to a second location.*

Which technically we are already at, but that doesn't mean I have to make things easy for these jerks.

I start to slip off the guy's shoulder and triumph fills me, but it's short lived. With a shrug of his big shoulder, I'm right back where I was. Trying to breathe through a squished diaphragm.

There has to be a way to get away, but it's not going to be squirming around like an eel on a hook.

Common sense starts to overcome my adrenaline fueled need to fight.

I can't fight my way past these three miscreants, especially trussed up like stage rigging. Letting my body go limp, I pretend to faint, hoping they'll talk openly when they think I can't hear them.

The only thing they do is joke with each other about the weakness of the female sex. They won't be joking when I cut their nut sacks off.

Eww. Okay, that would be really gross and lots of blood.

But they're not going to get away with this. Even if they get me all the way to the compound I won't give up. And I know Miceli will not give up on getting me back.

Another heave of that hard shoulder and I start to fall, landing on a hard surface. Then the sound of a car trunk closing tells me where I am.

They threw me into the trunk of a freaking car. My shoulder bangs against something hard.

Ouch. I mean, seriously. *Ouch.*

Despite my discomfort, hope surges through me and I use my bound hands to shove the darkened diver's mask from my face. My vision doesn't get a lot better.

Because there's no interior light inside the car trunk.

But my captors can't see me either, and not one of them thought to search me for weapons.

My taser is in my backpack, still sitting on the dock I got nabbed from, but I keep my kubotan in my pocket.

Lucky for me, it is in the opposite pocket from where I had my phone and the guy who took that away hit on the correct pocket the first time.

Honestly, I never expected to use the kubotan anywhere but in training classes with Miceli. I like having it though. It feels like a little bit of Miceli to carry around with me.

Right now, I kind of wish I had a sentimental attitude toward a gun.

The kubotan will have to do.

I have to shift to my other side, but I managed to get my bound hands inside my front right pocket. The wet denim of my shorts makes it hard to pull the kubotan out, but eventually, I get it.

Unscrewing the end to expose the hidden knife is pretty easy, but cutting the zip tie holding my wrists together isn't.

The knife is sharp and the tiniest nick draws blood. Pretty soon, it's not just water from my clothes making me wet, but I get the zip tie off.

It's a lot easier to bend down and cut through the ties on my ankles. I put the knife back in the kubotan, because I don't want to accidentally cut myself more severely.

The kubotan will be as good of a weapon against my attackers as the knife. Maybe better. The knife is too small to do a lot of damage, no matter how sharp it is. But I've gotten really good at using the kubotan on pressure points.

I would love to shove it right into one of their eyeballs. Which is not a pressure point and also gross. Escape is a way better option than fighting right now. I might get some good hits in, but I'm not going to win against those three with a kubotan.

I feel around in the trunk and find the hard thing I fell on. It's a box. Opening it takes a second and then I feel through the contents. It's a first aid kit. The scissors feel sharp, so I tuck them into my pocket as a secondary weapon.

There's a gauze roll and that tape you use to hold the gauze on or to wrap a sprain.

I tuck it into my other pocket before a more thorough search of the trunk reveals some kind of spray can. Don't know what's in it, but it could be useful.

Finally, I search for the inside trunk release. Afraid it has been removed, I put it off for last. Disbelief pours through me when my fingers slide over a release latch. It's right there.

We're still on the island, but I don't know where. And it doesn't really matter.

I am better off out there than in here, wherever out there is.

Knocking out the taillight to get an idea runs the risk of getting my captors attention from the noise. I don't want them to know I'm unbound and mobile.

The car lurches to a sudden stop and lots of yelling ensues. Near accident?

Whatever it is, I use the time we're stopped to wind gauze around the trunk latch so that when I pull the release, it doesn't pop up and alert the driver by showing in the rearview mirror.

Then I pull the latch, allowing the trunk to lift just enough to see out.

No cars behind us. Whoever they're arguing with must be near the front of the car.

I have two choices. Try to get help from him, or use the argument as a distraction to run. Not liking my odds either way, I choose to run.

For all I know they're arguing with someone who can't or won't help me.

I let the trunk open enough so I can slide my body out. I keep hold of the gauze, pulling the trunk closed behind me.

There's a clink as the latch catches again, but it's muted by the gauze and I'm hoping against hope they didn't notice it.

Staying low to the ground, I crawl away from the car. There's an alley about twenty-five feet back the way we came.

A truck and a minivan are parked on this side of the street. I use them for cover to get closer to the alley and then I run.

I don't bother to look back to see if I'm being chased because if I am, looking back will only slow me down. If I'm not, I still need to get as far away from them as I can.

A stich forms in my side and I'm panting when I finally slow down and try to figure out where I am.

I find a street sign and decide then and there, I am buying a LOTTO ticket this time for sure.

This is the street where the Shaughnessy warehouse is. The sound of a jet taking off tells me I'm close to the airport too. Which means not only is it the right street, but I'm in Queens and the warehouse can't be that far away.

People who are loyal to my family work at that warehouse. Even if I can't get down to the Bunker, they'll help me evade my attackers.

Considering what our nearness to the airport signifies, I shudder. They were going to smuggle me onto a private jet. I would have been in Pennsylvania before dinner.

With a new sense of urgency, I look around me. I'm not sure which direction the warehouse is and it takes me going the wrong way for two buildings before I realize the address numbers are increasing instead of decreasing. I have to turn around and start going the other direction.

Closer or further away from my pursuers? I don't know and right now if I think about it, it's only going to stress me out.

I'm only a couple of blocks from the warehouse when I see the car.

I quickly dodge behind a parked SUV. Did they see me? Ducking down, I peek around the back of the SUV.

The car is still crawling slowly along the street. A quick glance at the driver confirms that it's my captors.

I have to reach the warehouse. But my luck has run out because there is almost no cover between here and the building I'm aiming for.

If I run, they'll see me and, in a car, there's no chance they don't catch up to me. If I stay here, they might miss me. Do they know I'm headed for the warehouse?

Even if they do, if I wait for them to drive by and head back the other direction, I can go to one of the apartment buildings. Right?

I just have to stay where I am and out of sight. Shifting closer to the wheel, I hunch down, making my body as small as possible.

My heart pounds so fast, my chest hurts and I have to hold my breath so I don't start hyperventilating.

The sound of the car's purring engine grows louder, and louder as it gets closer. Am I visible? I can't check. If I move, I risk being seen.

The urge to run pushes my heart to an even more furious beat.

Gripping my kubotan tightly in my fist, I force my limbs to stillness.

The car drives past.

My legs turn to jelly and I fall on my butt.

Jayzuz, Mary and Joseph, that was close.

I suck in air, trying to calm my racing heart and crawl back onto my haunches. I risk a peek past the SUV and my heart just stops.

Because so did the car.

It's parked less than twenty feet from me, facing this direction. There's an entire car length between the SUV and the next parked vehicle behind me. If I run, there's a good chance they'll spot me.

If I stay here, one or all of them might decide to get out of the car and search the area on foot.

They definitely know about the warehouse. Did they check the routes to the apartment buildings first? Or do they have more people watching for me there?

The driver's door opens.

No. No. No.

Do not get out of the car.

Showing my mental push isn't pushy enough, the back passenger door opens too.

I want to run. Only if I do, they'll almost certainly see me. But if I don't run, there's no chance.

I turn and start sprinting away from the men in the car. There are shouts behind me. The sound of car doors opening and closing.

I'm so focused on the path in front of me, looking for an escape route that isn't there, I don't notice the line of black SUVs speeding in my direction until they're almost in front of me.

Recognition goes through me with the power of a lightning bolt. A very welcome lightning bolt.

It's Miceli. Not the driver. That's Allessio. Miceli is in the passenger seat.

The SUV rocks to a stop next to me while two more pass by, going fast. Miceli jumps out of the truck. His hair's askew and his tie is gone. Dark eyes devour me.

My feet are stuck to the pavement. Why can't I move?

I don't have to though.

Miceli reaches me from one second to the next. He's not gentle when he yanks me to him. His hold on me is so tight I can barely breathe. And it's exactly what I need.

"Oh fuck *mi dolce fiore*. You're okay. I'm never letting you out of my sight again."

Visions of my life as a barnacle stuck to the sea rock that is Miceli flash through my brain.

I should protest, but that image isn't an unpleasant one. At all. Inhaling deeply, I take in the scent of him. His aftershave that I love. His masculine scent. Even the stress sweat is good. Because it's him. And he's here.

And I'm not on a plane headed for a compound filled with chauvinistic misogynists who consider women property.

Adrenaline leaching from my system, my lizard brain accepts that I'm safe.

Safe.

My body gives a convulsive shudder.

CHAPTER 75: MICELI

"This is me being more trouble than I am worth."

"That is a lie." *Cazzo*. She has to know that. "You are worth *everything*."

I'm holding her too tight, but I cannot let go of this precious woman. The muscles in my arms refuse to loosen.

"I'm getting you all wet," she mutters against my chest.

Memory of the image she made standing there in a top nearly transparent from the water assails me.

Releasing her with one arm, I shrug out of one side of my suit jacket and then putting that arm back around her, I shrug out of the other. Then I put my suit jacket around her shoulders, surrounding her with me.

She looks up at me, vulnerability shining in her green eyes. "I can't believe you mafia guys wear suits in the summer. Who does that?"

"Suit jackets have their uses. They hide weapons nicely and–"

"Give you something to put around your fiancée when she's kidnapped by the bad guys and dunked in the bay?"

"Something like that."

I hold her away from me a few inches, but no more, so I can examine her. "Are you hurt anywhere?"

"I cut myself a little, getting the zip tie off. But it's not even bleeding anymore." She holds up her hand and shows me where she's nicked herself right below the palm.

I bring it to my mouth and kiss it. Then I lick along the shallow cut.

"You know we're not wolves or anything. I'm pretty sure that's not sanitary."

"I am incapable of hurting you, not even my saliva. We are perfectly chemically matched."

"I read that article too you know, and I am pretty sure the concept doesn't cover bacteria and infection."

Most women would be sobbing right now and if she did, I would hold her and think no less of her. But she's throwing out her usual snark.

I'm barely keeping up my end of the banter because all I want to do is to kill the men who took her and then fuck her over the pile of their dead bodies and prove to the world that she is mine.

"I should probably be offended I can feel you getting hard, but I'm not."

"What is there to be offended by? I will always want you. And sex is a primal response to vanquishing danger."

"I believe you." She wiggles against me.

"Watch out, or I'll strip you naked and take you here in the street."

"Kinky." She looks up at me, all humor drained from her eyes. "They threw me in a trunk. They were going to take me to the OAG compound and give me to Jed like I'm a rescue cat."

"Pusheen would eat them alive."

"She would. I want to punch every one of those miserable excuses for humanity in the nuts." She pauses. "With my kobutan."

"If that is what you want." I lift her into my arms and carry her to the SUV.

She stays snug in my lap as we drive the few feet to the other vehicles, where one of my envoy is blocking the back of the car and the other is blocking the side and front at an angle.

As soon as we arrived the car heading toward Róise tried to reverse direction, but they had no chance.

Just like this woman who has become my life, *mi dolce fiore*, had no chance against three trained soldiers with their fucking zip ties and DPVs.

All three *stronzos* have one of my men on each side, holding them in place to face judgment. To face *me*.

But it's my little spitfire that's going to confront them first.

The SUVs block the view from security cameras in the area. That doesn't mean we're not going to wipe them. Always better safe than sorry.

I nod to Allessio, who is holding one of the two younger men. "Keep him still."

Lowering Róise to her feet, I guide her arms into the suit jacket's sleeves and then roll them up so she has freedom of movement before buttoning the jacket.

There's still too much of her showing, but she needs her moment, and her needs supersede mine.

Not that I will hesitate to gouge out the eyes of any of the men around us who looks at her with lust. My men aren't that stupid.

The AOG bastards though...we'll see.

Róise pulls her kobutan from her pocket.

I shake my head. "These idiots let you keep it?"

No wonder she was able to get out of the zip ties.

"They didn't search me for weapons. The only thing they were worried about was my phone." She glares at the men. "They dumped it somewhere between Uncle Brogan's and the boathouse where we surfaced."

It's the first time she's referred to the mansion as her uncle's home and not her own. Something inside me settles.

"I'll get you a new one," I promise.

"But I liked that one. You got it for me."

"And that matters to you."

"I'll probably hoard every little thing you give me until the day we die. We might have to get a storage unit just for my sentimental memorabilia," she warns.

"Whatever you want, but I didn't notice a bunch of keepsakes in your things. Did your uncle's staff not collect all your belongings?"

"They did." She sighs. "I stopped saving things after my dad died."

Because the memories hurt. And she's willing to start collecting keep-sakes again. From me.

That atrophied organ in my chest fills with fresh blood that feels a lot like joy.

"What the fuck is this lovey-dovey talk? Our militia will take you fuckers out if you don't let us go *right now*," one of the two younger men mouths off.

"Watch your fucking mouth in front of my fiancée," I snarl. "You are already dead. After I execute your leader and that fucking asshole Jed for daring to lay claim to the woman who has given *me* her heart, I will raze the goddamn AOG to the ground and scorch the earth over their bones so it will never sprout again."

"I never said I love you." That's *mi dolce fiore* putting her oar in the water.

I scowl down at her. "You will."

"You kind of look like a demon right now." She winks at me. "It's sexy."

Fuck. This woman.

"You whore! The man you are flirting with is a criminal. You heard what he just said! He threatened to kill us." The other younger man spits at Róise.

I shift her out of the path of his saliva before backhanding him. Hard.

My ring leaves a gash on his cheek and the demon inside me revels in the spill of blood.

"What the fuck do you think a man who kidnaps a woman is?" Allessio demands.

He's furious with himself that they got Róise on his watch. If we had not gotten her back, I would have taken more than a finger for his failure. But she is here and safe.

I can forgive him. Maybe.

And only because I am as much to blame as he is. I was there too.

"You're not just a criminal," I say with disgust. "You're a stupid criminal. Because you tried to take what is mine and you will pay for that."

"Starting now." Róise wraps her hand around her kubotan like it's an icepick.

Just like I taught her. Then her thumb over the bottom of the stick, adding her free hand for more power.

This is going to hurt. Anticipation for the cries of pain coming have me almost smiling.

My fierce fiancée jabs straight into his solar plexus. "That's for carrying me around like a sack of potatoes and jamming your stupid shoulder into my diaphragm."

She's not done. Her next strike is his groin area. Right in the nuts, like she said she wanted to.

It's a good target for maximizing pain. The man shrieks.

She turns to the mission leader. "You were right about one thing. I desire the man I'm going to marry very much, but he doesn't need to try to rule over me to feel powerful." She gives me a heated look. "He's too strong to need to prop himself up like that."

I don't know what this *stronzo* said to Róise but it sure pissed her off. Her first strike is to his groin and the second to his temple, knocking him out cold.

"You think you're tough," the other younger man sneers. "You have to have a man hold me so you can get us."

"And you had to have *two men* hold me so you could put those zip ties on me, asshole." She strikes him on the throat with enough force to collapse his trachea.

He throws his head back, mouth gaping, but he's not breathing much less speaking.

"Oh, did I crush your windpipe?" Róise asks with fake sweetness. "That's too bad. I'm sure you have so much more to say."

"I'm so turned on right now."

Róise doesn't answer. She's watching the man struggle to get air but it's not happening.

She looks up at me with absolute trust tinged by panic. "Do something. I don't want to kill someone."

I pull out my knife and stab him directly in the heart. "There. Now you didn't kill him."

"Thank you."

My guys let him drop to the pavement.

But that's not enough for Ollie, who stomps his head. "Fecking AOG scum."

"What are you doing, man?" the only still lucid member of the kidnap team whines. "You can't just kill him."

"This is Cosa Nostra territory. I can do whatever the fuck I want." I dismiss him by turning my back. "Allessio."

"Yes, boss?"

I jerk my head toward the parked SUVs. "Get this mess cleaned up. I want all security and traffic cams wiped for a four block radius."

"On it."

I turn to one of my other men. "Take them to The Box. Make sure they can't try what those Lucchesi cowards did."

Our new policy is to use ball gags with all prisoners so they cannot bite their tongues off and choke to death on their own blood like the Lucchesi soldiers who attacked my cousin's fiancée did a couple months back.

"Ollie, you're with us."

Relief flickering in his eyes, Brogan's man nods. He needs to see that his former charge is safe. I get that.

I would have had him assigned to Róise's detail permanently after she moved in with me. However, she told me that her younger cousin is comfortable with the soldier and she didn't want to take Ollie away from Fiona.

But if there is one Irishman I would allow on my payroll, it's him.

CHAPTER 76: RÓISE

A sleek passenger helicopter is waiting for us on the roof of my uncle's warehouse, but Miceli wants me to change into dry clothes before we get on.

"It's a short flight," I argue, just wanting to get home. "Please. I'll even let you have a doctor look me over."

He's not impressed. "You know that's happening regardless."

"I want to go home."

Something flares in his eyes when I say that. "Whatever you want, *vitù*."

His life? Warmth spreads through me.

"Don't break out the Sicilian if you don't want our bodyguards to get a show on the helicopter," I tease, only half joking.

Miceli is to die for sexy when he starts speaking Italian, but when he uses the Sicilian dialect, I know his emotions are involved. And that's a bigger turn-on than any romance language could be, even uttered in that deep tone that goes straight to my ladybits.

"I would have to kill anyone who saw you in that state of passion," he says musingly, like he's considering it.

Laughing, I scoot around him and climb into the helicopter. The joy inside me is weird, considering what I just went through.

But I'm safe and I'm with Miceli. Two things to make me very happy.

Once we're buckled into side-by-side seats, he takes my hand and kisses the palm right above the shallow cuts. "I am sorry."

"What? Why are you apologizing?" Is he done with me?

Has he decided I really am too much trouble?

I cut my spiraling thoughts off. What is *wrong* with me?

Miceli cares about me and I'm beginning to believe he loves me. I mean, he called me his life. That's pretty big, no matter how I look at it.

I shake my head, dislodging the negative thoughts.

"I let you get kidnapped." He kisses my palm again. "But it will never happen again.

"It wasn't your fault. Gabriel Lion has to have someone on the inside of my uncle's organization."

Miceli nods. "The sonar would have picked up the three men and no alert was given. But I should have told you not to go to the boathouse. Your uncle should have an underwater patrol."

I want to say that's overkill. I'm pretty sure it is, regardless of what happened to me. "Maybe underwater robots?"

Like the kind they used to search for Nessie in Loch Ness. Sometimes, the Scots get it right. Not that I'll tell my *moma* that. The rivalry between Ireland and Scotland is alive and well in her heart, despite one of our forebearers being a Scottish immigrant in Ireland.

"I'll suggest it to him."

And by suggest, I'm pretty sure my fiancé means, argue until my uncle sees reason. Either that, or my days hanging out in the boathouse with my cousins are over.

"After what happened to me, he'll listen. It doesn't look good for a mob boss to have a family member kidnapped from under his nose. Besides, that could have been his grandson."

Uncle Brogan loves us all, but Fitz is *important* to him. The little boy is his heir and that's paramount to a man like Uncle Brogan.

"Yes." Miceli's expression changes and dark eyes devour me as the pilot lifts us into the air. "You were so fucking hot back there."

"You mean with the kobutan?" I tease.

It's not the first time he's implied seeing me with a weapon is a turn-on for him. I guess seeing me *use* that weapon is even more of one.

Because right now the air between Miceli and me is sizzling with restrained passion.

"I was just so angry. They thought it was okay to grab me and take me away from my family. Away from *you*. They're living under some kind of mass delusion if they all think I would marry that violent piece of garbage with a disgusting preference for women young enough to be his granddaughter."

"Tell me how you really feel," Miceli teases, but the expression in his eyes doesn't bode well for Jed or my grandfather.

"I feel like we need to get Aunt Hope out of there. She warned me this might happen and she had to have been taking a really big risk to do that."

His expression intense, Miceli laces his fingers through mine. "You knew this might happen?"

"Well, not *this*. Who would have foreseen something this extreme?"

"But your aunt warned you about something."

I nod. "She sent me a note."

"What did it say?" Miceli asks with a patience not reflected in his furious gaze.

"That my grandfather had not given up on the idea of me marrying Jed."

"Why didn't you tell me about this?" The controlled menace emanating from him is way sexier than it should be.

"When I got it, I didn't really trust either you or my uncle."

"And since then?"

He's asking if I trust him now. And there's only one answer to give him. "It slipped my mind since I've come to trust you." To love him.

I wince at the disbelief in his expression. "Security has been so tight," I try to explain. "I honestly didn't think it was a problem."

"It shouldn't have been," Miceli growls.

My body, which wants to celebrate winning over the bad guys and being free, thrums with desire. "No, it shouldn't. Do you and Uncle Brogan have any idea who is responsible for feeding intel to my grandfather?"

We didn't have plans to visit my family today. It was the spur of the moment. So, someone tipped off the team that tried to take me.

They had to have been waiting for just such an opportunity, but it only worked if they got apprised of my arrival.

Unless they were watching my uncle's estate, but that wouldn't account for the sonar alerts being ignored.

"Your uncle is holding the two men who were on the observation detail today."

"Two of them?"

"We won't know if it's both of them until after they've been questioned."

"By questioned, you mean..."

"I'm good at getting information." His tone sends a chill down my spine.

And excitement through my veins. There's definitely something wrong with how I react to Miceli's violent nature. But it's never directed at the innocent. Not like those guys today.

"They threw me in a trunk like a bag of junk getting donated." Not caring what I landed on, or if it hurt.

"Which was their second big mistake."

"What was their first?"

"Taking you in the first place. They forfeited their lives the moment they touched you."

One is already dead and Miceli is going to kill the other two as well. I can't make myself regret that.

Those men thought it was okay to kidnap me because they didn't believe that I have the right to make my own choices.

Even Uncle Brogan allowed me to choose. Yes, he pushed me toward one choice with coercion, but he would never have physically forced me into the marriage with Miceli.

Unlike Gabriel and Jed, Miceli would never physically force me to walk down the aisle either. He's ruthless and the mafia have some outdated attitudes about women, just like the Irish mob, but he respects my intelligence.

He respects me.

And that matters. A lot.

When we land on the roof of our building, Miceli doesn't let me walk, but lifts me out of the helicopter and swings me up into his arms.

Barking orders to security, he carries me inside the building and heads straight to the access to our penthouse. The elevator ride lasts only a few seconds and when we get to our place, four of his men accompany us.

He assigns one to the hall outside the elevator and another to patrol the outdoor space, with two inside the apartment.

I have a feeling this isn't a temporary aberration in our security. I'm going to have a lot more guards going forward and I get that, especially once I am the don's wife.

I tell him, "We are going to discuss having two soldiers in our living space."

"Later," he grits out.

Yeah, I don't want to fight right now either. There's something else I need a lot more than an argument with my fiancé.

Miceli carries me into the ensuite bathroom off of our bedroom. His expression on the verge of demonic, he lets me slide down his body until I'm standing on my own two feet.

He keeps one arm a tight manacle around me while reaching in to turn on the shower. "We need to wash all that salt water off of you."

The words are prosaic; the tension emanating off of him is not.

"Is this part of my new barnacle life?" Seeking more of his heat, I press against him, leaning my forehead onto his chest.

"Barnacle life?"

"Stuck to you like one," I explain, wriggling out of his suit jacket and letting it fall to the floor.

A hot shower sounds heavenly right now. Even with a guy whose expression and tone are a good match for someone who just escaped hades. Especially with that guy, if I'm honest with myself.

"I like that idea," he says gutturally.

Not a surprise. "You did threaten not to allow me out of your sight again."

Which is over the top and totally unrealistic. But still sends warm fuzzies through me. Despite what happened today, right now, I feel safe.

Protected.

Cherished.

His arm tightens convulsively. "It's not a threat."

"It's a promise?" I ask with dry humor.

"Spending time with me is not a punishment," he informs me in what is probably supposed to be a teasing haughty tone but is too gravelly for any real humor.

Turning my head, I rub my cheek against his chest. "No, it's not."

Without warning, Miceli steps back far enough to rip my shirt up over my head and unclasps my bra.

Still damp, the stretchy lace clings to my skin. My nipples pebble as he peels it away.

Pupils dilated with desire, he yanks the rest of my clothes off.

Craving reconnection with him at the most primal level, I tear at his clothing too.

Off. I want everything off.

Nothing between us. Just naked skin ready to meet naked skin.

It takes seconds to divest us both of our clothing and Miceli of his weapons. Including the time it takes him to slash through the sides of my underwear. He's not the only impatient one. His shirt is missing a few buttons too.

With nothing between us, he pulls us into the shower under the hot spray.

I can't help but notice one of his knives makes it into the shower with us.

Heat pulses between my legs, shivers of desire cascading along the backs of my thighs.

There are words I want to say. Words I want to hear. But right now, what I want most is to feel.

Him. Me. Us.

Grabbing his wrist, I bring the hand with the knife between my breasts and press his knuckles against my skin.

His eyes darken with primal heat and he drags the flat of the blade along the curve of my breast so lightly there is no chance he will cut me. Part of me wants him to, wants to be marked by him. As his.

"No," he growls. "I'm not cutting you."

I'm not surprised he knows what I'm thinking. He gets me like no one else does. Not even my grandmother and cousins.

"There's a scar from the day my mom died." A permanent reminder of that day. "Why can't I wear your scar?"

"I will not hurt you, *vitù*." There's no give in his voice.

"Tattoos hurt. People still get them."

"You are mine to cherish and protect. I will not give you pain."

I don't *want* pain. I want the result. The permanent mark.

"Then I'll get a tattoo."

"If you do, it had better be of my bloody thumbprint."

My arousal spikes. "Yes, that."

"For now, this will have to do." He presses his thumb against the tip of his dagger, drawing blood.

Then he presses it against my left breast. "Mine."

I nod, my throat too tight for words.

His hand travels down and presses against my center. I can't see the bloody print he leaves behind, but I know it's there.

It burns like a brand. I know it's an illusion created by my psyche, but I don't care. I can feel that thumbprint to the depth of my soul.

"Yours," I squeeze out of my uncooperative throat as I hold my hand up in offering. "Do it."

He's done this before. He cannot deny me.

A purely animalistic sound comes from deep in his chest before he does what I ask, pricking my thumb.

Once the blood wells, I place it over his heart. "Mine."

Then I press, leaving a crimson red smear before rivulets of water turn it pink, washing it away, bit by bit.

"I want my mark here," I tell him.

He offers me the knife, but I shake my head. "A tattoo."

"As you wish."

I force more of my life's essence from the tiny prick before it stops bleeding and press a print onto the underside of his big erection. "Mine."

"Do you want a tattoo there as well, *mi dolce fiore*?"

Atavistic pleasure settles deep in my belly. I don't feel sweet right now. "Would you get one?"

"Yes."

My thighs pressing tightly together as a shudder of arousal travels up my spine, I open my mouth to say *no*. Of course not. That's too much. Too primitive. Right?

Only what comes out of my mouth is, "Yes, I want that."

"Aphrodite, a true goddess who requires sacrifice to her love." His mouth slams down onto mine, locking my words inside me, his lips moving with feverish intensity to claim mine.

CHAPTER 77: MICELI

Róise's kiss is flavored with the same forceful need beating through my veins. She undulates against me, trying to press our bodies closer together.

I move the knife away from her skin without letting it touch her again and put it on one of the shelves built into the marble walls of our two person shower.

Cazzo. This side of her makes my cock so fucking hard.

She wants her thumbprint tattooed on me there. And I fucking want that too.

To be claimed by my goddess, for the forced vows between us to become something undeniably more.

Once both hands are empty, I fill them with her perfect, round tits and squeeze.

Her moan vibrates against my lips, the sound sending more blood rushing to my already engorged dick. My head pushes into the soft flesh of her torso.

Fuck, I love her body. All curves and no angles.

She reaches down with one hand and grips my hardon while the other tunnels into my hair, yanking it.

Hot urgency floods me at the small sting. She's so into this, she's not worrying about being nice.

Neither am I.

I drop one arm and hoist her up so my hand can reach between her generous ass cheeks. I spread them, letting water run down to her tight little pucker before I press just the tip of one finger inside her.

She fucking keens, her tongue thrusting against mine.

Tearing my mouth from hers, I groan. "I'm going to claim every one of your holes before I am done, *vitù*. Starting with this one."

Adjusting my hold on her, I open her pussy to me and thrust up, my cock so hard, I don't have to guide it inside her.

She's soaked for me, her tight heat sucking me into her body. "That's right," I praise. "Take all of me."

She only has one foot on the tiled floor and she's standing on tiptoe on that one. There's no leverage for her to meet my thrusts. All she can do is take what I give her.

And that's just the way I want it right now.

Thrusting into her with the power of a piston, I do exactly what I promised I would. I claim every single inch of her.

Ecstasy boils in my balls. *Cazzo*. I'm going to come soon. But not without her. "Be a good girl and touch that sweet little clit."

She mews, her head thrown back against the marble. "Please, Ares. You're the God of War. Fuck me harder!"

"So demanding," I croon, twisting my hips to grind into her on the next thrust. "Touch yourself, my sweet girl. *Now*."

Her hand comes between us and the next thrust forward brings my pelvis into contact with the back of her fingers.

"*Sì. Questa è la mia brava ragazza. Fai come ti è stato detto.*"

"That sounds so sexy, Miceli, but I don't know what it means."

And the expression in her emerald eyes says she wants to.

I oblige. "Yes. *Sì*. That's my good girl. *Questa è la mia brava ragazza*." I enunciate each phrase before saying it again in Italian. "Do as you are told. *Fai come ti è stato detto.*"

Her vaginal walls clamp down on my cock as I utter the Italian for that last instruction.

"Do that again," I order.

She does. Over and over as I thrust in and out of her, her fingers and my body forcing pleasure into her tender flesh.

"So close! Please, please, plea—" Her words cut off as I ram as deeply as possible into her welcoming body.

With a keening cry, she comes. Her channel tightens around me like a vise, her gorgeous tits flush with the blood rushing through her veins.

I let myself come inside her, the pleasure so intense my vision goes white for a few seconds.

Her head flops forward, resting again on my chest and fuck if that doesn't make me spurt again. There's so much trust in her release and the way she lets her body go boneless.

I will never let her fall and she knows it.

"Do not go to sleep. We're not done," I warn her.

She sighs. "You can wake me up."

"Not this time."

Taking her ass will be easier with her this loose and relaxed, although she'll be more sensitive. Handled right, that will only increase her pleasure.

And I know how to handle my woman.

I maneuver us so I'm sitting on the bench and she's on my lap, my still hard shaft firmly inside her tight pussy. The shower heads pivot when I press a button in the wall, so the warm water continues to rain down on us.

Her legs are spread over my thighs so I can touch her exactly where I want to. I press my forefinger and middle fingers into her mouth. "Get them wet, *mi dolce fiore.*"

Humming a little, she sucks my fingers languidly, sliding her tongue over and between them. When they are good and wet with her saliva, which is more slippery than the water cascading down onto us, I slide my middle finger in to the first knuckle.

She tenses and I wait to move it until she relaxes again. Then I prepare that tight channel to be claimed.

By the time I have both fingers buried inside her, she's moaning and writhing on my lap. Her pussy adds more viscous fluid to the mix of our cum inside her, drenching my cock.

Perfect.

When I lift her so I can pull out of one tight channel to take possession of another, she protests. "No, this feels so good, Miceli. I'm going to come again."

"Yes, you will, but with my cock buried in that tight little ass."

"My butt is not little," she argues.

I kiss her then say, "Your ass is perfect and your asshole is tiny."

Then before she can argue again, I put my erection slathered with her juices, her cum and mine against said tiny hole and push.

My head pops in and she gasps.

"Take me in." I release my hold on her hips and kiss the side of her neck, sucking up a love bite in a spot that sends her wild.

And also cannot be covered by anything less than a turtleneck or scarf, neither of which are summer attire in New York.

The primitive part of me revels in the knowledge that I am not just marking her inside, but where everyone else can see it too.

Her lips parted, her eyes glued to mine, Róise lowers herself slow centimeter by slow centimeter. Every few seconds, she rocks her hips to allow my engorged cock entrance into her primal channel.

The sounds she makes while she's doing this calls to the beast inside me, the one who makes being the God of War a natural fit.

But it's not bloodlust I'm feeling right now. It's pure, atavistic sexual lust.

When her ass is finally flush with my thighs, my muscles are shaking from the effort not to thrust up into her. "Ready?"

"Are you?" Her tone is pure challenge.

Is that a real question? *"Sì."*

My arm around her waist, I guide her body upward, going as slowly as she did, forcing her to feel every excruciating second of my cock sliding against her sensitive sphincter in retreat. I only allow her to withdraw about half the length of my dick before I force her back down.

Never once do I allow our gazes to break away from each other. For long seconds neither of us even blinks.

Then I draw her back up again, going only a little faster. I use the hold on her waist to control the depth and the speed of my thrusts. To control her body.

Because she lets me.

"Play with your tits, *brava ragazza*. Show me how much you love having me inside you."

"I do..." Her *do* turns into a sex filled cry as I slide my free hand between us and pinch the swollen bud at the apex of her folds.

Slamming my mouth down on hers, I do as I promised. Every thrust cements my ownership of her tight channel. Reconquering her mouth with my lips and tongue so I make sure that every hole carries the scent and taste of me.

Alternating between rubbing soft circles around her sensitive nub and lightly pinching it, I claim her in the most primal fucking way while driving her to accept that claim in the pinnacle of ecstasy.

I will not allow her body to deny me. Sweet and perfect, every atom of Róise is mine and after this, she will never be able to doubt that.

When she orgasms, her mouth goes slack against mine while her entire body tenses in the perfect rictus of pleasure.

Her ass muscles squeeze my cock and pleasure erupts from my balls, bathing her forbidden channel with my seed.

She is mine. Always and forever.

CHAPTER 78: RÓISE

Miceli pulls from my body with gentle slowness before shifting me so I'm sitting sideways in his lap. Then he washes me as carefully as he would a newborn.

Everywhere. Which destroys the baby metaphor but not the tender attention behind it.

My legs are filled with jelly instead of muscle and bone right now, so I don't even put up a token protest when he also dries me off.

I object though, when he slides a finger between my butt cheeks to smear ointment on my still fluttering sphincter.

"Shh. Let me take care of you, *vitù*."

Realizing there's no point in arguing when he's almost done, I nod.

There's so much approval and warmth in his smile, my heart flutters.

Miceli guides me to sit on the vanity bench before he starts picking up the impressive array of weapons littering the floor along with our clothes and the things I'd stuffed into my shorts' pockets from my trunk prison, thinking I might need them.

My fiancé checks *all three* guns to make sure there are no rounds in the chamber before placing them on the bathroom counter.

After he stacks as many knives beside the firearms, I shake my head. "I think I need a better personal arsenal."

"It is my job to protect you." Miceli looks me straight in the eye. "I might have failed today, but I give you my vow that I never will again. "

"You didn't fail. No one could have foreseen the guy working for Gabriel Lion on my uncle's payroll." I will never call that man grandfather again. "And you got me back."

"You were well on your way to saving yourself."

I shake my head. "They knew I was heading for the warehouse, though I don't know how they guessed I would go there and not one of the apartment buildings."

"I'll be sure and ask them," Miceli says grimly.

"The point is, I'd run out of options when you guys showed up."

"I have no doubt in your ingenuity." He leans down and picks me up bridal style. "You would've gotten away."

"Well, I'm glad you got there when you did."

He's all about what a badass I am. And I like knowing he thinks that, but the reality is, I'm a fine arts major, not a mafia soldier. No matter how much training in self-defense I have done over the years.

And none of those abilities had any impact on what happened to me today.

Miceli pulls the covers back and lays me down on the bed before joining me there and tugging the summer weight comforter over us.

He traces the contours of my face with a light fingertip. "Tell me everything from the second that asshole jerked you off the dock."

"Why? Don't you want to forget about it? It's probably not healthy for you to dwell on something you consider a failure."

"But it *is* healthy for you to talk about it. So, talk."

I mean to argue again. Say something about going to a therapist, or visiting my *mamo* which is pretty much the same thing.

But instead, when I open my mouth, words start spilling out. How the men took me, what it felt like underwater before I got the darkened diver's mask and access to oxygen.

"I was scared," I admit. "And angry. So angry."

Miceli kisses my forehead. "And so fucking brave. Keep talking."

I do. For more than an hour. I tell him everything in more detail than I even think I could remember. I can see the banked fury in his eyes, but not once does he interrupt me.

Not to ask about the random stuff I grabbed from the trunk now adding to the mess on our bathroom floor. Not even to curse the kidnappers out.

When I finally stop talking, the look of approval on Miceli's handsome face is a balm to my wounded soul. "Did I mention how fucking brave you are? And smart. You are so damn smart."

"I must be, I agreed to marry you." These words pop out without me thinking about it, but I have no desire to take them back.

Agreeing to be the sacrificial lamb in my uncle's alliance plans is the best decision I have ever made. It doesn't matter how we came together, Miceli is it for me, created to be the other half of my soul before I was ever born.

And I'm the other half of his. Whether he ever admits that out loud, or not.

Right now, his body goes completely still. For several seconds, he doesn't even breathe. He just stares at me like he cannot believe what I just said.

"It's true," I tell him.

And the feelings I have for him are real. My love for him is woven into the depths of my being at this point. There is no Róise without the love I hold for Miceli.

I am safe with him, both physically and emotionally.

It started all those months ago in Portland, but it didn't stop there. That very first time we had sex in his studio, the way he came back to give me stuff to put in my bath? To make sure I was okay.

It was so unlike the guy he portrays to the rest of the world, but it is the guy he shows me time and again. Even when we had to move the wedding date forward. He made sure *he* was the one to tell me.

To explain it.

And when I insisted on finishing school? He kept the promise he made in our contract. When I got kicked out of college, he could have capitalized on that to try to convince me to quit. Instead, he coerced the dean into accepting me back *and* apologizing.

Pretty much pretending I *hadn't* been kicked out, even though we both knew better.

Miceli didn't stop there, though. He found me an agent for after I graduate, so I don't have to give up my dreams.

He acknowledges my compromises and looks for ways to mitigate them, so I'm living a life I want, not one thrust upon me.

Yes, I stand up for myself. I am me, after all, but Miceli could make that really hard to do. Instead, he supports me. Even when that makes things harder on him.

Not only did he fire Giovanna for trying to hurt my feelings, but he made sure the interview with a massively popular and busy celebrity news reporter got rescheduled.

And the sex? It's not just off the charts; our souls connect when we are together like that. Maybe that's mystical, but it doesn't make it any less true.

He's not perfect. Not at all. He gets a little too much joy out of the dark side of his job as Genovese underboss. He's violent and unapologetically criminal.

And still, he's perfect for me and I'm done pretending that's not true.

"I love you, Miceli," I breathe.

My heart knows what it knows. I will never feel this way about anyone else.

He pulls my hand to press against his heart. "Do you feel that?"

"Yes."

"It beats for you."

"What are you saying?" Is he admitting he loves me?

"I swore to myself I would never fall for a woman like my brother or my cousin." He barks out a self-deprecating, dark chuckle. "I thought their obsession with the women they love, made them vulnerable, and weak."

"I don't know Salvatore very well." I met him briefly at his wedding, but that's all really. "But your brother is not weak."

"Neither am I. My love for you gives me strength. It gives me focus."

"Say the words, Miceli." I need the words.

"*T'amu*. I love you." He kisses me softly. "*Sempre e per sempre*. Always and forever."

Another kiss. My lips try to chase his, but he's not done.

"*Sei mio.* You are mine." This kiss is a little more forceful but no less emotionally devastating. "*Io sono tua.* I am yours."

"I love you so much, Miceli." My voice cracks on his name and a tear of joy slides down my temple.

He swipes it with his thumb, licking it off like even that single tear is precious to him.

"This..." He waves between the two of us. "It's not about blood alliances. It is about how my heart beats for you and you alone. I would give up the mafia for you."

Before, I thought that was what I wanted, but I realize now it's not. One, because my uncle is right. I am a Shaughnessy and nothing will change that. Which means that without the protection of a syndicate, I'm not safe.

Whatever children I have are not safe. And Miceli would *definitely* not be safe.

But two, a mafia underboss soon to be don *is* who I want to marry. "I don't need you to change for me to love you. And I don't need you to give up the mafia to make me happy. I *am* happy with you."

"I do not know what deity gifted you to me, but I will make offerings to them for the rest of eternity."

"To be clear, then, there will be no more of the *love isn't a word I use* crap? Because you *are* going to love our children."

"Every bit as fiercely as I love you," he vows.

My eyes burn with more joy-filled tears. The words are everything I need to hear. The final piece that assures me I made the right choice agreeing to marry this man.

"I fell in love with you that night in Portland," I tell him in a choked voice. "When I saw you standing in your brother's office and knew you were the man I was supposed to marry, I felt so betrayed. Not only by fate, but by my own feelings."

"You hid those feelings pretty well," he says with a wry twist of his lips.

"Self-preservation, but there is no one I ever want to touch me but you and I knew that then."

His eyes burn with violent intensity. "Good, because I would have to kill anyone who touched you."

"You're such a sweet talker."

His expression turns so serious. "I'm not a sensitive guy, no matter what people think about artists. You are the only one who touches my heart so deeply that I believe part of my soul still exists. I love you with everything inside of me and everything I have. Róise, you are my world."

His use of my name in this moment, with that admission feels like another claim on my heart.

~ ~ ~

Pusheen yowls at the door until Miceli lets her in. Then, she bounds up onto the bed, settling her long Maine Coon body along the side recently occupied by Miceli.

"She's a pushy beast, but I understand her need to know you are safe." He reaches down and pets *our* cat.

"She doesn't know I was kidnapped," I point out.

"I wouldn't be so sure about that."

I roll my eyes, but Miceli shakes his head. "Didn't you say that Troy was the soldier she jumped on in the hallway?"

It takes a second for me to remember what he's talking about. "Um, yes."

"Well, guess who was one of the men on sonar watch detail?"

"What a smart cat you are my beautiful Pusheen." I scratch her head and then yawn.

"Rest. I'll order us some dinner."

"Make it something we can eat in bed." I snuggle into the bed with my cat.

"We do not eat in bed."

"On the day *I* got kidnapped we do." There will be other times too, but I'll break him into the idea slowly.

"Why do I feel like this is not going to be a one-time deal?"

"Because you're smart?"

~ ~ ~

Pusheen is still in our bed when I wake up the next morning, but Miceli isn't. I get up to use the bathroom and find him in the en suite filling the tub.

I approve. "Good idea."

Sexy times in the shower are fun and all but right now the bath looks like heaven and a side of spicy tots.

"Your cousins are going to be here in an hour. I would have let you sleep otherwise."

"But you know I want to see them. Besides, I woke up on my own." Probably because he left the bed, but I don't mention that. "I swear I can feel every muscle and they all ache."

Exhaustion drags at my body from my epic adrenaline hangover too.

Miceli sweeps me up into his arms and then lowers me into the bath.

"You do that a lot."

"It's a family trait," he says with a shrug in his voice.

"Carrying your fiancée around like a bride is a family trait?" I scoff.

"Ask Catalina if you don't believe me."

"I will." After I visit with my cousins and then sleep for about three days.

Miceli climbs into the deliciously scented water with me and I lean back against his chest.

His hands pass over my body in languid strokes.

My eyes slide closed. "Feels nice."

It feels more than nice. It feels like I'm being cherished and I revel in it.

One of his hands travels up my torso until his thumb brushes the underside of my breast. He doesn't go any further but continues those unhurried touches on either side of my body. His big hands glide over my stomach, and then between my legs, washing my thighs. He doesn't go near my core.

I'm trying to decide if I'm disappointed or not when he moves down to caress under my knees.

The leisurely touches send tiny sparks of pleasure along my nerve endings. My eyes flutter closed and I slip into a place of half awareness.

My brain fills with pleasant, peaceful static as my muscles relax one by one until I'm a floating mass of goo.

Memories of yesterday are far away. Only Miceli's touch registers.

When he gently pinches both of my nipples between his thumbs and forefingers, I feel a corresponding pulse in my clit. I moan, reaching back to touch him too.

"Shh…just relax and feel *mi dolce fiore*."

With a soft sigh, I do and eventually the slow and gentle caresses bring me to climax.

"Feel better?" he asks.

"I do," I say with surprise.

I don't ache nearly as much as when I first woke up. How much is whatever he put in the bath and how much is the aftermath of my orgasm?

"That's a family trait too," he teases.

"That's *not* something I'm going to ask Catalina about."

Moma shows up with Kara and Fiona. She insists on fussing over me and is adamant I either lay on the couch or return to bed.

I know when I'm beat. I choose the couch.

"One of our own men was feeding information to Gabriel," Kara says, her tone filled with shock.

She should be shocked. The men allowed on the estates security detail are the most trusted among my uncle's soldiers.

"I bet your dad is livid." I take a sip of the strong Irish breakfast tea *moma* insisted on preparing for me.

She brought her own tin with her. It's no use telling her we have tea. It's not *hers* specially shipped from her hometown in Ireland.

"Mick and him are both on the warpath." Kara shakes her head. "I had to leave Fitz at the mansion with Ollie and the nanny."

"I'm surprised they let you all come then."

"That was *moma*."

I grin. My grandmother is a force to be reckoned with when she wants to be.

Moma sits by my legs and pats my calf. "Now, you'll tell us all about yesterday and drain the poison from your heart."

"I already did that with Miceli," I explain.

"You did, did you? Well, that's fine." *Moma* digs her knitting from her capacious purse. "He'll make a fine husband even if he is Italian. Now, you'll be telling us, or I'll hear no end of it from your cousins."

None of us are fooled. *Moma* wants the details as badly as Kara and Fiona.

Telling them is different than telling Miceli. My cousins interrupt a lot. *Moma* makes noises of disapproval and approbation where needed and I'm yawning halfway into the tale.

I don't know when I fall asleep, but I don't hear them leave.

CHAPTER 79: MICELI

The Box is more crowded than usual.

Sev stands against the far wall with Brogan Shaughnessy. Angelo is playing with his knives in front of our unwilling guest while Allessio leans against the wall directly across from him.

We've got one of the AOG soldiers strapped to a metal chair attached to the floor. We don't want it tipping in the middle of something important.

Unhinged stainless steel without seams makes for easy clean up too. Everything about The Box is designed so all DNA trace can be erased quickly.

Not that any law enforcement agency is going to find our interrogation and holding facility under the Oscuro Building.

But we don't take chances.

Which is why safeguards are taken on the extremely rare times when an outsider is brought in. Brogan Shaughnessy has no idea where he is and nothing in The Box reveals how many stories underground we are.

Allessio's murderous gaze doesn't shift from the man pretending not to be affected, but the sweat on Cleatus Jerome's brow and the pulse beating a rapid tattoo in his neck gives him away.

I move to stand in front of him without blocking Allessio's line of sight. "My friend there wants to cut you into tiny pieces for daring to touch his charge. What do you think I want?"

"I don't care what you want," Cleatus sneers.

"You will," I promise and look at Angelo. "Why don't you use one of those fancy knives and cut off Cleatus's clothes?"

Flipping a knife end over end, the Angel of Death saunters over to the AOG soldier. "Don't worry, Cleeeetus..." Angelo singsongs. "I know what I'm doing." He pauses and then grins maliciously. "If I cut you, it'll be on purpose."

"What kind of sickos are you? You want to see me naked?" Cleatus jeers.

"I want to see you dead," Allessio says with icy certainty.

I drop to my haunches so me and the militia solder are eye level. "But first you have some questions to answer."

"I'm not saying anything to you!"

Cleatus's bravado lasts until Angelo knicks his ballsac while cutting off his boxers. His screech echoes off the cold metal walls of the room.

By the time Allessio has cut off three of the AOG soldier's fingers, Cleatus is crying.

"I thought you'd be tougher, militia man. You're supposed to be trained to kill, right?"

"It doesn't take a lot to learn to kill," Angelo drawls. "But learning to accept pain is something else."

"All of this for a woman?" he demands with a sob. "Why?"

"You know who didn't cry the whole time you had her?" Disgust is written in every line of Allessio's face. "The fucking strong woman you kidnapped."

"Taking that assignment wasn't smart," Angelo says, like he's almost sympathetic. "Too bad you won't live long enough to improve your decision making skills."

"This pissant doesn't think for himself," Allessio dismisses.

I grab Cleatus's so far undamaged right hand and press my knife against the base of his forefinger.

"No, no. Please," he slobbers. "I'll tell you what you want. Just stop hurting me."

"I hope his friend holds out longer. I didn't even get to try my new clippers on his toes." Angelo's tone is not sarcastic. He sounds genuinely disappointed.

Cleatus stares at Sev's top assassin like he's a demon.

"The Angel of Death is a demon, right?" I ask of no one in particular.

"Yes, and why is that important?" Sev asks with raised brows.

"The pissant..." I like Allessio's word. "Is looking at our Angel of Death like he's a demon. It fits."

Cleatus wails.

Allessio chuckles darkly. "You've got a twisted view of the world, but yeah, it tracks, boss."

Cleatus tells us everything he knows about the AOG compound security, weapons stores and business.

The fact that it isn't a lot shows that at least someone there has a few working brain cells.

We move him to the wall manacles to serve as visual inspiration before Angelo and Allessio bring the AOG team leader in. Turns out Mordecai Jerome is Cleatus's cousin.

Our people had no trouble identifying them once we figured out which plane in the hangar they were supposed to be transporting Róise to Pennsylvania in.

They filed a flight plan. A real one with genuine names and airport destination.

The fucking arrogance. Or stupidity. I can't decide which one applies more.

As predicted, Mordecai takes longer to break, but in the end, he tells us what we want to know. Including the names of the men inside Shaughnessy's syndicate that are on Gabriel Lion's payroll.

The mob boss is livid there are two.

"Look at the positive side." Angelo wipes the blood from his blade on Mordecai's bicep. "Only one of them managed to infiltrate the detail assigned to your estate."

Brogan's scowl says he doesn't find that too much of a consolation.

Mordecai gives a hoarse yell causing us all to look at him again.

Angelo's blade is now sticking out of the bicep he'd used to wipe it off with. He shrugs when we all look at him and pulls it out. "Guess I wasn't quite done yet."

I'm not either.

I walk over to Cleatus's form dangling from the wall.

"You tried to take my heart from my body. Now I'll take yours." I shove the blade in, piercing the organ and then twisting until it's destroyed.

Piss mixes with the blood on the floor around Mordecai.

I don't bother repeating myself. He knows why he's about to die. Angelo might be our top assassin, but today I'm dealing the killing blows to our unwilling and fucking unwanted guests.

Mordecai manages a pretty good scream before his heart stops, but it does nothing to abate my fury at the AOG and its cult leader.

I fix steely eyes on Brogan. "Gabriel dies the same way, at my hand."

The mob boss glares at me. "He killed my brother."

"That was Jed and I'll let you kill him," I offer generously.

"Take the compromise. I don't want one of my new allies killed on an op because he got in the way of my brother's knife." Sev's tone doesn't invite argument.

Brogan shows his superior thinking skills to the AOG leaders when he nods in agreement.

After Brogan interrogates and kills the rats in his mob, we turn all the information over to our capo and his team of hackers.

Less than twenty-four hours later, we have the op planned.

We use low-flying helicopters to transport our teams to Pennsylvania. No fucking flight plans.

When we get there, allies have vehicles waiting for us.

In stealth mode, we hit the compound one hour after the moon sets, taking out the perimeter guards with two snipers and the gate guards with stun-and-kill techniques.

Domenico disarms their electronic alarm and surveillance setup once he has access to the computer at the gate. There will be no digital record of the carnage tonight.

The only soldiers living in the compound were hand-picked by Gabriel Lion. They're so far up his ass, he trusts them to protect him with their lives.

Well, tonight they'll pay that price, but they won't be able to protect him. The cult leader signed his own hit order when he tried to take *mi vitù* away.

We have six squads of five men. Splitting into two and three-men teams, we hit the key building in the compound simultaneously. My orders are to kill all AOG soldiers on contact with the exception of Gabriel or Jed. According to their now dead men, the leader and his lieutenant *should* be asleep in their own beds.

But I take nothing for granted.

Allessio and two more of my men make up my team. Our target is Gabriel Lion.

Zoey wanted to be here, but she's not made yet and every soldier on this mission is. We have all killed for the mafia and tonight we do it again.

Gabriel and Hope Lion do not share a bedroom. One of my men check to confirm the old woman is asleep while Allessio and I make our way to the primary bedroom and the man I plan to kill.

Eventually.

The door and frame are reinforced steel, but the walls on either side are plaster and wood. Allessio sets a charge on the wall to the right of the door. I set one on the left.

They blow simultaneously and with nothing left to hold it in place, it takes a single coordinated kick to send the door crashing to the floor.

Gabriel sits up with a shout, but all he's going to see are the dark shadows of our outlines. We're wearing night vision goggles. He's not. And we cut the power to the house before coming inside.

When I have a tactical advantage, I make sure I keep it.

"Who are you? What do you think you are doing?" He leans over and scrabbles for something beside the bed.

"Ah, ah, ah," I admonish and shoot the reaching hand.

He screams. "What do you want? Money? Weapons? Drugs? I'll give it to you."

Finally he asks a question I'm willing to answer. "What do I want?"

"Yes. Whatever it is. Do you want a woman?" He pauses. "A virgin?"

"You sick fuck." Allessio shoots Gabriel's kneecap.

Which elicits louder screaming, now accompanied by sobs.

"Sorry, boss," Allessio apologizes. "I know the kill is yours, but I've got sisters."

"Should have shot him in the fucking groin," my other guy says.

"Good idea." I aim and shoot right between Gabriel's legs.

"Good shot, boss," Allessio approves.

"Well, he's not a moving target." Unless you count writhing in pain.

A woman shrieks from the hallway, "Take your filthy hands off me. Let me go to my husband!"

My soldier drags her over the rubble of the walls and into the room, but doesn't let her go.

I grab her throat and squeeze. "Silence!"

She stops squawking, but glares up at me in the darkened room.

"Did you know?" I ask her.

She presses her lips tightly together.

I squeeze her throat tighter, cutting off her air. I count to ten in my head. Slowly.

And then I loosen my hold so she can speak. "Did you know that your husband had your son-in-law killed?"

"Gabriel wouldn't do that. Murder is a sin and he's a God-fearing man."

She's either deluded, or as big of a liar as her husband. I'm going with the latter.

"Help me, Mary-Hope," Gabriel sobs. "I'm dying."

Not yet, he's not. But soon.

"I need to call an ambulance," Mary-Hope says. "I can smell the blood in here. What did you do to him? Someone turn on a light."

I ignore the orders and her question to ask one of my own. "Did you know that Gabriel planned to kidnap Róise and give her to a man old enough to be her grandfather?"

"Jedidiah is a good man."

"Like your husband?" Derision drips from Allessio's voice.

"So, you knew?" I ask.

"It's not kidnapping when she belongs here. To us."

Not *with* us, but *to* us.

"You're as vile as your husband." Disgusted, I drop my hand from her throat and turn away. "Take her back to her room and watch her."

My soldier obeys, ignoring Mary-Hope's loud protests.

My plan tonight is not to kill the women in this cult.

Just Gabriel Lion and his little army. The women who have lived under his tyranny have been punished enough. But the temptation to end Mary-Hope is damn near overwhelming.

My plans for her are already in place though. Because she's not her husband's unwitting accomplice.

She helped him build the cult into what it is and bartered her daughters away for the sake of her husband's greed.

With cooperation from an FBI agent on our payroll, Mary-Hope Lion will be under investigation for her part in Gabriel's criminal enterprises starting tomorrow.

Except for a couple about to be frozen by the FBI, Domenico is draining the AOG and Lion's personal bank accounts tonight.

Mary-Hope will be destitute before morning and in prison by the end of the year.

Like my father always said, those of us who know how to operate outside the law are fucking aware of how to use it against our enemies.

"Are you ready to die, Gabriel?" I approach the sobbing man on the bed.

"No. No. I don't want to die. Call an ambulance."

"If I was going to call anyone, it would be the morgue. But when I'm done here, there won't be enough of you left to identify, much less bury." I shove my blade straight into his heart. "I am going to raze your compound to the ground and it will look like you fucking fanatics did it to yourself. Too bad you keep so much magnesium-based ammunition around."

Not as much as will be burning in the blaze that will turn him and his men to ash, destroying their legacy to their very fucking DNA. But the traces of it left after the fire will be attributed to the munitions in the building that's about to explode with a bunch of AOG soldiers in it.

"Too bad you won't be around to see your army destroyed." I twist the knife. "But you can die knowing there will be nothing left of you or the AOG by morning."

I make good on my word. By the time I'm done, the entire compound is blown up or burning, with just enough evidence left for the FBI to issue arrest warrants for men that no longer exist.

Their wives and children still have their bank accounts and twelve hours to get the hell out of Dodge.

I'm not a fucking social worker, but I don't make the innocent pay for the sins of the guilty.

Róise is going to be thrilled. Brogan is bringing her aunt and cousins back to Long Island with him.

Better him than me.

CHAPTER 80: RÓISE

Miceli walks like a cat, but I can sense his presence in the apartment before he walks through the door into the great room.

My throat is dry, my palms sweaty. My heart is beating so hard I can feel it.

I've been working so hard on the new décor, and this will be the first time that he sees it.

For the sake of security, Miceli insisted we stay with his family while the actual work was being done. Because I didn't want him to see anything before it was all finished, I agreed.

Staying with his family has been good for my relationship with Aria. We've gotten to know each other, and I like her. She likes me too, now. And I adore my sister-in-law Catalina almost as much as my cousins at this point.

Accompanied by a full security detail, I've been overseeing the workmen and transformation to our home. Miceli has been working in his office, but I wouldn't let him come up to the penthouse.

He's been complaining about not being able to see more of me because I'm up here while he's on a lower floor.

As of today, that can end.

Miceli walks into the room, his eyes on me.

He doesn't look anywhere else. He doesn't see his paintings on the walls or the new sofa and chairs. All he sees is me.

And my heart thuds for a different reason. Miceli De Luca loves me. I am the center of his world.

"What do you think?"

He gives me a look from head to toe, and his eyes darken with desire. "I like the yoga pants. They show your ass off but that T-shirt is too big for you."

"It's one of yours."

"You like stealing from my wardrobe."

"Yep. It's one of the bennies of being in a serious relationship."

He reaches me and draws me into his arms. "If by serious, you mean we're together until one of us kicks the bucket, yeah, I can see that."

"You and your morbid thoughts."

"Maybe you'll train me to stop thinking of death by the time our first kid is born," he offers.

I wrap my hand around the back of his neck, loving that I have the freedom to touch him whenever I want. "Well, I've got some time to do that since I'm not getting pregnant right away."

Something flashes in his eyes.

I put my hand up to stop him from saying what I know is going to come out of his mouth. Some morbid thing about how he needs to have an heir before too long in case he dies young.

"You are not dying young. I just got you. And I am keeping you forever. And if not, having a kid to train to be the next don will stop you from taking any chances..."

"I don't need any other reason than to know you are here waiting for me. I don't take the risks that will stop me from coming home to you."

"Good to know." Getting lost in his eyes, I forget what I'm supposed to be showing him.

We kiss.

But when he goes to pick me up to carry me to the bedroom, I remember. And I press against his chest "Wait. I want you to see."

"I want to see you too. "

Laughter bubbles out of me. "That's not what I meant. But it can be on the menu for later."

"I'm ready to feast now."

"Look around, my love, and tell me what you think."

He stops on his trek toward the bedroom. "Say that again."

Miceli calls me by all sorts of endearments. Aphrodite. His sweet flower. Good girl. But I haven't used any with him, except Ares. I don't know why.

No that's not true. I do know why. I didn't feel like I had the right. Maybe that doesn't make sense, but I know he is mine now.

In my family, endearments are special and only used with people you love. And I didn't want to reveal my love for him.

"My love."

That earns me another scorching kiss, but eventually I convince him to ooh and ahh over my hard work.

He likes the desk nook created by a bookcase divider open on both sides in the living room. "No more working in a spare bedroom?"

I shake my head. "You have an office two floors down if you need privacy or solitude to work. But this way, even if I'm studying over there and you're working here, we're still together."

I know he's going to like this. We're both a little obsessed.

The look of approval on his handsome face says I called it. "That's perfect. I didn't like being cooped up in one of the bedrooms while you were out here."

"But working on your laptop on the coffee table is not ideal."

He shrugs. "Worth it to spend more time with you."

"I don't care if I am supposed to be independent and want time to myself or if you're supposed to be hard and aloof with me. I want us to be just like we are. Always."

"Good because having you breathe the same air as me keeps me alive." He kisses me. "I love you." Another bone melting kiss. "I need you." He pauses, his dark gaze filled with emotion I never thought to see there. "You make my heart beat, and losing you would make it stop."

"Always with the morbid with you."

His laughter is still on his lips when he presses them to mine, but I insist that Miceli finishes his inspection of the great room.

"I like your touches, it feels like a ho..." He doesn't finish the word because his eyes have snagged on my portrait above the fireplace.

Then he sees the grouping of book cover paintings on the wall behind the dining room table.

"You hung up my art."

"Yes." I put my hand out to his. "Come with me."

I want him to see everything before we talk about that. We go back through the hall, but instead of going into the primary bedroom, I drag him down to the last room.

I open the door and step back and wait for his reaction.

The room is set up very similarly to the studio in lower Manhattan. There are two easels, cabinets for his paints, brushes, turpentine, linseed oil and everything else. Canvases of all different sizes lean against one wall.

The walk-in closet is now set up for storage of paintings as well as more art supplies.

He wiggles the doorknob. "There's no lock."

"This is your home. You don't have to lock away your need to paint from me." I don't want either of us to lock away any part of ourselves here.

"What if someone walks in here besides one of us?"

"If it means seeing my cousins and my *moma* elsewhere, so be it. If I see less of them, I'll deal. If it means not having your family over to visit, we'll visit them. But I want your heart here in our home."

"It already is. You're here."

"You're such a romantic for a big, bad mafioso." My sarcasm would be more believable if I wasn't giving him a totally sappy, gooey-eyed look.

"Only for you, *mi dolce fiore*. Only for you."

We christen his studio in the best way possible. Afterward he carries me to the bedroom and tells me he likes the new decor, even the mauve duvet cover.

The room is a mixture of mauve and midnight blue. On the far wall, here is a picture, but it's not a painting.

It's a blowup of one of the photos from the photo shoot. In it we were spinning, and my dress is flying around us. My hand is on his neck and his head is bent toward me.

And our love for each other shines like a thousand-watt bulb.

"It's us." He walks forward and touches the frame. "Our feelings are right there for everyone to see. This is the picture that should be hanging in the living room."

What am I going to do with this guy? "Could you maybe stop saying such perfect stuff? I like the painting in the living room. It's like a love letter from you."

Even though I didn't realize that the first time I saw it.

"I like it too," he admits.

"Good, because we're not hanging the painting where my legs are spread."

A wicked grin on his face, he turns back to me. "What will you give me to keep it for just us?"

"Anything you want." Because I want to give him *everything*.

"That's a generous offer." He twirls one of my curls around his finger and tugs. "But I will never allow another to see you in that way."

"I know," I say breathlessly.

He tugs me closer. "I don't want to keep our families out of our home."

"I don't either."

"I've been thinking about what you said about my father's portraits. I think that my family deserves to have the paintings that reflect his love for them."

"I do too. But are you ready for that?"

"I will be. Eventually, but I'm ready now for them to know about my own art. I know I will be a good don. I need to be sure that Sev sees me as I am though, before he names me as his successor."

"I'm pretty sure your brother sees everything in you already. He may not know about your paintings, but I wouldn't take for granted that he doesn't either."

Miceli shrugs, like his brother's opinion isn't what matters. "You know me in ways that no one else does, or ever will, *mi vitù*. They might see the paintings, but you see the heart of the man who painted them. A heart I believed no longer beat until I met you."

"I thought I hated you."

"But you've always loved me." His gaze dares me to deny it.

"Yes, but that doesn't mean you'll get away with murder with me."

"That is literally what I do. Get away with murder."

I can't help grinning, but I roll my eyes. "Not with me you don't."

"No." His expression turns serious. "With you there is no death, only life."

I wrap my arms around his neck. "I love you, Miceli De Luca."

"*T'amu mi vitù,* from now until eternity."

"*Sempre e per sempre,*" I reply in Italian.

Now and forever.

CHAPTER 81: RÓISE

I adjust the throw pillows on the couch for the third time in ten minutes.

Miceli's family is coming for dinner tonight. Aria, Severu, Catalina and even Giulia and her family are in town.

I should fluff the pillows on our bed. Pusheen likes to sleep there sometimes.

A strong arm wraps around my waist as I head in that direction. "Stop, *mi dolce fiore*. Everything looks great."

Sighing, I sag against him. "I just want it to be perfect."

"There's no such thing, unless we're talking about a certain sexy woman who left the Irish mob to become my wife."

Turning so I can see his gorgeous face, I smile. "There you go being perfect again, and we're not married yet."

"We will be soon."

That gives me so much more satisfaction than I ever believed it could.

"Yes, we will." Looking around the huge great room for anything out of place, I chew on my bottom lip. "But tonight, your family is going to see our newly decorated home for the first time."

"And my paintings."

Right. I shouldn't be nervous. I know it's going to be okay, but tonight, he's telling his family about his art and the studio he shared with his dad.

"You know what my studio here represents to me?" Miceli asks.

"A place where you can be yourself?"

"I am always myself," he declares arrogantly. "It represents your love for me. Your acceptance of all of who I am, not just the parts you are comfortable with."

"I do love all of you, even when I want to kick you in the shin." Miceli is a bossy, alpha male that has to be reined in sometimes, but he's *my* bossy, alpha male.

His lips tilt at one corner. "I never doubted it and that makes me a very lucky man."

"Remember that the next time we argue."

"Us argue? Never." This time his mouth curves in a fullblown grin.

"By never you mean the three days of war we waged before we settled on a compromise about the guards?" I don't want guards hanging out in the apartment all day, every day.

Miceli insists the full detail on duty be accessible to the penthouse.

"You must be referring to the three days of intense sexual passion we shared while discussing domestic matters."

I give him a look. "That air of innocence does not sit convincingly on your shoulders, Miceli, no matter what your doting mother told you."

But he's right about the passion. Every disagreement between us ends up with us naked in the bedroom, or on the sofa, or on one memorable occasion with me getting feasted on pressed up against the floor-to-ceiling window in Miceli's studio.

It was after that particular encounter, I agreed to the compromise of building a guard house on the west side of the terrace.

It means giving up some of our outdoor living space, but we have a lot of that. And the building will create a private balcony off the primary suite for me and Miceli, which we both like.

He wants to have sex in the hot tub. And I'm not against it.

Besides, we still have the south terrace that runs the entire width of our home for entertaining. The east terrace might be narrower than the one we're using for the guardhouse, but it's wide enough to install a play area for our niece and nephews.

Guilia and Raff have a little boy, Neri, who is a year younger than Fitz. They also have the most adorable baby girl named Sophia, but they're calling her Sophie.

"You're still okay with showing everyone your dad's paintings?" Some of the tension I'm feeling about this bleeds into my voice when I don't mean it to.

Enzo De Luca's portraits are on display in Miceli's studio and his family will see them tonight, too.

"You said you think my family will be fine with this."

Locking my hands behind his neck, I nod vigorously because I do believe it. Mostly. "And I meant it. But someone might say something that hurts your feelings and then I'll have to put castor oil in their after-dinner coffee."

He picks me up so we're eye-to-eye. "That's not going to happen."

"Because you're a big, tough underboss who doesn't get his feelings hurt?" I ask, locking my legs around his torso.

"No, because my family loves me."

I'm still getting used to this emotional honesty from him. It hits me in the feels every time.

"Even Severu," I remind him.

He rolls his eyes. "Even my brother."

"I'm glad you realize that."

"I've always known my brother loves me."

Which I'm sure is true, but there's knowing and there's *knowing*.

"Severu loves you as his brother, not just the God of War who always has his back." It still feels weird calling the Genovese don by his first name, but he insisted on it while we were staying with them.

Miceli doesn't answer, but he kisses me and that's answer enough.

We're interrupted by one of his men informing us that the De Luca family is on the way up in the elevator.

"I still don't like having bodyguards inside the apartment," I grumble as Miceli lowers me to the floor.

"They won't be once their guardroom is built." His gaze shifts toward the west terrace and then the east.

That look he gets sometimes comes over him.

"Stop it." I straighten the bodice of my dress and smooth the skirt.

Miceli runs his fingers through his hair to smooth. "Stop what?"

"Thinking about kids." I take one last look around the living area but it's too late to change anything now. "We've got at least three years."

"How do you know that's what I was thinking about?" he asks with a superior air that's a lot more believable than the innocence he tried a little bit ago.

"You get this look on your face."

"I'm pretty sure that look was for my plans to fuck you insensate on our private balcony."

"And not a single one of those thoughts ended with me pregnant?" I teasingly demand.

He shrugs.

Because of course they did.

The man wants me to have his baby, and not just to give him an heir. But I'm not getting pregnant before I finish school and he knows it.

The contract gives me another year on birth control after that, but I'm not worried about the terms of the contract anymore. If I want to wait five years, Miceli will wait.

Because he loves me.

But that won't stop him from fantasizing about planting a baby inside me.

~ ~ ~

Aria is the first person to come in, followed quickly by Giulia, Raff and their children.

Neri makes a beeline for Pusheen and our cat graciously tolerates the four-year-old's affection.

My mother-in-law insists on a hug *from me* before oohing and ahhing over the new decor. "It's gorgeous in here," she pronounces.

"Absolutely. Who would have thought this place could look so much like a home," Giulia asks with a smile, handing the baby off to Aria at the older woman's insistence.

My sister-in-law is beautiful and her husband can't keep his hands off her curvy figure. They're so in love, it would be sickening if it wasn't so amazing.

This whole mafia family is filled with couples that are deeply in love. Severu and Catalina. Salvatore and Bianca. Big Sal and Ilaria. The portrait on the easel in Miceli's studio shows how much his father loved his mother.

Catalina is the first to comment on my portrait hanging on the wall. "Oh, this is beautiful. You didn't tell me you were sitting for a portrait, Róise."

Before I have a chance to answer, Severu steps up close to the painting, and examines it. "M. A. D."

My heart starts beating faster.

He turns to Miceli. "You?"

The shock on my fiancé's face is comical. "How did you know?"

"I was our father's underboss and your don. Do you think there is anything about either of you that I didn't know?"

"You never said anything."

"It wasn't my secret to expose."

"It shouldn't have been a secret at all," I mutter.

"What are you talking about?" Giulia demands.

Aria looks confused. "What secret?"

"I painted the portrait of Róise," Miceli tells them all. "The paintings on that wall are mine too."

The next few minutes are filled with explanations, affirmations and even congratulations. But not one criticism.

Tears turn Aria's eyes glossy. "When I asked your father why you stopped drawing, he told me he'd taken care of it. It hurt that you'd lost that part of yourself."

"Then why didn't you say something about it?" Giulia asks her mother.

"It would have only hurt your brother more for me to acknowledge the loss, or so I thought." Aria smiles gently at Miceli. "I'm so glad you kept your art."

"I didn't mean that," Giulia says wryly. "I mean, why did you accept it when you thought papà had disciplined the art out of Miceli?"

Aria purses her lips. "He knew best how to raise his sons for the roles they would one day hold."

Giulia opens her mouth, like she's going to argue, but Severu interrupts her. "He knew enough not to take Miceli's art away from him. That's what matters."

"I guess." Giulia walks over to Miceli and hugs him hard. "You're an amazing artist, brother."

"Thank you, but so was dad."

They all go silent at that, shocked expressions on everyone's faces. Except Severu's.

"Show them your dad's paintings," I prod, knowing now is the time and not after dinner, like we planned.

His brother and sister are delighted with their portraits, but they want to see more of Miceli's work and he shares that with them too.

Aria stands in front of her portrait, looking like a woman holding onto her composure by a thread.

Stepping up beside her, I ask, "Do you want some privacy?"

"Not in here. I don't want to interrupt the children."

Hearing her refer to her son, the don, and the others as *children* makes me smile, but I nod. "Come on. You haven't seen the primary bedroom yet."

She turns and takes a stumbling step. I wrap an arm around her waist before anyone else notices. I just know Aria doesn't want them to see her like this.

She's a lot like *moma* that way. Strong for everyone else, but keeping her own struggles private.

I lead her out of the room.

"Miceli tells me Pusheen has her own room."

"She does." I stop in front of the door next to our bedroom. "Do you want to see it?"

The door is shut, but Pusheen has an access panel designed to look like part of the door. It's connected to a transmitter on the cat's collar and slides open when she bops it with her nose.

But Aria shakes her head. "Neri is probably in there already, playing with the cat."

She's right. We continue on to the bedroom.

"It's beautiful," Aria says approvingly, looking around, but then her gaze snags on the photo of us on the wall and stays there. "You look very much in love there."

"I didn't know it, but we were."

"I thought my husband had a mistress. I believed he loved me, but I thought he had someone else."

"Oh, Aria..." I don't know what to say. So, I hug her.

And after only a second of stiffness, she turns and hugs me back, a sob erupting from her.

"Oh, mamma." Giulia rushes across the room and throws her arms around us both. "Papa would never have betrayed you like that."

Aria tries to push us both away, rubbing at her cheek, but Giulia doesn't let her. "Stop, mamma. It's okay to be human. We love you."

"I love you, too." Aria turns into her daughter's embrace and I step back.

But Catalina's soft voice from near the door says, "Don't leave. You're part of this family too."

Guilia guides her mom to sit down in one of the armchairs.

Aria reaches her hands out toward us. "My daughters...all of my daughters. I am so blessed to have you."

I'm not her daughter yet, but she's not making the distinction, so I don't either. Catalina and I join Giulia on the floor near Aria's chair.

It's so reminiscent of times in my *moma* rooms with my cousins, it makes my heart hurt. In a good way.

I *am* part of this family, and not just because Miceli insists it is true.

"Papa loved you, but he thought his art was a weakness. That's what Miceli said," Giulia comforts her mom. "He didn't share it with anyone until he saw the same so-called weakness in his son."

"That kind of talent is not a weakness," Aria says fiercely. "I would have told him that if he'd ever shared that part of himself with me."

"Of course you would." I squeeze her hand.

"Are there other paintings?" Aria asks. "Where were those portraits stored?"

I tell her about the studio and all three women pepper me with questions. Catalina is just really curious. You only have to know her for a minute to figure that out.

But this is a part of Enzo I'm able to give to his wife and daughter that they didn't have before. "There are more paintings. They're all portraits."

"And Enzo painted them all?"

"Yes. The only portraits Miceli has ever painted are of me."

"Portraits as in plural?" Giulia asks, a mischievous glint in her dark eyes so like her brothers.

"One is very..." I look at Aria and blush.

She blushes too and hushes her daughter.

Catalina grins.

We've been chatting a while when the men join us, Severu holding the baby.

"Dinner is on the table," Miceli says.

"You served it?" Giulia presses her hand against her chest. "Watch out. I may faint."

"Don't pretend you cook any more often than I do," Miceli snarks. "You've got a housekeeper, maid and a cook, not to mention two nannies."

"Will you be hiring staff?" Aria asks, sounding more like her usual dignified self.

I nod. "But they won't live in. If we lived on Long Island," I tease Miceli. "And we had an estate like my uncles, maybe."

"This isn't exactly a studio apartment," Raff jokes.

And that's how the rest of the night goes. We have dinner, talk, laugh and enjoy each other's company.

When they leave, everyone hugs me and then Miceli.

Severu makes sure he and Catalina are the last to go. "You're going to be don soon."

Miceli nods, his expression turning wary.

"Don't think like our father. Your gift isn't a weakness. Don't hide it from your family."

His jaw taut, Miceli nods again.

Then they hug.

Catalina swipes under her eyes. "These darn pregnancy hormones."

"What's my excuse?" I ask, blinking away moisture.

After they're gone, Miceli wants to make love. In his studio.

I want to suck him off.

Win-win.

CHAPTER 82: MICELI

The dividing wall between the interrogation room and the outer room of The Box is recessed to make room for all the capos and their seconds.

Everyone is silent. The occasion is too serious for idle talk. We are all here to witness Lorenzo Ricci get his just desserts for betraying *la famiglia*.

Sev wants to do this before he turns off Don Caruso's life support and our shift in positions happens.

After I provided Sev with the final evidence to prove Lorenzo's decades of betrayal, he issued an order to bring the capo in. But when me and my team went looking, the *stronzo* was gone.

Turns out our cousin Salvatore had his own reasons for putting the capo on ice, but he didn't kill him. Which saved his life. Sev wouldn't have forgiven that.

He couldn't, family or not.

Salvatore's wife and his head of security are here too. That stupid fuck, Lorenzo, tried to cover his own ass by lying about Bianca and damn near got her killed.

She deserves to see him die, if that's what she wants. Under the same circumstance, Róise would not want to be here. She is strong, but not blood thirsty. She wanted her dad's murderer killed, but didn't want to see him die.

I asked before we left on the mission to raze the AOG compound.

"You are here today to witness the punishment of a traitor." My brother's tone is harsh and condemning. "Lorenzo Ricci has stolen money from *la famiglia* both in tithe and what he owes his own men from the profits of their enterprises."

"It looks like he's already been punished," Stephano Bianchi says.

Of course it's one of the older capos that put pressure on Sev to marry and have a kid last year. Too bad he's mamma's cousin, or I would arrange a nice little accident.

He's also Domenico's uncle and Dom is family loyal. Technically, the old bastard is related to me too, I guess.

Family. What can you do?

Severu shrugs. "One session of torture is not enough for such an offense."

He's right about that. No matter how satisfying that session was for Salvatore and me.

"Damn right." Domenico makes it clear he doesn't share his uncle's views.

Good man.

Sev acknowledges Dom's comment with a slight dip of his chin. "Because his offense was against the entire family, you are all here not only as witnesses but to participate in his punishment as well."

I'm not surprised when Salvatore is the first to step forward and punch Lorenzo hard enough to break the disgraced capo's jaw. The next man who steps forward does surprise me. A little.

It's Lorenzo's own son. "You stole from our people, forcing good and loyal soldiers to work outside the mafia to provide for their families."

Dario spits in his father's face before slapping him like a little bitch and turning to dismiss the older man like he is nothing.

The impotent fury that burns in Lorenzo's eyes is a pleasure to see.

Every capo and his second takes their turn doling out a punishment blow to the condemned man after his son is finished.

I am not a capo, so I stand back and watch, satisfied.

When the capos and their seconds are done, my brother orders me and Angelo to put Lorenzo on his knees.

We're not gentle cutting the zip ties holding him to the chair. Oops, I might have nicked him. Angelo seems to be having the same problem.

When we throw the betrayer down to kneel before Sev, he has four more cuts leaching his life's blood from his body.

My brother steps behind him, grabs Lorenzo's head and breaks his neck. "Lorenzo Ricci will have no funeral and no gravestone to mark his burial. He will return to the nothing he chose to become by breaking his oath to the Cosa Nostra."

Angelo activates the cover mechanism in the floor and as soon as there's a big enough opening, Severu kicks the dead capo over the edge.

The splash of his body landing in the chemical soup that will obliterate the man from existence is the only sound in the room.

"We are Cosa Nostra," Sev shouts.

"We are Cosa Nostra," we all shout back.

"Betray *la famiglia* and that is your fate." He points to the still open floor.

Salvatore isn't the first to step forward this time. It's Dario Ricci.

He kneels before Severu without being told. "I pledge my loyalty and my life."

Sev puts his right hand out, the one he wears his don's ring on. Dario touches his lips to the ring and then his forehead, sealing his vow.

The rest of the capos follow suit. This time, both Angelo and I join them, as does Pietro.

Soon, Sev will participate in a similar scene, but with the other dons of the Cosa Nostra as he is accepted as our godfather.

And I will become don.

As it should be.

The End of An Era

Don Caruso lays on his bed, completely still. Tubes and wires are keeping him breathing and alive, but the time has come to release him from this mortal coil.

Dons from two of the other five families are here as well. We don't congregate like this, but this is an extenuating circumstance.

Sev has unanimous support to step into Don Caruso's shoes after his death.

Other dons are already calling him for advice and even permission to do certain things. Every Cosa Nostra don in the United States will cast his vote for Sev when the time comes.

There is one capo here, the man that our godfather has named as his successor as Don of the Lucchesi Family.

No one speaks. Everyone's eyes are on the still man in the bed. The doctor stands ready for Sev's nod.

But my brother steps up to the bed, lifts the near lifeless hand, and bends one final time to touch his forehead to the godfather's ring.

The other dons follow suit. Only then does Sev nod toward the doctors. There is utter silence in the room when the woosh-woosh of the ventilator stops. Then comes the flat beep indicating the stopped heart of a once great leader.

Sev walks out of the room without acknowledging anyone else. I follow watching his back.

The vote happens less than 24 hours later, and my brother is named Godfather of the American Cosa Nostra.

Don Caruso's funeral will be this Saturday, but the five days of viewing the body beforehand will be used as an opportunity for Cosa Nostra dons and their underbosses to come and kiss the ring.

Severu's ring. My brother, the godfather.

A New Don

We're in the back room of Nonna Agata's, a restaurant as old as the Genovese Famiglia in New York.

Painted stucco walls are adorned with paintings of Sicilian landscapes in traditional ornate wood frames. Dark wood molding runs along the floor and ceiling, just like it did a hundred years ago.

For that same span of time, this is the place where the Genovese have named their dons and capos. The history of all those who came before me sits heavy in the air.

My father was given his ring here after my grandfather's death, and Sev after his. Both Dario and Salvatore's official ceremony to become capos happened here too. Just like their fathers before them.

Sev announced Salvatore's succession to his father's position when he promoted Uncle Sal to consigliere during a lesson in loyalty with all the capos, their seconds and a traitor who had sat at our table. But there still had to be a formal ceremony here.

Uncle Sal, Sev and I sit at the head table with our wives. Mamma is here too, on the other side of Róise. Ours is the only rectangular table in the room and set against the back wall.

Four large round ones filled with capos and their seconds face us.

Róise, Catalina, my mother and my aunt are the only women in the room. Giulia wanted to be here when she learned they would be, but she's part of the Vegas Cosa Nostra now.

While it's not the first time women are here to witness a new don receiving his ring, it is the first time in over three generations. And there is no way it would go over well to have a member of another Cosa Nostra family here to witness the sacred rite.

Everyone has a glass of predinner wine when Sev stands and lifts his. *"Saluti."*

We all raise our glasses and yell *saluti* before taking a sip.

"Alla famiglia." He takes a second sip.

Everyone toasts to the Cosa Nostra family.

"As you all know, Don Caruso chose to be both don and godfather." Severu waits for affirmatives to pepper the air before going on. "I do not choose to split my time or attention between two such important roles."

There is no surprise on any of the capos or their second's faces. They know why they are here, but that won't stop my brother from having his say.

It's tradition. And...it's Sev.

"Both for the good of the Cosa Nostra and the good of this family, as my father did before me, I appoint my successor."

I rise to my feet to stand beside Severu.

He lays his right hand on my left shoulder. "Miceli has been my right arm since before I became don of this family. Deciding whether to keep our God of War as my right arm or to put him in charge of this family was not an easy decision for me."

This is news to me. I didn't know my brother even considered a different course of action.

"But this family deserves the best and my brother is that," Sev goes on.

My chest tightens with emotion at his approbation, but my expression remains stoic. A don does not show his feelings.

A man might, with those he can trust, but never the don.

"Our father raised me to be don, to be patient. To be a diplomat when necessary. He raised my brother to burn down the city if necessary to protect this family. He will not be as patient with you all as I have been."

Remembering back to the day Salvatore was named capo, I think my brother is overestimating his patience.

"Miceli will lead this family into the future with strength, wisdom, and the ruthlessness necessary to keep a syndicate strong and protect the family."

Our family first, but to protect them I must keep the Genovese strong. I move my gaze from one person to the next, meeting the eyes of every single man in the room. Every capo. Every second in command.

Only then do I nod. "I will stand for this family until my death."

Always with the morbid. I can hear Róise's voice in my head, but thankfully she does not say it aloud.

Severu fixes the assembled crowd with a gimlet glare. *"Al nostro nuovo don."*

His toast to the new don is different from the others.

This is how he puts me forward to replace him. Everyone who joins the toast is voting in my favor.

Anyone who does not will die. At my hand. This family is mine to lead and to protect.

No one abstains from the vote.

CHAPTER 83: RÓISE

Miceli caresses my back as he walks behind me before moving around to stand in front of the head table.

It's a small touch, but it lets me know that I matter. Even in this incredibly heavy moment for their mafia.

I don't know if we have ceremonies like this in the mob, but I have never been to one. The capos stand as one and begin to come forward. I recognize the first man who takes a knee in front of Miceli.

It is his cousin, Salvatore. "I offer my life and my loyalty to you and the Genovese."

Miceli raises his hand and Salvatore bends his head over it. First, he kisses the ring. Then he touches the ring to his forehead.

"I accept your allegiance and loyalty." Miceli's voice is deep and commanding, sending a totally inappropriate frisson of desire through me.

I hope no one notices the way my breath catches as he takes one oath after another from all of these powerful men.

It takes almost an hour for every one of the men to make their pledge and kiss the ring. It is strange how the time both passes quickly and yet feels like it stretches to eternity as each man kneels in front of Miceli.

When the last capo's second stands and returns to his table, Miceli's uncle comes down from the head table and follows suit. Miceli told Allessio he would give his oath of loyalty later.

As part of Miceli's crew, he has already vowed lifelong loyalty to my fiancé, but that's not why Miceli wants him to wait.

After Big Sal, everyone stands again and lifts their glasses, shouting a toast to the new don.

The words about knock the air out of me, sending a chill down my spine.

This isn't a formality. This is life or death for their syndicate. Fidelity means everything and these powerful capos are offering theirs to Miceli.

I am about to marry the Don of the Genovese, the second most powerful man in New York, my uncle included.

And I am supposed to be his dona.

My knees want to give way, but I don't let them.

After the toast, Miceli beckons to Allessio.

Allessio jerks like he's surprised, but he approaches Miceli and drops to one knee in front of him.

Miceli accepts Allessio's vow of loyalty and then does something he did not do for any of the capos or his uncle. My don puts his hand out to lift Allessio to his feet.

Allessio stares at Miceli with confusion but takes the hand and stands tall beside his boss.

Miceli's lips tilt in a half smile. "I discussed who to choose as my underboss with both my brother and my wife."

The entire room goes quiet. You could hear the drop of a feather from an angel's wing, much less a pin.

All of the capos are looking intently at Allessio and Miceli.

"I choose Allessio as my underboss." Miceli turns his head so he can meet the eyes of each of his capos. "When he speaks, he speaks for me. When he acts, he acts for me. He is my right arm."

Salvatore lifts his fist in the air and shouts and the other capos follow, creating a cacophony of sound in the room and showing their approval for Allessio as the new Genovese underboss.

My shout is just as loud as anyone's.

This is what I want. I know Allessio will always have Miceli's back like Miceli has his brother's. There are men in the Genovese Cosa Nostra with more seniority than Allessio, but none more loyal to my fiancé.

That commitment might be matched by his brother and his cousin, but neither can be Miceli's underboss.

In my mind, Allessio is the only choice.

It wasn't easy to convince Miceli though, because he wants his best man leading my protection detail, but I also want the best man at his back.

There are a lot of men and women in the Genovese that would make excellent and conscientious bodyguards, but there is only one who can be the underboss Miceli needs.

I'm so glad that between us, Severu and I were able to convince Miceli of that fact too.

His brother suggested Angelo for my primary bodyguard, but the head enforcer/assassin is kind of intense, and I'm glad Miceli chose someone else.

Ultimately, he assigned the next in line after Allessio, two members from Angelo's crew and handpicked eight more. It feels like overkill to me, but that's Miceli, over the top. Especially when it comes to my safety.

The dinner that follows the ceremony is filled with jovial chatter and celebratory toasts. I don't know this group of men very well, but to my untrained eye, it does not look like there is a single person here that is unhappy Miceli is their don.

I am glad. Because my fiancé is not a man who will tolerate mutiny.

If any of the capos try to undermine his authority, my Aries will not choose diplomacy over violence. He will destroy any obstacle in his path.

That should not make me feel safe, much less aroused. But it really, really does. I know that with Miceli De Luca, I will always be safe. I will always be protected.

There will never come a time that me, or our future children, are not the most important people in Miceli's life.

I stepped in as a sacrificial lamb in this alliance, seething with frustration and desperately wishing for a way out.

Now, I would not change my place in the world with anyone, for anything.

My beloved owns my heart and soul and I am his queen.

We spoke our vows with blood on each other's skin and our coming wedding is a ceremony for other people. We already know the truth.

Miceli and I are bound for eternity.

He is mine and I am his and together we will lead the New York Cosa Nostra.

EPILOGUE

The Rehearsal Dinner

Róise

Putting my fork down, I shake my head at the waiter trying to put the pasta course in front of me.

"What's wrong, Róise?" my soon-to-be mother-in-law asks. "Would you prefer different pasta?"

Unable to stifle a grimace at the idea of eating yet another plate of food, I shake my head. "The *pasta alla norma* looks delicious, but I'm full."

"On antipasto?" Big Sal asks, his tone tinged with disbelief.

The thing is, we've been eating for three days. Apparently Sicilian prewedding celebrations include food. And lots of it.

The official festivities kicked off with a simple three-course dinner on Friday night for the two families. By breakfast the next morning, wedding guests had started arriving.

Every successive meal hosted by the De Lucas has had more and more guests and competed with the meal before it for the abundance of mouth watering food.

"Lunch did me in," I say apologetically.

There were five courses, and it took three hours to finish.

"That was hours ago," Miceli's uncle scoffs.

Aria waves a dismissive hand at her brother-in-law. "Leave her alone. If she doesn't want to eat, she doesn't have to. She's getting married tomorrow. Her stomach is probably tied in knots. I know mine was the night before my wedding."

With all the celebratory eating we've been doing, there's no room in my stomach for knots, but I appreciate the sentiment.

"Don't pester the girl," Big Sal's wife, Ilaria, says.

A warm hand settles against the back of my neck, strong fingertips digging into tense muscles. "Relax, *dolce fiore*. Only one day left and then we leave for Marseilles."

After the wedding and the reception following it. This time, the festivities will be hosted by my uncle. For the sake of tradition, I'm spending the night at the mansion with my family.

Maybe that has me a little stressed.

I like sleeping with Miceli. I feel safe with him. But *moma* won't budge. I'm sleeping in my old bedroom tonight for the last time.

Flicking a glance up at Miceli, I smile. "Is it too late to elope?"

"After all the work your grandmother and my mom put into the wedding? I like my head attached to my body, so I'm going with a yes."

Since becoming the don, Miceli jokes less. Hearing him tease me now makes my heart happy.

"Are you telling me the most powerful don in New York is afraid of his mother?" I tease back.

"Mamma might let me live, but your grandmother will have my guts for garters."

That sounds like something *moma* would say. "Did she threaten you?"

"It sounded more like a promise to me."

"She loves me."

Miceli's eyes darken with emotion. "So do I."

"I love you too."

Catalina

"Just call me the matchmaking don," my beloved husband says smugly while the bride and groom-to-be make googly eyes at each other.

"You're a godfather now and I'm pretty sure that's not a thing anyway."

"What would you call it? I have now orchestrated three happy couples in my family." He looks around the guests at the rehearsal night dinner like he's looking for a fourth victim.

"Um, I get you think you're responsible for Salvatore and Bianca's happy marriage, but Brogan Shaughnessy approached you about the alliance."

"And I picked my brother for Róise."

"You didn't even know her then."

"Unlike my brother, I read the background report on her and I knew Róise would be a good match for Miceli. He needs a wife who understands both the brutality of our world and the part of my brother no one else sees."

He's talking about the painting.

"You're not wrong," I admit. "But who's this third couple you're talking about? Are you plotting another marriage alliance?"

Severu's grin turns wicked. "Us, of course."

I can't deny he forced that wedding too, even if he had been engaged to my sister to begin with. I like to remind him of that now and again to keep my doting husband on his toes.

Opening my mouth to do just that, the baby kicks and I gasp instead.

Severu lays his big hand over my pregnant belly. "How's my son doing?"

"He's active." A little too active for all the food over the past three days.

While I didn't refuse any courses, I didn't eat more than a couple bites of each either. I was the one Uncle Sal was giving a hard time at lunch.

He's got a traditional Sicilian-American outlook. That means, he celebrates with food and gets offended by a guest who does not imbibe enough.

Lucky for both Róise and me, we're the hosts tonight, not Uncle Sal.

But since he's also dedicated and loyal to his family, he takes it personally when the bride doesn't eat her pasta.

Róise doesn't need me defending her though. She's got my mother-in-law and Severu's aunt staunchly on her side already.

I love this family, so different from my own. My husband might run a criminal syndicate, but he love and values me and cares deeply about the rest of his family too.

Just like they care about each other.

Even Uncle Sal, who is the first to offer the *per cent'anni* toast to Róise and Miceli.

For a hundred years.

Severu leans close to me after the toast. "Five centuries will not be enough with you. Wherever we are in the afterlife, I will be by your side into eternity."

The Wedding

Miceli

The soft strands of the Celtic harp accompany the bridesmaids and groomsmen as they walk down the aisle.

Mick escorts his wife, Kara, to the altar before going to stand on the other side of Sev. Sev is my best man, but he refused to walk any other woman down the aisle but his wife. And he adamantly opposed Catalina being forced to stand during the ceremony at six months pregnant.

Raph and Giulia are next. Now a mom of two, my sister glows with love for her husband. More importantly, he looks at her like she is the center of his world.

As she should be.

Next comes Bianca and Salvatore. Newlyweds married less than two months. I'm not the only one who notices that my cousin hesitates to let his wife go to join the other groomsmen.

But she whispers something to him, and he finally releases her.

Allessio escorts Fiona down the aisle at the last.

The harps fall silent, bringing a hush over the guests.

Then the tones of the uilleann pipes fill the cathedral as the wedding march begins.

And she's there. My bride.

My wife.

These vows we speak before the priest are superfluous for us. We have made our promises and sealed them in blood on each other's skin.

As she walks toward me, everyone else fades away. Her uncle, whose arm she is holding. The guests. Our attendants.

None of them register anymore as my beautiful angel in white makes her way toward me. Her veil does nothing to hide the emotion in her emerald gaze.

Love.

The rest of the ceremony goes by in a blur, though I speak my vows with a harsh voice that will carry to the very back of the cathedral.

Every guest here today will know that I am claiming this woman for my own and for eternity.

Róise

My grandmother's wedding dress rustles as I walk down the aisle toward my future.

Miceli is also my present. Last night, he serenaded me outside my window at the mansion. An Italian custom that gave him the opportunity to sneak inside and sleep beside me.

Mamo pretended not to notice the dent in the other pillow as she gave me the Irish linen handkerchief to tuck into my bodice. It will be used to make the Christening bonnet for my children one day.

Today, it will be used to soak up happy tears. I don't need the shamrocks embroidered in white silk floss around the hem of my gown to give me luck in my marriage with Miceli.

Our love is the only luck we need and it is as deep and abiding as the ocean.

The Honeymoon

Henry Caruso smuggled himself out of the U.S. with the help of a lot of cash and one of his few remaining friends.

Too bad for him that I am a tenacious hunter. I always find my man.

When I tracked him down to Marseilles, I asked Róise if she wanted to honeymoon in the South of France.

After I kill the former capo who thought he could usurp my brother and act in our territory without our leave, I will take my beautiful new wife sailing in the Mediterranean.

Two out of Henry Caruso's three bodyguards snore when they sleep. The drug in their wine with dinner guaranteed that no one is awake to witness me breaking into the villa.

Getting away from my own bodyguards was trickier, but I managed it. Leaving without my wife knowing took more effort but exhausting her with orgasms worked better than drugs and was a lot more fun.

It is our honeymoon, after all.

Tonight, I complete my last job as my brother's underboss, something I will not delegate to anyone else.

Henry Caruso thought he could challenge our family and now he will pay with his life for his arrogance.

Besides, I won the rock, paper, scissors challenge with Salvatore for the right to send the former capo to hell.

Disabling the alarm is easy with the new app Domenico installed on my phone and I erase the camera footage on the computer attached to the monitoring station, making sure I delete the backup to the cloud too.

Henry wakes up when I sit on his torso, but my knife is already in his heart when he starts struggling.

"You don't challenge a De Luca and win," I tell him, twisting the blade.

"Fuck you."

"No thanks, only my wife gets that privilege." I punch his face to shut him up.

But it's not necessary. I know what I'm doing with my knife, and he bleeds out internally before he can get another word out of his mouth.

~ ~ ~

"It's so beautiful out here." Róise lays her head on my shoulder.

We're on a borrowed yacht small enough for a skeleton crew but large enough for our security detail to have quarters nowhere near our stateroom.

It's also a big enough craft to sail into deep waters outside currents that might carry a weighted body to shore.

There's no chemical soup here to dump Henry's corpse into, so I'm going old school. I mixed the cement myself and his cement shoes are currently curing around his feet in the hold.

Later tonight, after I make love to my beautiful wife, Henry Caruso is going swimming with the fishes.

THE END

*If you enjoyed FORCED VOWS, please consider
leaving a review, or rating. Thank you!*

NAME PRONUNCIATIONS

In case you are curious, here is the pronunciation for the main family character names that are not Anglo-American phonetic:

Italian/Sicilian Names

Miceli: mee-chell-ee

Aria: ah-ree-uh (some more traditional members of *la famiglia* lightly roll the r, others do not when saying her name)

Severu: suh-veh-roo (lightly rolled r)

Giulia: joo-lee-uh

Salvatore: sal-vuh-toe-ray (lightly rolled r)

Irish Names

Róise: roh-shuh

Brogan: bro-gahn

Fiona: feen-ah

(Fi: fee)

Kara: care-uh

Maive: mai-y-ev

ITALIAN & SICILIAN GLOSSARY

Note: certain words are not italicized in the book because of their common use in American English. Also, these translations are not literal. They are the more common vernacular. Italian as it is used in Northern or Southern Italy (and Sicily) as the case may be.

accidenti – (positive) wow, gosh, my goodness (negative) darn, drat

alla famiglia – to the family

amore mio – my love

anima gemella – soul mate (no masculine form/same for either)

basta – stop, that's enough

bastardo – bastard

bèdda – beautiful (Sicilian)

biddùzza – beautiful (more endearing form Sicilian)

bella mia – you are my beautiful one, or listen to me i.e. in an argument to get the person's attention (alternate uses from Southern Italy)

bella ragazza – beautiful girl

bellissima - gorgeous

bisnonna – great grandmother

bisnonno – great grandfather

brava ragazza – good girl
bravo – well done
cara/o – darling
carina/o – cutie or pretty one
carissimo/a – very dear
cazzate – bullshit
cazzo – dick/fuck equivalent
caspita – yikes/wow
che bella – how beautiful
che bello – how handsome/how nice
che buono – how tasty
che palle – oh balls/fuck it equivalent
codardo – coward
dannazione – god damn it
delizia – when someone or something is yummy
Dio mio – my god
dolce fiore – sweet flower
dolce ragazza – sweet girl
dolcezza – sweetheart, honey (literally sweetness)
mamma – mom or mother
fottuto stronzo – fucking asshole (see also *stronzo del cazzo*)
giamope – fool (Sicilian and credited with being the basis for *jamook/giamoke*)
goomah – mistress or side piece
il mia lei – my her (possessive endearment for a woman)
il mio lui – my him (possessive endearment for a man)
la mia dia – my goddess
ma va' – no way
ma va? – really?
magari – I wish
mamma mia – oh, man
managgia – damn
managgia la miseria – damn it (literally misery or poverty)
manaja – damn (variant from Southern Italy)

marito – husband

meno male – thank goodness

mi vitù – my life (Sicilian)

moglie – wife

nonna – grandma/grandmother

nonno – grandpa/grandfather

oh merda – oh crap/shit

patatina – a small potato (it's a beautiful thing not like in English)

per favore – please

porca miseria – damn it

puffetta – it means a female Smurf

puttana – bitch

saluti – cheers (Sicilian)

sempre – always

sempre e per sempre – always and forever

stronzo/a – asshole (also another way to say bitch)

stronzo del cazzo – fucking asshole (see also *fottuto stronzo*)

tesoro – treasure

tesoro mio – my treasure

vaffanculo - fuck

vita mia – my life

vitù – (my) life in Sicilian

Phrases:

A accidenti. – (teasing or serious) darn him/her/you

Dammi il tuo cazzo. - give me your cock

Ho detto basta - that's enough, I said enough

Ho bisogno di te. – I need you.

Ho bisogno del tuo cazzo. – I need your cock.

Io sono tua. – I am yours.

Oh, sono qui! - Hey, I'm here.

Non fermarti! – Don't stop!

Prometto. – I promise.

Tu sei mia! –You are mine. (jealous: another man or woman involved)

Sei fuori! - Are you out of your mind?

Sei la mia anima gemelli. – You are my soul mate. (no masculine form – same for either)

Sei mio. – You are mine.

T'amu. – I love you. (Sicilian)

Ti amo. – I love you.

Uscire. - Get out.

Voglio il tuo cazzo. - I want your cock.

Zitto. - Shut up.

Acknowledgments

As always, a huge hug and genuinely heartfelt thank you to everyone who has helped me make this book what it is:

My husband, Tom, who listens to endless ideas, scene snippets and character revelations as I write and *still* reads the complete book from start to finish when it is done.

Andie, my amazing editor at Beyond the Proof who excels at catching dangling threads and inconsistencies. Her insights make my books better. Full stop. (And you all, she had some really good ideas for this one!)

Josephine Caporetto for her invaluable help on Italian phrases.

Two very special ARC readers who take the time to proofread after the copyedits are done before writing their reviews, Dee Dee & Haley. Massive hugs to you both!

Any remaining typos, mistakes, or translation errors are my fault and mine alone.

With more than 10 million copies of my books in print worldwide (Isn't that wild?), I'm an award winning and USA Today bestselling author with over 90 published books. My stories have been translated for sale all over the world and after a long career in traditional publishing, I've gone indie. I am loving the freedom to write the stories both me and my readers enjoy the most. My new steamy mafia romance series, Syndicate Rules features the morally gray alpha heroes and spice I love to write. I write contemporary, historical and paranormal romance. Some of my books have action adventure and intrigue. All of them are spicy and deeply emotional. I'm a voracious reader and love to talk about both my books and those I've read (or should read...good recs are always welcome) on social media. Welcome to my world where love conquers all, but not easily!

For info on my books and series extras, visit my website:
www.lucymonroe.com

Follow me on Social Media:
Facebook: LucyMonroe.Romance
Instagram: lucymonroeromance
Pinterest: lucymonroebooks
goodreads: Lucy Monroe
YouTube: @LucyMonroeBooks
TikTok: lucymonroeauthor

ALSO BY LUCY MONROE

Syndicate Rules

CONVENIENT MAFIA WIFE
URGENT VOWS
DEMANDING MOB BOSS
RUTHLESS ENFORCER
BRUTAL CAPO
FORCED VOWS

Mercenaries & Spies

READY, WILLING & AND ABLE
SATISFACTION GUARANTEED
DEAL WITH THIS
THE SPY WHO WANTS ME
WATCH OVER ME
CLOSE QUARTERS
HEAT SEEKER

CHANGE THE GAME
WIN THE GAME

Passionate Billionaires & Royalty

THE MAHARAJAH'S BILLIONAIRE HEIR
BLACKMAILED BY THE BILLIONAIRE
HER OFF LIMITS PRINCE
CINDERELLA'S JILTED BILLIONAIRE
HER GREEK BILLIONAIRE
SCORSOLINI BABY SCANDAL

THE REAL DEAL
WILD HEAT (Connected to Hot Alaska Nights - Not a Billionaire)
HOT ALASKA NIGHTS
3 Brides for 3 Bad Boys Trilogy
RAND, COLTON & CARTER

Harlequin Presents

THE GREEK'S ULTIMATUM
THE ITALIAN'S SUITABLE WIFE
THE BILLIONAIRE'S PREGNANT MISTRESS
THE SHEIKH'S BARTERED BRIDE
THE GREEK'S INNOCENT VIRGIN
BLACKMAILED INTO MARRIAGE
THE GREEK'S CHRISTMAS BABY
WEDDING VOW OF REVENGE
THE PRINCE'S VIRGIN WIFE
HIS ROYAL LOVE-CHILD
THE SCORSOLINI MARRIAGE BARGAIN
THE PLAYBOY'S SEDUCTION
PREGNANCY OF PASSION
THE SICILIAN'S MARRIAGE ARRANGEMENT
BOUGHT: THE GREEK'S BRIDE
TAKEN: THE SPANIARD'S VIRGIN
HOT DESERT NIGHTS
THE RANCHER'S RULES
FORBIDDEN: THE BILLIONAIRE'S
VIRGIN PRINCESS
HOUSEKEEPER TO THE MILLIONAIRE
HIRED: THE SHEIKH'S SECRETARY MISTRESS
VALENTINO'S LOVE-CHILD
THE LATIN LOVER 2-IN-1 with
THE GREEK TYCOON'S INHERITED BRIDE
THE SHY BRIDE

THE GREEK'S PREGNANT LOVER
FOR DUTY'S SAKE
HEART OF A DESERT WARRIOR
NOT JUST THE GREEK'S WIFE
ONE NIGHT HEIR
PRINCE OF SECRETS
MILLION DOLLAR CHRISTMAS PROPOSAL
SHEIKH'S SCANDAL
AN HEIRESS FOR HIS EMPIRE
A VIRGIN FOR HIS PRIZE
2017 CHRISTMAS CODA: The Greek Tycoons
KOSTA'S CONVENIENT BRIDE
THE SPANIARD'S PLEASURABLE VENGEANCE
AFTER THE BILLIONAIRE'S WEDDING VOWS
QUEEN BY ROYAL APPOINTMENT
HIS MAJESTY'S HIDDEN HEIR
THE COST OF THEIR ROYAL FLING

Anthologies & Novellas

SILVER BELLA
DELICIOUS: Moon Magnetism
by Lori Foster, et. al.
HE'S THE ONE: Seducing Tabby
by Linda Lael Miller, et. al.
THE POWER OF LOVE: No Angel
by Lori Foster, et. al.
BODYGUARDS IN BED:
Who's Been Sleeping in my Brother's Bed?
by Lucy Monroe et. al.

Historical Romance

ANNABELLE'S COURTSHIP

The Langley Family Trilogy
TOUCH ME, TEMPT ME & TAKE ME
MASQUERADE IN EGYPT

Paranormal Romance

Children of the Moon Novels
MOON AWAKENING
MOON CRAVING
MOON BURNING
DRAGON'S MOON
ENTHRALLED anthology: Ecstasy Under the Moon
WARRIOR'S MOON
VIKING'S MOON
DESERT MOON
HIGHLANDER'S MOON

Montana Wolves
COME MOONRISE
MONTANA MOON